Purple Palette
for
MURDER

A Meg Harris Mystery

The Meg Harris Mysteries

Purple Palette for

MURDER

A Meg Harris Mystery

R.J. HARLICK

DUNDURN
TORONTO

Cover image: © istock.com/shaunl
Printer: Webcom

Library and Archives Canada Cataloguing in Publication

Harlick, R. J., 1946-, author
     Purple palette for murder / R.J. Harlick.

(A Meg Harris mystery)
Issued in print and electronic formats.
ISBN 978-1-4597-3865-2 (softcover).--ISBN 978-1-4597-3866-9 (PDF).--
ISBN 978-1-4597-3867-6 (EPUB)

     I. Title. II. Series: Harlick, R. J., 1946- . Meg Harris mystery.

PS8615.A74P87 2017   C813'.6   C2017-901259-2
                                                     C2017-901260-6

1 2 3 4 5   21 20 19 18 17

 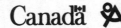

We acknowledge the support of the **Canada Council for the Arts**, which last year invested $153 million to bring the arts to Canadians throughout the country, and the **Ontario Arts Council** for our publishing program. We also acknowledge the financial support of the **Government of Ontario**, through the **Ontario Book Publishing Tax Credit** and the **Ontario Media Development Corporation**, and the **Government of Canada**.

Nous remercions le **Conseil des arts du Canada** de son soutien. L'an dernier, le Conseil a investi 153 millions de dollars pour mettre de l'art dans la vie des Canadiennes et des Canadiens de tout le pays.

Care has been taken to trace the ownership of copyright material used in this book. The author and the publisher welcome any information enabling them to rectify any references or credits in subsequent editions.

— *J. Kirk Howard, President*

The publisher is not responsible for websites or their content unless they are owned by the publisher.

Printed and bound in Canada.

VISIT US AT

dundurn.com | @dundurnpress | dundurnpress | dundurnpress

Dundurn
3 Church Street, Suite 500
Toronto, Ontario, Canada
M5E 1M2

To Jim

ONE

"Is the fawn still there?" I asked Jid, who was picking his way through the tall ferns in front of us.

Yesterday I'd accidentally discovered the tiny newborn while tramping along a trail that meandered through the forested hills behind my cottage. Or more correctly, Shoni, my seven-month-old standard poodle, had stumbled onto the defenceless baby deer while chasing a squirrel. Fortunately, I was able to stop her from doing any harm. I didn't linger, knowing the mother would return once we were gone.

But this morning, while picking up the mail from my box at the end of my road, I noticed the legs of a dead deer protruding out of the ditch on the other side of the main road. It proved to be a doe, a lactating one that had been run over. I immediately thought of the fawn. If its mother was this dead deer, it wouldn't survive the coyotes, wolves, and other predators that called this forest home.

"I don't see it yet," Jid replied, moving the chest-high fronds aside.

His full name was Adjidamò, meaning "Little Squirrel" in Algonquin, but he preferred to be called Jid. He hated to be reminded that he was small for his thirteen years.

"Are you sure this is the right place?"

I pointed to an enormous granite boulder covered in lichen and moss rising several metres from the forest floor. "It was hidden in the ferns to the right of that rock."

If the fawn's mother were alive, it would be gone. Sensing that her baby had been discovered, she would've moved it. Barely able to walk during the first couple of weeks of life, a fawn had two things going for it: it had no scent, and it remained absolutely still. The mother could safely leave it for many hours of foraging without fear of predators seeking it out. Until someone like me stumbled across it and left behind a scent, which would attract the curious.

"If you see it, don't go any closer."

He hitched up the waist of his baggy jeans, which had crept downward from their usual resting spot midway down his bum. In an effort to keep up with the older boys at school, he had recently adopted this ridiculous fashion statement.

"I know," he replied, not bothering to hide the impatience in his voice.

Of course he would know. Having spent his entire short life in these Quebec woods, he knew considerably more about its inhabitants than I ever would. He also had a way with animals, like a whisperer, if such a person existed.

One time when we were hiking with Sergei, my sadly missed standard poodle, we surprised a black bear, a large one, not at all happy at being accosted by a frenetically barking dog. I froze, convinced the dog would shortly be dinner. But Jid continued walking toward the animal, easily four times his size, and spoke to it in a calm, soothing tone as if they were buddies. For several nervous seconds I was terrified the bear would pounce. By the time the boy had calmed Sergei, the bear had settled down too. He grunted and took one last look at us before loping into the forest shadows.

"I see something." Jid pointed to the middle of the ferns.

I could barely make out a faint cinnamon colour amongst the sun-dappled green. It could easily have been dirt or last fall's dead leaves.

"Go closer. I want to be certain it's still there." I stayed where I was, a good three or four metres away. "Don't touch it."

"I know, I know." He parted the fronds and inched forward. "It's still here. Oh, it's so cute. So small. This is the first time I ever see a baby fawn."

"The first time for me, too. Does it look sick or injured?"

"Nope. It looks okay. It's staring at me. What should we do?"

"I don't want to remove it in case the dead deer isn't the mother."

"Yeah, but it's still here. You said that wouldn't happen if she was alive."

"I know, but I worry about taking it away before being absolutely certain that the mother is dead. If we remove it, that'll jeopardize its ability to survive when it's old enough to be released."

"Yeah, but the injured birds and raccoons Janet saves don't have any problems when she lets them go."

"I know, but this tiny deer would become so used to us, it would no longer be afraid of humans. It would be an easy target for hunters."

9

"We could tie a red ribbon around its neck and tell everyone not to shoot it."

"I wish. No, we should give the mother one more day. If the fawn's here tomorrow, we'll assume the dead deer is the mother and take it to Janet, okay?"

Janet Bridgford, a retired veterinarian, had moved into a nearby farm a few years ago and established a wildlife refuge. People in the area, including the Migiskan Reserve, had taken to bringing her sick and injured wildlife. I'd done it a few times myself.

At the suggestion of my husband, Eric, I'd been helping her out a couple of days a week over the last few months. He viewed this as a way to get me out of the house and out of my funk. Though I enjoyed working with these helpless creatures, it wasn't proving the cure Eric hoped it would be.

I still found myself summoning up all the fortitude I possessed to get out of bed each morning. Sometimes I didn't. When I did, I only wanted to curl up in the sofa in front of the fire and watch the flames lick the glass. To be clear, it was the fire in the living room and not the den, once my favourite room for relaxing. I hadn't gone near that room, not even to look through the doorway, since The Nightmare.

"Yeah, but is she going to be okay? I could stay here and guard her," Jid replied.

"And keep the mother away at the same time." I watched a woodpecker track up a tree above the spot where the fawn was hiding. "You called her a she."

"I can't tell, but she looks like a girl to me. So cute. Bye, bye, little fawn. I hope you're gonna be okay." He hitched up his jeans and tiptoed away.

The ferns rustled behind me as I headed back through the underbrush to the trail.

"Uh-oh, she's getting up. What do I do, Auntie?"

"Just keep walking."

"But she's following me."

I turned to see the tiny creature, its white-spotted body barely larger than a snowshoe hare, wobbling on matchstick legs toward the boy. It bumped up against a fern and almost toppled over, but miraculously stayed upright. So endearing and so incredibly helpless. A wolf would devour it in one bite.

As much as I wanted to gather it in my arms and take it with us, I feared it would put her in more danger, so I said, "Speed up, and hopefully she'll stop following us." He had me thinking it was a girl too.

I picked up my pace. It was a sparkling late spring morning in early June with the forest bursting with new life. Unfortunately, the new life also included black flies — swarms of them. Before setting out, I'd liberally doused myself with anti-bug juice, which was working, marginally. Though the temperature required jackets and fleece, the sun spoke of the summer to come.

The trail meandered through an ancient maple forest. When my great-aunt Agatha lived at Three Deer Point, she had operated it as a sugar bush and produced some of the best maple syrup in west Quebec. But she shut it down several years before her death. When I inherited the property, I had thought of reviving it, but so far hadn't got around to it and likely never would.

I was tramping along the trail, admiring the shy blooms of spring peeking through the dead leaves, when I realized it was too quiet behind me. I turned around and, as suspected, didn't see the boy.

"Jid, where are you?" I called out.

"I'm here," came the answer from beyond the ridge I'd just crested.

"Hurry up. I have to get back to the house. I'm expecting a call from Eric."

My husband had flown to Yellowknife a little over a week ago to meet with the chiefs of various Northwest Territories First Nations and to spend time with his daughter, Teht'aa. She was having man problems and needed a father's shoulder to cry on. He had tried to cajole me into going with him, believing it would do me good to get away.

He was right, it would, but I couldn't do it. I couldn't leave my forest sanctuary. I'd only just begun to find a sort of calm within myself, though an uneasy one. I wasn't ready to summon the nerve to venture out into the big bad world. Mind you, Three Deer Point had proven to be no less bad.

"I can't go faster," he replied.

"Why not?"

"Kidi can't keep up with me."

"Kidi?"

"That's what I'm calling the baby deer. It's short for *kidagàgòns*, fawn in Algonquin."

I scrambled back over the rise to discover Jid creeping along at a crawl with the tiny fawn teetering a few metres behind him. The damage was done. We wouldn't be able to leave her now.

"Do you think she can walk all the way back to the cottage?" I asked.

"I think so. But if she gets tired, I can carry her."

"Will she let you near her?"

"Yeah, she's already nibbled my fingers."

So much for telling him not to touch her. "Okay. We'll take her to Janet's. She'll know how to take care of the poor thing."

"I can help her." His brown puppy eyes twinkled with eagerness.

"I'm sure you can. Look, I have to run. Can you manage on your own?"

"You bet." The fawn tottered up to him, stretched her head into his groin, and nipped. "Ouch, you're not supposed to do that."

"She's hungry. Janet will have some special milk to feed her. After I finish talking to Eric I'll come back for you, okay?"

"Yeah, sure. Say hi to Shome for me."

"Will do."

Though Eric wasn't Jid's *mishòmis*, meaning grandfather, Jid used the shortened version, *shome*, as an endearment, the same way he used "auntie" for me, though we bore no blood relationship.

By the time my rambling timber cottage loomed into view, I could hear the phone ringing. I leapt up the back stairs and snatched up the kitchen phone before it stopped ringing.

"So how's my one and only today?" I gasped between breaths.

"Ah ... Mrs. Odjik?"

Whoops, it was a man, but not Eric. Thank god he couldn't see me blushing. "Actually, it's Meg Harris, but I do answer to Mrs. Odjik."

"My apologies. I believe Eric Odjik is your husband." His voice wasn't familiar.

"That's right."

"My name is Derrick Robinson. I'm your husband's defence attorney. He has been arrested for murder."

TWO

I was in a state of shock from the moment I hung up the phone until I boarded the plane for Yellowknife. I became a robot going through the motions of preparation.

Eric. *Murder?* Impossible! No way! A horrible, god-awful mistake.

I didn't know how long I remained slumped in Aunt Aggie's rocker trying to make sense of what the lawyer had told me. A man dead. Teht'aa's boyfriend. Eric charged with his murder. Teht'aa beaten up, lying close to death in a hospital in Yellowknife.

I was too stunned to take in everything. I only knew I had to shove my own fears aside. I had to get to Yellowknife. I frantically set about booking the earliest flight. I dismissed options that had me flying through Toronto and Calgary. I found one direct flight, which would get me there the quickest. The only problem was the flight was leaving in four hours from Ottawa, a two-hour drive away. Taking check-in time into consideration, that gave me less than an hour to pack and sort out Shoni.

Then Jid walked through the door. I had forgotten about him.

"I have to go away. Collect your things, and I'll take you to your aunt's."

For the past month, Jid had been living at Three Deer Point. He preferred staying with us than with his aunt, his legal guardian. Eric and I were hoping that it would soon be permanent. We had put in a request to adopt the orphan boy.

"Where are you going?"

"To Yellowknife. Eric needs me." I was afraid to tell him that his hero was in big, big trouble.

"Can you do it? You haven't left this place since … you know what." A shadow of fear washed over his face.

I closed my eyes and breathed deeply. "I have to."

Jid had also survived The Nightmare, but had handled it much better than I could. Maybe because he talked it over with his Shome. I hadn't been able to talk about it to anyone, not even my husband.

We gripped each other's hands in shared memory, until Jid broke free. "What about the fawn?" he asked.

"Right, the fawn. We'll take her to Janet's. Call her to let her know."

Shoni whined in her cage, anxious to greet us. Right, the puppy. "Can you take Shoni with you to your aunt's?"

"I suppose, but I don't know if she'll get along with Joe's husky mix. Do I really have to stay with Auntie Anne? I could stay with Mikey."

Mikey was his best friend. When life at his aunt's house became too stressful and we were away, Jid stayed with Mikey. Jid's older cousin was a bully. Usually he could handle it, but occasionally it became too much and he needed to escape.

"Will his mom take the puppy too?"

He nodded vigorously. "Yeah, she really likes dogs."

"You'd better call her. No wait. I'd better do it." I snatched up the phone.

"She's not there. Mikey said they were going to his aunt's place this morning."

"Do you know the number?"

He shook his head.

"Look it up while I pack, and don't forget to call Janet."

I raced upstairs to my bedroom. With a desperate craving for solitude after The Nightmare, I had taken over Aunt Aggie's old bedroom. It was only supposed to be for a few weeks, but close to six months later, I hadn't yet gathered my nerve to move back into the master bedroom with my husband. Initially, he'd been patiently understanding, as only he could be. Whenever he tried to bring it up, I deflected him. I couldn't bring myself to tell him why I couldn't share a bed with him. Lately I'd sensed a resigned acceptance and a distancing, which only made me more depressed. Maybe, just maybe I would be able to talk to him in Yellowknife about what really happened that terrible night when my world was turned upside down. He knew some of it. He'd cleaned up the blood. But he didn't know everything.

Figuring north of 60 had to be colder than the forty-five degree latitude temperatures of Three Deer Point, I threw in mostly winter clothing with a few summer t-shirts on the off chance summer would arrive while I was there. Unfortunately, today was wash day, and I hadn't yet gotten around to doing it, so I had to pack a few dirty items. I threw in a Ziploc bag of detergent, intending to wash them in my hotel room.

Speaking of hotel rooms, I needed a place to stay. But with no time to make a reservation before I left, I would have to chance that there would be a vacancy somewhere in that northern capital. Of course, Teht'aa wouldn't mind if I stayed at her apartment. And Eric had a hotel room, except I couldn't remember the name of the hotel. But enough. I'd worry about it when I arrived.

"Janet says it's okay," Jid yelled from downstairs. "She got mad at me for taking the fawn."

"Don't worry, I'll explain how it happened."

"Your message light's flashing. Want me to check the messages?"

"Don't bother. Only people wanting money from me." No one else called me besides Eric.

I ran down the hall to the bathroom, rolling the suitcase behind me. I added some toiletries, strapped everything in, and zipped up the case.

"Did you find the aunt's phone number?" I called out as I stumbled down the stairs. "If so, dial it for me."

The phone line was ringing when Jid placed the receiver against my ear. All I heard was the voicemail greeting. I left a message for Mikey's mother explaining my difficulty and asked if she minded keeping the boy for a few days. I left the same message on her own phone.

"Do you have all you need for the stay over?"

"I need my computer and stuff for school. How long you gonna be?"

"No idea. I'm hoping this is all a big mistake, and we'll be returning on the next flight."

"Big mistake? What's happened to Shome?"

Oh, dear. How much should I tell him? "Shome has been arrested."

"You mean he's in jail?" His eyes grew in size.

"Yup, though by the time I get there, I'm hoping the charges will be dropped and he'll be free to go."

"What did he do?"

I hesitated. Should I pretend I don't know? But Eric was like the father, the grandfather the boy had never had. I would have hated for him to find out from someone else. "The police think he killed someone."

"No!" His face filled with horror. "Not Shome! He would never kill anyone."

"That's why I'm going to Yellowknife. I want to convince the police that he could never hurt anyone, let alone kill someone."

"I want to go too."

"I wish you could, but you'll miss school."

"Fuck school."

"Jid! Your language."

He shrugged sheepishly.

"Someone needs to look after Shoni and ensure Kidi is doing okay."

"Yeah, I guess."

"So quick, get your stuff. We've got to leave, or I'll miss my plane."

While Jid ran upstairs, I checked the front of the house to ensure the doors and windows were securely locked, then headed back to the kitchen to collect the puppy, now yelping full voice in her crate. Without thinking, I let her out the back door. It was only as I was collapsing her crate that I remembered the baby deer. But I needn't have worried. When I opened the back door, I discovered the two of them sniffing noses. For the moment Shoni was bigger than the fawn, but in a few short months, she would be lifting her head to reach the deer.

I gathered the dog's food and bowls, along with her favourite ball and chew bones, and placed them at the back door beside my suitcase. I tried Mikey's home phone and his aunt's one more time but failed to reach anyone, which left me in a quandary. I couldn't leave Jid and Shoni unannounced on their doorstep. I had little choice but to take him to his aunt's house.

Janet came to his rescue. After giving us a long lecture on the perils of removing the poor wee thing from its habitat, she offered to put up the boy and the puppy. Since the fawn had already bonded with Jid, it would be important for him to maintain this connection. Besides, she could do with the extra help in caring for the other wounded creatures. I swore Jid thought he had died and gone to heaven, he was grinning so broadly.

With a hasty goodbye and a "Get Shome out of jail!" from Jid, I drove as fast as my ancient Ford pick-up would allow. I had two and a half hours to catch my flight. I prayed there were no traffic jams on the bridge crossing the Ottawa River and that my truck wouldn't break down. Miraculously, the gods were listening. I slid into the airport parking lot with twenty-five minutes to spare. I ignored the angry scowl on the check-in clerk's face as I puffed up to the counter. Once again the gods were looking out for me as I breezed through security. They were on the final boarding call for my flight by the time I reached the gate. I helped myself to a free newspaper from the stand before presenting my boarding pass and scurrying down the walkway.

THREE

I collapsed gasping into my seat. My heart was pounding so hard, I barely heard the announcements in both official languages. I closed my eyes and felt the plane rumble down the runway, then lift into the air.

Eric, my love, I'm on my way. In five short hours I'll be with you.

I tried and failed to banish the images of him sitting in a cold, bleak cell, wearing orange, with his feet shackled. I couldn't imagine the level of despair he would be feeling.

Yes, I could. I was feeling it myself.

"Would you like some coffee?" A voice cut through my thoughts.

I opened my eyes to see the attendant peering down at me. "Some tea would be nice, with milk. Thanks."

Although a double vodka with tonic would be more in order.

But I couldn't go there. I'd been dry for almost two years, thanks to Eric. Though the urge had been over whelming after The Nightmare, he had ensured that I didn't come within seeing or smelling distance of alcohol of any variety, including rubbing alcohol. He had gone as far as to give up his nightly glass of single malt and remove every bottle of beer, wine, and liquor from our house. In time, the urge had waned until I rarely thought about it.

Until now. I could almost taste the fiery comfort of the vodka sliding down my throat.

My neighbour's voluminous thigh brushed against my own. I flinched and tried to move beyond touching distance, in doing so rubbing against the man on the other side. I felt panic rising. I steeled myself to stay seated while I clamped my elbows into my sides and clenched my legs together until I no longer felt either neighbour. I breathed deeply, counted to a hundred, and tried to convince myself that no one was going to hurt me.

A distraction. I needed one. Desperately. But my view outside was blocked by my well-padded neighbour hunched over her Kindle.

Yes, reading would do the trick, but in my haste I hadn't thought to bring a book. Then I caught sight of the newspaper jammed into the pocket in front of me. I wrenched it free, opened it, and gasped.

Eric's soft grey eyes stared back at me from the front page under the headline "GCFN Grand Chief Arrested For Murder."

Of course. As the newly elected Grand Chief of the Grand Council of First Nations, all media eyes were on him. I was so glad I'd told Jid rather than having him find out this way. But what would this do to Eric's standing as chief? He would be shattered if forced to resign. He had worked so hard for this opportunity to help his people.

In the photo, my husband was wearing his full regalia and the cherished moosehide jacket once worn by his grandfather and holding the ceremonial eagle feather given to him by a former chief of the Migiskan Anishinabeg, the Algonquin community he belonged to and that he had been band chief of for over ten years. In the photo, he was beaming, having just been elected Grand Chief.

I had willed myself to forget about The Nightmare and go with him to Vancouver to share in that moment, but at the last minute I balked. I hadn't had it in me to plant a smile on my face and be charming to all his supporters, who would have been scrutinizing me, looking for any misstep, and wondering what kind of wife I was to such a remarkable man. He hadn't been happy, but he'd understood.

I had stayed glued to my computer, watching the election unfold, and had sent a congratulatory text the minute his name was announced. But it wasn't enough. I should've been at his side, beaming alongside him and showing the assembly that he had his wife's full support.

Now this. Poor Eric. The front-page headline killed any hope of keeping the ignominy quiet. Everyone would think him a man capable of murder. I had to help him. I might not have been able to face an assembly full of supporters, but I would do what I could now to prove his innocence.

The first thing I learned from the article was that Eric wasn't in Yellowknife, but in a remote fly-in community by the name of Digadeh, which begged the question: What in the world was he doing there? Not wanting to burden the GCFN coffers with the high cost of northern flights, he had arranged for the chiefs of fly-in communities to meet him at the main Dene Nation offices in Yellowknife.

The murder had apparently happened yesterday. We'd missed our daily phone call, though I'd tried to reach him twice. I had put it down to a dead phone battery. He had a habit of forgetting to plug it in. But it looked as if he'd had another reason for not answering.

The article merely identified the murder victim as male with his identity pending family notification. Yet the lawyer had said it was Teht'aa's boyfriend. As far as I knew, the man lived in Yellowknife, so maybe the lawyer was mistaken.

The article made no mention of how the man had been killed, though it did report that the RCMP weren't looking for any other suspects, which in police-speak meant they had sufficient evidence against Eric.

Things were going from bad to worse.

But I didn't know how much worse until a name embedded in a later article caught my eye. Teht'aa Bluegoose. Too used to her married last name of Tootoosis, my eyes had passed over it before I remembered that she'd reverted to her maiden name after moving to Yellowknife. Though the article didn't make the connection to Eric, I knew it was her.

"How Many More Native Women Need to Die Before Something Is Done?" shouted the headline. My heart sank until I read that Teht'aa was still alive. While the other two women discussed in the article had been found dead, one in Edmonton and the other in Vancouver, she had been found badly beaten and unconscious three days ago in a back alley of Yellowknife. At the time of writing, she was still in a coma at the Stanton Territorial Hospital, with her condition listed as critical.

Three days ago! Why hadn't Eric told me when we'd talked two days ago?

Although the article made no link, I knew with chilling certainty that there was a connection between Teht'aa's beating and Eric's arrest.

When we chatted on the phone a little over three weeks ago, she was bubbling with excitement over her new job at CBC North. She'd been lured away from the aboriginal network APTN and was scheduled to start next week as an evening news announcer for Canada's public broadcaster. She would be devastated if this assault jeopardized her job.

The phone call, though, had had a sombre side to it. She'd finally broken up with her boyfriend. Eric and I had seen it coming and were thankful she had finally removed the blinkers and seen the man for what he was: a bully and an abuser. He, however, didn't want the relationship to end and had been hounding her to get back together. She'd sought her father's advice on how to deal with him. Another reason for Eric's trip to Yellowknife. He had intended to speak to the man and get him to leave his daughter alone.

Something had gone horribly wrong.

FOUR

We landed in brilliant sun, as brilliant as the sun I'd left behind. Though it was close to seven in the evening my time, the time difference had me adjusting my watch to five o'clock. Nonetheless, the sun seemed farther from the horizon than I was used to seeing at this hour.

After crossing the seemingly limitless expanse of Great Slave Lake, I was surprised to spy smoke rising from the forest on the shore of a bay opposite the grid of Yellowknife. During the flight, my neighbour had pointed out two other fires, remarking that it was an unusually early start to the forest fire season. She blamed it on the unseasonably hot and dry spring they were having.

The plane landed as smoothly as it had flown and taxied up to the low single-storey airport building, easily a tenth of the size of Ottawa's sprawling structure. The warm air hit me as I descended the staircase to the tarmac. I hastily doffed my down jacket. It looked like I wouldn't be needing it or any of the other winter clothes I'd brought.

I picked up my luggage under the hungry eyes of a stuffed polar bear guarding the baggage carousel and headed out the main door in search of a cab. While I waited, I called the lawyer using Eric's spare cellphone, which I'd remembered to bring at the last moment. I didn't reach him, so I left a message before hopping into a taxi to go directly to the hospital. Since Eric couldn't be with his daughter, I would be there for her.

Teht'aa and I hadn't always been close. Our relationship had started out on a rocky footing. I was jealous, believing she was Eric's girlfriend before discovering their true relationship. She was highly suspicious of whites and wanted her father to stop seeing me. Eventually, though, we overcame our initial animosity and became the best of friends. Considering our closeness in age, a little more than ten years apart, we were more like sisters than stepdaughter and stepmother.

Eric had been a teenage heartthrob playing Triple A hockey in Medicine Hat. Teht'aa's mother came from a remote Dene community in the Northwest Territories. They met at one of his games and fell in love. When she became pregnant, she fled back to her northern community and had no further contact with him. Eric never knew he had a daughter until Teht'aa, then in her twenties, approached him at a gathering. She'd been an integral part of his life ever since.

He would be devastated if she died.

My first view of Yellowknife whipped past the window. I'd been expecting rustic log cabins huddling under the towering trees of a northern forest. Instead I saw strip malls, big box stores, and acres of mostly empty parking lots that looked remarkably like the outskirts of any town in Canada. I caught a glimpse of the rocky shoreline of a small lake. The smooth pink granite was dotted with clumps of trees, none of which met my definition of towering.

A quick call to Janet assured me that Jid was doing well and was being a big help, when he could be persuaded to leave Kidi's side.

"I think the wee thing can't be more than a week old and would've died if you hadn't brought her in. She is indeed a 'she.' She is readily accepting the goat's milk Jid is feeding her. I have high hopes that she will survive."

"I'm so glad, and many thanks for all your help."

"I'm happy to do it. By the way, I heard about Eric on the news. I'm so sorry. It has to be a horrible mistake. He's too good a man to be treated this way. I assume it is your reason for this last-minute trip."

I should've told her before I left, but I had been too focused on getting to the airport to go into lengthy explanations. By the time I disconnected the call, the cab driver was braking to a stop in front of the hospital's main entrance. There seemed to be two main wings, three storeys each. STANTON TERRITORIAL HOSPITAL read the sign over the portico, which likely meant it served the entire Northwest Territories.

I hopped out of the cab, pulled my suitcase out of the trunk, and headed to the door. I was so intent on seeing Teht'aa that I paid no attention to the couple standing near the entrance until it was too late.

"Are you Meg Harris, wife of Chief Odjik?" the man asked, approaching me.

He was dressed in what goes for business attire these days and carrying a photo of Eric and me. I assumed he was the lawyer. I acknowledged I was before noticing the woman coming up behind him holding a TV video camera with "CBC North" stamped along its side.

The man raised his other hand to reveal a microphone. "Are you at the hospital to see his daughter, Teht'aa Bluegoose?"

Somewhat nonplussed, I wasn't certain I should answer, then decided it couldn't do any harm. "Yes, I am."

"Can you give us an update on her condition?"

"I'm sorry, I don't know." I felt the breeze nudge my hair, way overdue for a cut. I tucked wayward strands behind my ears in an attempt to look presentable. "As you can see, I've only just arrived. Now, if you don't mind, I would like to go inside to see her."

The two of them blocked my way.

"Do you believe there is a connection between her assault and the death of her boyfriend? I assume you know your husband has been arrested for his murder."

Time to go. Clamping my lips shut and holding my head down, I barged my way through using my suitcase as a battering ram. I didn't care what it looked like on film.

"Do you think your husband is guilty?" he shouted.

I pushed the door open and sighed with relief at the silence when it clicked closed behind me.

"Are you okay, dear?" the grey-haired lady in a mauve angora sweater behind the reception counter asked as I approached. "I hope they didn't bother you too much. They've been standing there since I came on an hour ago."

"I'm fine, just glad they didn't follow me inside."

"Oh, they could never do that. They aren't allowed. I have the strictest orders to call security if they do. So what can I do for you, dear?"

"I'd like to know which room Teht'aa Bluegoose is in."

"I'm sorry, we're not allowed to give out that information. Only to family." A marked chill descended.

"But I am family."

She surveyed me carefully. "Are you sure, dear?"

"Look, I'm her stepmother. She is the daughter of my husband."

"What is his name?" She consulted a piece of paper.

"Eric Odjik."

"Can I see your identification?"

Drat. All my identification was in my name. Though I had wanted to change my name to his, Eric had objected, saying it was traditional for Algonquin woman to keep their own names in marriage.

Fortunately, I remembered that my dental plan card was under Eric's name. I showed it to her.

"That's perfect, dear. You can never be too careful. Your stepdaughter is in the Intensive Care Unit on the third floor. I hope she is going to be okay. I hear she is in a bad way. Such a beautiful young woman. I enjoy watching her on the television. Give her my best, will you, dear?"

After thanking her, I followed her directions to the elevator. On the third floor I encountered the same scrutiny. But since I had already been through it once, I was prepared.

"She is only allowed two visitors at a time," the nurse said. "Since she only has one at the moment, it will be okay for you to go in."

"Who is there now?" I asked, surprised. I had thought Eric and I were her only family.

"An uncle. You likely know him."

Not having the foggiest idea who it could be, I pretended I did. "Could you tell me her condition?"

"You need to speak to her doctor. He is in surgery at the moment, but I will let him know you're here."

"Thanks."

"She's a delight to watch on TV," the nurse continued. "What a shame that this should happen to her. I hope it doesn't cut her career short. It's amazing what plastic surgeons can do today."

With that I opened the door to the ICU.

FIVE

I faced a room crammed with humming machines, pulsating screens, and a jumble of tubing and wiring. I had no idea which of the four beds Teht'aa lay in. I dismissed the bed over which a man and a woman hovered. The patient was too small and the hair too blond. The silent mound of a man occupied another bed.

Before I could choose between the other two beds, a nurse from the central nursing station approached and led me to the one I had been about to reject. I couldn't believe that the slight, unmoving figure whose head and face were encased in bandages could be Eric's beautiful daughter. If any native woman were to embody the words "Indian Princess," she did, with her high, sculpted cheekbones, flashing mahogany eyes, and Julia Roberts smile. Her long, satiny black hair was the envy of any woman. It looked as if the long tresses were no more.

Instead of lying flat, her bed was slightly raised, putting her in a half-sitting position. She seemed to be connected to more machines than the other patients. Wires extended out from under her blanket to what looked to be an electrocardiograph. A blood pressure sleeve was wrapped around her upper arm, while a wire extended from a clip on her finger to another machine. Particularly disturbing were the tubes running out of her mouth to a machine I suspected was a ventilator.

"How badly injured is she?" I asked.

"You'll have to speak to her doctor," the nurse replied.

"Can't you give me an idea? I only know what I've learned from the news. Seeing her lying so still with all these tubes and bandages is making me very nervous. Is she in danger of dying?"

The nurse smoothed her pink floral scrub top over her ample frame and sighed. "I'm not supposed to do this, but she lives near me in Old Town. She always says hi and often stops for a chat. I hate to see what some bastard has done to her." She scanned the chart.

"The bandages on her face are hiding a broken nose and a crushed cheekbone. She has a bruised kidney and a couple of broken ribs, which punctured her lung, causing it to collapse. It has been re-inflated. Her left arm has a compound fracture."

"What about her head? The paper said she was in a coma."

"She had a depressed skull fracture and underwent surgery to alleviate the pressure on her brain. The doctor is keeping her in an induced coma to minimize brain damage."

"Is she going to die?"

"Only the doctor can answer that, but I can tell you that her condition was recently upgraded from critical to serious."

"So that means she's going to be okay?"

"According to her chart, her blood pressure, oxygen saturation levels, and heart rate have improved. Though not yet within normal ranges, they're much better than yesterday."

"Does she have any brain damage?"

"We won't know until she comes out of the coma."

"When does that happen?"

"Sorry, I can't help you there. Dr. Yausie makes that call. He should be here within the hour."

"Do you know how she was hurt or who did it?"

"I don't know. All I can say is I hope the guy is locked away forever for what he did to her. But it won't happen. It never does. Guys beat up gals, go to jail for a few months, come back out, and beat them up again. It's a never-ending vicious circle that no one does anything about."

She said this with such vehemence that I suspected her of being yet another woman with first-hand experience. She checked the monitors and the intravenous line going into the back of Teht'aa's hand before returning to the nursing station.

The vibrant Teht'aa I knew was not the woman lying so corpselike on the sterile hospital bed. I only knew she was alive from the slight rise and fall of her chest as she drew in a breath and expelled it.

"Oh, Teht'aa, I'm so sorry."

I pulled up a chair beside her. I wanted to clasp her hand but was afraid to in case I disturbed something, so I gently stroked her uninjured arm instead.

"You're going to be okay. Eric's going to be okay," I whispered over and over again, praying it was true.

What a trick the gods had played on us. One day everything was nirvana — well, almost — and the next, a living hell. If his daughter were to die, Eric would be destroyed. And if he were convicted of murder, I doubted I could carry on.

"So you're Eric's wife," a voice rasped.

Startled, I looked across the bed to discover an old man sitting in a chair partially hidden by the folds of the blue-striped curtain separating Teht'aa from her neighbour.

"You must be Teht'aa's uncle," I said none too politely.

He sat as immobile as Teht'aa, his arthritic hands resting on the bony knobs of his knees protruding through the thin denim of his jeans. His lightweight windbreaker hung open to reveal a red plaid flannel shirt buttoned to his chin. Loose-hanging folds of skin hid the top buttons. Wisps of grey hair caressed the collar. A navy ball cap with "Tlicho Wolves" stamped in red across the front hugged his head, though I couldn't decide which stuck out farther, the brim of the cap or his nose. His black eyes assessed me from the maze of wrinkles covering his deeply bronzed face.

He didn't answer.

I had learned in my conversations with Algonquin elders that a response was not always immediate, so I waited, embarrassed by my earlier rudeness. I continued to stroke Teht'aa's arm.

Finally, he said in slow, measured words, "Yup. I'm Joe Bluegoose, Teht'aa's *go'eh*. Eric calls me Uncle Joe."

It was my turn to be silent while I tried to place him in Eric's life. The name was vaguely familiar, and then it came to me. This man had once been the single most important person in my husband's life. He had helped him reclaim his Algonquin heritage.

"You must be the uncle of Teht'aa's mother. Eric told me her name, but I'm afraid I've forgotten it."

"Charmaine."

"I gather she died in a car accident."

He grunted.

"Such a tragedy to die so young and leave a baby behind."

Another grunt.

I waited for him to say more, and when he didn't, I asked, "Have you spoken to Teht'aa's doctor?"

The same grunt as before.

I was beginning to think we had exhausted our conversation when he spoke up. "You family. Why you take so long to come to Eric's daughter? She is here three days."

"I'm sorry. I only found out this morning and came as fast as I could from my home in Quebec. Do you know who hurt her? Was it her boyfriend?"

"Eric is no murderer," he rasped. "What you do about it?"

My response was interrupted by the sound of powwow drumming coming from my purse. I scrambled to retrieve the phone and started to answer when the nurse tapped me on the shoulder. "No cellphones allowed. Take it outside."

I sped out of ICU in time to hear only a dial tone. When I checked for the caller's name, another nurse told me I had to go to the lobby. Down the stairs I flew and almost collided with a man leaning over the reception counter admonishing the dear who'd been so helpful.

"I demand to see Teht'aa Bluegoose."

"I'm sorry, only family are allowed to visit."

"I'm her goddamn boyfriend. Now tell me where in the hell she is in this godforsaken hospital."

SIX

Boyfriend? I thought he was dead.

From the man's unkempt blond hair and unshaven face to the scuffed hiking boots on his feet, he looked as if he'd crawled out of a hole. Not to mention the smell. His jeans were filthy, though the white T-shirt was remarkably clean under a mud-streaked, down-filled vest with feathers leaking out of it like a plucked turkey. His blue eyes were bloodshot, as if recovering from a bender.

"Look, *meine Frau*, I've been in the bush prospecting and only found out about my girlfriend today. So tell me her room number." He spoke with a slight German accent.

The woman glanced in my direction as if debating whether to turn him over to me.

I took the decision out of her hands and approached him.

"Hi, I'm Teht'aa's stepmother, Meg Harris. How can I help you?"

"You don't look like a stepmother. Way too young and pretty." A band of brighter than white teeth spread across his face. "I'm Hans Walther." He held out his hand. "You can take me to her."

I couldn't bring myself to touch him, so I pretended I hadn't noticed the hand. I continued walking into the lobby, where several chairs were occupied with people, some with worried expressions on their faces, others lost in sleep.

"You are married to her father, Eric Odjik," he said, coming up behind me.

At least he knew that much.

"I'm afraid I've never heard Teht'aa mention your name."

The two media people were still stationed outside. They ignored the old man pushing a walker and a woman hugging flowers who were inching past them. Instead the reporters kept their eyes trained on me.

"Let's get out of the way." I led him to an alcove behind a wall that blocked the reporters' prying eyes. "I'm told that her boyfriend was killed yesterday."

"Do I look dead to you?"

"How do I know you are her boyfriend?"

"Excuse me. Is my word not good enough?"

"You could be a reporter using this as a ruse to get to her."

"Looking like this? I didn't have time to change. I came directly to the hospital when I heard. Go ask her. She'll tell you who I am."

"I'm afraid that's not possible." I noticed he hadn't yet asked about her condition.

"Don't tell me, she told you she didn't want to see me. She was only joking."

"She's in a coma. When she wakes up, I'll let her know you want to visit and let her decide if she wants to see you."

I heard him mutter "bitch" under his breath before

he smiled at me and said, "Can you tell me her room number? I would like to send her flowers."

"Flowers would be nice. Have them delivered to the hospital, and they will ensure she receives them." The phone vibrated in my hand as the drumming started up again. "Sorry, I have to answer this."

I wasn't certain the man would leave but, as if making a decision, he nodded and held out his hand. "It was nice meeting you, Meg. Please tell Teht'aa I love her and want to see her."

Once again I ignored it.

I was saying "hello" into the cell when I heard him add, "Please wish her a speedy recovery from me."

He strode out the main door, where he was immediately accosted by the journalist. He flashed a broad smile into the camera and began talking.

"Am I speaking to Meg Harris?" came a male voice over the phone. "This is Derrick Robinson."

"Good. I'd like to know when I can see my husband. I'm at the hospital."

"How's his daughter doing?"

"Not good. I'm waiting to speak to her doctor to find out more. Do you know who did it?"

"As far as I know, the RCMP haven't officially identified a suspect. She had a restraining order out against a former boyfriend, so I believe they are pursuing that avenue."

"I'm confused. I just met a man who insists he's Teht'aa's boyfriend, but you told me the murder victim was her boyfriend."

"That's what your husband told me, although the police haven't yet released the name."

"Could you tell me why they think my husband killed this man?"

"He was found near the body with the murder weapon, a knife, in his possession. What the police call an open-and-shut case."

"There is no way Eric killed him."

"That will be for the courts to decide. I've already suggested to your husband that he should consider making a deal."

"Is that lawyer-speak for a guilty plea?"

"Yup, for a lesser sentence. They have charged him with first degree, which is twenty-five years minimum."

I gulped. "No way. He's not going to plead guilty. I won't let him."

"It's his prerogative, but I would advise the guilty plea given the evidence against him."

"Do you mind telling me how you came to be his lawyer?"

"Sure. I'm Annette Drygeese's son-in-law."

"And she is?"

"You don't know? She's the administrator for the GCFN offices here in Yellowknife."

"How long have you been practising law?"

"About five years, but given the number of cases I've handled, it's got to be equivalent to twenty years."

"And how many of these cases have been for murder?"

"A couple … well, they were domestic, pretty open-and-shut, so I guess you could say this is my first real homicide case, though it's kind of open-and-shut too."

Time to find a new lawyer. "I need to see my husband. When can I do that?"

"He's currently at the detachment in Digadeh, but the RCMP intend to bring him to Yellowknife within the next day or so."

"Can I talk to him on the phone?"

"Sorry, it's not permitted."

"Then I'll go to Digadeh and see him there."

"The RCMP won't let you."

"But I need to talk to him."

"For the moment only his lawyer can communicate with him. I can pass on anything you want to tell him."

The second after I hit the hang-up icon, I was dialling the number for my sister. An Ontario superior court judge, she would know who the best defence attorneys were.

"Sally McLeod," Jean proposed after we had gone through sisterly pleasantries and I'd explained the situation. "She ranks among the top defence counsels I've had in my court. Though she now works out of Vancouver, I know she's licensed to practise in the Northwest Territories. I imagine her caseload is full, so I'll call to see what I can do to persuade her to make room for Eric."

I hung up more than a little gobsmacked by my sister's willingness to help. Our relations could be described at best as passively tolerating each other, yet here she was offering to smooth my way. But it wasn't me she was helping. It was Eric. He had won her over with his dimples, smiling eyes, and sympathetic manner, just as he had won me over.

SEVEN

A wisp of a man clad in doctor's white and surgical greens with the *de rigueur* stethoscope slung around his neck was reading Teht'aa's chart when I arrived back at her bedside. On the way, I'd stopped at the nursing station to warn them against Hans Walther. I suspected he wouldn't let up until he was standing over her.

But for the faint rise and fall of her chest, Eric's daughter lay as deathlike as when I'd left her. The monitors blinked the same numbers, drew the same wavy lines. Nothing had changed. I patted her arm and told her I was back. Useless, I knew, but I couldn't ignore her. I had to do what I could to try to connect, to let her know that I was here.

"When is she going to come out of the coma?" I asked the doctor.

His piercing black eyes peered at me through horn-rimmed glasses. "And you are?"

Was this guy even old enough to be a doctor? He could be my son, if I'd bothered to have any. "I'm her stepmother, and you are?"

"Dr. Chan, resident for Dr. Yausie, the surgeon."

He returned his attention to the chart.

"I assume Dr. Yausie is the doctor who operated on her?"

"Yes." He continued reading.

"Are you allowed to tell me how she is doing, or do I have to wait for Dr. Yausie?"

"Tell her," Uncle Joe ordered from his chair in the folds of the curtain. "She understand your fancy words better than old man like me."

He glanced at me again and this time added a smile. "Sorry, I didn't mean to ignore you. Dr. Yausie has gone for the day. I'll give you an update after I've examined Ms. Bluegoose."

He did what doctors usually do, poked and prodded his patient and double-checked the machines, while the pink-floral nurse hovered behind him. He listened to Teht'aa's chest, glanced at the readings on the ECG, and listened to her chest again.

Ten minutes later he was finished. Dr. Chan motioned for Uncle Joe and me to join him at the nursing station. When I watched the old man struggle to rise from the chair, I wasn't so sure if it was a good idea. But after shaking out the kinks in his legs, he hobbled to the counter, where he dismissed with an impatient wave the chair being offered by the nurse at the station.

The update was short and to the point, with minimal medical bafflegab. The depressed skull fracture had caused minor hemorrhaging and swelling in her brain. She had been put into a drug-induced coma to minimize damage. Since her latest CT scan indicated that the swelling had subsided, they'd reduced the level of sedation this morning and planned to take her off it completely this evening.

"How long before she wakes up?" I asked.

"It can take a number of hours."

"Maybe I should also be asking if there is a danger she won't wake up."

"The probability is high that she will regain consciousness. The damage to her brain was minimal. But I have to caution you that there is always a risk that she might not."

"Do you think she will have any long-term effects?"

"Until she fully wakes up, it is hard to say. The human brain is a finely tuned instrument. Some patients fully recover after more severe damage than your daughter's, while others with less damage have long-term effects."

"Teht'aa gonna be okay," Uncle Joe declared. "She Tlicho. I smudge for the Creator. He make sure she wake up." Trembling fingers struggled to extract a small leather pouch from his jacket pocket.

"Sorry, sir," the nurse interjected. "I've already told you that you can't burn anything in here."

"Yah, yah, I know." He waved his hand again in dismissal, but the jut of his jaw told me that he was going to ignore her.

"Uncle Joe, with all the oxygen tanks in this room, lighting a match could make us go up in flames. You can hold the ceremony outside and capture the smudge in a bag and cleanse Teht'aa with it."

"Sorry, not allowed," the nurse persisted. "The smoke will bother the other patients. You can hold your smudging ceremony in the healing room and keep the smudge within its walls."

Though he merely grunted, I could tell that he had decided to accept the rules.

"What about Teht'aa's other injuries?" I asked Dr. Chan.

"You should speak to Dr. Finkelstein about those. Dr. Yausie and I only operated on the cranial injury."

He must've seen the look of exasperation on my face, for he continued, "Reading her chart, I would say that the only injury that could have a long-term effect is the compound fracture in her arm. I see Dr. Finkelstein put a metal plate on the ulna. But I suggest you talk directly with him. He can give you a better prognosis."

"Thanks, I will. Do you have any idea what caused these injuries?"

"I understand she was beaten."

"But with what? Surely a fist couldn't have done such damage."

"Sorry, I can't help you. I haven't watched enough *CSI*." He grinned but stopped when he noticed neither Uncle Joe nor I was smiling. "I suggest you talk to the RCMP."

"Do you know who's looking after her case?"

He shook his head. "Wilma should be able to help you." He nodded in the direction of the nurse behind the counter. "Now, if you will excuse me, I have another patient to attend to."

"I have a name here. Sergeant Ryan." Wilma held up a business card. "We're to call her when Teht'aa wakes up." She wrote down the information and passed it over. Noticing the phone in my hand, she continued, "You can't use your phone in here."

"Yeah, yeah, I know."

Uncle Joe was breathing heavily beside me. I didn't think he was up to doing the smudge but felt I should ask. Once again we were hit with the rules. I was beginning to think regulations were all this hospital cared about.

"You have to follow the schedule posted outside the healing room," the nurse said. "Besides, there isn't enough time. Visiting hours end in ten minutes."

I glanced at my watch. "Wow, almost eight o'clock, later than I thought. No wonder I'm so hungry. It's well past dinner time for me. But first I have to find a hotel room. Maybe you could recommend one?"

"You stay at Teht'aa's," Uncle Joe said.

"I don't know where it is. Do you?"

"I take you."

"What about a key?"

He opened his palm to reveal a silver ring crammed with assorted keys and a BMW key fob.

"Does that belong to Teht'aa's car?"

The old man's dark-brown eyes twinkled. "Nice, very nice."

Great. Exactly what I needed, some wheels. "I suggest we spend the remaining time with Teht'aa and then call a cab."

"No, I drive. BMW is in parking lot. It fun to drive." A huge grin with more gaps than teeth spread across his furrowed face.

EIGHT

If I questioned Uncle Joe's ability to get us to Teht'aa's apartment intact, I was answered by the ease with which he manoeuvred the metallic blue M3 out of the hospital parking lot. He might be a tottery old man on foot, but behind the wheel he was a confident young one with a penchant for speed. A couple of times I squeezed my eyes shut, gripped the dash, and waited for the jolt of the bump that never came when he swerved around a corner a little too sharply.

While he drove, I called the lawyer my sister recommended and the policeman in charge of Teht'aa's case. Since it was well past business hours, neither answered. But within seconds of leaving a message for Sally McLeod, she was returning my call. Within another second I was hiring her as Eric's defence attorney and promising to transfer ten thousand dollars to her office bank account. Not having anywhere close to that amount in my account, I made a mental note to call my broker to redeem one of the bonds I'd inherited from Aunt Aggie. I also agreed to meet Sally at the airport coming off the first flight tomorrow morning from Edmonton, where she'd just finished a trial with a not-guilty verdict, she added.

If I didn't hear from Sergeant Ryan tonight, I wouldn't wait for her call in the morning. Instead, I would be at the detachment at 6:30 a.m., the time her voice greeting said she'd be in the office. In addition to an update on Teht'aa's case, I was hoping she would provide information on Eric's case.

With little traffic on the main road, we sped through the downtown core of Yellowknife, past the two or three blocks of drab government buildings varying from a few stories to about ten. The sidewalks were mostly empty but for a clutch of people milling about in front of the post office and across the street at an A&W. We came to a screeching halt in front of a sign proclaiming we'd arrived at the Vietnamese Noodle House.

Uncle Joe smacked his lips and declared that whenever he was in town he treated himself to a Vietnamese meal.

He patted his stomach and grinned. "Good for waistline."

As if he had to worry. His bony hands suggested he didn't have an ounce of fat to spare. But if he was on the thin side, it wasn't related to his food intake. He gorged as much as I did on the shrimp rolls, chicken satay, vermicelli soup, and other tasty Vietnamese dishes all ordered by him, except for the chicken satay. I had a hankering for the peanut sauce of satay and persuaded him to order it. I could see he had set dishes he always ordered and didn't like to stray from these. But he tucked into the satay as heartily as I did, so perhaps he would add it to his list.

We continued along the main road, down a long decline lined with gaily painted clapboard houses and a motel or two crammed into the few building spots the rocky terrain would allow. To the right I could see the blue expanse of Great Slave Lake, dotted with the odd island and what looked to be a straggle of houseboats. At the bottom of the hill, where the road flattened, we passed several gift shops, one sporting a sign that read "Ragged Ass Lane," which had me wondering about the northern tale behind its naming. Though the buildings declared that civilization had taken over this shore of the lake, the ever-present mounds of impenetrable Precambrian granite reminded me that the vast, empty wilderness was only a few blocks away.

We came to a halt beside a pale-blue three-storey building clinging to the side of a rocky outcrop with a steep wooden staircase zigzagging up the side.

"Here the key," Uncle Joe said. "Teht'aa live on top floor."

"No elevator?" I asked, angling my head back to see the narrow landing at the top of the stairs. "Aren't you staying here too?"

"My old legs don't do stairs. I stay with my son in N'dilo."

"Where's that?"

"Island at the end of this road. N'dilo is Yellowknives, like we're Tlicho or Dogrib people."

"But you're all part of the Dene, right?"

"Yup, guess Eric learned you a thing or two."

"Is it far? Because I am hoping to be at the police station by six thirty tomorrow morning."

"No problem. I get up with sun. I go fishing with my grandson. I bring you some. Plenty whitefish in the lake."

"Sounds good as long as you aren't late. Do you have a phone number I can reach you at?"

He rhymed off his cell number. I was finding this old guy more amazing with every minute. No lying back and waiting to die for him. He was going to enjoy life to the fullest until his time came. No wonder he meant so much to Eric.

He left me in a squeal of dust and gravel with my bulging suitcase planted beside the bottom stair. Another glance up the three flights to Teht'aa's landing had me wondering whether I was up to the challenge. But I made it with only a modest amount of puffing along with strategic stops at each landing to admire the view. And what a view it was overlooking the deep blue of what I took to be an arm of Great Slave Lake extending toward the haze of the distant horizon. A canoe was setting out from a dock for one of the houseboats hugging the rock islands. Beyond, I could make out the spiralling cloud of smoke from the forest fire we'd flown over.

At a shade past nine thirty, I was surprised by the amount of daylight until I remembered that in this part of the world it was the time of year for endless days, when the sun only briefly dipped beneath the horizon.

I inserted the key into the lock of the landing's sole door. It sprang open before I had a chance to turn the key.

Did Teht'aa have a roommate?

"Hi, anyone there?"

I pushed the metal door farther open and called out again. Silence was the only answer, apart from a motorcycle whining full throttle along the road below me. Maybe in the Great White North people didn't lock their doors.

I hesitated. Every jangling nerve in my body was telling me to call the police. But I was afraid of making myself look a fool. A wimpy southerner who couldn't handle the North's idiosyncrasies.

"I'm coming in," I shouted and gingerly stepped into a small vestibule and waited until I was convinced I was alone. I kept my cell in my hand, ready to dial 911, which I later discovered would have been futile because Yellowknife hadn't yet implemented the service.

I picked my way through the boots and running shoes scattered over the tile floor and entered a large living area with two picture windows focused on the lake view. Eric's daughter wasn't known for her tidiness. Magazines and books were strewn over the glass coffee table beside a mug half-filled with old coffee.

I smiled at the sight of the dark-green soapstone carving of a polar bear rising on its hind legs from its place on the table. I'd bought it during my trip to the Arctic and had given it to Teht'aa when we finally decided we actually liked each other.

Several articles of clothing, including the jacket of the blue suede suit she'd bought in Ottawa, were scattered over the sofa. It seemed like yesterday that she was bragging about the purchase of this chocolate-brown leather chesterfield with matching armchair. She'd bought it at the Edmonton Mall at the kind of discount price one couldn't turn down and had borrowed a friend's truck and trailer to transport it the thousand or more kilometres to Yellowknife.

The kitchen was the usual mess I had come to expect from Eric's daughter, who only believed in washing dishes when she ran out of clean ones. Mind you, until Eric moved in, I had been no different. In addition to the stacked dirty dishes, she hadn't bothered to close several drawers or pick up the items that had tumbled onto the floor.

Though I hated cleaning as much as she did, my threshold for dirt was lower. If I was going to stay here for any length of time, I would have to clean it up, but I'd worry about that tomorrow. Right now, all I wanted to do was sleep. By Quebec time it was well past my bedtime. I headed down the hall.

I peeked into the bedroom on the non-view side of the apartment and saw a single bed with an IKEA desk and set of drawers. It was too neat to be Teht'aa's bedroom. The room across the hall was more in keeping with her style. The duvet on the queen bed was half on, half off, with pillows bunched on the broadloom. Most of the dresser drawers were open, with clothes spilling out. One drawer lay upside down on the floor. But I was too exhausted to do anything about it. After ensuring the front door was securely locked, I crawled into her bed.

Only as my eyes were drifting shut did I wonder if her apartment wasn't *too* untidy. My thoughts wandered back to the partially opened front door. But I was asleep before I could connect the dots.

NINE

One second I was deep asleep, and the next I was on high alert. A sudden bang had invaded my dream, forcing me to claw my way to the surface. I strained my ears to hear more than the looming silence. A truck rumbled on the street below. Of course, a backfire. I allowed myself to relax until I caught the sound of footsteps in the apartment.

Not again! Panic consumed me. I flung the covers over my head and tried to pretend I was elsewhere. I stopped breathing and listened to the footfalls echoing down the hall toward me. The person hummed as they drew closer. *Please, God, transport me somewhere else.*

"Hey, Tee, whatcha doin'?" shrieked a female voice. "I gotta bottle of Johnny. Let's party."

Not a man. Thank God.

I poked my head above the covers.

"You sure ain't Tee. Who the fuck are you?"

The woman was leaning against the door jamb, or should I say clinging, since she seemed to be having difficulty staying upright.

"I'm Teht'aa's father's wife. Who the fuck are you?" I might as well throw it back at her. I felt the fear slowly draining away.

In the twilight of dawn, I could only see a mass of black hair and the outline of a slim, almost elfin figure with a large bag slung over her shoulder and the shadow of a bottle hanging from her hand.

"Ya don't say. I heard about you. Where the hell ya come from?"

"I arrived from Ottawa this afternoon."

"Where's Tee?"

"She's in the hospital."

"Fuck, I forgot. That motherfucker of a boyfriend beat her up. She gonna be okay?"

"I hope so. So who are you? I didn't know Teht'aa had a roommate."

"Not 'xactly a roommate. She lets me sleep here when things ain't goin' too good. I'm Gloria." She lifted the bottle up and drained a hefty amount. "Want some?"

"No," I shot back to drown out the yes.

"Sorry I woke ya up. Guess I'd better get to bed." She turned a little unsteadily and headed across the hall to the other room.

I lay back and tried to sleep before my bladder convinced me it was full. On my way to the washroom, I noticed Gloria's door was open. I poked my head in and asked, "You didn't happen to leave the front door unlocked last time you were here?"

The glow of a cigarette marked where she lay in the bed. "Not me. I ain't been here in a while. Look, don't tell Tee you seen me smoking, eh? She hates the smell."

"Keep the door closed and open your window." I wasn't fussy about the smell either. "When were you last here?"

"About a week ago. I was visiting my kid. Why you ask?"

"The door was open when I arrived tonight, but I expect Teht'aa doesn't lock it."

"No way. She's real careful. Always locks it up tighter than a virgin's cunt. Whoops, sorry. Better talk like a lady, eh?" She broke into a raucous laugh that turned into a fit of coughing. When she finally stopped, she asked, "How long she gonna be in the hospital?"

"Too soon to tell. We don't even know if she's going to wake up from the coma."

"Fuck. I didn't know she was that bad."

"You said her boyfriend beat her up."

"Yah, that's what I heard."

"What's his name?"

"Frank. I could never figure out why such a nice lady like Tee would go out with such a jerk." She lifted the bottle to her mouth and took another long draught. "Sure ya don't want any?"

I shook my head. "I met a man today who insisted he was her boyfriend. Hans Walther was his name."

"He did?" Her cigarette glowed. "Where d'ya see him?"

"At the hospital."

"What was he doing there? He hurt or something?"

"He wanted to see Teht'aa."

Another glow of her cigarette. "Nah, he's not her boyfriend. Frank was."

"Why did he insist that he was?"

"He's got the hots for her. But she don't like him."

"Do you know about the murder at Digadeh?"

"Yah, I heard. That's where I'm from. Tee too. And Frank."

"I thought she came from a town called Wolf River."

"We call it Digadeh now.... it's Tlicho. Means the same thing ..." Her voice petered out into a whisper followed shortly by soft snoring.

I retrieved the burning cigarette before it set us both on fire, ignored the uncapped bottle on the night table, opened the window to let the smoke escape, and shut the door behind her.

Though the amount of daylight made it seem like six in the morning, my watch said it was only a few minutes past three. Not sure I could go back to sleep, I was tempted to join Uncle Joe on his fishing expedition, but couldn't muster up the energy, so I returned to bed.

The loud drumming of the phone woke me up. It was Uncle Joe saying he didn't mind waiting, but the cop might be gone by the time I got to the station. It was shortly after seven thirty. I threw on clothes, grabbed my purse, and down the stairs I fled.

"I'm so sorry," I said, buckling up the seatbelt. "Have you really been waiting for an hour? You should've called earlier."

"You need sleep. Besides, I'm old man. I can wait. Shelagh say you need some food in your stomach." He passed me a thermos mug of still-warm coffee, a large piece of bannock, and a container of fried fish, along with a fork.

"Is this the fish you caught this morning?"

"Was good morning. We caught two whitefish and an inconnu."

I sampled some fish. "Delicious. Please thank Shelagh for me. Is she your wife?"

"Nope, Mary died fifteen years ago. Shelagh's my son's wife." He put his foot on the gas and off we zoomed, barely missing a car that had turned onto the road.

"Do you know Gloria?" I asked between bites of bannock.

"You talking about Claire's daughter?"

"I guess. I left her sleeping in the apartment. She says she's from Digadeh."

"Yup. Claire and Charmaine were sisters."

"So she's Teht'aa's cousin."

"Yup. Teht'aa looks out for her. She's had a rough go. Better she stay in Digadeh, but she don't want to."

"Is that where you live?"

"Yup. These days. I used to live in Alberta and Saskatchewan. Met Eric in Medicine Hat when working on the pipeline. When old, better to live in place where you come from." He honked the horn and waved at a man driving a shiny red pickup passing us in the opposite direction.

"That's George. He from Digadeh too. Ice road closed. He have to keep his fancy new truck in Yellowknife now." He chuckled.

"Ice road?"

"Yah. In winter, when river and lake ice real thick, they make a road to communities that don't have no highway going to it. It goes to diamond mines too. Plane only way to get there now. And it don't take trucks." He chortled as he swerved around a stopped car.

"Are you originally from Digadeh?"

"Digadeh only a summer camp when I was born. I'm seventy-five. Not bad for an old man, eh?" He thumped his chest. "Heart like boy." He grinned. "When I a boy, no one live in Digadeh all the time. We live on the land, move from camp to camp. We follow the caribou. No caribou now. They make Digadeh permanent in 1970s, when I live in Alberta. They build a store, church, and houses for the families. A lot easier living in a permanent house than setting up camp, eh? But not all families do this. Not my sister."

He braked to a stop to allow two young boys to cross the road.

"I was a boy, like him." He pointed to the smaller child clutching the hand of the older one. The boy couldn't be older than six or seven. "RCMP come to our camp and take me and my brother and sister away. It was many years before I come back here."

"What kept you away?"

"Saint Anne's. There ten years."

"Is that a school?"

"Yup, residential school run by nuns and priests." He spat. "They don't let us leave."

I cringed at the term "residential school," schools that were set up by the government to remove the "Indian" from these poor children. Only now, 150 years after the first such schools were established and twenty years after the last of them was closed, were we learning through the Truth and Reconciliation Commission set up by the government about the life-altering damage they had inflicted on generations of children and their families.

"Not even for summer holidays?" I asked.

"They afraid we never come back." He chuckled. "They right. My brother and me escape two times. But we got lost. They found us and send us back. When school finish, Larry and I don't go home. No reason to. Our parents dead." He screeched to a halt at a light turning red.

"You know Eric's at Digadeh," he said.

"I know. Tell me, is the victim's name Frank?"

"Yup. A bad 'un. Had it coming."

"Was Frank Teht'aa's boyfriend?"

"Don't know. They cousins."

"How could he be her boyfriend, then?"

"Not real cousins. Connie adopted Frank. She's my sister Florence's girl."

"What do you know about Hans Walther?"

"The prospector? Friend of Teht'aa too. Frank had problems with women. She shoulda stay away from him."

"Did Frank assault Teht'aa?"

"Eric say Frank did it."

"How do you know?"

"Told me."

"When did you see Eric?"

"At the hospital two days ago. He say he go to Digadeh to see Frank. I told him don't go, but he stubborn fool. Too angry to listen."

Hours later, Frank was dead and Eric was arrested for his murder.

Like his lawyer said, an open and shut case.

Damn.

TEN

Using Teht'aa as his excuse, Uncle Joe left me at the entrance to the police station in the downtown core. When I brought up the earliness of the hour, he sheepishly admitted he was allergic to cops and would wait in the hospital lobby until he was allowed into ICU. I soon discovered he'd dropped me off at the wrong door. It turned out the building housed both the RCMP divisional headquarters for all of the Northwest Territories and the detachment for Yellowknife. I found myself being squired through a labyrinth of anonymous halls until I was left at the reception counter for the detachment.

Sergeant Ryan was about Teht'aa's age, with short-cropped white-blond hair and the kind of athletic build that had me trying to suck in my stomach. After meeting me at the front reception, she led me along a narrow hall to a door that opened onto a windowless room, bare but for two straight-backed chairs and a metal table.

"We can talk in here." The police officer swung the door wider. "We prefer to meet with relatives in friendlier surroundings. I was intending to meet you at your hotel. I guess you didn't get my message."

I slipped Eric's cell from my purse and noticed the flashing icon. "Sorry, I didn't check."

She pulled out the nearest chair for me and brought the other around to the same side of the table. She dropped the file folder she'd been carrying onto the table and sat down. "I'm so sorry about your daughter. Is she still in a coma?"

"Actually she's my stepdaughter, my husband's daughter, but you probably know that."

She acknowledged with a curt nod.

"The doctor is stopping the sedation, so she should wake up sometime today."

"Good, we need to talk to her."

I noticed a camera peering down at us from high up on the opposite wall. "Are we being recorded?"

"Not unless you give me a reason." Her thin lips barely cracked a smile in her otherwise impassive face. "I'm afraid our detachment is overcrowded, so this interview room is the only private room available. By husband, you mean Eric Odjik."

I nodded.

"You know he's been arrested for murder."

"Yes, but he didn't do it. He'd never kill anyone."

She gave me a polite shrug, as if she'd heard this many times before, and asked, "How can I help you?"

"I'd like to know more about Teht'aa's assault. I gather the man murdered at Digadeh was the man responsible."

"All I can say is that we are following up on various leads."

"So you haven't stopped your investigation?"

"No."

Good. If the murder victim had nothing to do with Teht'aa's injuries, there went Eric's motive. Still, Eric had told Uncle Joe that Frank had done it. But I wasn't about to mention this to the sergeant.

Instead I said, "Do you have a motive yet for the attack?"

"It was a sexual assault. The motive is pretty straight forward."

"Does that mean Teht'aa was … ah … raped?" I could barely get the word out as I tried to suppress the rush of panic it released. "I … ah … thought she'd just been beaten."

"Unfortunately not."

"But she has a fractured skull, a broken arm, and other injuries not usually associated with … ah … rape."

"She likely put up a good fight and got someone good and mad at her."

"Yeah, Teht'aa's not exactly a shrinking violet. Do you think she knew the man?"

"As I said, we are following all leads. Let's just say most of the sexual assault cases we investigate are domestic."

"So that means a boyfriend or husband?"

"Or family member. What can you tell me about the men in her life?"

"I met a man yesterday who said he was her boyfriend. Hans Walther is his name."

"Tell me about him." She extracted a notebook from her shirt pocket.

I told her the little I'd learned and ended by saying, "It might be worthwhile checking out his alibi. It's possible he made a brief visit to town and returned to the bush after he assaulted Teht'aa."

"Any other men?"

If she didn't already know about Frank, I wasn't going to tell her. "Not that I know of."

"Do you know if she frequents any of the bars in town?"

"Sorry, I know next to nothing about her social life here, but I would be surprised if she spent much time in bars. She was sick and tired of the bar scene. The only men she ever met in bars were after one thing, and it wasn't her brain."

"I'll second that." This time Sergeant Ryan's smile added more life to her face. "What about female friends?"

"She's mentioned someone by the name of Sylvia several times. They hike together. She worked with her at APTN. Sorry I don't have a last name for you."

"It should be easy enough to get. The next is a rather delicate question, but it needs to be asked. Do you know if she is into rough sex?"

"You mean like bondage and stuff like that?"

"Yes."

I thought back to that terrible time a couple of years ago when Eric almost died and shuddered. "No, she'd never get involved in anything like that."

"What about prostitution?"

"You've got to be kidding. She had a good-paying job and is about to start a new one at CBC. Why are you asking these questions?"

"Just covering all angles. You probably don't know that she was found in an alley behind the Gold Range Motel, known for its hourly rates."

"Oh. Is it close to her apartment in Old Town?"

"Actually, it's only a few blocks from here. If Yellowknife were said to have a rough area, this would be it. Do you know if she's still involved in drugs? I see she pleaded guilty to possession seven years ago but didn't serve time."

This was news to me. The only charges I knew about were dropped when she agreed to attend a healing circle. "As far as I'm aware she has been drug-free for the last few years."

"What about alcohol?"

"No more than most people. Can you tell me anything about how she was found and when?"

"One of the homeless women who hang out in the alley behind the motel found her and notified the motel's manager. The call came in at 2:33 a.m., the morning of the sixteenth. We're not certain when the actual assault occurred, but we know it was after 9:45 p.m. the previous night, when she was seen leaving her apartment." She opened the folder and brought out a sheet of paper. "It says here that she's lived in Yellowknife two years."

"It's probably closer to twenty months. APTN sent her here to handle its NWT news coverage. Before that she was living and working for APTN in Ottawa, and prior to that her father's house on the Migiskan Reserve in Quebec."

"I've seen her on TV. She's certainly a beautiful woman. I hope her injuries don't put an end to her career."

"I hope so, too, but that's a worry for the future. Right now the most important thing is for her to wake up with no permanent brain damage. I imagine you know that she was born and raised in the Northwest Territories."

"Yes, in the Dene community of Digadeh. Apart from her father and yourself, we aren't aware of other relatives." She pulled out another sheet of paper. "No, that isn't entirely correct. There's an uncle, great-uncle by the name of Joseph Bluegoose, but we haven't been able to locate him."

"He's in Yellowknife. Staying with his son." *Sorry, Uncle Joe, but finding Teht'aa's attacker is more important than keeping the police away from you.*

"Do you have the co-ordinates?"

"No, but he spends most days at the hospital. There's also a cousin in town. Her name is Gloria."

"Do you have contact information for her?"

"I just left her sleeping at Teht'aa's apartment. But that's all I know about Teht'aa's relatives." If they didn't yet know that their murder victim was also related, that was their problem. "She never talked about her childhood. Why do you need this information? The key thing is to catch the man who did this."

"As mentioned, most assault cases in NWT are domestic, so the first step in our investigation is to determine the men who knew her, including relatives."

"You should be asking people in Digadeh."

"We are. I have a constable following up there, but as with any small community, when it feels threatened the tendency is to close ranks and not divulge much information, particularly to the cops." Another smile inched across her freckled face.

"By the way, I assume you've checked out Teht'aa's apartment."

"My partner and I did."

"I'm surprised you didn't clean up after your search."

"What do you mean?"

"There was stuff strewn all over her apartment."

"That can't be. We left it exactly the way we found it. While Teht'aa would never get an award for good house-keeping, it was no messier than my own place." Another wisp of a smile.

"The door was also unlocked."

"Impossible. I distinctly remember double-checking that it was locked." The cop pushed her chair back with a grating noise that set my teeth on edge. "I'd better check it out. You come with me."

I glanced at my watch. "How long will it take? I have to meet someone at the airport in a couple of hours."

"No problem. If you don't have wheels, I'll drive you there."

I had a feeling being picked up in a cop car wouldn't go over well with Eric's new lawyer. "Thanks, I can take a cab."

ELEVEN

This time Teht'aa's door was firmly locked, the way I had left it. While I searched through the jumble in my purse for the key, the sergeant slipped on a pair of latex gloves and examined the outside of the metal door, concentrating on the area around the lock.

"See anything?" I asked.

"Nope, no sign of forced entry. Do you have the key?"

I passed it to her. Ordering me to stay outside, she unlocked the door and stepped into the vestibule. Only when the door closed behind her did I remember.

I hastily reopened it and called out, "Don't forget Teht'aa's cousin Gloria is sleeping in the back bedroom."

"Her last name Bluegoose?" she asked with a hint of suspicion.

"I've no idea. Why do you ask?"

"We have a warrant out for her arrest."

And I'd been sleeping in the bedroom across the hall from her.

"What's it for?"

"She's up on prostitution charges and hasn't abided by the conditions of her release."

At least it wasn't murder.

The last glimpse I had of the cop before shutting the door was of her striding purposefully toward the bedrooms.

Though the sun had begun to heat up the day, a cold wind blowing from the lake had me trying to warm up my hands in my pockets. Feeling somewhat exposed perched on the narrow landing with its ten-metre drop to the street, I sat down on the hard-packed dirt of a flower planter. Through the railing I was surprised to see a string of people going in and out of the house across the street, until I realized it was a bed and breakfast. A tantalizing whiff of bacon and something sweet, like cinnamon buns, told me it also housed a café. Good. I wouldn't have to rely on my own dreadful cooking.

Beyond, the lake glistened and rippled with the wind. A red canoe was setting out from one of the houseboats. The paddler was having a challenge dealing with the waves and the wind. As much fun as it would be to live in one of those, I'm not sure I would like to be at the daily mercy of the vagaries of subarctic weather.

My eyes followed the ribbon of the main road. It ran through the flats of Old Town, past a collection of abandoned log shacks, and up the hill to the scattered skyscrapers of Yellowknife, skyscrapers only because they towered above everything else. Far off to the left of the downtown core, I could make out a high, thin tower that didn't appear to be an office building or an apartment.

"Beautiful view, isn't it?" a male voice suddenly said behind me.

I turned to see an RCMP officer stepping onto the landing. "Fabulous. But what is that high building beyond the downtown core?"

"That's all that remains of Con Mine, one of two gold mines that made Yellowknife a boomtown. That's the headframe, all twenty-five storeys, the highest structure in the Northwest Territories. It sits atop one of the deepest shafts in the world, over a mile deep."

"Is the mine still in operation?"

"It closed in 2003, but cleaning up the site continues to be a major headache. Arsenic trioxide, a byproduct of gold mining, is very toxic and difficult to get rid of. They managed to clean up the tailing ponds, but the area continues to test high for arsenic. But the site isn't anywhere near as polluted as the Giant Mine site, which is behind us on the opposite shore of Back Bay. Do you remember the Giant Mine explosion?"

"Is that the one that killed several striking miners?"

"Yup, nine of them. It was one of the largest murder investigations in RCMP history. A mine employee was later convicted. When the mine finally closed, it left over two hundred million tonnes of arsenic buried underground, enough to kill everyone on Earth several times over. After nearly twenty years of mostly talk, the government has yet to come up with a solution for dealing with it. In the meantime, we Yellowknifers have to trust that none of it is leeching into Back Bay and ultimately our drinking water. Gold mining is dirty business."

"Is that you, Gus?" The sergeant's blonde head appeared around the door. "I hope you brought your kit. Looks like we have a b and e here."

"Left it in the truck." The black crown and yellow band of his police cap was the last I saw of him as he tripped down the stairs.

She turned to me. "Mrs. Odjik, you can come in now. Don't touch anything. I want you to tell me if it looks any different from what you saw last night."

"What about Gloria? Did you arrest her?"

"She isn't here."

"Amazing. Given the condition she was in early this morning, I didn't think she would surface until midafternoon."

I followed the police officer into the cluttered living room.

"Is this how you found it?" she asked.

"Yeah. I guess it wasn't like this when you were here."

"Nope. Since you've been in the apartment, we need to get a set of your fingerprints."

Gus tramped into the room carrying a black suitcase-like container. "I'll do it on the kitchen counter."

Within minutes he had captured all ten fingers and two thumbs on an electronic fingerprint machine, along with my photo, and had sent them off into the big black cloud without setting off alarm bells.

While Gus snapped photos of the living room, the sergeant led me into Teht'aa's bedroom. I felt somewhat embarrassed at the sight of my unmade bed, particularly when I noticed that Gloria had made hers before leaving. I wondered if her cop antenna had warned her about their pending arrival.

"Do you think it was the man who assaulted Teht'aa?" I asked.

"Too early to tell. I don't suppose you can tell us if anything was taken."

"Sorry, this is the first time I've been in the apartment."

70

"Look around anyway. No matter where we live, we all have personal items that move around with us. See if you can tell if any of Teht'aa's are missing."

I chuckled at the photo of her father and me lying face up on her dresser. We were standing on a sandy shore, looking drenched beside an overturned canoe. It was taken during a canoe trip that was more memorable for what I found than for the whitewater paddling.

I was about to reach for Teht'aa's jewellery box lying on the floor when Ryan brushed me aside. "Don't touch anything." She lifted up the delicate birch bark box with an intricate floral design made from dyed porcupine quills. It had been a gift from an elder on the Migiskan Reserve as a thank you for the time Teht'aa had spent driving the woman to and from Ottawa for doctors' appointments.

The policewoman opened up the box. It was filled with jewellery.

"Can you tell if anything is missing?" she asked.

"I'm afraid I'm not very familiar with her jewellery, but since I see a couple of pairs of gold earrings, including a pair with diamonds and a gold bracelet, I'd say it's likely nothing was taken."

Her flat-screen TV, Blu-ray player, and satellite receiver were where one would expect them to be, in the living room. Then I realized her desktop looked decidedly empty.

"Did she have her laptop with her when she was found?"

"No, it was on her desk when we checked out her apartment after she was finally identified. Gus," Sergeant Ryan hollered, "did Johnny pick up the computer?"

"Not yet," came the shout from the back of the apartment.

"Damn him. There goes our chance to check her email and Facebook for possible leads."

"You can get that info from her cellphone, can't you?"

"No cell. Her purse is missing, along with her wallet. Main reason for the delay in identification, that and her facial injuries. We figure the cell was with the purse, since we didn't find it here."

"So her assailant stole her purse."

"Possibly, but she was found in an area where homeless people hang out. So could be one of them took the purse."

I glanced at the empty desktop. "Don't you think it strange that the only item taken from here is her computer?"

"If there is one thing I've learned after fifteen years of policing, it's that the people who commit crimes often do it for the craziest of reasons. I've investigated B and E's where the only items taken were everyday household things you could buy at Walmart. Do you notice anything else missing?"

While I studied the living room, Ryan jotted in her notebook. Last night I'd noticed a coat hanger hanging empty from a hook in the middle of the wall over the sofa. At the time I hadn't thought much about it, other than it was a strange place to leave a hanger. But today in the light of day I realized I'd seen this unique coat hanger before. Covered with red and orange braided ribbon, it was used for hanging only one item.

"I don't see her deerskin dress. It's a very old dress that was once worn by her Algonquin great-grandmother. It's very valuable."

"Do you have any photos of it?"

"I know we have one at our home in Quebec of her wearing it at a powwow. It's likely she has the same photo here."

"If you could search for it later, that would be good. If you don't see anything else, I'm going to have to ask you to leave, while we process the apartment. Do you have some place to go?"

"As mentioned I'm meeting someone up at the airport." I glanced at my watch. "I should be leaving now. How long do you think you'll be?"

"It's hard to tell. Give me a call when you plan on returning. But on second thought, you might want to consider checking into a hotel. Since the perp didn't force entry into the apartment, it suggests he or she has a key."

TWELVE

While I accepted the sergeant's offer for Constable Teresko call-me-Gus to drive me to the airport, I turned down his offer to take me and my friend to wherever we were going afterward. I thought Eric's defence attorney might not fancy riding with the police who'd arrested her client.

But I needn't have hurried. Sally McLeod's flight from Edmonton was delayed by thirty minutes, so I settled into one of the hardback seats in the arrivals area under the hungry eye of the polar bear guarding the baggage carousel.

I took the opportunity to make some calls, the first to Janet, but was only able to leave a message for her to call me.

I reached Uncle Joe buying himself a coffee in the hospital cafeteria. Despite the sedation having been completely stopped, he hadn't noticed any signs of Teht'aa waking up. After drinking his coffee, he planned to head to the Healing Room to smudge the Creator into nudging his grandniece awake. I took a moment to say my own silent prayer to whichever gods would listen.

I also called Derrick, something I'd been putting off. He surprised me when I told him about hiring a new lawyer.

"Good," was his immediate reaction. "Your husband is a nice man, and I'd hate to see him go to jail. He's going to need bigger guns than I can muster. I'm not really a defence attorney. But I'm happy to help out in whatever capacity I can. I know a lot of the players in this town. I've done wills and real estate deals for most of them."

"Sounds good. I'll run it by Sally and get back to you."

"You talking about Sally McLeod, the lawyer who won the Bedford case?"

"I don't know about the Bedford case, but yes, Sally McLeod is her name."

"Wow. You definitely got yourself one of the top defence attorneys in Canada."

"Any further word on Eric?"

"The RCMP are sending a plane to bring him back to Yellowknife later today. I'll let you know when he arrives."

"Where will they take him?"

"He'll likely be detained at the detachment."

"Will I be able to see him?"

"Sorry, no visitors until after the show cause."

"Show cause?"

"That's the bail hearing. It'll likely be tomorrow or the next day. I guess you won't be needing me for that, eh?"

"It's Sally McLeod's call. She's arriving in another twenty minutes. I'll have her call you, okay?"

"Yah, sure, thanks. By the way, your husband says hi. He's glad you're in Yellowknife, but he doesn't want you wasting time on him. He said he can get himself out of this mess. He wants you to do what you can to ensure his daughter is receiving the best care."

"Tell him I'm on it. You can also let him know that she's doing well with Uncle Joe by her side." I decided not to mention the lingering coma. My husband had enough to worry about. "Tell him I love him and I'll see him soon, and I know damn well he didn't do it."

I hung up feeling the tears trickle down my cheeks. Was I ever going to be able to hug the only man I'd ever loved, or were we going to face years looking at each other through bars?

Someone jerked the seat behind me, tearing me away from my morbid thoughts. New arrivals were spilling through a gate and crowding around the baggage carousel. But the flight from Edmonton was another ten minutes away. A man standing against the wall kept glancing at me as if he knew me. While he looked vaguely familiar, I couldn't place him, so I didn't feel compelled to smile back. Besides, I was in no mood to talk to anyone.

Eric had me wondering if Teht'aa was getting the optimal care her injuries demanded, especially the brain injury. Though I was certain the medical care was good, Yellowknife wasn't likely large enough to attract specialized medical talent. Dr. Yausie had been introduced as a surgeon, not a neurosurgeon. I suspected the hospital didn't have one. I would have to do what I could to ensure a neurosurgeon became involved in her care.

"Sorry to bother you, but are you married to Eric Odjik?"

I looked up into light-brown eyes partially hidden by a fringe of coal-black hair. The man who had been staring at me brushed the hair from his eyes.

"You likely don't remember me, but we met during one of your husband's visits to Yellowknife when he was campaigning for the GCFN Grand Chief. I'm Reginald Mantla, Grand Chief of the Tlicho."

I tried to recall the visit. "Sorry, you've caught me at a bad moment. We must've met at the feast that was held in honour of Eric's visit."

"You've got a good memory. It was held at Behchoko, about an hour's drive from Yellowknife. As I recall, you were a pretty mean drum dancer."

"I remember now. You enticed me to join the circle. It made the evening extra special for me. Thank you. Do you live in Behchoko?"

"These days I'm spending most of my time in Yellowknife, but normally I live in Digadeh, another Tlicho community."

"Oh," was all I could think to say, not wanting to bring up the murder.

But he did it for me. "Let me tell you how sorry I am to hear about your husband. But I imagine everything will be straightened out."

"It had better be."

"I greatly admire your husband and look forward to working with him in his new role as GCFN Grand Chief."

A pregnant pause. Neither of us wanted to voice what was uppermost in our minds, that it might never happen.

He glanced over at another set of new arrivals filing through the gate. "I see my wife and son. It was good meeting you again, and please let Eric know that I am more than willing to offer any support he needs. I feel badly that it happened in my community."

He greeted a plump blonde woman with a young boy shyly clinging to her side. I remembered chatting with her at the feast. We'd carried on a heated discussion about the merits of huskies versus poodles. Neither of us was willing to budge.

As I watched him tousle his son's curly hair and lift the child, shrieking, into the air, I remembered something else about the man. He'd wanted the job of GCFN Grand Chief and had come a close second to Eric.

I then noticed a slim, unsmiling woman in no-nonsense business attire striding through the gate on foot-crunching high heels. She pulled out her cellphone. A second later my phone rang.

THIRTEEN

It was Sally McLeod on the phone, but she wasn't the woman I'd thought. She, too, was wearing the *de rigueur* business suit, but her pale-blue Chanel suit and off-white silk blouse were considerably less formidable. With her well-rounded figure, soft grey hair, and twinkling blue-grey eyes, she presented more of a grandmotherly image than that of the foremost defence attorney in Canada. But maybe that was her secret.

"My dear, I know you're terribly worried, but we are going to get your husband off, you hear? So put a smile on those lips." She squeezed my hand. "Now let's go to the car rental counter. I hate having to rely on cabs."

If I'd thought she was going to rent the fanciest car in Yellowknife, I was wrong. We climbed into a discreet white Yaris, the cheapest economy to be had. Which, when I thought about it, was fine by me. I was probably paying for it.

"I'm dying for a decent cup of coffee. The slop they served on the plane didn't come close to being drinkable." She deftly manoeuvred the car around a stopped vehicle and onto the main road. "I'm sure you want one too."

"I'd love one, along with a muffin. But I'm afraid I haven't been in Yellowknife long enough to discover the best place for coffee."

"No problem. I know the town as if it were my own. My daughter and the grandkids live here. Your choice. Tim Hortons or McDonald's? Too small a town for Starbucks." She whomped on the gas to pass a slow-moving car and almost hit bottom at a sudden dip in the road. "Sorry about that. I always forget about these dips, a northern specialty. They're caused by the permafrost melting under the roadbed."

After picking up our coffees, a chocolate donut for her, and a fruit explosion muffin for me at the drive-thru window, we drove back onto the main road.

"We could've drunk our coffee at Tims, but Yellowknife's a small town with the usual big ears. Since your husband is well known, I thought it best we talk in private. We'll go to one of my favourite spots."

I was wiping the last crumbs from my mouth by the time we came to a stop in a parking area overlooking a park next to the lake. While most of the opposite shore was wilderness, directly across stood an impressive stone building with a couple of black Quonset-style roofs rising above the flat roofline.

"The Prince of Wales Northern Heritage Centre," she said. "Worth a visit."

"I'm sure it is, but I won't have time. I don't plan on sticking around once Eric is freed."

She fixed me with a chilling blue stare. "As much as we'd like to hurry it up, the court system has its own schedule. It can sometimes take up to two years to go to trial."

"You've got to be kidding. Are you saying that Eric will be in jail all that time?" I shuddered at the thought.

"That's why we're going to push for release, but more on that shortly. Follow me."

She opened the car door and climbed out clutching her purse, the coffee cup, and the bag with the donut. Carrying my own cup, I traipsed behind her down a set of concrete steps to a bench overlooking the water. A metal sculpture of stylized dancers cavorted beside it.

"The sculpture is by T-Bo," she said, sinking onto the bench. "He was actually a Thibault, but since no one up here could spell the French-Canadian name, he shortened it."

"Have you talked to my husband yet?" I sat down beside her.

"I will today when he arrives in Yellowknife. I'll want to talk to his current lawyer. Have you had a chance to let Derrick know of my involvement?"

"This morning, and he was fine with the change."

"Good. If you don't mind the cost, it'll be useful to keep him on retainer. I could use eyes on the ground for when I'm not here."

I'd happily have paid for a hundred lawyers if they were needed to free Eric.

"As I said, my first job is to get him released. I imagine the show cause will be tomorrow or the next day. How high are you prepared to go with bail?"

"As much as it takes. Don't worry about the money. I have investments I can tap into. And if need be, I can sell some land."

"There'll be no need to sell any land. Normally, bail is very low in this court, but since Eric is out-of-province

81

and an important man, the Crown might ask for more, but likely not more than five thousand, ten at the most. We don't go in for high bail amounts like they do in the States."

"Do you really think they will release him?"

"With a murder charge, it's less certain. Unlike other charges, the onus is on the defence to prove why he should be released. But he's an upstanding citizen with no priors. His only criminal conviction was for assault in '85, plus a few traffic violations, nothing to cause the court concern." She munched on her donut. "Ah, I see you didn't know about the conviction."

No, I didn't. "Do you mean he spent time in jail?"

"He was probated for time served plus community work. I imagine it was youthful hijinks. He was twenty and no doubt feeling his testosterone. It was either a bar brawl or a fight over a girl. I wouldn't take him to task on it. The important point is that it is his only criminal charge … until now. Right now the charge is first-degree murder, but I'm going to get it reduced to manslaughter."

"How likely is that?"

"A lot depends on what he's told the police. But if he's a smart man, and I think he is, he would know to keep his mouth shut. He'll need a surety for his release."

"What's that?

"A person who is responsible for ensuring he meets whatever conditions the court attaches to the release. Normally it would be you, his wife, but you don't live in the territory. We'll need someone from here. I gather his daughter lives in Yellowknife, but since the police are linking her assault to the murder, I wouldn't recommend her. By the way, how's she doing?"

"The doctors have stopped sedation, so we are hoping she'll come out of the coma today, tomorrow at the latest. I think Uncle Joe would be the best choice. Though he's not directly related to Eric, they have known each other since Eric was a young man, and he's Teht'aa's great-uncle. But does this mean that Eric won't be able to come home?"

"Part of my negotiation with the Crown. Where do I find Uncle Joe?"

"He's at the hospital. We can drive there afterward."

"I still want to recommend you as a surety if I can get the court to agree to allow him to travel to your home. Any criminal offences in your past?" She raised her eyebrows, but I had a feeling she already knew the answer. This woman had done her homework on Eric; likely she'd checked up on me too.

"Nope, nothing official. I was once charged with impaired driving, but my lawyer got me off."

"So you're a drinker."

"Not anymore. Haven't had a drink in almost two years."

"You're not going to go off the deep end on me, are you? It's difficult times like these that make that urge to drink all the stronger."

I vehemently shook my head, though just the mention of the word "drink" had me salivating.

"I should know," she continued. "I had a problem too, twenty years ago. I've been alcohol-free since. So if you feel the urge, get on your phone to your sponsor."

"Sponsor?"

"You went to AA, didn't you?"

"No, Eric was my AA. I guess you could call him my sponsor."

"Then call me. I'll talk you through it, okay?" She patted my hand. "You've been dry for two years. Let's keep it that way."

She drained the last molecule of her coffee. "Now, enough talk. I've got a lot to do before your husband arrives, so let's go see this Uncle Joe of yours."

I left her waiting in the car while I talked to Uncle Joe. She'd parked at the hospital entrance, near where the reporter had accosted me yesterday. Thankfully, I didn't have to run the gauntlet today. But if the man were to learn that Eric was arriving this afternoon, I had no doubt I would see my husband on tonight's news with his head covered as he was being pushed into a paddy wagon. Poor Eric. I hoped he would be saved from this indignity.

When I arrived at Teht'aa's bedside, Uncle Joe was leaning back in his chair with his eyes closed. She was as still and as silent as yesterday, while the machines continued to hum, seemingly content, beside her. The only change appeared to be the transference of the IV needle from her right to her left hand.

I mumbled a greeting and patted her arm. "You're going to wake up, aren't you."

I thought I saw an eyelid move, but when it wasn't followed by another flicker, I knew it was only wishful thinking.

"Don't you worry. She gonna be okay," Uncle Joe said, rising from his chair. "She strong, like my sister."

"I hope you're right." I glanced at the couple hovering over the girl in the next bed. "Let's go out in the hall where we can talk in private."

At first the old man refused to be a surety, saying he'd do anything for Eric, even go to jail for him, but he couldn't do this. In case a criminal past was the obstacle, I queried him about it, but he acted as if I'd insulted him. Finally, he admitted he'd been surety for a nephew, and it had cost him no end of trouble.

"Stupid kid kept staying out after curfew and hanging with kids he not supposed to. What does the stupid kid do? He steals bag of chips and can of Coke from the Northern store and gets caught. It cost me plenty grey hair and a canoe load of moose."

"You won't have to worry about Eric not obeying his conditions."

"Ha! When he hotshot hockey player, he think rules not for him. He drive too fast and total fancy new car. He get in lots of fights and he get my niece pregnant. Now he hotshot chief. It no different."

Ah, the secrets we keep. No wonder Eric said little about his early hockey years. "He's a grown man now and the most law-abiding citizen I know. He'll abide by them."

"If he don't come to court, it cost me big money."

"He'll be there. But if it makes you feel any better, I'll put up the money, okay?"

"You good woman. I do it."

FOURTEEN

I spent the rest of the morning with my eyes trained on Teht'aa, watching for a flicker of an eyelid, a twitch of a finger, any movement, no matter how infinitesimal, that would tell me she was waking up. But as the minutes ticked into an hour and then another with still no sign of life other than the steady rise and fall of her chest, I started losing hope, convinced that this was her future. I agonized over what it would do to Eric. But whenever I raised my concerns to Uncle Joe, he insisted in his calm, steady way that she was going to be okay.

"She strong." He kept squeezing his hand, as if it held something. "When Teht'aa little girl, she trip over rock and break leg. We were out on the land hunting caribou, many days from a doctor. Florence, my sister, know healing ways of *ik'oò elii*. She use caribou bones to keep leg straight and wrapped strips of hide around it. We put Teht'aa in canoe and paddle many days to doctor at Rae. She very brave little girl. She didn't cry. The doctor say Florence do very good job. The leg was straight and healing good. He put fancy cast on her leg. We put Teht'aa back into the canoe and paddle back to camp. When cloudberries ready for picking, she running over the rocks with her cousins. Don't worry. She gonna be okay. The Creator look after her. I have *dzodiì* to make sure." He opened his hand to reveal a stub of dried vegetation. "Rat root, strong medicine. It very special to Tlicho."

"Like sweetgrass or tobacco is to the Algonquin. Do you smudge it?"

"Some people do."

"After Teht'aa's mother died, did she live with you?"

"No, with Florence. Charmaine was her daughter. Florence don't like to live in Digadeh. She like to live on the land like ancestors, harvesting caribou, moose, fish, and berries. When I was away working, I sometimes came back with my family. We go out on the land with Florence and follow the trails of ancestors. Sometimes we follow Idaà Trail all the way to Sahtu, what you call Great Bear Lake. Plenty big whitefish in Sahtu. They were good days. Good for my boys to learn Tlicho ways." He gave the rat root another squeeze.

"So why didn't you stay there?"

"Life too hard. We too used to living in nice house and going to store for food. Fun to do for a few weeks." He shrugged apologetically.

"Glad to hear our white man ways aren't all bad."

He laughed and patted his niece on the arm. For a nanosecond I thought I saw her skin twitch, but when it didn't happen again I put it down to an autonomic response.

"Did Teht'aa ever live in Digadeh?"

"Not much after she go away to school."

"So she went to residential school too."

"No, they closed Saint Anne's. They build new school in Edzo, another Tlicho community. She go there, much better living near own people. No nuns or priests. They let her speak Tlicho."

"Teht'aa must've been quite young when she went off on her own."

"Think seven or eight. But she brave girl. She don't cry. She go home for holidays and summer vacations, not like at Saint Anne's. She smart. Get special award when she graduate high school. Florence proud *Mamàcho*."

"Does that mean grandmother?"

"Yah. *Mamàcho*. Good word. When Teht'aa came back to Digadeh, it's hard for her. She didn't want to go out on land with Florence. So she stay with her Auntie Claire, Gloria's mum. But Claire drank too much. Make it difficult for Teht'aa. Think one of Claire's boyfriends caused trouble too. Teht'aa leave and go to Edmonton to school. Only come back for short visits with Florence."

"Did Teht'aa meet her husband at school? She's never really talked about the marriage other than it was short."

I wondered if she could hear our conversation. It gave me a strange feeling to be talking about her as if she weren't lying on the bed between us.

"Don't know. He was Cree. Came from a reserve near Edmonton. Met him once. Didn't like him. She young when they married. She didn't know much about men. And he was a bad 'un."

"What did he do? Abuse her?"

He grunted a yes.

Something else Teht'aa and I shared, except I didn't have the smarts to leave. I put up with my ex's abuse for fourteen years, ten months, and eleven days, letting him pummel me into the ground until the only way I could escape was through alcohol.

"Tell me about her mother. Eric has never said much about Charmaine, although I got the impression that he really loved her and was heartbroken when she left him."

"Charmaine was beautiful. Îeht'aa looks like her. One look at her and Eric was a goner." He chuckled. "She Florence's youngest. Born on the land like the others. She go to residential school like her sisters. RCMP take them from her. Florence don't see her kids for many years. She say she don't know them when they come back to Digadeh. They more white than Tlicho. They forget how to speak Tlicho and forget Tlicho ways. She very upset. Her girls have hard time. They don't want to live on land with Florence, so stay in Digadeh. Charmaine hated it, wanted to leave. So Florence tell her she have to come live with me and Mary in Medicine Hat.

"I like to go to the hockey games in Medicine Hat. Charmaine come with me. She meet Eric there. They made a nice couple. She very beautiful. He handsome hockey player."

Though it was more than thirty-five years ago, I couldn't help but feel a tinge of jealousy. "How long did they spend together?"

"Think it little more than a year before she got pregnant and return to Digadeh. I was sorry it didn't work. They good for each other. She help him get to know his Indian heritage. He give her a better future than the boys at Digadeh. He was a good worker and wasn't a drunk. Good husband material. But I guess you know that, eh?" He laughed.

I laughed too, but didn't tell him what was uppermost in my mind, that I was glad the relationship was a distant memory when Eric came into my life. I didn't think I could live under her shadow.

"Charmaine and I had big fight. I want her to marry Eric, but she didn't want his white man's life. When she live with me in Medicine Hat, she didn't like the way the people treat her because she was Indian. She not want this for her baby. She only marry Eric if he live at Digadeh. But hockey was his life. Best player on the team. NHL scouts looking at him. One night an important man come to a game and want him to play hockey for Canada."

"Wow! For the Olympics?"

"World Junior Championship. A very big honour."

"Amazing, and he's never mentioned it. What a modest man."

"It was very hard time for him. He so upset, he don't play very well."

"I imagine it was a very difficult choice for him. In those days hockey defined who he was. It helped him deal with the problems he faced with his adoptive family. I'm surprised Charmaine didn't understand this."

"She was afraid. Your world scare her. She speak English and watch TV, but she don't understand your ways. If she marry Eric, she have to live like white man. I think he also afraid to live like an Indian."

"I expect he was, since he only learned after meeting you that he was an Indian and not the Italian his adoptive parents insisted he was. I guess their relationship was doomed from the beginning. A little like Romeo and Juliet, eh?"

"I was more mad at Eric than Charmaine. I thought family and being Indian more important than hockey. I so mad I don't talk to him for many years. Never told him about Teht'aa or about Charmaine's death."

"I know, but he forgave you long ago. You hold a very special place in his heart. He looks upon you as the father he never had. His adoptive father certainly wasn't a father to him. He's particularly grateful to you for helping him discover his Algonquin roots and reconnecting him with his grandparents."

"They very nice people. I glad he still had real family. He good man. You very lucky woman."

"Don't I know it. Now we have to make sure he doesn't go to jail."

At that precise moment, the reassuring beat of the heart monitor suddenly changed to an alarming single tone, which set off more alarms.

FIFTEEN

The nurse rushed toward us. I jumped out of my chair, letting Teht'aa's limp hand drop to the bedcover. Shit. Had Teht'aa's heart stopped beating? Uncle Joe remained sitting on the other side of her bed, tenderly stroking her arm as if nothing was happening. He didn't even raise an eye to the nurse.

She didn't stop. She sped past to the neighbouring bed, the one with the young girl, and whisked the curtain closed behind her. Another nurse slipped through to join her, while her parents scrambled out into the middle of the room. Clutching each other, they kept their eyes rooted on the commotion coming from their daughter's bed.

Only then did I notice that Teht'aa's heart monitor continued to beat with reassuring regularity.

"Code Blue," clamoured the loudspeaker.

A flurry of pink floral and white burst through the door as a nurse and a doctor pushed in a cart carrying the kind of equipment I'd seen TV doctors use to shock a heart into restarting.

"Move," the doctor shouted at the parents, almost ramming the cart into them.

The cart and the staff disappeared behind the curtain, while the parents shuffled out of the way. Tears streamed down the mother's cheeks. I motioned them to join us and offered the mother my chair. But she ignored it and continued clinging to her husband's arm as the monotonous drone of the monitor voiced its harrowing message.

"Okay, everyone stand back," a female voice ordered.

A whining sound was followed by a deadened thump. "Again!"

The parents gripped each other harder. I found myself holding my breath as I listened to another shock going through the young girl.

"Again!"

I couldn't imagine what her parents must be feeling listening to their daughter, who'd barely begun her life, dying.

The single unnerving buzz continued, and then it changed to a tentative intermittent beat that grew stronger.

"We have a pulse."

Both parents sighed. Unable to stand any longer, the mother collapsed into my chair. "Thank God," she whispered. Her husband placed his hands on her shoulder and kissed the top of her head.

"Our Christie was supposed to be medevaced today," he said. "But the plane was diverted for another patient. She's on the heart transplant list, but I'm not sure how much longer she can hold out."

Before I could offer my sympathy, the curtain was shoved aside and the female doctor approached the parents. "She's okay for now, but we need to get her to Edmonton. Rita's on the phone finding us another plane."

Without a backward glance, the two clinging figures returned to their daughter.

"I know about this little girl," Uncle Joe said. "She granddaughter of man I took caribou hunting many years ago. He had a heart problem too. Died from it."

"At least he lived long enough to have a family and enjoy life. It looks as if his granddaughter won't have that chance."

"It in the hands of the Creator. When her time come, it come."

Was that how he felt about his grandniece? I was afraid to ask.

"Mrs. Bluegoose?" came a voice from behind me.

I turned to see a grey-haired man of about Eric's height whose surgical greens were straining at the waist. He was flipping over the pages of Teht'aa's chart.

"Actually, my name's Meg Harris, Teht'aa's stepmother. You must be Dr. Yausie."

He nodded and turned his glance to the old man. "Good to see you, Joe. How's that hernia of yours?"

"Never come back after you open me up." Grinning, he patted his stomach.

"I want to talk to both of you about Teht'aa. I gather her father can't be here." So he knew. At least I wouldn't have to explain Eric's absence.

"He's arriving in Yellowknife today. You might be able to talk to him over the phone. I could get his lawyer to set it up."

"Good to know, but as long as you are comfortable making decisions for your stepdaughter, I don't think it will be necessary."

"It depends on the decision." I knew there was one decision I would never be able to make.

"I'm wondering if either of you has seen any movement from Teht'aa while you've been sitting here?"

"Nope, I haven't. Uncle Joe?"

He shook his head slowly. "She been so still. She gonna be okay, Doctor?" This made my heart skip. Despite his appearance of optimism, Uncle Joe was as worried as me.

"You haven't seen any small movements like her eyes opening or hands, fingers moving?

We answered a regretful no in unison.

I dug my fingers into the back of Uncle Joe's chair while we watched the doctor poke and prod Eric's lifeless daughter. He lifted one eyelid, then the other, shining a light into each in turn. He had the nurse unwrap the bandage around her head and check the sutures. Poor Teht'aa. Her luxurious long black locks were gone. But if she never regained consciousness, it wouldn't matter. And if she did, a token price to pay for her life.

"Teht'aa, open your eyes if you can hear me?" the doctor said.

Nothing.

He tried again, and again no response.

Turning to us, he said, "If she hasn't regained consciousness by tomorrow morning, I'm considering medevacing her to Edmonton, where they have neurosurgeons on staff. While all her vitals look good and the CT scan is showing no further intracranial hypertension, I'm concerned that she isn't yet showing signs of coming out of the coma. It's been over twelve hours since I stopped the pentobarbital. Usually by this time we start to see signs of consciousness."

"Why not transfer her today?" I asked. "It looks like she needs a neurosurgeon to check her out now, not tomorrow."

"Like I said, her vitals are good and there is no longer any swelling in the brain, so I am optimistic that she will come out of the coma soon."

"How certain?"

"Every patient is unique. Some people take longer to heal than others, and so it is with the brain. As you know, it's the most complex organ in the body. While the medical field has learned much about the workings of the brain, there are still aspects that we don't understand. I wish I could tell you exactly when she will regain consciousness, but I can't."

"All the more reason for her to see a specialist as soon as possible. I would like her flown to Edmonton today."

"To make this happen, she needs a fully equipped air ambulance. I'm afraid none are available for today, but staff have reserved one for tomorrow." He glanced at the curtain separating us from the young heart patient next door.

"Have they been able to find one for her?"

"I don't know. She's not my patient. But I think you appreciate that her need is more pressing."

"I do and wouldn't want Teht'aa to take her place. But maybe my stepdaughter could share the plane if they're going to the same hospital."

"Sorry, that's not possible."

"Is there a privately owned plane I could charter?

"It would be a significant cost."

"I can handle it. I love Teht'aa as much as my husband does and would hate to see her suffer serious brain damage. If getting her to a neurosurgeon one day sooner lessens the risk, then I'm more than willing to cash in some bonds."

"I pay too," Uncle Joe piped up. "I have savings."

"Good," replied Dr. Yausie. "I'll let Rita know. Now, if you'll excuse me, I have to attend to another patient"

"That's very kind of you, Uncle Joe," I said, resuming my seat beside the bed. "But it's not necessary."

"We see. I want to help."

"Perhaps you can help another way. Since I don't want to leave Eric, I am hoping you can go with Teht'aa to Edmonton."

"My granddaughter is going to have baby. Is why I come to Yellowknife. But for Teht'aa, I go. Your husband need you." He pushed himself out of the chair. "Nothing more we can do here. I need a bowl of noodle soup. You do too."

SIXTEEN

I braced myself and waited for the crunch when Teht'aa's Bimmer came within inches of striking a left-turning car. When it didn't, I readied myself for the next near miss. You'd have thought I'd be used to Uncle Joe's kamikaze driving by now.

We were racing to the airport after our lunch at the noodle place, which, by the way, Uncle Joe had to pay for, because in my rush to leave this morning I'd forgotten my wallet. While I was slurping the last of my vermicelli soup, Sally had called to tell me that Eric's plane would be landing momentarily. She would be consulting with her client at the detachment and would also try to arrange a visiting time for me, though she wasn't hopeful. Visitors weren't normally allowed before the court appearance. She insisted that there was no point in my going to the airport. He'd be taken straight from the plane to the RCMP van, giving me no opportunity to speak to him. The most I could hope for would be a glimpse, which was better than nothing, so off Uncle Joe and I sped.

We arrived at the airport in time to see a white twin-engine plane marked with the red, yellow, white, and blue stripes of the RCMP about to set its wheels down on the runway. Instead of driving straight to the terminal, Uncle Joe veered past.

"Where are you going?" I kept my eyes on the plane until it disappeared behind the terminal.

"The RCMP hangar. They take him there."

"How do you know?"

"RCMP bring my nephew there every time he arrested."

"Every time?"

"Thirty, forty. I lost count. Mostly for assault. He get drunk and beat up whoever handy. Mostly girlfriends."

"Sounds like he spends most of his time in jail."

"He get off a lot. He got fetal alcohol syndrome. Can't control his temper, so judge easy on him."

"His poor mother. She must feel guilty for drinking during her pregnancy."

"She didn't want him. Took off and left his grand-mother, my wife's sister, to look after him. The kid not a bad guy, just can't stay away from booze. They got him on a healing program. He stopped drinking. Hasn't been in trouble for a good year."

We were driving along a road that paralleled the run-way and had already passed several low industrial build-ings and Quonsets, some sporting the names of airlines.

"But he's always going to have anger issues and other problems related to the syndrome. It's not going away."

"He good hunter. Spend much time on the land away from people, hunting for elders. See the SUV in front of us? It's the RCMP coming to get Eric."

I noticed for the first time that the white SUV we'd been following bore the RCMP markings, complete with the Mountie on the horse. The vehicle slowed to turn in to a side road next to a low-rise building with blue metal siding. As we turned onto the road, I saw a sign that read "Yellowknife Air section, RCMP 'G' Division." The SUV pulled to a halt in front of a gate in a chain-link fence. Beyond I could see the tarmac. Uncle Joe jerked the car to a stop within inches of the cops' bumper.

I heard the engines before I saw the police aircraft emerge from behind a government jet parked on the tarmac. It taxied past us. I stuck my hand out the window and waved in case Eric could see me. But the hope of watching him leave the plane was quashed the second it disappeared behind the RCMP building. Only the tail remained in view.

Soon my love, soon.

An angry Sergeant Ryan hopped out of the passenger side and motioned for us to leave.

"It's me, Meg Harris," I hollered as I walked around the back of Teht'aa's car. "I've come to see my husband."

"Sorry, no can do, it's against regs. Gus, I'll get the gate."

She strode to where a padlock dangled from a thick chain.

"Please, I really want to see him."

"Not allowed." She slapped her pockets as if searching for something. "Fuck. Gus, did you bring the key?"

We both whirled around at the sharp squeal of tires behind us. A CBC van swerved around the corner and lurched to a halt behind Teht'aa's car. The male reporter I'd met at the hospital jumped out of the driver's side and sauntered toward us, while the same camerawoman hefted her heavy equipment onto her shoulder and started filming.

"Sergeant Ryan, are you—"

"Josh, you know you have to go through media relations."

He flashed a set of pearly whites, doubtless his ticket onto the TV screen. "Come on, El, you know me. Hell, we were drinking at the same bar last night."

"Along with fifty other people. Now, I'd appreciate if you could back your van out onto the road."

"I just have a few questions which you can answer quicker than Yves. After all, the Digadeh murder is your case."

"Christ, Josh, what planet do you live on? You know I can't discuss a case. Now, please return to your vehicle." Ignoring the camera trained on her, she strode toward him, stopping centimetres from the microphone.

He held his ground. "Is there a connection between the Frank Chocolate murder and the sexual assault on Teht'aa Bluegoose?"

I held my breath for the answer.

"Josh, are you going to leave nicely on your own, or do we have to escort you off RCMP property?"

Gus sauntered up beside her, crossed his arms over his Kevlar vest, and stared down at the much shorter man. Josh looked as if he were about to speak, then, thinking better of it, waved at his camerawoman to stop filming and strode back to the van.

The two officers kept their eyes trained on the vehicle as it reversed onto the main road. But it didn't drive away; instead, Josh parked it on the shoulder within full view of the cops and the gate.

"I am going to have to ask you to leave too, Ms. Harris."

"Can't I let my husband know I'm here?"

"You'll get your chance later. Now go."

I watched the constable slide the gate open and for one crazy second thought of running through it. Maybe I could help Eric escape. Maybe we could race across the runway to the distant line of trees and flee this nightmare. But as if reading my thoughts, the sergeant rested her hand on her gun holster. I shoved the ludicrous idea aside and retreated to the car.

"You wave to him from here," Uncle Joe said, parking the BMW in front of the CBC van.

I watched the RCMP SUV disappear around the corner of the building in the direction of the plane.

Poor Eric. How humiliating. To arrive so ignominiously in one of his favourite towns. I was very glad Ryan had ordered Josh away. He wouldn't be able to capture Eric climbing, manacled, out of the plane and broadcast the video for the world to see.

In what seemed less time than it took to blink, the white RCMP SUV was speeding through the gate and swerving onto the main road. By the time it streaked past us, I was standing by the car, waving. It drove by too quickly for me to pick out Eric. But I thought I saw a shadowy figure in the back seat nod in my direction. It was only as I watched the back of the cop vehicle disappearing around the corner that I realized a nod would have been all Eric could manage. His hands would be cuffed.

I felt the coolness of tears tickling down my cheeks at the same time as I sensed someone's eyes on me. I looked up into a camera lens and a microphone ready to capture my words.

"Fuck."

SEVENTEEN

I didn't care if my mother would be turning in her grave at my less than ladylike response. I was ticked and told the reporter so. With visions of my tear-stained face filling up the TV screen, I stopped short of saying exactly what I thought of his privates.

The old man's infectious laugh had me joining in as we zoomed away from the pointed camera.

When I finally stopped giggling, I said, "God, I needed that."

"That guy no good. People don't like him. Teht'aa taking over his job."

"Let's hope she can. But I hadn't realized she'd be going after the news in addition to reading it."

"Teht'aa says CBC office pretty small in Yellowknife after many budget cuts. The news announcer do the big stories."

"The arrest of the Grand Chief of GCFN for murder is certainly a big story. It would also get Josh's face splashed on TV screens across the country. Maybe he wants to use it to find another job."

Uncle Joe turned into the hospital parking lot.

"Do you mind if I take the car?" I asked. "I need to get my wallet at the apartment, and I want to see Eric."

Although I'd heard nothing yet from Sally, I decided to go to the detachment and camp out on their doorstep, if that was what it took to persuade them to let me visit my husband.

"But first Teht'aa. I want to see how she's doing and find out if they've found a plane."

Eric's daughter seemed as deathly still as this morning and the morning before. However, when I told her that her father had returned to Yellowknife, I thought I saw her eyelids flutter.

"Flutter your eyes again if you can hear me."

I wasn't certain, but they might've moved.

"Did you see that, Uncle Joe?"

"See what?"

"Her eyelids move."

"Nope.

Nonetheless, I felt more optimistic that Teht'aa would soon be joining us.

The news on the medevac front was less promising. All private air ambulances in the Territories and Alberta were in use. The only possibility was a plane that was currently evacuating someone from northern Saskatchewan to Regina. If the province had no other priority requirements, the airline would send the airplane to Yellowknife. But they wouldn't know until late afternoon, and given the distance it would be late evening before the plane arrived. Meanwhile, the hospital had booked an air ambulance for tomorrow at noon.

My initial reaction was to cancel the charter and go with the hospital's booking. But though the medical staff assured me that Teht'aa's condition was stable, they couldn't assure me that it wouldn't take an unexpected change for the worse. So I gave them my credit card information for the deposit and left Teht'aa — my stepdaughter, my sister, my best friend — under her great-uncle's watchful eye.

Before setting off for her apartment, I tried Sally's number but was routed to voicemail. I hoped this meant she was sitting across a table from Eric, plotting his release.

I had assumed the way to the apartment was straightforward. But I hadn't paid enough attention to Uncle Joe's route and found myself driving around in circles in a neighbourhood of crescents that seemed more befitting of a city suburb than a town surrounded by hundreds of kilometres of wilderness. Even if I'd known her address, I didn't have the foggiest idea how to plug it into the fancy navigation system. Driving a fifteen-year-old pickup with wind-up windows didn't exactly equip me with the required know-how.

I would've stopped and asked, but the sidewalks were as empty of people as the road was of cars. A search of the glove compartment and door pockets only turned up a map of Edmonton and an unpaid parking ticket.

I was stopped at a junction agonizing over whether to turn left or right or continue straight ahead when I finally saw a vehicle. It was backing out of the driveway of one of the largest houses on the street, about a half block behind me. I swerved around in a U-turn. You gotta love the turning ratio of these Bimmers. With my hand on the horn, I managed to stop the SUV before it turned onto another street.

"What do you want?" the blonde woman yelled, powering down the window of a Grand Cherokee I could've sworn was Eric's, complete with the metallic champagne colour, except his Jeep was parked at the Ottawa airport.

A curly-haired child peered at me from the back seat. The child seemed familiar, as did the woman.

While I tried to place them, she beat me to it. "You're Eric's wife, aren't you? We've met before."

"Of course, Reggie Mantla's wife. I was chatting with your husband this morning at the airport. Is this where you live?"

"Yeah, we bought it about six months ago. We used to spend more time in Digadeh, but since Reggie's work frequently brings him to Yellowknife, as does my job, we decided to move here full-time, which has turned out to be a good decision now that Reggie is taking over the top spot at GCFN." She stopped to soothe the child, who'd started whimpering. "By the way, I'm sorry to hear about your husband."

"That's quick. Eric has only been arrested for a couple of days. Doesn't your husband need the endorsement of the assembly to take over?"

"He came in second in the election, so it's natural that he assumes control."

"Tell him not to get too settled. Eric will be free in no time."

"Not from what I hear. It's pretty obvious he killed poor Frank."

Not bothering to wait for my reply, she rolled up her window and drove away.

"No, he didn't, and I'm going to prove it," I yelled after her.

I hopped back into the car, slammed the door with more force than needed, rammed it into drive, and took off after her. I figured she knew where she was going. Though I was making her nervous, I hugged her bumper until we reached an intersection that finally looked familiar. We parted company without a goodbye wave on either part. She drove straight through, while I turned right onto the main road, which I knew would take me through the downtown core, down the big hill, and into Old Town.

Instead of police cruisers parked outside Teht'aa's building, there was another unwanted vehicle. The CBC van. I debated driving past but decided that I wasn't going to let Josh keep me from doing what I had every right to do. Unfortunately, the only free parking was in front of the van, forcing me to walk past him to reach the stairs. Avoiding eye contact, I walked along the opposite side of his vehicle to where he was standing.

"Mrs. Odjik, do you have a moment?" he shouted.

I hastened my pace. He ran behind the back of the van to block my passage. I swerved onto Teht'aa's neighbour's driveway and made a beeline for her stairs.

"Please, I just want to talk. I promise I won't record it."

He was alone, without his camerawoman. Regardless, I continued walking.

"Look, I'm really sorry about Teht'aa. It's a terrible thing to happen to her. I want to help."

"Why? If she doesn't survive, you get to keep your job." I started up the stairs.

"I'm leaving anyway. I have a new job in Regina," he called out from the bottom step. "I have something that belongs to Teht'aa. It could relate to the assault."

"Give it to the police."

"Like you saw, I don't have the best relationship with them. It'd be better coming from you."

"Okay, what have you got?" I shouted back from the height of the first landing.

He glanced over at the couple walking on the opposite side of the street. "I'll come up there."

"No!" I was never going to let a strange man into my apartment, my house, whatever … not ever again. I ran back down the stairs.

EIGHTEEN

I thought it would be something substantial, a solid lead to the man who attacked Teht'aa, but all Josh gave me was a purple flower. Not the kind that grew out of the ground, but one that had been crafted from a soft, bristly material.

"It's moosehair," he said.

He slid his fingers over the tightly packed tufts that had been clipped short, dyed purple, and sewn onto a piece of suede that had the golden colour and suppleness of moosehide. There was one complete flower with a couple of green, tufted leaves and three petals of another one that looked as if it had been ripped apart.

"It's Dene. They decorate vests, moccasins, and purses with these flowers."

"Where did you get it?" I held out my hand.

He dropped the flowers onto my open palm. The hide felt as soft and silky as deerskin.

"I found it in the parking lot across from where Teht'aa was attacked."

"Why do you think it belongs to her?"

"We were out drinking together a couple of weeks ago. She was picking my brains about the job. This fell out of her purse. When I picked it off the floor, she snatched it out of my hand." He stopped talking as an elderly woman walked behind us. She was struggling with a young boy intent on extricating his hand from her grasp.

His eyes followed the pair. "The terrible twos. My kid's going through those too." He watched them for another few seconds before turning back to me. "As I was saying, Teht'aa acted as if she didn't want me to see it."

"How do you know this is the same piece?"

"I remember the purple colour and the unusual tufts. Moosehair isn't used much anymore. Today, most Dene embroidery is done with coloured beads."

"Like the centre of this flower." I fingered the clear beads and watched them catch the afternoon sun's rays. "How lovely. They sparkle."

"I also noticed this mark." He pointed to what looked to be a tiny bird made from yellow thread that had been embroidered into one of the corners of the hide.

"Why do you think it's related to her attack?"

"I found it when I was reporting on the incident. It was lying on the ground near where I'd parked my car. This morning I noticed these spots."

I could barely make out the faint reddish brown colour soaked into the tufts of two petals. But the spots on the hide were more pronounced. "It looks like blood."

"That's what I thought."

"Why didn't you hand it over to the police?"

"I didn't think it important until I saw the blood this morning."

"So why give it to me?"

"I don't want to get involved. Me and my family are moving to Regina next week, and I don't want anything to delay it." He stopped to answer his phone. After a short conversation of no's and yes's, he hung up. "I've got to go. You do whatever you want with it, just keep my name out of it."

"It might not be possible."

"You'll figure out something, because if you do mention my name, I'll release a video of your husband offering a GCFN member a bribe to vote for him in the election."

The van began to move while I was trying to absorb his blatant attempt at blackmail. Before I could question him about the video, he peeled off in a squeal of rubber, a whisker-length from hitting the BMW. But he braked to a stop beside the grandmother and the boy, who was now sitting on the ground, shrieking his refusal to walk any farther. Josh hopped out of the van, lifted the suddenly quiet child into the passenger side, helped the grandmother climb in, and drove off. So he wasn't all bad. But he was still a bastard to me.

I thrust the petals into my pocket, muttering, "What in the world am I supposed to do with this?"

I knew I should give it to Sergeant Ryan. But she would want to know how it came into my possession. Once I gave her the journalist's name, I had little doubt that he would carry out his threat. The national coverage would be too tempting and the last thing Eric needed.

But I found it hard to believe that the video was of Eric. He was the most honest man I knew. He became band chief for the Migiskan Anishinabeg Reserve on a platform of cleaning up corruption. He refused to pass out the usual bottles of free booze for votes, and it worked. They elected him six times.

If anyone had bought votes, it was that man Reggie. During the campaign Eric had caught wind of some underhanded dealings related to his main opponent, but he was unable to obtain sufficient information to report it. To be on the safe side, though, I would wait until I had a chance to talk to him before doing anything about these bloody petals.

I lumbered up the three flights of stairs, cursing the journalist with each stomp on the wooden steps. With my heart pounding, I was gulping in mouthfuls of air by the time I reached the top landing. Maybe doing this several times a day would get me in the kind of shape Eric kept telling me I should be in.

Remembering Sergeant Ryan's caution, I pulled the doorknob to ensure it was firmly locked. I also rang the doorbell and called out that I was coming in, which, let's face it, was not the brightest move. If an intruder really were inside, all this noise would only serve to warn him to hide. I waited a few minutes in the vestibule for the silence to continue before gathering up enough nerve to walk into the living room.

The police had not only left the mess the way I'd found it, but they'd also added to it. Liberal amounts of dark-grey powder were sprinkled over a variety of surfaces.

I checked the spare bedroom to see if Gloria had returned and was startled to discover her softly snoring, lying fully clothed on the bed with a blanket half on, half off her. A strong odour of alcohol permeated the room.

A tad early in the day, I thought, shaking my head. If she kept this up, what kind of state would she be in when she reached my age — that is, if she survived that long. I pulled the blanket up to fully cover her and closed the door behind me, though why, I couldn't guess. If the doorbell and my shouts hadn't woken her, my padding around the apartment certainly wouldn't.

After retrieving my wallet from Teht'aa's bedroom, I returned to the kitchen to make a cup of tea. Nothing calmed twanging nerves like a soothing cup of hot black tea. I moved Teht'aa's clothes off the couch, took a long, slow, warming sip of coffee, then placed the mug on the coffee table beside the stone bear before pulling out Eric's cell. I'd try Sally again in case she hadn't seen my earlier message. But before I could click on her number, she was calling me. Except when I answered, it wasn't her.

I heard a long, lingering sigh before the words, "Hi, my love. It's me."

"Oh, Eric. It's you. It's really you. How are you?" Banal words, but my emotions were in such a swirl that I didn't know what else to say.

"Miskowàbigonens, my little red flower. It's so wonderful to hear your voice."

My heart twisted at the sadness in his. "When am I going to see you? I want to hug you."

"I'm so sorry to cause all this trouble, to make you come all this way when you're not ready. I hope it wasn't too stressful."

"Oh, Eric. Forget about me. I'm fine. It's you I'm worried about. Are you okay?" I tried to shake the vision of him sitting shackled in a cold, inhospitable room.

"I'll survive. I want to know how Teht'aa's doing. Is she going to make it?"

"She's still in the coma, but the doctor's optimistic that she has no brain damage. I've chartered an air ambulance to transfer her to Edmonton tonight. If that doesn't work out, the hospital has one booked for tomorrow noon. Either way, she'll get the proper neurosurgeon care she needs."

"You'll go with her," he said more as a fact than a hope.

"But I want to be with you."

"Don't worry about me. She needs you more than I do."

"Okay," I said, not wanting to argue. But as far as I was concerned, Uncle Joe would be the family member going with her. "Can I come visit you?"

"No," he replied a little too quickly, as if he were ashamed to have me see him in jail. "I appreciate you hiring Sally. She's obviously a top lawyer. But you could've saved your money. Derrick would've been fine."

"No way," I replied with horror. "He doesn't have the experience or the smarts to keep you out of jail."

He sighed and remained quiet for few seconds before saying, "Sally says if all goes well tomorrow, I should be free to walk out the door."

"I assume she means after the bail hearing. Does she know the time yet? I want to be there."

"Please, I'd rather you didn't come. It's likely to be a circus with all the media. I don't want you exposed to it. Besides, you should be on your way to Edmonton. Tell me, how bad is her face?"

"It's hard to tell because of the bandages. But I have a good feeling she's going to be okay, and her beautiful smile will be gracing the TV screens in a few short months."

"I love your optimism." Another deep sigh. "Christ, what a mess I've made of things."

"Shhh … don't think that way. We'll talk about it tomorrow. Look, Eric, I'm going to the bail hearing. Uncle Joe can go with Teht'aa. I want to be the one friendly face in the crowd."

"I don't want you to. I'll come to you afterward — that is, if they release me. Where are you staying? At the hotel or at her apartment?"

At least he no longer wanted me going with his daughter. "The apartment. Eric, everything's going to be okay, you hear? The police will find the real culprit."

"The Mounties think they already have their man."

Neither of us laughed at the famous words. Eric called me an optimist. But I wasn't the true optimist — he was. No matter how bleak things appeared, he would be the one giving it a positive twist. Not this time. I'd never heard him sound so low, so defeated.

"If they won't search for the killer, I will."

I could hear Sally saying something to him in the background.

"I guess we should cut this short. I'll see you at the bail hearing." I paused. "Eric, I love you."

NINETEEN

I felt emotionally drained. The pall of black clouds advancing over the lake made my spirits fall further, while the steaming hot tea was failing miserably.

Teht'aa so badly injured, she might not be able to take up the dream job she'd fought for. Eric charged with murder, his cherished goal of being a fair and equitable spokesman for his people a tattered ruin. He was right. It was a mess.

Yet less than a week ago, life was on the upswing.

Teht'aa, ecstatic about her new job, had beat out two other candidates, both white, both male, to become the first native female announcer for the CBC. Eric was getting into his stride as Grand Chief after an arduous year-long campaign in which not every candidate played by the rules. And I was making progress, albeit slowly. I'd managed to quell the jitters so that the horror of that godawful night no longer ruled my dreams.

We had thought the bad times were behind us, if not the memories.

So what had we done wrong to make the gods angry?

I swallowed another mouthful of tea. Outside, the blackness had spread over the lake, turning its blue brilliance into dull, light-sucking grey. Rain was on the way. I knew I should go back to the hospital, but I didn't think I could watch Teht'aa's corpse-like body without succumbing completely to despair.

I threw the rest of the tea down the drain and surveyed the dark confines of the narrow kitchen, wondering in which cupboard my stepdaughter kept her booze. A bracing slug of vodka would sure lift my spirits. I'd even accept Scotch, rye, any liquor as long as it contained sufficient alcohol to dull the pain. I checked two cupboards without success and was about to open a third when I heard the drum-roll ring of Eric's cell.

"Auntie, it's me," came Jid's breathless voice through the airwaves.

I'd expected it to be Eric and I felt a tinge of relief that it wasn't. As much as I wanted to hear his voice again, I didn't think I could summon up the optimistic support that would be needed right now.

"Hi, how's it going?"

Bubbling over with excitement, Jid told me about the latest happenings in his life. He'd been invited to play the striker position for the Migiskan Ravens, the senior boys soccer team, a level up from what he'd played last year.

"How's Shoni doing?" I asked, and off he went without taking the time to catch his breath. The puppy and the fawn had become the best of buddies, with Shoni sneaking into the stall to play with her. Janet let him give the bottle of milk to Kidi, which she slurped up while Shoni lapped up the dribbles falling onto the straw.

As I listened to him prattle on, bursting with the joie de vivre that only the young can feel, I felt my spirits rise.

Everyone needs a child in their life to put their own into perspective. I was pondering the best way to bring up his hero without deflating this exuberance when I realized I was listening to silence.

"Jid, you still there?"

I could hear his breathing and the puppy whimpering, followed by rustling.

"Shoni, woof, it's your momma," the boy said in the background.

"Hi, Shoni, it's me." I felt a little silly yelling through the phone at a dog.

More rustling as he returned to the phone, but the silence continued.

"Jid, you okay?"

More silence and then, "The TV says Shome is a murderer."

"He's not. You and I both know Eric would never kill anyone."

"Yah, that's what I told the boys at school. I even got into a fight."

"Did you win?"

He laughed softly. "Yah, but I got a black eye."

"Good. Because we're going to win, even if we get a couple of black eyes, maybe some scrapes and bruises. We know Eric didn't do it, and we're going to make sure the police prove it, okay?"

"I guess."

"Jid, I know it's hard, but it's important we don't give in, for his sake as much as ours. We have to keep smiling for him. We have to keep fighting, okay?" I felt I was saying this as much for myself as for the boy.

"Yah, I'm good. How's Auntie Teht'aa? She gonna be okay?"

"She's going to be fine. Shome and I will be bringing her home soon, and we'll have one big family reunion, okay?" I prayed the gods were listening.

"Are Shoni and Kidi invited too?"

"Of course, it wouldn't be a family reunion without them."

I set the phone down, feeling more upbeat and more ready to do what I could to save Eric. I even felt I could manage a return to the hospital. And then Gloria padded back into my life.

One could never say that she entered it silently. Her shrill curses bouncing off the hall walls provided sufficient warning. She stumbled into the living room almost as if she didn't know it was there.

Night had been kind to her. In the harsh reality of daylight, she looked like she'd risen from the dead. Her skimpy rayon dress, two sizes too large for her, was twisted around her tiny skeletal frame. Its faded yellow colour did nothing for her sallow complexion. What might have been a beehive of cascading ringlets at the start of last night was a tangled mat of purple and dark-brown hair. Under the streaks of mascara I could see that her features were striking, almost those of a classic beauty, but the sneering twist of her smile did nothing to bring that beauty out. The biggest surprise and the saddest was her age; she was barely into her twenties. Last night I'd assumed she was well past her youth.

"Tee never keeps any booze in this shithole. You got any?"

And a good day to you, too. "Nope."

She shoved a hank of purple hair behind her ear. "Can you loan me a twenty? I'll pay you back."

I eyed her with suspicion. "Would Teht'aa loan you the money?"

Her eyes flashed annoyance as she flopped onto the other end of the sofa.

"You got a cigarette? I'm all out."

"I don't smoke. Nor should you."

She jerked off the sofa, stomped over the bare wood floors to the hall closet, and searched the pockets of a puffy pink jacket. "Fuck," she snarled when she came up empty. She returned to the couch.

"I was surprised you weren't here when the police came this morning."

"Police? Fuck. Were they looking for me?"

"Not really, but I gather they have an arrest warrant out for you."

She brushed that off with an indifferent shrug. "How's Tee? She gonna be okay?"

"We don't know yet. She's still unconscious. Would you like to visit her?"

She shivered. "No, I'm good. I don't do so good in hospitals. What did the cops want?"

"I was worried that someone had broken into this place."

"Yah, maybe. Tee ain't the neatest, but it ain't usually this bad."

"The RCMP suspect the thief got in using a key. Do you know who has keys?"

"Her dad's got one."

"I doubt he'd be robbing his own daughter."

"Yah, I guess. I'm pretty sure Frank had one, 'cause he was here without Tee one time when I came in."

"I suspect he was dead by the time this place was robbed. Anyone else who might have a key?"

She shook her head and glanced at the rain beginning to splatter against the window. "Good. We need it. It's been too fucking dry. Already started some forest fires." She turned her brown gaze back to me. "I ran into Frank the day before he got killed."

"Here?"

"No, at Digadeh. We were at a party. He was acting nervous, like, smoking one cigarette after another and getting real drunk like something was really bothering him." She started rubbing her upper arm as if it bothered her.

"Did he say what it was?"

"Nah."

"You know some people think he was the one who put Teht'aa in the hospital. Do you think it's possible?"

"Yah. He used to hit her, you know, like men do when they want to show you they're the boss."

Didn't I know it, but it was something I learned when I was a good deal older and not in my twenties like she was. "How did he take the breakup?"

"He was mad."

"Mad enough to hurt her?"

"Maybe. You sure you don't got a smoke?"

"Why don't you stop?"

"Fuck off. I don't need no mother."

I should've kept my mouth shut, but she looked so young and so in need of a mother.

She turned her attention back to the rain while she rubbed her arm again. "You know, I saw Tee's dad in Digadeh?"

"When?"

"Day Frank was killed. He was walking from the airport. Wanted me to show him where Frank lived."

"Was that where Frank's body was found?"

"Yup."

TWENTY

"Shit, shit, shit," I muttered as I retraced the route to the hospital, this time without the detour. Exactly the kind of evidence the RCMP would use to solidify the case against Eric. Though I was tempted to send Gloria off on a holiday to Mongolia or some other place equally off the beaten track, I felt confident it wasn't necessary. She wasn't about to call the cops, and I sure wasn't going to mention it.

The wipers flicked the rain back and forth off the windshield. They'd come on automatically while I was searching for the right gizmo to turn them on. I could get used to these modern gadgets. Maybe it was time to finally trade in my poor old rattletrap, if it would let me, for something jazzy like this Bimmer.

The rain was fleeting and not enough to soak the land. By the time I drove into the hospital parking lot, the sun was drying the puddles.

As I skirted the nurses' station, a new nurse, one I'd not seen before, stopped me to tell me that the air ambulance couldn't make it to Yellowknife this evening. It was needed for a priority emergency medevac in Saskatchewan.

But she assured me that Ms. Bluegoose was confirmed for tomorrow's transport.

"I should also let you know that she had a neurosurgeon consult this afternoon."

"How's that possible? I thought there wasn't one in Yellowknife."

"About an hour ago Dr. Yausie consulted with Dr. Steeves via the Internet. He's the neurosurgeon who will be looking after your daughter in Edmonton. It's so amazing what can be done with technology today, all that sharing of the CT scans and other diagnostic images. Not like when I started out in nursing, when everything had to be couriered. It could take days, especially when it got lost in the mail room." She twittered as she tucked a silvery curl behind her ear.

"What was the conclusion? Is she going to come out of the coma?"

"I'm afraid I can't answer that, but I can page Dr. Yausie, if you like."

I gave her the go-ahead and continued walking to Teht'aa's bed, where I found Uncle Joe nodding to sleep in his chair with his hand resting on the arm of his grandniece. I tiptoed around to the other side of the bed and took up my station. Any hopes I had of seeing signs of her awakening were quashed by her immobility. Maybe her hand was in a different position, but the nurse would've lifted it to check on the IV connection. The rest of her body lay as firmly fixed as it was this morning. The only positive sign was the regular humming of her machinery.

The young heart patient had been replaced by a much older and heavier woman whose two equally beefy daughters hovered on either side of her bed, wringing their hands. She too was in a coma, although the readings on her machines didn't appear as normal as Teht'aa's.

I must've nodded off too, for I started at a sudden tap on my shoulder. I opened my eyes to see the grey-haired nurse peering down at me.

"A man by the name of Hans Walther is waiting outside and would like to talk to you," she whispered before placing a vase of long-stem red roses on Teht'aa's eating table.

I started to tell her that I wanted nothing to do with the man, but I changed my mind, thinking it wouldn't hurt to talk to him. He might have something useful to say.

The dishevelled prospector was cleaned up today in a pair of crisp blue jeans, if jeans could be called crisp. A brown leather jacket was slung casually over his Oxford-shirted shoulder. His scraggly beard was gone, revealing a cleft chin of the Dudley Do-Right variety. His dirty blond shag had been transformed into a respectable businessman's haircut.

"Frau Odjik, I am sorry to bother you again. Is it possible you will permit me see Teht'aa?"

"Sorry, it's not my call. The hospital only allows relatives. But you already know that."

"*Ja*, but perhaps you could convince them."

"If you were her boyfriend, it could be argued that you were family. But I gather you're not."

"Who told you this?"

"I'd rather not say."

"It was Gloria, wasn't it? She is much trouble. She lies and causes Teht'aa many problems. She steals her things. I don't know why Teht'aa allows her to stay in the apartment."

"Because she's family, and Teht'aa wants to help her." Though as I said this, I was mentally going through the items in my suitcase, wondering if there was anything of value that Gloria could use to trade for a bottle of alcohol or a package of cigarettes.

"I am very worried. I fear my Teht'aa is in danger of dying."

"Not any longer. The doctor's optimistic about her recovery."

"I am glad that the man who injured her is dead. I never liked him."

"So you knew Frank."

A porter pushing a bed with an old man hooked up to an IV squeaked past us too closely, forcing me to brush up against the German. Without thinking, I shoved myself away with a force I didn't know I had.

"Are you okay?" he asked, moving closer.

My hands burned where they had touched him. I backed farther away. "Sorry. It's nothing. I'm fine. You were saying something about Frank."

"*Ja*. I met him a few times. He didn't treat Teht'aa the way a man should treat such a precious jewel."

When you're in love, I suppose anything goes. "The police haven't yet determined that he was the man who assaulted Teht'aa."

"Of course he did. He was very angry when she turned him down."

"That sounds like a marriage proposal."

"*Ja*, and she said no, as she should."

Shit. More ammunition in the case against Eric. Something else to let the police find out on their own.

"You're blocking the door. Get out of the way," ordered a male voice behind me.

Before I had a chance to move, I found myself being grabbed by Hans. Reason snapped into panic. I had to flee the monster. I pushed and scratched. When I felt resistance, more panic set in.

"Let me go," I screamed.

I stopped when I felt cool air against my face. I scurried away and didn't stop until there was a hallway separating me from the man.

"Are you okay?"

A nurse stood anxiously beside me. Only then did I notice others, equally concerned, staring at me.

"Did he hurt you?" she asked.

I took another gulp of air and tried to calm my clanging nerves. "No, no he didn't. Please, it's okay, really."

"Are you sure?"

I sucked in more air. "Yes. Please, it's just me. Go on with your business." I waved them away as I felt the blush of embarrassment flood my face. How could I be so stupid?

"I'm so sorry." Hans stepped toward me.

I backed up until I felt the wall. "Please, stay there. It's nothing to do with you. I'm sorry. It's me."

"I didn't mean to scare you. The bed was coming straight toward you. I didn't want you to get hurt."

He made another step toward me.

I slid along the wall. "Just go, okay. I'll be fine."

I usually was after these panic attacks. But it would take time for my nerves to settle and my breathing to return to normal.

"I would like you to keep me informed on Teht'aa's progress. Here is my card." He hesitated with the card in his hand, unsure of what to do with it.

"Leave it on the floor, okay?"

He placed it next to the wall. With a brusque goodbye, he disappeared into the stairwell.

I continued leaning against the wall, willing myself to calm down while people passed, eyeing me suspiciously. This was so ridiculous. I was acting like he'd tried to attack me, when all he'd done was push me out of harm's way. *Come on, Meg, it's time to get over it.*

Finally I felt settled enough to retrieve the card.

As I bent down to pick it up, the nurse emerged from behind the ICU door. "Good, there you are. Dr. Yausie is available to speak with you."

TWENTY-ONE

"You worry too much." Uncle Joe rubbed his trembling fingers along the piece of rat root lying on his palm. "Teht'aa gonna be okay. She be in Behchoko for her five bucks."

"Five bucks?"

"Treaty money."

"Sorry, you got me."

"It's in our treaty. Canada must give every Tlicho five bucks every year. Not much now, but buy many bullets, tea, flour, and other stuff at Fort Rae in early days."

"Seems rather paternalistic, if you don't mind my saying."

"It's very important to my people. Is obligation Canada must respect. Also good excuse for a feast." His black eyes twinkled. "We have very big feast, lots of drum dancing and handball games on Treaty Day. People come from all Tlicho communities."

"When is it?"

"In July, what we call Soòmba Nàzhèe Zaà, Treaty Month."

"Let's hope Teht'aa can join the celebration. From the way the neurosurgeon in Edmonton was talking, it might be possible." I smoothed out a wrinkle in her pale-blue bedcover. "He doesn't see anything in the CT scan that would suggest permanent damage. He's convinced it's a matter of time before she wakes up. But you heard him say that only an MRI would confirm his diagnosis. I think we should have it done."

"But the fancy machine is in Edmonton," he said. "Much better she stay here with her own people. The Creator look after her here."

"She'd be with you. You could make sure the Creator was watching over her, keeping her safe."

He dropped his gaze to the rat root in his hand, then shifted it onto his grandniece. He remained quiet for so long, I began to think he hadn't heard me.

I was about to repeat the suggestion when he turned his deeply lined face back to me. "She gonna be okay. Edmonton too far away. She stay here."

We shall see, I thought to myself. If there was no improvement in the morning, I would insist that they medevac her.

I focused my attention back on the still figure lying on the bed. A hollow wisp of her once-vibrant self, she created barely a ripple above the flatness of the bedcover.

"Come on, Teht'aa, move. Give us a sign that you're coming back to us. Do it for your dad. He'll be here tomorrow … I hope."

As if on cue, an eyelid fluttered. I waited for another flutter. And it did. "Look, look, she's moving."

"Where?" the old man asked.

"Her left eyelid. See, there it goes again. Teht'aa, can you hear me? It's me, Meg."

"She doing that lots this afternoon. Her arm twitch too."

"Teht'aa, move your eyelid if you can hear me."

Both of us leaned over and watched. But this time there was no answering flutter, not even a twitch.

I tried not to feel disheartened. Eyelid movement, no matter how involuntary, was a step in the right direction.

I removed my jacket and draped it over the back of the chair. "Uncle Joe, how can you keep your jacket on? Aren't you hot?"

"Hot, cold. It make no difference to an old man like me. This special jacket." He ran his hand over the dark navy nylon fabric. "Shelagh, my son's wife, give it to me. I don't want her to think I don't like it." He did, though, unzip the fleece-lined windbreaker and shook it open to reveal his heavy red plaid flannel shirt.

"Are you sure Hans Walther isn't her boyfriend? He certainly thinks he is."

"Crazy guy. Spend too much time on the land."

"But your people have lived on the land for eons, and I don't think they're crazy, apart from you, that is."

"Me an old coot, eh?" He snickered, showing a gap-filled smile. "It's different for white people. You not use to being all by yourself with only trees, water, and rocks to talk to. You got to have buildings, cellphones, cars, all that fancy stuff."

"If that's the case, I'll take over Teht'aa's car and let you walk."

He snorted.

I noticed a scrap of white paper on the floor near the bed's front wheel. Retrieving it, I recognized it as the business card Hans had given me. It must've slipped out of my pocket. It identified him as the president of Walther Aerial Exploration International, with offices in Yellowknife, Canada and Munich, Germany. I assumed this meant he searched for mineral deposits by plane and not by tramping endless miles through the bush.

"I see that Hans is a pilot."

"Yah, he bring Teht'aa to Digadeh when Florence sick. I seen him getting supplies at the Northern. Think he was prospecting nearby."

"So he owns a plane."

"He was showing it off the time he bring Teht'aa, taking folks up for a ride. Lots of fancy equipment. But it was no big deal. We fly in planes all the time. Only way we get in and out of Digadeh, except in winter when we got the ice road."

"You know what this means."

"He fly plane? I don't know." He shrugged.

"It punches a hole in his alibi. He told me he was in the bush when Teht'aa was attacked. But with his own plane, he could've easily flown into Yellowknife from wherever he was prospecting. Do you think he could've done it?"

"Like I tell you, I don't like the man, but she never say he beat her."

Regardless, this was one piece of information I was going to pass on to Sergeant Ryan. Weakening the case against Frank would weaken the case against Eric.

"Teht'aa's popular today." The grey-haired nurse placed a vase containing a large arrangement of yellow lilies, white carnations, and purple daisies next to Han's red roses. Curious, I pulled out the card and was surprised to read, *Wishing you a speedy recovery. Reggie and Tony.*

"Tony?" I asked Uncle Joe.

"His wife. Real name Antoinette. She only use it when she talking to bigwigs."

"I guess we're not bigwigs. Why would they send Teht'aa flowers?"

"Reggie's her chief. Just making sure she vote for him next time." He chuckled.

"I had a run-in with her on the street this morning. She sure treated me like dirt."

"She wanted Reggie to be Grand Chief more than he did. She was real mad at Eric when he won. Said he cheated."

"From what I hear, it's more likely Reggie was the one cheating. Did you know that he has appointed himself acting Grand Chief? Rather quick, don't you think?"

"Eric set him to rights. Hey, look at that. Her arm moving." So were the fingers of the other hand, the one belonging to the broken arm. "Come on, Teht'aa, you can do it. Wake up."

The part of her face that wasn't covered in bandages grimaced as if in pain.

"Good," the nurse said, padding up beside me. "She's starting to feel pain, which means she's coming out of it. Could you please move to one side?"

I stood at the bottom of the bed and watched her test the IV needle to ensure it was firmly in place before she replaced the empty IV container.

"How long has Reggie been Grand Chief of the Tlicho?"

"About five years. Before that he was chief of Digadeh for many years. Took over from his dad. His granddad was chief before that."

"So he essentially inherited the position, even though it's an elected office."

"Folk like to respect tradition. They say his ancestor was one of the great medicine men of the Dene. Reggie wasn't a bad chief. He got things done, most of the time. I liked his dad better. Had more respect for Tlicho ways."

"How did he get to be Grand Chief?"

"Tlicho got self-government now. Grand Chief very important job. Much responsibility. Need to know much and work good with white people. He got good education. He promise big things and say he know many important people. Lots of people vote for him. They also like the free cigarettes and gas he give out." He laughed.

"So he paid for votes."

"He didn't. Mining company did."

"Amounts to the same thing, doesn't it?"

"Don't matter if he do a good job."

"So he's done a good job."

"Some people think so. Some not. Self-government give us control over minerals in our traditional lands. Mining companies say we got lots. They want to build mines. Reggie says we need to do this."

"I imagine he would, since he seems to have a cozy relationship with one of them."

"Many elders don't want mines."

"Why not? It would bring in much-needed revenue."

"Yah. But mines destroy land, scare animals away, and kill the fish. Look at what gold mines do to Yellowknife. Too much pollution. A girl die from eating snow near the mine. We want to leave our land like when the Creator gave it in our care. We can get money other ways."

"Excuse me," the nurse said. "I would appreciate if you both could go elsewhere for the moment. I want to change her dressings."

"Happy to. I see it's almost dinner time, so we should be leaving anyway." I gave Teht'aa's arm a farewell pat. "I'd love to be here when she wakes up. Do you think it's going to be soon?"

"Hard to tell. Sometimes when they start moving like this, it happens quickly. I or the nurse who comes on duty after me will call if she looks close to regaining consciousness."

"That would be wonderful."

"But keep in mind, it's likely she won't recognize you. They're pretty groggy, with some memory loss. It usually returns, but it can be a bit disconcerting at first."

"I don't care, as long as she's awake."

With Uncle Joe following close behind, I left with more spring in my step than I'd had since receiving that fateful phone call from Derrick.

TWENTY-TWO

I wanted to decline. I was in no mood for socializing, particularly with people I didn't know. But Uncle Joe was so insistent on my coming to his son Malcolm's house for dinner, I felt I couldn't turn him down. It was the right decision. They wrapped me in the warmth of their large and loving family. Without hesitation, his daughter-in-law Shelagh folded me, a stranger, into her ample bosom as if we were long-lost friends. For a couple of hours I was able to shove my worries aside and enjoy their company, though I couldn't help but think that this family gathering was incomplete without Teht'aa and Eric.

Houses didn't come cheap in Yellowknife. Teht'aa had been very discouraged when she discovered the only house she could afford to buy was a trapper's one-room cabin on the outskirts of the town. Though she'd been attracted to its lakeside location, the lack of electricity and running water dissuaded her.

So I was surprised at the size of Malcolm's home in the Dene community of N'dilo, an island extension to the peninsula Old Town straddled. I'd been expecting a discreet bungalow and instead found myself entering a spacious log house built on a granite outcrop overlooking Yellowknife's Back Bay. The winged, two-storey structure with its expansive picture windows and high, vaulted ceilings could rival the rustic elegance of ranchers' lodges featured in architectural magazines. Although its logs were new round cedar from British Columbia and its design decidedly modern, I felt a pang of homesickness for my century-old, squared-timber house standing atop its own granite cliff.

This prompted me to wonder about Malcolm's job. I found out when his father asked when he'd be returning to the mine. Turned out his son worked in one of the diamond mines close to the Arctic Circle. Because of the isolation, employees worked two weeks on with two weeks off. Malcolm was just starting his second week off.

"He's been working for them fifteen years," Shelagh added, her face beaming with pride. "Right after he graduated from University of Alberta."

"You have a lovely house to show for it."

"Thanks. We pinched our pennies for many years. Papa Joe has helped out too." She wrapped her arms around the old man and gave him a noisy kiss on the cheek.

Eight of us, including three of Malcolm and Shelagh's five children, plus the husband of the very pregnant daughter, crowded around the kitchen table. The spacious modern kitchen rivalled my own country kitchen in size, but the two double-door refrigerators and state-of-the-art six-burner induction stove put my aging appliances to shame.

We gorged on caribou stew and bannock with a side order of smoked whitefish that had been grilled on the outside barbeque. But as much as I was enjoying it, I felt guilty at the thought of Eric eating jail fare. Tomorrow night, though, if everything went the way his defence attorney said it would, I'd be treating my husband to the best food Yellowknife had to offer.

Earlier, while Uncle Joe and I were en route from the hospital, Sally had finally returned my call. Eric's bail hearing was scheduled for tomorrow afternoon. In the morning, she wanted Uncle Joe and me to go to the courthouse to sign documents as sureties. We decided to do this separately so one of us could be with Teht'aa when she regained consciousness. Though the nurse hadn't yet called, I was still feeling optimistic that come morning Teht'aa would be with us in mind as well as body.

Lost to my own musings, I didn't hear the question until the old man shouted in my ear, "Malcolm wants to know if you are related to Father Harris."

Malcolm, scraping the last of the stew from his plate with a piece of bannock, was a carbon copy of his father, including the distinctive nose, except twenty-five or so years younger, with unblemished black hair and a face that spoke of a much easier life than his father had lived.

"Sorry. Who's Father Harris?"

"He's a fixture in Yellowknife. Worked at Saint Anne's before they closed it."

"That's the residential school your father went to, isn't it? Did you go there too?"

"Fortunately for me and my brother, we were living in Medicine Hat, so I went to a regular school. Not that it was an entirely happy experience. My cousins weren't so lucky. They went to Saint Anne's."

"Did they have a bad time there?"

He glanced at his father, whose face remained studiously impassive. "They never said. Since your last name is Harris, I was wondering if there was a connection."

"I doubt it. I've never heard anyone in my family mention any relatives living in the Northwest Territories. I also suspect from the honorific that he is a Catholic, and I'm afraid the Harris side of my family is diehard Protestant, if religious at all."

"I thought he might've dropped by the hospital to see Teht'aa. For some reason she feels sorry for the man. He's a bit of a sad sight. He spends most of his time walking the streets looking out for the homeless."

"A noble cause in itself. I take it he doesn't have a church."

"I imagine he's retired. He's about Dad's age. Have you met Gloria yet? He keeps an eye on her for Teht'aa."

"Gloria and I have had a few, shall we say, encounters. What's her story?"

"Dad, you should probably tell it. You know more than I do."

"No different than a lot of kids today." He concentrated on savouring his last spoonful of stew before ripping off a piece of bannock to mop up the rest.

"I know you don't like to talk about it, Papa Joe," interjected Shelagh. "But we shouldn't hide these things. Meg's family. She should know about the family, good or bad."

Following the others' example, I tore off a piece of bannock and let it soak up the remaining sauce on my plate while I waited. I wasn't going to push Uncle Joe. I figured he would tell me when he was ready. The caribou stew had been delicious, almost as good as Eric's moose stew. The bannock was tasty too. Silence reigned but for the sound of scraping bannock and smacking lips as the others joined me in the wait.

"One of your best, Shelagh." Uncle Joe patted his stomach. "Hits the spot."

"You always say that, Papa Joe. I could cook a dried-out moosehide and you'd say the same thing." She laughed a light girlish twitter that belied her age. "Meg, I suppose you could call Gloria another of our lost souls. Teht'aa, bless her, was trying to help her. Robbery, drunk and disorderly, prostitution, I swear there wasn't—"

"You talkin' about that slut?" piped up the younger boy.

I put the age of the three children to be early to mid-twenties. While the other son and the pregnant daughter bore the stamp of their father, this son had not only the laughing brown eyes of his mother, but also her propensity to put on weight.

"I see her picking up johns all the time behind the Gold Range," he continued between mouthfuls of fish. "She's so fuckin' scrawny it'd be like fuckin' a toothpick."

"Christopher, your language," his mother shot back.

"You too hard on the girl," Uncle Joe broke in. "She had her troubles, but life not been easy for her."

"As if it's been easy for the rest of us," his daughter-in-law retorted. "My mother was a drunk too, so drunk the authorities took me away and put me into care. I was even younger than Gloria was. And I never saw my mother again. At least she got to see her mother."

"You have strong medicine power, Shelagh. You can overcome anything."

"You and your stupid medicine power. It doesn't exist anymore. It disappeared when the church took over our lives."

Her chair scraped on the tiled floor as she pushed away from the table and started collecting the dirty plates. Being well trained by my mother, I rose to help, but she motioned me to stay put, so I passed the dirty plates down to her end of the table.

"But it still there. We just don't know how to recognize it anymore," Uncle Joe said. "Sadly, Gloria not born with much medicine power. She not equipped to deal with bad things life throw at her."

He helped himself to the last morsel of fish before the plate was whisked out of reach, savoured its smoky flavour, then pointed his fork at me. "Like I tell you, Gloria is Claire's daughter, my sister Florence's middle girl. Claire had problems. After Saint Anne's, she forgot how to be Dene. She didn't want to live in Digadeh. But she had problem in Yellowknife too. Florence try to help, but Claire think her mother a stupid Indian. Treat her badly. She ended up a drunk with three kids by three different men.

"Gloria and older girls were in and out of care. Sometime they live with Florence. But Claire take them away. She don't want her girls near her mother. Once Gloria live with me and Mary. Only ten year old, but a handful, kept running away, stealing things from the Northern. She were too much for Mary. By then Mary had the cancer. When Claire off the booze she a good mum. But she couldn't stay away from it. Gloria was living with Claire in Yellowknife, when they find Claire in snow bank. Drunk, she passed out and froze to death."

"I remember," Malcolm added. "Happened about ten years ago. The police contacted me because I was the only family member living in Yellowknife. I had to deal with getting the body shipped to Digadeh for burial. I'll never forget how my cousin looked. She used to be a very pretty woman, but a lifetime of drinking and living with men who beat her had changed her beyond recognition."

"What happened to Gloria?" I asked, eyeing the home-made chocolate cake that was making its way to the table.

"She fifteen," Uncle Joe answered. "Almost too old for care, so authorities send her to her grandmother. She like Florence, so live with her until Florence get sick. When they take Florence to hospital in Yellowknife, Gloria go too and stay in Yellowknife when Florence come back to Digadeh. Gloria smart girl. She like school. So she learn enough to get a job. But it don't last. She find easier way to make money."

"What happened to her sisters?"

"The oldest died. Got sick. The other live here. She got that fetal alcohol disease, like my nephew. Has tough time. Lives on the streets mostly."

"FASD. Fetal alcohol spectrum disorder," Shelagh added. "Unfortunately, we have a high incidence amongst our people because of the high rate of alcohol addiction. The disorder manifests itself in low intelligence and various behavioural and emotional conditions, such as an inability to control anger. We have a FASD program at the hospital where I work that helps those affected to better manage their lives. But it's for kids, and unfortunately Gloria's sister is too old to benefit." She slid an enormous slice of chocolate cake onto a plate and passed it over to me.

My initial reaction was to pass it on to one of the men, but then I decided I needed some comfort food.

"Gloria doesn't have it, does she?"

"Claire was in jail when she pregnant with Gloria. Not much booze in there, eh?" Uncle Joe chortled.

"I gather Gloria has a child. Is this history repeating itself?" I asked.

"You're talking about Anita," Shelagh answered. "A real sweetie, about five years old. She lives in Digadeh with Florence. Gloria loves her, and from what I've seen she's a good mother. But thank goodness she's smart enough to know her child is better off with Florence. She visits her daughter fairly often. Teht'aa's been trying to convince her to stay in Digadeh, but she won't."

The silence returned as we concentrated on gobbling up every last crumb of cake. It rivalled the cakes my family's cook baked when I was growing up. I was waffling over whether to have a second helping when the phone decided for me.

It was the nurse from the hospital. Teht'aa had woken up.

TWENTY-THREE

Teht'aa was awake. Thank God. And she no longer needed to be medevaced. But I wasn't jumping up and down with joy, not yet.

Although her eyes were open, they weren't focusing on anything or anyone. They would drift from her great uncle to me and back again but didn't seem to register our actual presence. She spoke mostly gibberish, something about needing her blueberry, which she said over and over again. She also kept asking, "Where am I?" and "What's happened?" but paid no attention to our answers.

At least she was trying to talk this morning. Last night, when the nurse had allowed me to spend a few minutes with her, she had been mostly silent with the occasional groan of pain.

It was as if she was with us, yet wasn't. The nurse had tied her arms to the bed because she wouldn't stop trying to pull the IV needle from her hand or remove the bandages from her face. The nurse assured us that this was normal, that within a few hours Teht'aa should be more aware of her surroundings. On the plus side, most of the machines were gone. The ventilator had been removed, along with the ECG. But she was still hooked up to the machine that monitored her heart rate, blood pressure, and oxygen intake.

I had been sitting with her for most of the morning, apart from my visit to the courthouse, and had seen only marginal improvement. When I finally left her in the care of Uncle Joe, she was sleeping and had been for the last couple of hours.

I wanted to arrive at the courthouse in plenty of time for the start of the bail hearings. In my latest phone call with Sally, she reiterated her client's request for me not to attend. However, once she'd performed her duty as his lawyer, she let drop that the hearings started at two o'clock and that Eric's case was the second on the docket.

Unsure of the length of time it would take for the first case to be heard, I decided to be there from the start. Unfortunately, Sally had forgotten to tell me the number of the courtroom. I only discovered after I'd entered the courthouse that there were several. Thankfully, a person leaving the elevator was able to direct me to the one on the main floor where the show cause hearings took place.

With no little amount of trepidation, I opened the door, expecting to find the kind of dark, cavernous room one sees in the movies, with tiers of seats for spectators. I was hoping to sit unseen in a back corner behind other spectators. No such luck. The room was bright, with only a few rows of seats. There was no place for me to hide.

A man in a uniform guarding the door raised his eyebrows in question. I mumbled something about attending a bail hearing and sat down on one of the hard plastic chairs in the back row. The room was almost empty but for a murder of sombre-suited men and women sitting in the first couple of rows. They too glanced at me questioningly but turned their eyes to the front when a side door opened. They hastily stood up as a perfectly coifed woman wearing black robes strode across to the judge's bench, leaving the Canadian and NWT flags fluttering in her wake. She sat down to face us. Everyone bowed and resumed their chairs, except for me. Uncertain of court protocol, I'd only decided to stand after I noticed another person who looked more like a spectator than a lawyer standing. I was partway up when everyone sat down.

The first defendant, a bored-looking young man with a bad case of acne, was escorted by a guard through a more solid door than the one to the judge's chambers and took his seat behind a wall of glass. The judge started reading out the charges and the conditions of release, and so began the first hearing.

Though the proceedings were new to me, and the case, a robbery with an assault using a dangerous weapon, in this case bear spray, had the potential to be interesting, if not a tad farcical, I paid little attention. I was more interested in it ending quickly. I tried to peer through the narrow window in the prisoner's door to see Eric waiting. But all I saw was the occasional face of another guard standing behind it.

As the case progressed, more people entered the room, most of them lawyers and others looking equally officious. I waited for Sally to arrive. The hearing finally ended with the defendant being denied bail, primarily because this was his twenty-seventh charge and he had a history of noncompliance with previous release conditions.

I tried to assure myself that this wasn't the case with Eric. He was an upstanding citizen with only one prior conviction, a thirty-year-old one at that. Surely the judge wouldn't hesitate to release him.

After we rose for the judge to leave the room, I expected Eric's lawyer to take her place in the front row. When Sally didn't appear, I checked to see if she was waiting in the lobby and found it empty. When the judge raised his gavel again and still no Sally, I grew more anxious. When a defendant who was not Eric was escorted into the room, I knew something was wrong.

The guard noticed my confusion and asked if he could help.

"I thought the hearing for Eric Odjik was supposed to be up now," I whispered while the judge read out the charges.

The man scanned the list attached to his clipboard. "I don't see his name. Are you sure his show cause hearing is this afternoon?"

"His lawyer told me it was. Could it have been changed at the last minute?"

"It sometimes happens. Let me check the dockets for the other courtrooms." He leafed through other pages. "Here it is — upstairs in courtroom three. Eric Odjik ... the name's familiar. Isn't he the man charged with the killing at Digadeh?"

I mumbled, "Yes."

"That explains it. Bail hearings for prisoners charged with murder are held in front of a superior court judge. The cases being heard in this courtroom are for lesser charges and are in front of a justice of the peace. You his wife?" Not waiting for an answer, he continued on. "You better hurry. It's likely started. Take the elevator to the second floor. It's the first door on the right. Tell the deputy-sheriff in charge I sent you."

With a hasty thank you I fled out the door, worried that the hearing would be over by the time I arrived. The wait for the elevator didn't help, but with no stairs in sight, I was forced to watch the seconds tick by. Finally one arrived and up I went.

I was so annoyed at Sally for not telling me and myself for not asking that by the time I reached the door to the right courtroom, I forgot that I needed to be quiet. I opened it with too much force and stepped inside with too much noise. Every eye in the room, including Eric's, swivelled in my direction. If the floor had suddenly opened up in front of me, I would gratefully have jumped in. Instead I smiled apologetically at my husband, gave him a nervous wave, and tiptoed to the closest empty seat.

For a second his face lit up, then it turned to stone. Hunching his shoulders forward, as if trying to hide, he twisted around to face the judge. Oh my poor, dear, sweet Eric. He wasn't angry at me. He was embarrassed. He hadn't wanted me to see him defeated, because defeat was all I read in his posture. Normally he held himself so confidently and proudly, ready to take on whatever challenge life flung at him. But not this time. It was as if he had given up.

I could feel the tears seeping down my cheeks. I brushed them away.

Eric, I won't let this happen to you. You may have given up, but I haven't.

TWENTY-FOUR

I straightened my shoulders and sat more upright, daring anyone to call my husband a killer. But no one paid any more attention to me.

All eyes were trained on the judge, a man of about the same age as Eric, midfifties, with the same amount of grey in his black hair, except it was trimmed to a short judicial length and not flowing over his shoulders like my husband's. Wearing black robes with a red border and red cuffs and a matching red vest, he towered above the rest of the courtroom, behind the elevated bench bookended by two lower stands in the same dark-brown wood. Directly below him sat the court reporter. On his left was the jury stand, empty for this hearing. I hoped I would never see it occupied. The richness of the wood lent this courtroom the aura of authority that was more in keeping with my image of a judicial court than the plastic and metal of the courtroom below.

In front of him, at the table to his right, sat Eric's defence team, Sally and Derrick, both appropriately garbed in their black robes. Sally was standing, expounding on some technical point. One of the Crown prosecutors sitting at the other table seemed more focused on his laptop, while the other leafed through sheets of paper.

And Eric, my poor, sweet, innocent Eric, sat all alone behind them in a glass-enclosed booth. This, above everything else, finally drilled into me the direness of his situation. I was still trying to absorb the enormity of this prisoner box after my initial shock. At least he wasn't wearing prisoner orange.

The rows of spectator seats were for the most part occupied. I was surprised to recognize Reggie sitting a few rows back from the front. Was he here to ensure that his rival stayed in jail? Or should I be more charitable and say that he had come to offer moral support?

Josh and others I took to be his media buddies sat at the end of my row and the one in front. The CBC journalist acknowledged my presence with a nod and nudged the woman beside him. Her stare was so penetrating that I jerked my eyes back to the front and wondered how in the world I was going to escape her microphone. A casually dressed man with black plugs in his earlobes was curled over a sketchpad, drawing. No doubt a likeness of Eric would be appearing on the front pages of the nation's papers tomorrow.

Given the number of journalists present, Sally had better have an escape plan. No way did I want my husband to spend his first minutes of freedom being hounded by the pack.

Sally finished speaking and sat down. I expected the Crown to rise to give their side and was surprised when they remained seated. All eyes were on the judge. Ignoring us, he riffled through some papers. It looked as if I had arrived at the end of the hearing. Eric remained rooted to his chair, shoulders hunched in dejection. He didn't glance at his lawyer when she sat down. Instead I sensed his body tense in expectation. I willed him to turn around so I could give him a smile of hope. But he remained facing forward, away from me and everyone else in the courtroom.

Finally, the judge stopped reading and looked up.

"I will give my decision in three days. Meanwhile, Eric Odjik remains in custody. The court is adjourned."

In a swish of black silk, he strode through the judges' door, followed by the clerk, who firmly closed the door behind them.

"No!" I shouted.

I pushed my way through the departing crowd, intent on getting to my husband. By the time I reached the front, he was shuffling through the prisoner door, sandwiched between two guards. Before he vanished completely, he stopped, forcing his guards to stop. He scanned the courtroom and eventually found me. Once again his eyes lit up with love and, he smiled, but not enough to reveal his dimples. He shrugged as if to say "I'm sorry" and was gone behind the closing door. Only then did I realize the cause of his constrained movements. My poor, dear sweet Eric was still shackled, like a dangerous criminal. Something inside of me twisted.

Barely able to hide the despair in my voice, I asked Sally, "Why didn't the judge let him go?"

"Let's get out of here. I need a coffee."

Using her briefcase as a battering ram, she shoved her way through the throng with me at her heels and Derrick acting as our rear guard.

An arm reached out to stop me. "Meg, I'm so sorry." I read sympathy in Reggie's face, not triumph. Maybe I'd judged him too harshly. "I wasn't expecting this. None of us were. I and a number of other chiefs had even given his defence attorney character statements."

"Thanks."

"Please, don't despair. I'm sure this is just a momentary hiccup. He'll be out on bail in three days' time."

"You'd better be right."

"Look, if there's anything I can do, let me know. You're probably in need of some friendly company. Why don't you come for dinner tonight? I need to check with Tony first to make sure we're free. I know she would love to have you."

Yeah, right. "Thanks, but I need to be with Teht'aa. She has finally come out of the coma, so I should be with her as much as I can, particularly now that it will be another three days before her father can be with her."

"That's wonderful news ... about the coma, that is. Does she remember much?"

"Her mind is pretty hazy, but I expect within a day or two she'll be back to her old self."

"Terrific. When do you think she'll be up for some visitors?"

"I imagine as soon as she is moved from ICU. I'll let you know. Oh, and thanks for the flowers. They're beautiful."

"I'm glad she liked them. One thing I'll say about Teht'aa: she doesn't hesitate to speak her mind. She's good at reminding me of my duties as Tlicho Grand Chief. Whenever she has some burning issue, she's on my case." He laughed. "Don't get me wrong. I enjoy her sparring. She's even managed to convince me to change my mind, like this latest business about mining on Tlicho territory. I don't suppose you know where she is with her investigation, do you?"

"Investigation?"

"Yeah, into the mining industry. A hot topic around here, when a good portion of NWT jobs depend on it."

"Sorry, I've no idea."

"I see your lawyer waving to you from the door. You'd better get going. And don't forget, anytime you want a reprieve, drop by our place." He passed me his business card. "The address is on the back."

I pushed my way to Sally waiting next to the courtroom door, all but blocked by the people streaming through it.

"Hang on to me and keep your head down," she ordered. "And your mouth shut. Not one single word, you hear."

I hung on to her robe as she rammed her way through the crowd. Lights flashed. Reporters shouted. "Mrs. Odjik, is your husband guilty?" a female voice cried out.

"Outside, everyone," a male voice yelled. "You know you're not supposed to conduct interviews inside the courthouse."

Two deputy sheriffs brushed past me and started moving everyone from the hallway.

"Where's your car?" Reggie asked.

"Out front on the street," I replied.

"Mine's out back. Follow me."

I grabbed Sally's arm.

"Come on, we're going this way."

He led the three of us across the lobby to a door that was being unlocked by a deputy sheriff. We fled through it and down an empty hallway. A woman's whining voice drifted out to us as we scurried past an open doorway. We kept walking to the end of the hall and down a stairwell to emerge outside with, thankfully, not a reporter in sight.

"I can take you to wherever you're going. You can come back later to pick up your car."

"Thank you, Reggie," Sally answered. "You're very kind, but we can take it from here."

The three of us watched his champagne-coloured Jeep turn the corner before Sally spoke up. "A good way to escape the mob. He was so intent on helping us that I didn't want to let on I was already coming this way. Men. You gotta let them think they're on top. You never know when they'll come in handy." She chortled.

Derrick pretended he hadn't heard.

I ran to catch up to the two lawyers as they walked toward Sally's rental parked halfway down the street.

TWENTY-FIVE

"So what in the hell happened?" I wrenched the teabag out of the teapot a little too vigorously, splattering hot tea over the table and me. "I thought it was a simple matter of rubber-stamping Eric's release."

Apart from an elderly bald man hunched over his beer at the bar, the three of us were sitting in an empty café a goodly distance from the courthouse, well out of range of prying media.

"It was never a sure thing," Sally answered after taking a lingering sip of a foamy latte. She pulled her smartphone from her purse and placed it face up on the table.

Derrick mumbled agreement as he poured beer into a glass.

"So why did you lead me to believe it was?"

"I didn't want you getting all depressed on me." She scrolled through her messages.

"Screw that. I want you to tell me exactly what's going to happen to my husband."

"My apologies, but to tell you the truth I wasn't too certain myself which way this judge would go. He's a tough-on-crime judge, but he sympathizes with the local indigenous population and will verge on the point of leniency when their cases come before him. I'm still holding out that he'll release Eric."

"I imagine the earlier criminal charges are a factor in the delay, wouldn't you say, Sally?" Derrick added, after taking a similarly lingering sip of his beer.

"But that was years ago, when Eric was barely out of his teens," I interjected. "He's been the poster boy for upstanding citizenry ever since."

"Not quite." Her cell buzzed. She read the message before continuing, "He has a more recent arrest for DUI but was never formally charged. Ah, I see you didn't know about this one, either."

Not only did I not know, but he was supposed to be the one who could handle his liquor. "When did this happen?"

"Twelve years ago."

Good, before I knew him. "But if he was never charged, isn't that supposed to mean it never happened?"

"Unfortunately, the arrest record is still there. But I doubt these arrests are causing the delay. I imagine it's the flight risk, given the seriousness of the charge. You see, murder charges are treated differently from other charges. The onus is on the defence to prove why the defendant should be released, unlike lesser charges, for which the onus is on the crown to prove why the defendant should not be released."

"So what are the chances the judge will come down in favour of letting Eric go?" I asked.

"I wish I could be more optimistic, but I think it's fifty-fifty. What do you think, Derrick?" She scanned another message and tapped in a response.

"You're the boss, Sally. You've been through this many times before. But since you're asking, I believe if Eric's official residency were the Territory, Justice Demarco wouldn't hesitate to decide in his favour. But since his official residency is several thousand kilometres away, with little to prevent him from leaving on the next plane other than the guarantee of Joseph Bluegoose, who isn't even a relative, I agree with you. Though I might nudge it up to sixty-forty, given the number of testimonials we were able to get from some key people with NWT residency."

Sally's cell dinged again. Glancing at the message, she said, "Now if there is nothing else, I need to get back to Vancouver."

"Aren't you going to be here when the judge gives his decision?"

"Derrick will be attending. My presence isn't needed. We've done all we can at this point." Her phone buzzed again. She scanned it before rising from her chair. "Now I really must be going. Meg, I'll drive you back to the courthouse to retrieve your car. The media should be gone by now."

"I thought you were going to tell me more about the case against Eric." I remained seated. I didn't care if she had other things going on. Right now she was working for Eric and for me.

"Normally we can't discuss cases to protect client confidentiality, but your husband gave his approval to share everything with you. Derrick knows as much as I do, so he can bring you up to date." She dashed off to pay our bill.

"No, I'm not leaving until *you* tell me what you know," I shouted after her.

"Look, Mrs. Odjik, I can bring you up to date," Derrick said. "She has a big trial starting tomorrow and needs to get back to Vancouver."

After paying the bill she headed to the exit.

"I don't care. I'm probably paying for her time until she gets on that damn plane, so I want to hear from her."

"Are you coming?" she called out, holding the door open.

"What time does your plane leave?"

"In two and a half hours."

"Okay, I'm going with you to the airport. Two hours should be enough time for you to bring me up to date."

"But I need to … okay, all right. It can wait. I'm yours until boarding time. Now let's get going."

At my insistence, she drove straight to the airport, rather than making the detour to pick up the car. She, with contributions from Derrick, recounted everything they had learned from my husband.

The day the police had finally identified Teht'aa, Eric had been on a hunting trip with friends and didn't learn of the attack until he returned to his hotel in the evening. Both lawyers mentioned the emotion in his voice as he recounted the first sight of his daughter lying deathlike on the hospital bed, her head and face hidden by bandages, connected by wires to a plethora of machines. At that point the doctors were giving her a 50 percent chance of survival.

My poor, poor Eric. How awful for you that you had to face your dying daughter alone. I should've been with you. I would've come, if only you'd let me know. But maybe you did call, I thought as an image of my phone's blinking message light came into focus. *Maybe you tried several times and anxiously awaited my return call, a call that never came. While I, too afraid to let the world in, pretended that the message light wasn't blinking.*

According to Sally, Eric believed from the outset that Frank was the culprit. I learned for the first time that during an earlier visit he'd found his daughter trying to cover up bruises on her face with makeup. Though she refused to admit she'd been hit, he'd seen enough battered women to know the signs. In the past he wouldn't have hesitated sharing this with me, but not this time. I had little doubt that this was another example of his wanting to shield me. I wondered how many other burdens my husband had carried alone in the past months. And I was too blind to notice.

Well, Meg, Ms. Harris, Mrs. Odjik, Margaret, whatever you want to call yourself, it's time to stop being so damn selfish. Time to stop thinking only about yourself. Time to stop letting The Nightmare rule your life and Eric's. Time to start being an equal partner in this marriage.

From Sally I learned that Eric had gone straight to Frank's apartment after leaving the hospital. Failing to find him there, he spent much of the night roaming the streets of Yellowknife, checking bars and other likely spots for the man or for information on his whereabouts.

"In the morning your husband received the call that sent him to Digadeh," she said.

"Why didn't he let the cops go after the man?"

"My question exactly. Apparently there was no time. The daily flight to Digadeh was leaving in less than hour, so he took it, intending to notify the RCMP upon his arrival."

We hit one of those permafrost melt dips in the road a little too fast. If it hadn't been for the seat belt, my head would've hit the roof. She could give Uncle Joe a few tips on speeding, if that were possible.

"Did he?"

"Unfortunately, neither of the community's two constables was at the detachment, so he left a note. It's included as evidence in the case against your husband."

"Don't tell me. He wrote that he was looking for Frank, who beat up his daughter and put her in the hospital."

"More or less, except he did ask the police to arrest the man."

"So why didn't he wait for that to happen?"

"He was worried Frank would escape before the police could act on the note. Apparently someone he met on the road told him that Frank was heading into the bush."

I watched a plane rise up into the electric-blue sky and disappear into the billowing white of a cloud.

"So what happened? Did Eric try to stop him?"

"Eric doesn't remember."

"Doesn't remember! Why not?"

"He says he blacked out. When he came to, he was lying beside Frank's body with his bloody knife in his hand."

"Someone must've knocked him out."

"The RCMP had the Health Centre nurse check him out. She couldn't find any evidence that he'd been hit on the head."

"Did she perform any other tests? He could've passed out from the extreme stress of the situation."

"Does he have any underlying medical conditions?"

"No, he received a clean bill of health from his latest physical about six months ago. But you never know. He might have an underlying medical condition that wasn't detected."

"I will ask that he undergo a thorough medical examination. But if we are unable to find hard evidence for the blackout, we won't be able to use it as a line of defence. In fact, at the moment, I have very little to use for my defence. It could be the best way to go is to plead manslaughter. We could argue that in trying to stop Frank from escaping, he accidentally killed him." She wheeled the car into a parking spot and turned off the engine.

"No way. I refuse to believe that my husband killed a man."

"Right now he is charged with first-degree murder. If I am not able to mount a credible defence against this charge, your husband will be going away for twenty-five years. But if we have the charge reduced to manslaughter, I would negotiate for an early release of three years."

"You are supposed to be the best defence lawyer in Canada. I will not let you plead him guilty to manslaughter. Either you mount a proper defence, or I will find another lawyer."

"Sorry, my dear. Your husband is my client, not you, and he wants to plead guilty to manslaughter."

TWENTY-SIX

All the way to the hospital I couldn't stop muttering, "You stupid idiot. How can you give up so easily?"

This man wasn't my husband. The Eric I knew was a fighter.

His life was paved with causes he'd taken on, fought hard for, and for the most part won. His only reason for running for election as Migiskan Anishinabeg band chief was to correct the wrongs of the past and help his community become more viable, both economically and socially. When he was confident that his people were well along the road to making this happen, he took on the challenge of overseeing the Grand Council of First Nations with the intention of moving as many of the serious issues facing its members toward resolution as he could. This job had barely begun. He had too much vested interest to give it up now without a fight.

Pleading guilty made absolutely no sense. I refused to believe that he had anything to do with the killing of Frank Chocolate. So why take the easy road? To avoid the risk of spending twenty-five years in jail? Not likely. The man I married would fight the first-degree murder charge with every bit of ammunition he could muster. He would push his lawyer to do everything within her power to prove his innocence.

So damn you, Eric, why aren't you going to fight?

Well, if you won't, I will.

I bounded up the stairs to the ICU floor with more zest than I'd felt since hearing the staggering words about his arrest. Hoping Teht'aa was fully conscious, I would start with her. If she said someone other than Frank attacked her, I was on my way to proving his innocence.

But it was not to be. Although her eyes shone with recognition when I entered the room and she clasped my hand with surprising strength while voicing her gratitude at my putting my fears aside to be with her, she expressed only confusion when I finally felt it appropriate to ask about the attack.

"Are you sure you don't remember who did this to you?" I persisted.

"I'm sorry, Meg, I wish I could. I want to see the monster caught as much as you do." Her heart rate and blood pressure readings on the vitals monitor rose slightly before dipping back down to normal.

"Is there anyone you know who would be capable of doing this?"

She started to shake her head in answer, then stopped. "Oooh, that hurts too much." Using her unbroken arm, she reached up and gingerly patted the bandage swaddling her head, then touched those on her face. "I guess I don't look too hot, eh?"

"At the moment, you'd give a zombie stiff competition, but in a few weeks' time, you'll be back to your beautiful self."

She flashed one of her signature smiles, then grimaced. "Ouch, that hurts too."

"Could it have been Frank?"

"Why do you ask that?"

"Your father thinks he hurt you a while back."

"He's wrong. Just because he saw a bruise on my face, he thinks the worst."

"He loves you. He doesn't want to see you get hurt."

"For your information, I did it to myself, okay? I accidentally hit an open drawer when I was picking something off the floor. By the way, where is Dad? Surely he's returned from his hunting trip."

"Didn't Uncle Joe tell you?"

"Tell me what?"

She didn't need this kind of a shock after five days in a coma, but if I didn't tell her, she wouldn't stop bugging me. "Sorry, Teht'aa, there's no easy way to say it. He's in jail, but he should be out Friday."

"Jail? Dad? What for?" She tried to sit up but winced and collapsed back onto the pillow.

I swallowed. "He's been charged with murder."

"*Murder?*" Her voice rose several octaves, along with her blood pressure. "Who?"

"Frank."

"Fuck, fuck, fuck." Her heart rate was spiking too. But mine probably had too when I first heard the news. Still, I thought it best to wave the nurse over.

"Are you sure Frank wasn't the man who attacked you?"

"Is that what Dad thinks?"

I nodded. "Someone told him Frank did it."

I squeezed up against the bed to let the nurse pass behind me.

"You're upsetting the patient," the nurse interjected. "You should leave."

"No, she can't," Teht'aa cried out. "I have to find out about my father."

"I understand, but you need to rest. We don't want you to have a setback," the nurse answered.

"Not knowing will make me more upset."

The nurse picked up a small pill container from the bedside table and a glass with a straw. "Take this. It will help calm you." She tapped a tiny white pill onto Teht'aa's open palm and held the straw close to her mouth, waiting for her to swallow the pill.

"You'll have a few minutes before it takes effect."

She scrutinized the monitor one last time before returning to the nurses' station. Either Teht'aa was over the initial shock, or the pill was having an immediate effect, for her vitals were starting to lower.

"Fuck, I can't believe Frank's dead. And Dad is supposed to have killed him? No way. I don't believe it. When is this supposed to have happened?"

"Saturday."

"But Frank wasn't even in Yellowknife. He was supposed to be in Digadeh."

"That's where he was killed."

"Are you saying Dad was in Digadeh too?"

"Yup. Do you know if Frank was in Digadeh the night of your attack?" I crossed my fingers.

"That was last Wednesday, right? God, I can't believe I was out cold for five days." She yawned and shut her eyes for a second. "Frank told me he'd booked the Thursday flight."

"That means he was still in Yellowknife Wednesday night, so he can't be ruled out as a suspect. Damn. I'd been hoping."

"Why?"

"If someone other than Frank attacked you, it would help your father."

"Because the police think he killed Frank because of me?"

"Right. So can you think of anyone else? What about Hans Walther?"

"Hans? How do you know about him?"

"He's been wanting to visit you. He says he's your boy-friend."

"No way," she sputtered, then yawned again.

"Could he have attacked you?"

"He can be a little fierce, but no, I don't think so." Her mouth opened in yet another yawn. "Could you do something for me? Next time you come could you bring my computer? It's on my desk in the apartment." Her eyelids drifted closed.

"Oh dear, I'm afraid I have bad news. It was stolen."

"What?" Her eyes shot open. "Can't be. You need to get it back."

"I'm sure the police will do their best to locate it. But if not, your insurance will cover the cost of a replacement."

"I don't care about the computer. I need what's on it. You have to find it for me." Her eyes closed. "It's the only copy ... I have of the data."

"What data?"

"Story ... I'm working on. It's ... it's about ... *dzìewà*...." Sleep silenced her.

TWENTY-SEVEN

M y phone call found Uncle Joe at his son's house. After leaving his grandniece, he'd taken his son's truck to catch lake trout for their evening meal. But despite my love of freshly caught fish and the warm reception by his family yesterday, I turned down his invitation to join them. I wanted to focus on helping Eric. Besides, I couldn't justify enjoying a delicious meal and lively company while my husband languished alone in a cold, sterile cell, eating tasteless prison food.

On the bright side, Derrick had left a message while I was with Teht'aa. My husband had been transferred to the Correction Centre, which meant visits were allowed. Finally. The lawyer was trying to arrange one for tomorrow afternoon. At last I could be with him, hug him, kiss him, if allowed, and we'd talk. Oh, we'd talk. He'd tell me everything he knew about Teht'aa's attack and all that followed, and I'd do my utmost to persuade him to give up this ridiculous idea of pleading guilty.

Before heading back to the apartment, I decided to check out the place where the police said Teht'aa had been found, hoping it might give me some insight into the assault. With the downtown core concentrated in a six-block area — mind you, they were large blocks — it didn't take me long to find the butt-strewn piece of asphalt in the alley behind the Gold Range Motel where she'd almost died. A piece of yellow police tape tied to the handle of a waste container confirmed I'd found the right place. With images of a bleeding and battered Teht'aa foremost in my mind, I gingerly stepped over the area while several smokers eyed me with suspicion from behind the container.

In the broad daylight of a northern evening, it seemed an innocent enough place, despite the litter. But when night arrived, it would take on a more ominous feel. Apart from a single light at the back door of the motel, I didn't see any other building lights or streetlights. At the end of the alley was the liquor store I'd passed driving here. While it was busy at this time of day, it would've been closed when Teht'aa was attacked. The same would apply to the rest of the buildings, low-rise and commercial, backing onto the lane. A parking lot, mostly empty, stretched between the alley and the next street. I doubted there would be any traffic, foot or otherwise, after business hours. Not exactly a place that a single woman would want to visit late at night.

So what in the world had Teht'aa been doing here?

I started at the sound of a soft voice behind me. "Lady, please, you got a cigarette?"

I turned around to find a scrawny middle-aged woman with hanks of black oily hair tickling her chin. Her shoulders were hunched under a faded yellow nylon jacket with a broken zipper. She clutched it closed to keep it from billowing open in the wind. Hope tinged the wrinkles etched in her broad face.

"Sorry, I don't smoke."

"Maybe a twenty to get some?" She bit her lower lip.

I reached into my purse. "Do you spend time here?"

"Yah, I guess. Here and there." A dirty, bare toe poked through the frayed hole in her running shoe.

"Were you here last Wednesday night?"

"What night that?"

"Wednesday, a week ago tomorrow."

"Yah, I guess. I don't remember."

"She's here most days. This is her hangout, eh Lucy?" An elderly man approached. He was about Uncle Joe's age, but with more flesh on his bones, less hair on his head, and a surer gait. A gauze bandage covered one of his cheeks. "But since she can barely remember what she did an hour ago, she's not going to remember last week." He spoke with a faint British accent. "I'm Father Harris. Perhaps I can help you?"

"My stepdaughter was assaulted in this alley last week."

"I see. You must be Eric Odjik's wife. I'd heard that you were in town. I'm sorry about Teht'aa. Lovely woman. I have been praying to our dear Lord that she will survive this terrible tragedy."

"Maybe your prayers have worked. She has regained consciousness. By the way, I'm Meg and a Harris too. Someone thought we might be related, but I don't think so. My family is Protestant, and as far as I know none of my far-flung relatives ever wandered this far north."

"You never can tell. An ancestor might have found the right path." His mournful face brightened slightly with a wisp of a smile. "But I'm from Britain originally, arrived in the early 1960s, so unless your family still has ties to the old country, I agree it's not likely."

"I'm afraid my family ties to Britain date back to the early 1800s, when the first Joseph Harris arrived as a member of the British army. So any connection we had to England has long since been severed."

"You say your stepdaughter is out of the coma. Has she identified the man who did this terrible thing to her?"

"Unfortunately not. She doesn't remember. But I'm hoping with time that she will."

"Yes, right. I will pray for her speedy recovery. Now, if you don't mind, I must continue my rounds."

"Rounds? Do you come by here regularly?"

"Yes, most nights. We have too many lost souls wandering the streets of Yellowknife, lost souls like Lucy and her friends." His eyes shifted to the bedraggled woman walking with a slightly lopsided gait back to the garbage container to join the other two equally bedraggled women. "I like to ensure they have a place to sleep for the night, particularly when the temperatures are below freezing."

"Were you here last Wednesday?"

"The police have already asked me that. Unfortunately, Wednesday is my night off, so I would not have been able to help your daughter. I'm sorry."

"No need to be sorry. Since you know this alley and the people who frequent it, can you think of any likely suspects? Maybe someone who has a history of sexual assaults?"

Touching the bandage on his face, he stared blankly at me for a few seconds before answering. "I wish I could help. You must understand that it has taken me many years to build up the trust of these people. If I betrayed this trust, my work would become all but useless. But to ease your mind, the lost souls I work with are for the most part only interested in getting their next drink. I suspect whoever did this terrible deed was likely a frequenter of this motel. It does have a reputation."

We both turned to face the anonymous back wall with its two rows of curtain-covered windows, except for one room with the curtains pushed aside.

"Maybe someone in one of those rooms saw something," I suggested. "But I imagine the police have already checked it out."

He continued to stare at the windows. "I imagine they have."

Lucy shuffled out from behind the container again and shambled toward us, while her two friends continued to watch from their sanctuary.

"Maybe Lucy can remember something."

"I doubt it. I'm afraid years of drinking have done too much damage. I suspect she was also born with fetal alcohol syndrome. How old do you think she is?"

"I'd guess in her fifties."

"She was thirty-two in March. Life has not been kind to her. I knew her mother, another lost soul. She attended the school where I taught." He sighed. "I also knew her aunt."

"Are you talking about Saint Anne's?"

"Yes. How do you know?"

"Teht'aa's great uncle mentioned it. Joseph Bluegoose. You might know him?"

"We've met. Now if you don't mind, I really must be continuing on with my rounds. I have more lost souls to check on." He held out his hand. "It's been nice meeting you, Ms. Harris. I will start reciting a special prayer for Teht'aa in my evening prayers to help speed her recovery."

"Thank you. Every bit helps. Before you leave, perhaps you could do something for me." I pulled two bills from my wallet. "I was about to give Lucy these twenties when you arrived. I'd really hate for her to spend it on booze, so do you mind ensuring it's used on something she really needs, like new socks or shoes?"

"I wish it were that easy. I think the longest she has kept a pair of socks is a week. Shoes a tad longer. Personally, I don't think she likes them. But thank you, I will ensure the money is put to good use."

He slipped the bills into his pocket and, turning to leave, collided with Lucy, who'd crept up behind him.

She winced. "My foot!" She hopped around on her good one while she tried to hold the injured one, lost her balance, and collapsed onto the hard asphalt.

My head knocked against Father Harris's as we both bent over to help her. Rubbing our respective heads, we apologized in unison. Fearing another collision, I deferred to him.

"Sorry, child," he said to Lucy. "I didn't mean to hurt you. I'll help you up." He held out his hand, but she ignored it.

"*Dzìewà*, Father," she said, smiling. "Like the other one."

The priest jerked away as if he'd been burned. "*Dzìewà?*" I'd heard this word before.

"*Dzìewà*." She held up a piece of moosehide covered in purple embroidery. It looked familiar.

"What are you doing with that?" he asked.

I reached inside my pocket and found it empty. "It's mine. It must've fallen out." I held out my hand for Lucy to give it to me, but she ignored me.

"Nice." She rubbed the tufted petals against her cheek. "Soft. Home."

"Do you recognize it?" I asked.

"*Dzlewà.*" Her lips creased into a gap-toothed smile.

"Do you know what she's saying?" I asked Father Harris.

"Blueberry. It's the Dene word for blueberry. May I look at it, Lucy?"

So the word Teht'aa had spoken as she fell asleep was blueberry. But what did blueberries have to do with a story?

Lucy continued caressing the petals. "My pretty flower."

"Please, give it to me," the priest persisted. "I won't hurt it."

She glanced up at him and smiled shyly. "You promise?"

"I do."

She gave the petals a last kiss and passed it up to him.

He brushed his fingertips softly over the embroidery. "Beautiful work. Dene. These tufts are made from caribou hair."

"I was told moosehair."

"Older handicraft like this one are generally made from caribou, when caribou was the mainstay of Dene life. The skin is also caribou. See how soft and supple it is. You rarely see such fine workmanship anymore." He sniffed it. "It still has a faint smell of smoke from the traditional tanning process. Such a shame that it's ripped. Where did you get it?"

"It belongs to Teht'aa."

"Ah, I see."

"Someone found it over there after her attack." I pointed to the parking lot behind us. A man walking away from his car waved at Father Harris, who waved back.

"You think it's related to the attack," he said.

"Maybe. See these brown spots. I think they might be blood. Maybe it fell out of her purse as she struggled to defend herself. But if she was attacked behind this motel, I don't know how it ended up on the other side of the alley."

"I suggest you hand it over to the police. They are in the best position to ascertain its importance. I could do it for you, if you like."

"*Mamàcho* makes pretty purple flowers like this." Lucy struggled unsteadily to her feet and tried to snatch the embroidery back from the priest, but he moved it beyond her reach.

"Does she mean her grandmother?" I asked.

"Yes. I know her," the priest replied. "A wonderful woman."

"When I was little, *Mamàcho* take me to see purple flowers," Lucy continued. "Very pretty. They twinkle like stars. She showed me how to make pretty flowers. But I forget. It was a long time ago."

Without another word, she turned to her friends standing protectively behind her. They'd crept out from their hideaway when she'd fallen. As one the three women turned their backs on us and shambled back to their garbage container.

"Lucy!" the priest called out. "Here." He tossed her a partially filled package of cigarettes, which landed at her feet.

"Thanks." Beaming, she bent over to retrieve it. After extracting a cigarette for herself, she passed the package on to her friends.

"Does she have a home?" I asked.

"There's a women's shelter she sometimes uses."

"She must have a Dene community she can go to."

"Digadeh, where her grandmother lives. But I doubt she ever visits. Her grandmother is a holy terror when it comes to alcohol. Well, I must be off. Nice meeting you. By the way, I'm sorry to hear about your husband. Not an easy time for you. If you want to talk about it, my door is open."

"Thanks, but I'm okay. I don't expect him to be in jail much longer."

"They're letting him out on bail, are they?"

"I'm hoping so. But what I really meant was that they will be dropping the charges. He's innocent."

"I know how difficult it is to accept that a loved one committed one of God's ultimate sins. But if you can find it in your heart to forgive him, particularly since there seems to be just cause, it would make it easier for both of you. Now I really must be going."

I felt my anger rise but held my tongue as I watched him slip the piece of caribou hide into his pocket. He started walking away.

"Aren't you forgetting something?" I called out. "Teht'aa's embroidery. I'd like it back."

"Yes, right. So sorry. Just my old brain not working. It really is a marvellous piece of workmanship."

He gave it one last look before handing it over.

TWENTY-EIGHT

While Lucy and her friends focused on smoking the cigarettes the priest had given them, they continued to cast furtive glances in my direction. When another cigarette butt was flicked onto the wedge of filthy asphalt where Teht'aa had lain dying, I shivered. It felt too much like a desecration.

Their differences were so great, I found it hard to believe that Lucy and Teht'aa had grown up in the same small community. Though close in age, Lucy's ravaged face suggested that she was a good twenty years older. Without a mother and effectively no father, Teht'aa would've had just as difficult a time in her early years. But she'd had Uncle Joe to help guide her and, from what he said, a loving grandmother. Like Lucy, Teht'aa had had her battle with addictions, both drug and alcohol, but she'd overcome them to establish herself as a top broadcaster.

There was likely one aspect that differentiated the two women: their mothers. Eric had said that from the moment Charmaine had learned she was pregnant, she stopped drinking. She wanted her baby to start life as healthy as possible. If Father Harris was correct in his FAS diagnosis, then Lucy's mother hadn't stopped drinking. So from the second she was born, Lucy had been ill-equipped to handle the curveballs life would throw at her.

Since this was Lucy's regular hangout, the odds were good that she had been here when my stepdaughter was attacked. The trick was to get her to remember. But even if she couldn't, I wondered about her two friends. I bet they spent just as much time at this dreary location. Maybe one of them would be better at remembering.

As I walked toward them, one of the woman broke away and started running down the alley.

"Give 'em back," Lucy shouted and sped after her. She caught up, grabbed the woman's jacket, and pulled with more strength than I'd have thought possible. The woman fell backward onto the ground. Lucy pounced, pulling her hair and punching her. The woman fought back. With arms and feet flying, the two of them tussled on the hard ground while the third woman stood back and watched, sucking on the remnant of her cigarette.

I was about to intervene when Lucy jumped up, holding the cigarette package over her head in triumph. Within seconds she was taking off in the direction of the liquor store with her friends fast on her heels.

Deciding it was pointless to chase after them, I walked over to where I'd parked Teht'aa's car. I would come back later. My phone rang as I was putting the gearshift into drive. When I realized it was Sergeant Ryan, I stopped the car on the odd chance she had X-ray eyes or ears.

Not bothering with opening niceties, she said, "We have finished processing your husband's room at the

Explorer Hotel. You can now remove his effects. The management would like you to do it today."

I'd totally forgotten about his hotel room. "Okay, I'll come now."

"The manager will let you into the room. You'll need to show him some ID to confirm your identity. You'll also have to settle the bill." I could hear a voice in the background. She covered the phone for a few seconds before returning. "I'm afraid I've got to go."

"Wait, I'd like to ask you how the case is going?"

"Sorry, I can't speak about it to you."

"No, I'm asking about Teht'aa's assault. Your call found me at the place where she was attacked."

"That's fine by us. We've finished processing the crime scene."

"I was wondering if you had talked to the homeless women who hang out here. They might've seen something."

"We interviewed three women."

"Was one of them Lucy?"

"I don't have my notes with me, but the name sounds about right. I'm afraid none of them are credible witnesses. They were drunk and pretty hazy on their activities that night. We're not even certain if they were in the alley when the attack took place, though one of them thought she remembered seeing your stepdaughter. Unfortunately, she was mistaken about the clothing Teht'aa was wearing that night. If you don't mind, I have to go."

Though I'd never stayed in the hotel before, I felt as if I knew it. Invariably, while we were on the phone, Eric would make a comment about the spectacular view he had from his room. Sometimes it was the glow of the setting sun on the two small lakes across the street, or the air being so crystal-clear he could see across an arm of Great Slave Lake to the distant wooded shore. Finding it perched on a rocky knoll high above the main road, I could see why it had such views.

Though I was anxious to get his belongings, I made one quick stop before seeking out the manager. Eric had jokingly taken a selfie of himself in front of the giant polar bear who ruled the lobby, saying it was the closest he'd ever get to the North's most dangerous predator. In the photo his head seemed to be on the verge of being devoured by this mammoth stuffed bear. And mammoth it was, towering a good six or more feet above me. Of course, I had to take a selfie of myself about to be consumed by this beast.

But the mirth stopped the second I crossed the threshold of Eric's room. Though it was a typical, impersonal hotel room, it spoke of my husband's presence. His belongings were scattered over the room, as if he'd left it only a few hours ago, instead of three days ago. Since it was messier than his normal tidy standards, I assumed the cops were the guilty party. Even the bed was unmade. The police had likely kept hotel cleaning staff away.

I lay down on the bed he'd slept in and buried my face in the pillow, hoping to breathe in his smell. But I smelled only stale air and a slightly chemical odour, doubtless from the products the cops used in their forensic analysis. I wrapped myself in the blanket and tried to imagine him lying beside me. But all I could picture was him trying to keep warm under a thin blanket on a cold, hard prison bunk.

I dropped his suitcase onto the bed and spread it open. I pulled his brown corduroy slacks out of the closet and was about to toss them into the suitcase when I realized he would be needing them. My poor husband had likely been wearing the same clothes since his arrest, unless they'd made him wear one of those orange prison uniforms you see on TV, a thought that had me cringing.

I folded the slacks up neatly, set them aside, and added a shirt still wrapped in the hotel laundry packaging. I placed a couple of pairs of unworn socks and underpants on top. I would give them to him tomorrow. The rest of his clothes, mostly dirty, I threw into the suitcase, intending to wash them at Teht'aa's. He would need clean clothes when he was released.

As they had done with his clothes, the police had left his toiletries scattered over the bathroom counter, along with patches of a dark-grey fingerprint powder, which left me confused. Since Eric had every right to be in this room, I had no idea why they would be dusting for his fingerprints. A hunt for his toilette kit eventually found it buried under a pile of towels in the bathtub. I threw everything into it and headed back to the main room.

I collected the rest of his belongings — keys, some loose change, a collection of receipts, the book he was currently reading, Thomas King's latest, several jam-packed file folders, and a number of loose documents — and crammed everything into his briefcase. Though his wallet was missing, along with his cellphone, I assumed they'd gone with him to Digadeh. I didn't think the same assumption could be made of his computer, also missing. But I could see the police wanting to check its contents in search of more evidence.

The last item I almost missed. It was tucked away in the top drawer. When I spied the wedge of pale-gold hide peeking out from under the Gideon Bible, I wasn't even certain it belonged to Eric until I pulled it free. It was a match to the fragment of caribou hide that Josh had passed on to me, purple tufted petals and all.

I extracted that one from my purse and laid the two of them side by side on the desk. They fit together perfectly. On Eric's piece the four complete purple tufted petals, along with a single green leaf, matched the three purple petals and green leaf on Teht'aa's piece to form a complete flower with a sparkling beaded centre. Eric's slightly larger fragment had two fully intact purple flowers with a couple of green leaves and a stem that I thought might belong to another flower, which suggested there was at least one more missing piece of hide. The main distinguishing feature of each piece was the tiny bird embroidered on one corner. On Teht'aa's piece it was yellow. On Eric's it was red.

It appeared that the police hadn't been as thorough as they should've been. I knew I should hand the two fragments over, but at this point I would have had too much explaining to do, something I didn't want to get into until I knew more. I was hoping Teht'aa and Eric would tell me. Besides, I had no idea whether these purple flower fragments had any bearing on the case.

TWENTY-NINE

Eric's hotel bill was a hefty one. I didn't mind paying for the days he used the room, but it rankled to have to pay for the three days it took the police to carry out their investigation. I was tempted to send them their portion of the bill.

With my stomach growling that it was past dinnertime, I decided to try the hotel's restaurant. Eric had praised its variety of northern game dishes. But a perusal of the menu dissuaded me. Though the descriptions of the items had my mouth watering, they suggested that the dishes would be more substantial than I felt like eating now. I was also feeling poor after handing over a fair chunk of money to the hotel. Knowing that there would be an even heftier lawyers' bill to come, I decided to return to Uncle Joe's cheap noodle house.

As I was leaving, I almost collided with Hans, who was coming in to the hotel. Garbed in a camel-hair coat and grey flannels, he looked more like a prosperous businessman than a prospector.

"Meg, I have heard the good news about Teht'aa." He beamed. "I am so happy. Do you think they will let me visit her?"

I backed out of reach, worried his exuberance would include a hug. "Not as long as she's in ICU, but the nurse said she will be moved to a regular hospital room. Since she's still very weak, I could check to see if she will be allowed visitors."

"Please do. She will be so happy to see me."

Though I wanted to retort "not likely," I bit my tongue.

"I am coming in for a drink at the Trapline. Please join me."

"Is that the bar? I don't drink, but if they serve food, I'll have something to eat." Though I wasn't keen on the man, I couldn't pass up this opportunity to learn more about him.

Rather than choosing one of the empty tables near the stone fireplace with its inviting fire, Hans steered me toward the bar tucked against the back wall. The way he greeted the buxom bartender and strode without hesitation toward the second bar stool from the end told me that he'd adopted this bar as his own. He pulled out the adjacent high-backed wooden chair for me.

I wasn't a fan of bar stools. I usually struggled to climb onto them. I could never drag them close enough to the counter, so I ended up leaning over farther than my back liked. Invariably, my feet dangled as if they were a couple of lost puppies in search of a home.

But this time, with an extra lift and a forceful shove of the chair from Hans, I found myself comfortably seated within easy reach of the granite counter. I was tempted to order the poutine with cheese curds and minced bison smothered in gravy but could feel Eric's disapproval from his jail cell, so I ordered the seafood chowder and a small Caesar salad.

Hans swirled the olive around in his glass and nodded in the direction of the bartender. "Jill makes the best martinis in the north. I miss them when I'm in the bush, so I make up for it when I'm back in Yellowknife. Are you certain you won't have one?"

I could almost taste its clean smoothness sliding down my throat, but I vigorously shook my head and tried not to look at him enjoying his first sip. "Do you spend much time in the bush prospecting?"

"As much time as I can when the ground isn't buried in snow."

"What minerals are you looking for?" The soup, with large chunks of Arctic char, scallops, and shrimp, was proving to be very tasty.

"Whatever my client wants, but lately it's been diamonds."

"Diamonds. Sounds exciting. I gather there are several diamond mines in the Territories?"

"Four, and they produce some of the highest quality diamonds in the world. They also have the added benefit of being ethical diamonds."

"They follow the rules?"

"In a way. These mines must abide by Canadian labour regulations, resulting in a much safer working environment. This isn't the case in other countries, where the death rate for diamond workers can be high. The buyer is also assured that the diamonds weren't used to purchase arms. Many of the world's diamond mines are found in unstable regions and used by rebel armies. I'm sure you've heard the term 'blood diamonds.' A lot of innocent people are killed because of those diamonds."

He drained his martini and slid the glass toward the bartender for a refill.

"How can you tell the difference? Diamonds all look the same to me."

"Easy. Every gem-quality Canadian diamond is inscribed by laser with a unique identifier, plus they have an accompanying certificate, so there is no confusing them with blood diamonds. Make sure the next diamond your husband buys you is a Canadian one."

"I'm afraid we're not into diamonds."

I showed him my gold wedding band engraved with a delicate line of flying Chee Chee–like geese. Eric had wanted to buy me the standard diamond ring, but I persuaded him not to. I had a jewel box filled with diamond brooches, earrings, and rings that had once belonged to my great-aunt and my mother, none of which I wore. Sparkling gems weren't my thing.

"I have this image of you tramping through the woods, geologist's pick in hand, eyes glued to the ground in search of elusive minerals. But I gather from your business card that most of your exploration is done from the air."

"I do it both ways. Using the plane is the most efficient way, but I love being in the bush, so I spend much time on the ground checking out possible deposits that I identified from the air."

"Have you found any diamond deposits, or gold for that matter?"

He slowly sipped his second martini, but instead of answering my question, he asked, "How long do you expect to stay in Yellowknife?"

He probably didn't want to admit he'd failed.

"Until Teht'aa can manage on her own," I said. "And my husband is free. How long have you known Teht'aa?"

"Since she arrived. The second I saw her beautiful face on TV, I knew she was the woman for me."

It didn't sound like he was prepared to accept her rejection. So was he the sort of man who would use physical force to try to bend a woman to his will? I sensed he was.

"When was the last time you saw Teht'aa?"

"Before I went into the bush. We came here. She likes Jill's martinis too." A surprisingly warm smile spread across his face.

"Did you come here the night of her attack?"

The smile vanished, along with the warmth. "Like I told you and the police this morning, I was in the bush. And I have my flight plan to prove it."

Damn. "Maybe you know why she would go to the alley behind the Gold Range Motel? It doesn't seem her sort of place."

"Lucy, that no-good whore. She hangs out there." His thin lips sneered with icy Teutonic disdain. "I've told Teht'aa on numerous occasions to stay away from the woman, but she refuses to obey me. Insists the woman isn't responsible for her actions." He tossed back the second martini and nodded for another.

"Do you know where I might find Lucy? I'd like to talk to her."

"I doubt you'll get a sane word from her. She's drunk most of the time."

I was beginning to wonder about his own sobriety.

"Do you have access to Teht'aa's apartment?" he asked.

"I'm staying there."

"Good. I left something there and would like to retrieve it."

There was no way I wanted to be alone with this man in the apartment. "Tell me what it is and I'll get it for you."

"Better I do it. You don't know where to look."

"Just tell me where it is."

"It will only take me a second to retrieve it."

"How do I know it isn't something that belongs to Teht'aa?"

The baby blues that had smiled so warmly now flared with anger. "How dare you? It is women like you that cause such problems."

Deciding it was time to exit, I pulled my wallet out of my purse to pay for my meal. Not wanting to wait for the bill, I calculated the amount, placed it on the counter, and jumped down from the chair.

"Where did you get that?" Hans shouted. He reached for the embroidery inside my purse and plucked it out.

"Give it back."

He held it away from me. "Tell me where you found it."

"Why do you say found?"

"Because I know it doesn't belong to you." He spread it out on the counter to reveal two purple flowers, the partial one and the tiny red bird. "Where are the rest?"

I stuck my purse under my arm to ensure he couldn't see the other piece. "You tell me. You seem to know more about it than I do. Now give it back."

"Not until you tell me who gave it to you."

"No one did. I found it."

"Where?"

"It's none of your business."

I watched him clench his jaw and for a terrifying second thought he was going to hit me. Instead he scrunched the embroidery into a ball and jammed it into his coat pocket.

"Hey, that's mine." I reached for his pocket, but he swatted my hand aside and strode out of the bar.

I raced after him. Before I was halfway across the lobby, the front glass doors were closing on his Gucci heels. I sprinted across the driveway after him, took the stairs two at a time to the upper-level parking area, and finally caught up to him as he was climbing into his truck. I grabbed his coat. He karate-chopped my arm and pushed me so hard, I fell onto the ground.

I froze.

"Get out of the way or I'll run over you," he shouted.

The truck engine roared into life.

But I didn't hear any of this as I struggled to contain my rising panic. It was only when I sensed the truck was about to move that I roused myself enough to scramble out of the way.

"Okay, you can have it." I rubbed my sore arm, the same arm my ex had broken a lifetime ago. "Just tell me why it's so damn important."

"*Gut*, you don't know." He powered up his window and put his foot on the gas.

I watched helplessly as his black pickup swerved past the hotel entrance, narrowly missing a taxi, and veered out onto the main road.

THIRTY

I sat in the car, hanging on to the steering wheel while I struggled to calm down. I was annoyed at myself. Once again I'd let a man run roughshod over me without so much as a whimper. The minute Hans hit me, the old panic had set in. The nightmare images I'd fought to bury gyrated around my head. I breathed slowly in and out the way the therapist had taught me years ago when my brother died. Gradually, my nerves began to relax and the trembling slowed down.

I was confused. There seemed to be no reason for Hans to steal the embroidery. It might be old and possibly rare, but surey any value it once had had disappeared when it was ripped into pieces.

At least I still had Teht'aa's.

If nothing else, I'd learned something from this encounter. Hans was a man who wouldn't hesitate to hurt a woman. I didn't care if he had an alibi. He would stay on my list of suspects. I'd even put him at the top.

I needed to do what I could to get Lucy and her friends to recall the night of the assault. I debated seeking them out but decided that at this hour of the evening they would be well into the booze, and if not yet passed out, close to it. I'd wait until morning, when the chances of finding one of them sober were higher.

Though I didn't fancy being alone in the apartment, particularly if there were spare keys wandering around the town, I didn't want to approach Uncle Joe about staying at his son's house. I wasn't in the mood for their chattiness. I could stay in a hotel, like Sergeant Ryan had suggested, but I wasn't in the mood either for a cold, impersonal room. I was finding comfort in being surrounded by Teht'aa's things. Besides, I should wash Eric's clothes. I would just make sure the door was securely locked and put something against it to prevent entry.

Unlike the curving streets around the hospital, I found the downtown grid easy to navigate. From the hotel it was a simple matter of retracing my steps one block to the main drag, turning left, and following the longest and straightest road in Yellowknife down the big hill to Teht'aa's apartment.

Before turning, I stopped to pick up groceries for breakfast at a large and well-stocked supermarket. I noticed Lucy's pale-yellow jacket amongst a group of people hanging out in the parking lot, but decided not to approach her. I would stick to my plan of tracking her down in the morning.

As I descended the hill, I was so focused on admiring the orange glow effect the setting sun was having on the distant shore that I almost ran over a fox. Only at the last moment did I see his dark body trotting across the road. By the time I came to a full stop, he'd scampered into a stand of trees without giving me a backward glance.

Yellowknife may have been a booming town of almost twenty thousand souls, but it was still only a fox's trot away from wilderness.

The sight of the apartment's dark and vacant-looking windows had me reconsidering my decision. After all, Malcolm's house was only a five-minute drive away. But I needed to stop being such a wimp and face my fears head-on. Besides, I felt the chances of the thief returning were almost nil. He'd already stolen what he wanted.

With grocery bags in hand, I clambered up the three flights of stairs and stopped to catch my breath on the landing before unlocking the door. I supposed what was helping me grapple with my fears was the continuing daylight. Close to ten o'clock, and night's blackness seemed no closer than it did an hour ago. I was wondering if it would descend at all.

I opened the door and flicked on the hall light. "Gloria, you here?" I called out and wasn't surprised when she didn't answer. Nighttime was her time, and she was no doubt out prowling the streets.

But she had been here. The mess was gone. The drawer had been restored to the desk, the magazines neatly stacked on the coffee table, and the clothes removed from the sofa. I half expected to see Teht'aa's laptop lying on the desk, but it wasn't. She had even cleaned up Teht'aa's room and made the bed. *Thank you, Gloria.*

I was dead tired, only wanting to bury myself in sleep. But felt I should wash Eric's clothes first and mine too. It was such a struggle to keep awake through the wash cycle that by the time I threw the wet clothes into the dryer, I decided sleep took greater priority than waiting to fold the dried clothes. Before slinking off to bed, I rechecked the front door to ensure it was firmly locked and placed a kitchen chair in its way. I didn't remember my head hitting the pillow.

I struggled to escape as the sound of his approaching foot-steps bounced off the hall walls. I strained and pushed against the rope binding my wrists, but it remained as tight as when he first tied me to the chair. The footsteps stopped in the doorway. My heart thudded. His leer-ing smile loomed out of the darkness. His ice-blue eyes gleamed with lust. Frantic, I tried to push the chair away from him and toppled it over, landing like a trussed chicken on my back. He hovered over me, licking his lips, grabbed the front of my shirt, and ripped.

I screamed and screamed.

And realized there was an echo. I wasn't the only one screaming.

"She's dead," someone shouted.

I tried to move and couldn't. My arms, my legs were trapped.

A light suddenly blinded me. I squeezed my eyes shut.

"What in the fuck's wrong with you?"

I opened my eyes. For a few more seconds confusion reigned, until reason took over and I knew I was safe.

"You okay?" Gloria's worried face leaned over me, her eyes red from crying.

"Yes. It was just a nightmare." *Shit.* I thought I had finally buried it, but it was back.

"Yah, I get them too. What's with the chair blocking the door?"

"It was supposed to be added security. I guess it didn't work."

"Almost. I really had to push hard. I think I broke it." She undid the top of a plastic water bottle and held it out to me. "Do you want a swig?"

I almost gagged on the fumes. "No thanks, but I could do with a cup of tea."

I tried to get up but found myself wrapped in blankets. Gloria helped loosen them for me.

"Did you say someone was dead?" I pulled my nightie down and slipped on a sweater in an effort to make myself more presentable.

"Yah, my sister just died." Her eyes brimmed with tears.

"I am so sorry." She stood there so forlornly that without thinking I wrapped my arms around her and hugged her. Her body felt so frail and small. "Let's have a soothing cup of tea. It'll make you feel better."

She glanced at the bottle in her hand, then placed it on the dresser. "Yah, *Mamàcho* always says tea's the best pick-me-upper in the world. Better than booze."

As I walked to the kitchen, I was surprised to see the dull grey light of dawn seeping through the living room window. A streak of orange above the distant shore confirmed that night was almost over. I hadn't thought I'd slept that long. And I hadn't. Less than four hours. The clock on the stove was saying it was only three thirty. Back home it would still be pitch black. These short nights could take some getting used to.

After plugging in the kettle and adding a couple of teabags to the teapot, I retreated to the sofa, where Gloria had already curled up with a fuzzy blanket she'd brought from her room and her pink jacket draped around her shoulders.

"Please, tell me what happened to your sister?"

"Someone killed her."

"How awful for you. Do the police know who did it?"

"Probably some fuckhead john. I told her she shouldn't pick up guys on the street. It's not safe. Look what happened to Tee. But she wouldn't listen."

"What a minute, are you saying Teht'aa was attacked because she was picking up a guy on the street?"

"No, but it coulda happened."

"But surely Teht'aa wasn't selling herself. She had a good job."

Gloria shrugged. "A girl can always do with a little extra cash. But I don't know if she was. Just is, I found her a few times in bed with guys who didn't hang around all night, like guys do when you love 'em and shit like that." She tucked a wayward tendril of black hair behind her ear.

"Do you know who they were?"

"Nope, never saw any of them. Just heard them leaving."

"How many are you talking about?"

"Not many, maybe five or six. But could be more. I don't stay here every night."

I thought back to Sergeant Ryan's line of questioning. Surely Teht'aa wouldn't go that far. With her tendency to favour jerks, I knew she wasn't fussy with whom she shared her bed. But she would never look for payment. She had too much self-respect.

The kettle began to whistle. I returned to the kitchen and poured boiling water into the teapot, then placed a double-folded dishtowel over it to keep it warm and set the timer.

"Sure a bitch Lucy being dead and all," Gloria muttered when I returned to my seat. She must've noticed me shivering, for she offered me part of her blanket.

"Did you say Lucy?"

"Yah, my sister ... my dead sister."

"Does she ... ah ... live on the street?"

"Yah, that's what got her killed. I kept telling her she had to stop drinking and get off the streets, but she wouldn't listen. Just 'cause she's older, she thinks she knows it all." She paused. "I guess I should be saying 'was,' eh?" More tears trickled down her cheeks.

"I'm so sorry. It's going to be hard for you." I put my arm around her shoulder and hugged her.

Apart from the two women being slight, I'd noticed nothing about Lucy to suggest she was related to Gloria. I studied Gloria's face, looking for similar features, but Lucy's had been so ravaged by her hard life that any family resemblance had been wiped out.

"Yah, I suppose, but I didn't have much to do with Lucy. I got more to do with Tee." She pulled a cigarette from a crumpled package. "Don't tell Tee, 'kay?"

"I won't, but air the place out. I'm no fan of cigarette smoke either."

"Thanks." She turned away to light the cigarette.

"I heard that Teht'aa looked out for your sister."

"Yah, Tee's good that way. Takes care of family. Lucy had a tough life living on the streets."

"I saw her outside the grocery store last night. Do you know when it happened?"

"Uncle Joe said they found her a couple of hours ago behind the Gold Range Motel."

"The same place Teht'aa was attacked."

"I guess."

"Do you know how she died?"

"Uncle Joe said the cops think she was strangled."

"How awful. Did Uncle Joe have anything else to say?"

"I'm supposed to go identify her. He said he'd pick me up around noon and take me there … to the hospital. I think that's where they keep bodies."

"It's going to be hard for you. Would you like me to come too?"

"Would you really do that for me?

"Of course."

"But you're wh—" She paused and bit her lower lip. "But you don't even know me."

"No, but I'm also family."

"Yah, right." She smiled, a soft wistful smile. "But I'm okay. Uncle Joe'll be with me. You need to be with Tee."

The timer dinged.

THIRTY-ONE

When I returned to the living room with the two mugs of steaming tea, Gloria was staring silently out the window at the orange streaks spreading across the sky. A curl of smoke rose from the chimney of a houseboat partially hidden in the shadow of the island.

"Nice, eh?" she said, creating her own smoke. "I like sunrises. Reminds me of when I was little, when we stayed at the summer camp. Uncle Joe would wake me early and take me to a special rock to watch the sun come up. He said it was quiet time, time to talk to *Nòhtsi*." She circled her hands around the hot mug and took a tentative sip. "That's what we call God. Some people call him the Creator too."

"I like dawn too, but I'm rarely up so early." I punctuated this with a yawn. "By the way, thanks for cleaning up the apartment."

She shrugged. "No big deal."

"Do you have any idea who might've broken in?"

"Nope."

"Do you think it could've been the guy who attacked Teht'aa?"

"What's Tee say?"

"She can't remember. Could any of the guys who slept with her have been her attacker?"

"Like I said, I never seen any of them. But I don't know why you're asking. Frank did it. And now he's dead."

"What about Hans?"

"What about him?"

"Could he have attacked your cousin?"

"Nope."

I rubbed my arm where he struck it last night. "He strikes me as the kind of man who abuses women."

"No way. He's a gentleman. Treats a woman good. Besides, Frank did it."

"How do you know? You weren't so certain when we talked about it earlier."

"People say he done it."

She turned her attention to her tea and to the sun flooding into the room. It outlined a profile that reminded me of her cousin, including the slight bump on the upper bridge of her nose, a bump Teht'aa used to rub to try to smooth it out. It was a profile whose firm chin spoke of an underlying strength, like Teht'aa's.

"Gloria, do you know anything about a piece of embroidery with purple flowers?"

She turned her head so abruptly that she almost dropped her mug. But she hesitated a moment too long before saying, "Don't know what you're talking about." She resumed drinking her tea.

Yeah, right. I went to the bedroom and retrieved the piece Josh had given me.

I spread the delicate work out on the coffee table. A sudden ray of sunlight brought the three-dimensional flowers into sharp relief, revealing every single tuft of purple-dyed caribou hair. Reflections from the flowers' sparkling, beaded centres danced on the ceiling. For the first time I noticed that each petal was edged with a delicate line of purple beads, which also sparkled in the sun. The green stems and leaves were made from another material that reminded me of the porcupine quills the Algonquin used. It was an exquisite piece of embroidery that seemed to have taken on a life of its own.

She sucked in her breath. Her hand hovered over the shimmering flowers as if she was afraid to touch them.

"It's the same, but isn't," she whispered. Her fingertips followed the raised outline of each petal. "Lucy's piece had only one flower and a couple petals like these."

For a moment I thought she'd forgotten about me, so absorbed had she become in the handiwork, until she raised her head and asked, "Where did you get this?"

"You said Lucy's piece. Are you saying your sister had one like this?"

"Yah, she showed it to me a long time ago, when she still lived at Digadeh. But hers had a tiny blue bird, not a yellow one like this one."

"What do you know about it?"

"Nothing," she said a little too quickly for my liking.

"I think you do. Look, it might have something to do with Teht'aa's assault. It was found close to where she was attacked."

She jerked her head up, her eyes wide with alarm. "No, no. It can't be."

"Please, tell me what you know. It might help find the man who attacked her."

She sucked deeply on her cigarette and blew out a stream of smoke. "Does this belong to Teht'aa?"

"I believe it does. See these spots. It could be her blood."

"Fuck." Followed by another stream of smoke. "I don't know much. Just know it has something to do with an island where a boy died a long time ago. It's sort of a memorial thing my *Mamàcho mamàcho* made. Lucy called it *dzièwà.*"

Dzièwà. That word again. Father Harris said it meant blueberry. "Does *Mamàcho mamàcho* mean great-great-grandmother?"

"Yah, I guess." She picked up the supple hide and rubbed it gently over her cheek. "It's so soft." She placed it back on the table, spreading it out once again in the sun. "Lucy said *Mamàcho mamàcho* made it a long time ago, when they used to follow *ekwò.* That's caribou in Tlicho."

"Do you know how many pieces there are? I've seen another one with a red bird, so there are at least three."

"Lucy never said. I didn't know Teht'aa had one until you told me."

"Do you know who gave Lucy her piece?"

"*Mamàcho.* And if she finds out I know about it, she'll kill me. It's supposed to be a secret. That's what Lucy said."

"Your *Mamàcho* is Uncle Joe's sister, Florence, right?"

"Yup. Teht'aa's *Mamàcho* too. And Frank's."

"Do you know if Lucy still had hers?"

"I don't know. The only time I seen it was that time she showed it to me." She brushed her fingers over the soft petals again. "It'd be cool to see the whole design."

"I imagine the original was very beautiful. Your great-great-grandmother was a highly skilled artist. What a pity it was destroyed. You said that it was a memorial for a young boy."

"Yah, that's what Lucy said. She said *Mamàcho* told her a story about it. We Tlicho are always telling stories. *Mamàcho* is kind of like the storyteller in our family. She's always telling them whenever we're sitting around a fire. She wants us to remember where we come from."

"Did your sister tell you the story?"

"Sort of, but it was a long time ago and it was in Tlicho, so I don't remember much." She rose from the sofa with her empty mug in hand. "You want more tea?"

"Sure, if there's enough."

After placing the two refilled mugs on the coffee table beside the embroidery, she resumed her spot beside me on the sofa and tucked her legs under before covering herself with the blanket. The sun had risen higher and was bathing us both in its yellow warmth. But it wasn't enough to take the chill out of the early morning air. I pulled the blanket up higher.

She lit a cigarette and took a thoughtful drag before continuing, "The story was about some kind of a sacred island way far away in *hozìi*,"

"*Hozìi*? What's that?"

"What you call the Barrens. It's way up north. No trees grow there, just bare rock and lots of lakes and rivers. Anyway, the story tells about the time *Mamàcho mamàcho* found the island. One summer *ekwò* didn't come to the summer hunting grounds and the family was starving. My great-great-grandfather took them to a special place his father had told him about, where *ekwò* sometimes go in bad years.

"They followed a very old ancestor trail. After many, many days they found *ekwò*. While the men were hunting, the women went to an island in the middle of a big lake to pick blueberries. It was also covered with pretty purple flowers she'd never seen before. They sparkled in the sun. But *Nòhtsi* was angry. A big storm came up and splashed big waves over the island. Her little boy drowned. *Mamàcho mamàcho* made this embroidery to remember him."

"What a lovely but sad story. However, I don't understand why it should be kept a secret."

"They don't want anyone going there. Lucy called it Dzìewàdi, Blueberry Island. It's sacred, see. Lucy told me *Nòhtsi* get mad if I tell anybody. But I don't believe in any of that shit, not anymore. You know this flower isn't like most Dene flower designs."

"How so?"

"These have seven petals. Mostly they have five, sometimes six petals."

"Maybe your great-great-grandmother was being creative."

"Frank thought she was trying to tell us something."

"With seven petals?"

"I dunno." She surveyed the embroidery again. "Maybe the boy was seven when he died."

"Sounds plausible." I rubbed my finger over the little yellow bird and thought of the red one. "Do you know if Frank's piece had a red bird?"

Another cloud of smoke. "Dunno. Never saw it."

I would have to ask Eric if he got it from Frank. If he did, it would mean another connection to the murder victim. Whether this was good or bad, I had no idea, but doubtless the police would find a way to use it against him.

"Do you have any idea why Hans would be interested in the purple flowers?"

She jerked her head around. "Hans? Whattya mean?

"The red bird piece I mentioned. Hans stole it from me."

"What were you doing with it?"

"I found it." I decided to keep the location to myself.

"Fuck." She crushed her cigarette into the saucer she'd been using as an ashtray.

"Why would he take it?" I asked again.

She stood up, causing the blanket to slide to the floor.

"You know something. Tell me."

"Can't." She kicked the blanket aside. "Look, I'm really sorry, eh?"

Her eyes pleaded for understanding before abruptly turning away. She thudded down the hall to her room, slamming the door behind her.

A minute later I heard her muffled voice and wondered who she had called.

THIRTY-TWO

After Gloria finished her phone call, I half expected her to come flying out of her room and race off to whomever she'd called, doubtless a man. Instead the silence grew until it was interrupted by gentle snoring.

I opened a window to dilute the smoky air with fresh, returned to the sofa, and wrapped myself completely in the blanket. The sun continued its rise into day, though as far as I was concerned at five in the morning, day was a good couple of hours away. I couldn't be bothered to make a fresh pot of tea, so I nursed the dregs of cold tea in my mug.

I was too wired to sleep. Gloria had left me with more questions than answers. The purple-flowered embroidery was important. Her strange reaction told me that much. But I was left confused over its role in this whole sorry mess. I was hoping Eric would have some answers, but I wouldn't be able ask him until this afternoon. Teht'aa should be able to fill in more gaps, but with her memory loss, she might not be able to. Besides, I couldn't visit her for another five hours.

At the moment Uncle Joe was the best option. Since the embroidery involved his sister's family, he might know something about it. And more importantly, he was likely awake for his early-morning fishing trip. But I was too late and found myself leaving a voicemail instead.

I was in wait mode with nothing to do. Too restless to eke out the minutes inside, I bundled up and headed out to commune with the new day.

The street was quiet as only a street can be at this early hour. I walked past houses still shuttered with sleep. Curls of smoke rising from chimneys spoke of toasty warmth inside. A curtain flicked open in the upper window of a townhouse. A man scratching his hairy chest peered out at the waking day, then turned away without noticing me below. A car drove up beside me, startling me for a moment. The driver waved a good morning as he continued past.

I came to the bridge Uncle Joe and I had driven over on our way to his son's house. I was partway across it when I decided I didn't want to walk that far. I paused for a moment to watch the water twitch underneath the bridge before turning back. The narrow channel connected the bay on Tcht'aa's side of the peninsula to another smaller bay. I watched a plane taxi through the water to the float plane base at the end of the channel.

Rather than taking the other shore road back to the apartment, I took the road that carved its way through the middle of the peninsula and found myself climbing up to the best view in Yellowknife, the Bush Pilot's Monument, perched atop a massive rock outcrop. According to a bronze sign, the monument paid homage to the bush pilots who opened up the north in the 1920s and 30s. Staring down at the many rooftops interspersed amongst the trees and rock, it was hard to imagine that less than eighty years ago, this was all barren wilderness. Mind you, the wilderness was still within striking distance and stretched thousands of kilometres north through the vast boreal forest and the treeless tundra to the Arctic Ocean, with only a handful of communities in between.

More chimneys were announcing that their households were getting on with the day. The traffic on the only road to downtown had increased to a handful, with one contrarian, a metallic blue truck, going against the flow. Probably a shift worker returning home after a long night at work.

I made my way back down the flight of stairs and eventually to Teht'aa's street. I noticed the same blue truck parked in front before I began my second lofty stair climb of the morning, both of them before breakfast. If nothing else, I would go home well exercised. To prove the good effect this stair-climbing was having, I was barely puffing by the time I reached Teht'aa's third-floor landing. I was feeling rather pleased with myself until my hand dug around my pocket for the key and came up empty. I'd forgotten to bring it.

I had a moment's hesitation over ruining Gloria's sleep before I placed my finger on the button and pushed it several times. The shrill ring echoed through the apartment. I pressed it again.

Without warning, the door sprang open and someone slammed me back across the landing into the railing. My fingers clawed at the rough wood as I struggled to keep from falling backward. For a few anxious seconds I hovered precariously over the jagged granite three stories below before I managed to push myself upright and away from the railing.

I leapt toward the stairs in time to see a man heading down onto the next landing. I clambered down after him only to see him running along the street below. A minute later the blue truck swerved onto the road and vanished in the direction of downtown.

Fearful for Gloria's safety, I shoved the rising panic aside and raced back up to the apartment. Heat wafted out the open door, but nothing else stirred.

"Gloria!" I shouted. "Are you okay?"

Silence.

I stepped gingerly into the vestibule, closed the door, and waited.

I caught the faintest of sounds coming from the back of the apartment.

"Gloria, you okay?"

"Fuck."

She was alive. Thank god.

I found her half-sitting on the hall floor, rubbing her head.

"Fuck, what happened?" she groaned. "My head hurts like shit."

"Someone broke into the apartment. Did you see them?"

"Fuck, no. I was out cold when something woke me up. I opened my door and wham, something hit me. Next I know, I'm lying on the floor. Fuck, what's going on?" She stared at the blood covering her fingers.

"Here, let me have a look."

The scalp wound wasn't extensive, but would produce a good-sized egg. I placed a wet face cloth on it to help staunch the bleeding.

I then noticed the bear carving lying on the floor.

THIRTY-THREE

The ambulance arrived within minutes of my call, along with the police, who were the problem as far as Gloria was concerned. Because of the outstanding arrest warrant, she had tried to pull the phone from my hand to stop me from making the call. When that hadn't worked, she'd attempted to flee, but the blow to her head had left her dizzy and barely able to stand.

After a preliminary examination by the paramedics and brief questioning by the police, she was whisked off to the hospital along with a police guard. Though I'd wanted to go with her, Sergeant Ryan wouldn't let me. Instead the cop questioned me for the next hour, while two others went through the apartment yet again with their dirty dusting powder and other forensic tricks.

Like the previous break-in, they found no evidence of forced entry, so the possibility of a stray key became more certain. But they would need to follow-up with Teht'aa to determine other possible key holders. Though given the numerous men that seemed to wander in and out of her life, there could be a number of stray keys.

When it came to describing the intruder, I was of little help. I'd been so caught up in saving myself that I'd paid little attention to the individual, other than to note it was likely a male. My impression was of height and a certain heftiness judging by the heavy sound of the footsteps running down the stairs, which spoke more of a man than a woman. I was able to remember that he wore dark clothing but couldn't recall the exact colour. I had no impression of hair or colour, so he must've been wearing a hat.

I'd been hopeful that the truck would provide the best clue for identifying the man. But when I tried to recall the make, I couldn't, other than to say that it had too many dents and too much rust to be a recent model and was more substantial than my own truck. Although the metallic blue colour would help reduce the number of possibilities, Sergeant Ryan thought it would only reduce it to a few hundred. Given their shortage in manpower, it would take them several days to check them out.

"Looks like the perp used the handiest heavy object," the sergeant said as she examined the dark-green stone sculpture. "I see several good fingerprints where the perp placed his hand to strike the victim. Let's hope he's in RAFIAS." She dropped it into a large Ziploc bag.

"How soon will you know?"

"Likely in a few days, but forensics is a bit overwhelmed at the moment, so it could take longer." She passed the bag to another cop before continuing. "I would like you to go through the apartment and identify anything that is missing."

"I'll see what I can do, but like I told you last time, I'm not familiar with Teht'aa's things."

But it proved easy. Nothing had been disturbed in Teht'aa's bedroom, and the kitchen was equally untouched. The living room looked exactly the way I'd left it before going on my walk, right down to the blanket bunched up on the sofa, Gloria's pink, puffy jacket and matching pink scarf draped over the chair, and my empty mug on the coffee table — except, of course for the blank space where Teht'aa's bear had once stood. I also realized there was another glaring emptiness.

"It's gone," I said. "The embroidery is gone. He took it."

"I sense you know who," the sergeant said.

"Hans Walther."

I filled her in on as much as I was prepared to divulge about the two pieces of caribou hide with the embroidered purple flowers. I concentrated more on the theft of the first piece than their provenance. Reluctant to mention how'd they come into my possession until I learned more about them, I merely told her that they belonged to Teht'aa's family. I didn't hesitate, however, to tell her in great detail about Hans's theft of the other piece.

"So you see he has to be the person who took this one too." I paused. "And tried to kill Gloria."

She nodded as she wrote furiously into her notebook. "We'll bring him in for questioning. By the way, we've cleared him of your stepdaughter's assault. He had an alibi."

"So he told me. But I understand Gloria's sister, Lucy, was murdered last night. With the attack on Gloria this morning, don't you think there is too much coincidence at play? You might want to look at him for the murder."

"It's not my case, but I understand the evidence points to an altercation with one of her homeless buddies. It's not the first time someone has been killed over a bottle of booze." She resumed writing in her notebook.

"Do you know if they found a piece of purple embroidery in her belongings?"

"You mean like the two pieces you're talking about?"

"Yes. When I was in the alley yesterday, she talked about the purple flowers. And since she is a member of the same family, it's possible she also has a piece. I believe there are at least three of them, and there could be more."

"I'll mention it to my colleague handling the case, but it seems a pretty flimsy motive for murder."

"No flimsier than booze. Don't forget Gloria was almost killed because of this embroidery."

"Yeah, I suppose."

She placed her pen into her shirt pocket and snapped her notebook shut. "If you can't think of anything else, we'll be on our way. I also recommend you change the locks. I don't think you want any more unwanted visitors."

The door had barely closed on the RCMP when Uncle Joe pushed it open, panting. Without a word, he collapsed onto the sofa and stayed there while he struggled to regain his breath. His face was so scarlet that I feared he was about to have a heart attack. I brought the phone near in case I had to call for another ambulance.

Finally, he gasped, "What going on? So many cops. You okay?"

I told him about the intruder and Gloria's attack.

"You can't stay here. Too dangerous. You stay with us."

The thought of being enveloped in the warmth of his family tempted me sorely and helped to allay the rising panic I'd been trying to ignore. Only now was it sinking in

211

that if I had been sound asleep in Teht'aa's bed, I could've ended up in the hospital with Gloria, or worse.

No, I couldn't stay here, alone. But I didn't want to stay with Uncle Joe either. I liked my privacy. I didn't do well staying with strangers.

"Thanks for the offer, but I'll go to a hotel."

"You need to change lock on the door."

"Yes, that's what the cop said. Can you recommend anyone?"

"Malcolm do it."

Before I could decline, he was calling his son, who said he would change it as soon as the hardware store opened.

The old man's breath was finally settling down to normal, but his face remained red.

"Are you going to be okay, Uncle Joe?"

He waved a dismissive hand. "Just an old man. Not used to so many stairs. But ticker good." He slapped his chest. "Doctor say so. You got coffee? It do the trick." He flashed a yellow-toothed grin.

My coffee-making skills weren't exactly stellar. In the early months of our relationship, Eric had patiently endured my hit-or-miss coffee, until finally he could abide it no longer and offered to take over the coffee-making duties. Over time I had learned a trick or two from watching him. I tried them now.

While I waited for the coffee to finish, I made my breakfast: two pieces of toast with cream cheese lathered onto them and topped with a hefty dollop of strawberry jam. I offered the same to Uncle Joe, but he declined.

I watched nervously as he grasped the full mug with two hands, both shaking. The hot coffee sloshed around the rim of the mug as he brought it to his lips. I was convinced more coffee would end up on him than in him.

"Hot." He blew on it before taking a sip. He smacked his lips. "Good."

Imagine that.

He took another sip before placing the mug on the coffee table. "Do you think this man is same who hurt our poor Teht'aa?" He brushed away the drops splattered over the front of his jacket.

"I do. Hans. But unfortunately he has an alibi for Teht'aa's attack, which the police have already confirmed."

I munched on the toast. Not exactly healthy, but tasty and it would fill me up.

"Maybe he do it. Maybe not. He like a bull moose. He make lots of noise and like to charge, but he no killer."

"But he could've killed Gloria with the carving."

"You tell the RCMP?"

"I did."

"Good." He brought the shaking mug back up to his lips, this time with less spillage.

"Uncle Joe, three women from your sister's family have been attacked within days of each other. Do you have any idea why?"

"Nope."

"Could it have something to do with the purple embroidery?"

He slurped his coffee before shaking his head. "Lots of old Dene handiwork. Some with red flowers, some with yellow ones and some with purple ones." He let his nylon jacket fall open to reveal the front of a hide vest covered in red and yellow flowers. "My mother made this."

"This piece with the purple flowers seems to be specific to your family. Both Gloria and Lucy know about it. Gloria said it was made by their great-great-grandmother many years ago. A piece of it was found where Teht'aa was attacked."

"It women things. I know nothing about women things."

"Eric had another piece. I found it in his hotel room."

"Show it to me."

"I told you, Hans stole it from me yesterday. He took the other one this morning. Do you know why he wants them?"

He continued slurping his coffee. "Is good, but maybe next time you add more coffee."

So much for improving my prowess in coffee-making. "Gloria says your sister Florence knows about it."

"Maybe."

"If she has other pieces, she could be in danger too."

He put his mug down. "Hans gonna hurt my sister?" At last I had his full attention.

"Possibly. You need to warn her. Does she live in Digadeh?"

"She stay at the family camp."

"Is that near Digadeh?"

"A day and a half by boat."

"You should call the RCMP in Digadeh and alert them."

"Hans don't know where camp is."

"What if he finds out?"

"My grandson protect her. He good hunter." He placed his empty mug back on the coffee table. "Now we go. Gloria need us."

THIRTY-FOUR

We drove to the hospital in separate vehicles so I could drive straight to the Correction Centre afterward. But if his wistful glance at me stepping into the BMW were anything to go by, Uncle Joe would've much preferred leaving his daughter-in-law's Ford Focus behind and coming with me. As it was, he set out to prove her car was equally speedy by squealing away from me at the outset. Though I didn't rise to the challenge, I maintained a steady pace behind him with only a slight increase of pressure on the gas pedal. I managed to beat him to a parking spot only because he turned into a row that was completely full.

While the old man shuffled down the hall to emergency, where Gloria had been taken by the paramedics, I grabbed the elevator to ICU and was stopped short by an empty bed. For a heart-stopping moment I thought the worst until the nurse informed me that Teht'aa had improved enough to be transferred to a regular bed.

I found her in a crowded ward, sandwiched between two beds, one empty, the other occupied by a plump middle-aged woman who turned out to be a big fan. Teht'aa was awkwardly autographing the woman's breakfast menu when I entered the room. I say awkwardly, for with her broken right arm she was forced to use her left hand, which could only manage a jagged sprawl of a signature.

"I guess I'm going to have to practise writing with this hand. The doctor says it'll be six weeks before the cast can be removed. Thank God for computers, eh? Speaking of which, have you found it yet?"

"And a good morning to you too. You look wonderful."

She did, despite her face and head still being swathed in bandages, though the one on her face had decreased in size, allowing her smile to blossom. She no longer moved with the lassitude of near death but had the life and energy of renewed health. I leaned over and kissed her on the forehead.

"Not yet," I admitted somewhat sheepishly. But I didn't admit that I'd been too focused on her and her father to put any effort into the search. "Speaking of break-ins, your apartment was broken into again this morning."

I pulled the hard-back chair closer to the bed and brought her up to date. Though she was upset by the attack on Gloria, she was more sanguine about it than I was.

"It's her lifestyle," she said. "I keep trying to convince her to leave it. I found her a part-time job in the video library at the APTN station, but she didn't last more than a couple of months. Too boring, she said."

She pressed her fingers gingerly over the bandage covering her cheek. "God, I feel like a wreck. How bad does it look? No, don't tell me. So far I've managed to avoid the mirror when I've gone to the can."

"The key thing is you are alive and acting like the Teht'aa we love. And apart from memory loss, you seem to have your brain intact."

"If I have to do one more stupid cognitive test, I'll scream."

I squeezed her hand and was surprised by the strength of her answering squeeze.

"You think the break-ins were directed against Gloria and not you?"

"Why me? I wasn't there, and I've got nothing that anyone would want to steal. No, it has to be one of the many johns in Gloria's life."

"Don't forget it was your computer that was taken and nothing of hers."

"Probably a cheap bastard. Didn't want to buy one."

"And your great-grandmother's deerskin dress."

"Oh no. That's missing too? Dad's going to be upset. But who would want it, other than a museum? The museum in Ottawa once offered me five hundred bucks for it, nothing more. Hardly worth the effort to steal it."

"The same could apply to another item that was stolen this morning. A ripped piece of caribou hide with tufts of purple-dyed caribou hair made into flowers."

"What was it doing at my place?"

"Your colleague, Josh, gave it to me. He found it behind the Gold Range Motel where you were attacked. He thought it belonged to you. Does it?"

"What colour was the bird?"

"Yellow."

"Why did he think it was mine?"

"He said he saw it in your purse last time you had a drink together."

Instead of acknowledging that, she turned her focus to the glass of water on her side table. She brought it to her lips and sipped slowly from the straw.

"I found a similar piece in your father's hotel room. It had a red bird. What do you know about it?"

"Nothing."

"I don't believe you. You know about the birds."

She glanced over at her roommate, who dropped her eyes guiltily to the magazine she had been reading. "Can't tell you."

"So maybe you can tell me why your friend Hans is so interested in them. He stole the red bird piece from me last night and the other one this morning."

"How's Dad doing?"

"No, you're not going to change the subject." I was starting to lose my patience. "Tell me what's so damn important about these embroideries."

"Meg, please, just let it be. It's nothing to do with you."

"But it is. I think these embroideries are behind your assault, and that concerns me."

She laughed. "Ridiculous. A sex pervert raped me ..."

There was that word. She said it so easily. I could barely think it, let alone say it.

"And tried to smash my head in so I couldn't identify him. It had nothing to do with a piece of embroidery."

"Good. You remember the attack."

"Not exactly. It's still a big black hole. But that's the only thing that makes sense to me."

"I don't suppose anyone's told you about your cousin Lucy."

"Lucy? What about her? Has she been tossed into jail again?"

"No. Sadly, she's dead. Murdered."

She sighed. "I can't say that I'm surprised. I've been expecting it. She led such a miserable life. I tried helping her, but apart from a few bucks for booze and cigarettes, she wouldn't take anything else from me. When I first came to Yellowknife, I made the mistake of enrolling her in an addiction program, but she never showed. I tried it a couple more times and then gave up. Do the cops know who did it?"

"Not that I know of, but the interesting part is she was killed where you were attacked, behind the Gold Range Motel. Maybe it's the same guy."

"It's possible, but like I told you, I have no idea who the bastard was. And if he raped Lucy, he is one sick bastard. She wasn't exactly pin-up girl of the month. Whoops, sorry, shouldn't have said that."

There. She'd said that word again. "Maybe sex wasn't the motive. She knew about these purple flowers too. Might have even had her own piece. So maybe the embroidery got her killed."

"Fuck."

"Gloria said your great-great-grandmother made it."

"How does she know?"

"She also said that Frank had a piece that he found in his mother's house."

"Look, I'm not feeling so hot. Do you mind going?"

From the way she refused to look me in the eye, I sensed ill health was the least of her concerns. "Do you want me to call the nurse?"

"No, I'll be okay."

"Will you let me stay if I promise not to talk about the embroidery?" I'd leave it for the moment. I was hoping her father would know enough to fill me in.

"Thank you," she whispered. "I appreciate your understanding. It just is … I promised *Mamàcho* that I would never talk about it."

"So it's a family secret?" Perhaps it was, but I felt more was at play, like fear.

"Yes. So please can we talk about something else?"

I patted her hand. "It's all right. I won't—"

I was interrupted by the sound of footsteps stopping at the door. The rumpled figure of Father Harris stood leaning partway into the room.

"Sorry to bother you, Teht'aa, but I see you have a visitor. I'll come back later."

Before she could reply, he backed out and was gone.

"Should I call him back?" I asked.

"No."

"A sad old man. I met him behind the motel last night. He was checking on his lost souls."

"Yeah, his rounds. I call it his guilt trip. I figure he's trying to make up for all the abuse that happened at Saint Anne's."

"Are you saying he was involved?"

"I have no idea. No one ever talks about it. But just teaching at the school and doing nothing about the shit makes him guilty in my books. I can't for the life of me understand why he doesn't go back to England or wherever he's from. No one wants him here."

"He left so many years ago, he probably thinks of Yellowknife as his home."

"Yeah, but I heard he went to a parish in Edmonton after the school closed. So why come back north? But, hey, who gives a shit? I don't. Have you seen Dad yet?"

"I'm seeing him this afternoon. Why don't I take a photo of you so he can see how well you are doing," I said, remembering the phone in my pocket.

At first she pulled up the sheet to hide her face but eventually relented. I managed to snap a good one that lessened the jarring effect of the bandages. I didn't want to overly worry Eric. I even had her smiling, though only after one of my dreadful jokes. But she refused to look at the picture, saying it was something to be viewed after she was fully recovered.

"Look, I need to pee. Do you mind helping me to the can?"

I had barely started before the nurse arrived and took over. At the same time, another bed was being wheeled into the room.

A familiar face peered at us from above the sheet. "Hi, Tee. You're looking good. It looks like I'm joining you. We're gonna be a matched pair." She patted the bandage around her head.

Uncle Joe shuffled in behind her.

THIRTY-FIVE

Fortunately, the thump to Gloria's skull had caused little damage other than a sore head and a good-sized egg, but as a precaution, the doctors wanted to monitor her for the next twenty-four hours before allowing her to leave. The nurse had no sooner settled her into the bed next to Teht'aa than Uncle Joe declared, "We give thanks."

While the nurse sputtered her objections, he had me gathering up two wheelchairs. We loaded our patients into the chairs with the help of the nurse, still protesting, and wheeled them down the hall. We stopped in front of a closed door with a schedule tapped underneath a sign that read "Healing Room/Chapel." Without so much as a knock, Uncle Joe barged in.

There was a reason for the schedule. If the old man had stopped to look, he would've seen that the room was booked, notably to Father Harris. We stopped him in mid-sentence praying over a frail elderly man in a wheelchair with his hand-wringing wife huddled in a chair beside him.

"I beg your pardon. This is a private matter." The priest looked up. "It's you … I'm so glad to see you looking so well, Teht'aa."

"We need the room," Uncle Joe demanded, waving his hands at the priest to move him and his supplicants out.

"Please, give us ten minutes."

I turned Gloria's chair around to wheel her into the hall.

"You stay," the old man ordered, then pointing at the priest, hissed, "You, go."

"Please, Uncle Joe, we can wait outside," I pleaded.

Neither Gloria nor Teht'aa said a word. They merely stared at the priest, Gloria with the same fixed dislike as Uncle Joe. Teht'aa's expression was more of bemusement.

The priest mumbled some hasty words over the sick man and patted him on the arm. Stuffing his battered bible into his jacket pocket, he wheeled the man out of the room, careful to avoid colliding with Gloria's chair parked directly in his way. The man's wife tottered beside him. "Sorry, sorry," she muttered.

"Uncle Joe, that was awful. We weren't being respectful," I said when the door clicked closed behind them.

Ignoring me, he motioned for me to take up the plastic chair he'd pushed beside Teht'aa's wheelchair, while he positioned Gloria's to face us. He dragged another chair to form a quasi-circle, as if you could make a circle with four points.

The old man retrieved a large abalone shell from a bookcase. One shelf held an assortment of shells and small pottery bowls. Another contained several beautifully crafted birch-bark containers. Judging by the aroma wafting from them, they held sweetgrass, cedar, and sage, the herbs traditionally used for smudging. On another shelf, feathers of varying sizes jutted out from several glass jars. Uncle Joe selected a large brown-and-white one that reminded me of the eagle feathers used in Algonquin smudging ceremonies.

A wooden cross with the figure of Christ looked down upon us from the back wall above a narrow wooden table set up as an altar. The other walls sported colourful works of gyrating creatures by indigenous artists.

Uncle Joe lowered himself into the empty chair. "Tlicho way is to feed the fire, but they don't like fires in the middle of the floor, might burn the place down, eh?" He chuckled. "So we smudge like I seen the Cree do. But we use good Dene medicine, rat root."

He extracted the piece of root I'd noticed him rubbing from time to time and placed it in the middle of the pearl-grey interior of the shell, on top of the soot from previous smudgings. He attempted to light it with a match taken from his pocket. After several false tries, a wisp of smoke finally rose from the shrivelled root. He gently blew on it and fanned it with the feather. Soon he had a good smudge going.

He closed his eyes and mumbled in Tlicho. When both Teht'aa and Gloria crossed themselves in Catholic fashion, I assumed he was praying and closed my eyes also. Unsure of what gods were listening, I mumbled my own thanks for Teht'aa's survival and a prayer to wish the both of them a speedy recovery.

"Meg, my legs too tired. Can you take the smudge around the circle? Everyone supposed to wash in the smoke. Make us better people."

My nose twitched at the acrid smoke rising from the burning root. Accustomed to the sweetish scent of the more traditional ingredients, I found it jarring and not soothing the way the smudge was supposed to be. I hoped this wouldn't upset the Creator.

Before taking the shell from Uncle Joe, I washed the smoke over my head and body with my hands. I held the smudge for him to do likewise. Once finished, I walked over to Teht'aa, who without hesitation cleansed herself in the smudge. Gloria's eyes arched with uncertainty, but she mirrored our movements and shrugged with a so-what when she was finished. However, she closed her eyes, moved her lips as if in prayer, and crossed herself.

I returned to Uncle Joe and passed the smudge back to him. He mumbled more Tlicho prayers before saying, "Good, *Nòhtsi* happy. He make you better. We go."

I helped him out of the chair and kept the door open as he wheeled Teht'aa into the hall. I followed behind with Gloria, who exclaimed, "Uncle Joe, you really believe in that old shit?"

I winced at her impertinence, but the old man merely smiled. "They made me a Catholic at school. I said my prayers like a good Catholic boy. But I always left gifts for *Nòhtsi* to show my respect. Still do. I figure the more gods you keep happy, the better it's gonna be, ain't that so, Teht'aa? No one drum dances like you, girl."

She laughed then winced with a groan. Touching the bandage on her face, she said, "I'll be glad when I can finally get this thing off. On the other hand, I'm not sure I want to see what's underneath."

"Don't matter," Uncle Joe replied. "You same Teht'aa inside."

"I guess, but CBC might not want me anymore."

I watched the nurse settle Teht'aa into her bed. "Don't give CBC another thought. Your immediate focus is on getting better."

"And finding the bastard who did this."

"You still have no idea?"

"Like I said, I don't remember a thing."

"And you don't think any of the men you know could've done it."

"No way, none of them ever beat me up this badly."

"Beat you up?"

"Come on, Meg. Don't look so grim. I'm kidding."

I wasn't so sure.

"The police believe someone used a key to break into your place. Do you remember who has one?"

"Precisely the question I wanted to ask," came the words from behind me. I turned to find Sergeant Ryan, looking official in her Mountie uniform, standing at the bottom of Teht'aa's bed. "I'm so glad you are much improved, Miss Bluegoose. I wonder if you mind answering some questions."

Teht'aa self-consciously touched her bandage. "Sorry for looking such a mess. I guess you want to know what I remember of the attack. Well, it's short and simple. Nothing. But go ahead, fire away."

"Why don't you answer Mrs. Odjik's question first?"

"You mean about the keys? Uncle Joe has one."

"That's the one I'm using," I said.

"Okay. Dad's got one. Gloria, I gave you a key, didn't I?"

"I lost it, remember? I use the one you keep on the hook under the top stair."

I felt more than heard the cop groan. "Who knows of its existence?"

"It could be anyone," Teht'aa replied. "Sorry."

"What about Hans?" I asked.

"Yah, I imagine he knows about it. But like I said, it's no big secret. Half of Yellowknife probably knows about it."

Another lead to Hans shot down.

THIRTY-SIX

I left Eric's daughter being wheeled down the hall by the Mountie, away from the eavesdropping ears of her roommates to a consultation room. I hadn't been invited, but that was fine. Teht'aa would tell me what transpired later. Meanwhile, I had Eric to visit.

According to Derrick, normal visiting hours were on the weekend, but he had persuaded the warden, a friend of his, to allow me to see my husband three days early. It was a one-time exception. If the judge refused to release Eric, I would be forced into this weekend schedule. A thought that made me more determined to do what I could to get him out of there.

Though the directions from Derrick were simple, only two turns, I gave myself plenty of time in case I became lost. The first was a right turn onto Kam Lake Road, which I thought would take me far into the bush. But I found myself surrounded by suburban homes when I made the second turn onto the gravel road of the Corrections Centre.

I arrived twenty minutes early, including a stop for a burger. I debated bringing Eric one, knowing he would be fed up with tasteless prison fare, but I was worried it would be confiscated and could jeopardize my visit.

My first visit to a prison, I expected to see a forbidding, windowless stone structure surrounded by utility-pole-high fencing, with razor wire and guard towers strategically placed along the perimeter. Instead I drove up to a perfectly ordinary two-storey building covered in Yellowknife's ubiquitous metal siding, with actual windows, the kind that let lots of light in, and no surrounding fence. The only fence within view was a screen-like mesh expanse that stretched from the building I was about to enter to another wing of the facility. I felt marginally relieved. Eric wasn't locked away in an inhumane dungeon. Nonetheless, it was still a jail.

I remained in the car, becoming more nervous as the minutes ticked by to the appointed hour. I didn't know what to expect. While Eric had sounded his usual confident self on the phone, he hadn't acted it at the courthouse. Would he be embarrassed? The way I was feeling. Would we have to talk through a mesh, or would we do it over a phone, like on TV? Would we be able to touch, or would we be forced to press our hands against the mesh?

I didn't know if he wanted to see me. He hadn't been pleased with my presence at the courthouse. Yet Derrick had arranged this visit. So my husband must want it too.

I watched a man leave through the front door. Though he was casually dressed in jeans and a windbreaker, he carried a briefcase and walked with the confident swagger of a lawyer. Doubtless visiting a client. And speaking of lawyers, I turned at the sound of a tap on the passenger window to find Derrick's inquiring face peering through the glass.

I put down the window. "I didn't know you were coming."

"I'm only here to ensure everything goes smoothly. You shouldn't have any problems, but one never knows. Your husband really wants to see you."

Thank goodness.

"You ready?"

But he didn't need to ask. I was already standing outside the car.

"You'll have to go through security. Make sure you don't have any sharp objects, keys, cigarettes, or anything that looks like it could be drugs, like prescription bottles. Cameras and other electronic products are also not permitted."

"Not even a cellphone?"

"Definitely not. You can't even take in a SIM card."

"But I have photos of Teht'aa."

"Print it out and show it to him on your next visit."

Next visit! "But he'll be released on Friday."

"Sally and I are both hoping Justice Demarco will grant release, but this delay in his decision is highly unusual. So prepare yourself for a no decision."

Any optimism I'd felt vanished.

"I'll leave my purse in the car."

"No, bring it. You'll need to show some ID. You can leave it in one of the lockers at the security desk."

With Derrick holding the door open, I entered the prison feeling as if I were going to a funeral and not the joy I should be feeling on finally being able to be with the only man I had ever loved. The sombre atmosphere of the main foyer didn't help. I dutifully signed myself in at the security desk, locked my purse into a small metal locker, and passed through the metal detector without a murmur. My heart pounded as I walked up the stairs to the visitors' room on the next level with Derrick by my side. Though the stairwell seemed airy and bright, I couldn't ignore the underlying oppression of incarceration.

My spirits rose when the lawyer opened the door to a grand hall with high ceilings and sun pouring through the windows. Rather than finding cold metal chairs lined up before a wall of mesh, I saw work tables and molded plastic chairs scattered about the room. Indigenous artwork brightened up the soft-brown walls. The room reminded me of a hall at a community centre where people came to enjoy themselves.

But I didn't see Eric.

"Take a seat." Derrick motioned to a nearby chair. "They will be bringing your husband in shortly."

I walked toward the windows, to the chairs and tables flooded with sunlight. Eric loved the outdoors. This would be as close as I could get him to it. I sat down and waited.

Within minutes, my husband walked through another door with a prison guard behind him. His usual flowing mane was tied back into a ponytail. At the sight of his rumpled clothes, the same as the ones he had worn yesterday, I realized dumb me had totally forgotten to bring the suitcase with the change of clothes.

He walked a few steps into the room and stopped as if uncertain. I hesitated, too. I tried to read his expression, but his granite-like stillness gave me no clue to his thoughts. Only his soft grey eyes hinted at the emotion he was feeling. He was scared. He was afraid that I would no longer love him. The tears betrayed his love for me.

I started walking toward him. At the same time, he moved toward me. Our paces quickened. Like some love-sick movie, we met in the middle and stood for I don't know how long clasped as one, until someone coughed, and coughed again when we didn't move. I stepped back, wiping the tears from my cheeks and noticed Eric doing the same.

"Come, my love." I held out my hand. "Let's sit in the sun."

THIRTY-SEVEN

With so much to say to each other, but not knowing where to start, Eric and I stuck to the safe topics like the state of our health, my living arrangements — not his — and the safest of all, Teht'aa. Thankfully, I could give him good news, which brought the first real grin to his face, though it wasn't enough to cause his dimples to erupt. I decided not to mention the photo, convincing myself that he would be seeing her in person in two days.

The guard and the lawyer remained in the room but kept a discreet distance, enough to give us a sense of privacy. Derrick studied a document from his briefcase while the guard gave the appearance of being absorbed in his thoughts. However, when I reached into my pocket to pull out a memento for my husband, he marched over, demanding to see it. But he merely raised an eyebrow when he saw it was only dog treats, Shoni's, left forgotten in my pocket.

I knew they would bring life to Eric's eyes, and they did. I pictured the two of them relaxing in front of the fire, the puppy stretched out on the sofa with her head on Eric's lap while he combed his fingers through her soft poodle coat.

For a brief moment I forgot I was in a prison, and from the bemused smile spreading across Eric's face, he had too.

But I had to shatter the illusion. "Sally said you intend to plead guilty to manslaughter. Is that true?"

He stopped playing with the treats and leaned back in his chair. "It's for the best."

"Best for whom? Certainly not for you or me."

"Meg, you're stronger than you think. You can handle our separation, as can I. If I'm good, and I will be, I'll be out in three years."

"Fine, but everything you have worked for will be beyond your reach. The community won't want you, a convicted killer, helping them anymore."

He shrugged.

"Are you saying you killed him?"

He remained stonily silent and shifted his gaze to the view of the prison grounds outside the window.

"Well, I don't believe it, and I'm going to do all I can to prove your innocence."

"Meg, please don't. You have a tendency to get carried away and can stir things up a little too much. I don't want you to this time. People might get hurt."

"People, what people?" The guard jerked his head in our direction. I guessed I'd spoken a little too shrilly, so I lowered my voice. "As far as I can see, the only people who are going to get hurt are you and I if you continue on this ridiculous path."

"Please, Meg, trust me." He reached for my hand, but I moved it away. "When Teht'aa is well enough to leave the hospital, I want you to take her back to Three Deer Point and get on with your lives."

"What's going on, Eric? I know you didn't kill Frank, so why do you want to ruin your life?" I had a sudden thought. It was the only reason that made sense. "You're trying to protect someone."

He firmed his lips in resignation and flicked one of the treats across the table before saying, "Please try to understand. Our time together is precious. I don't want it to end in anger, so let's talk about something else. Tell me how Jid is doing."

"Who is it? Who are you trying to protect?"

"Meg, please don't." His eyes pleaded. "If you keep at it, I'm going to ask the guard to return me to my cell."

I took a deep breath and willed myself to calm down. "I'm sorry. I didn't mean to upset you. But you're the most important person in my life, and I can't bear to see you suffer for something you didn't do."

His only answer was to raise my hands to his lips, kiss them, and whisper, "I love you."

But if he thought I was going to lie down and accept his guilty plea, he had learned nothing about me over the past seven years. No way was I going to stop trying to find the person who killed Frank.

It was my turn to lean back into the chair. "I'm trying to settle in my own mind some of the events surrounding Frank's death. Sally has told me pretty much everything that you told her, but I still have some questions. May I ask them?"

"I suppose."

"It's about the phone call you received identifying Frank as the man who assaulted Teht'aa. I'm curious about who it was."

He sighed. "I don't know."

"You didn't ask?"

"They left a message on my voicemail. And no, I didn't recognize the voice. It sounded like a male, but I'm not entirely certain. There was too much background noise."

"An anonymous call. Sounds suspicious to me. Your phone didn't identify the caller?"

"Not a name, just a phone number, one I didn't recognize. But to tell you the truth, I didn't care. I was so angry at the damage that had been done to Teht'aa, I wasn't thinking straight."

"Did the police trace the call?"

"My cell is missing. I know I took it to Digadeh, but according to Derrick, it wasn't on me when I was found."

"What did the message say?"

"It was short. Frank assaulted Teht'aa and had fled to Digadeh. That's how I knew where to find him. But enough, let's talk about Jid."

He reached across the table for my hands. This time I gripped them firmly.

"He's incorrigible, isn't he?" Eric said, chuckling after I recounted the episode with the fawn. "That's what I love about the boy. It will be wonderful to finally bring him officially into our small family. I don't imagine you've heard anything more on the adoption."

"No. But have you thought about the impact a guilty plea could have on our chances? A convicted murderer might not be the kind of father the authorities have in mind."

His shoulders slumped. "No, I hadn't."

"Not only will you hurt us, but you'll also hurt Jid. You'll shatter him, you know? You're his idol. He believes totally in you. He's had a difficult enough time trying to come to terms with the tragedy of his real father without having to deal with your betrayal."

"Please, don't say anymore," he whispered. "I know you're right. Forgive me."

I moved my chair beside his, wrapped my arm around his shoulders, and held him tightly. "No matter what happens, I will always love you, Eric. But, please, think your decision through very carefully."

"I will."

With renewed hope, I kissed him gently on the cheek and leaned my head against his. And so we sat until I noticed Derrick glancing at his watch. Our time was coming to a close, and there was one more very important topic I needed to discuss.

"Eric, what can you tell me about the purple embroidery I found in your hotel room?"

He eyed me warily. "You'd better ask Teht'aa about it."

"I was hoping you could tell me something about it. I think it could be connected to the attacks on her cousins and possibly her."

"Are you talking about Gloria and her sister?"

"Yes."

He sat up. "Don't tell me they're dead."

"Unfortunately, Lucy is, but not Gloria. Why would you think they were dead?"

"Their lifestyles. Plain and simple. Although Teht'aa had little success in trying to get Lucy to change, she felt she was having marginal success with Gloria. Was Gloria badly hurt?"

"Fortunately not. Despite being attacked with the stone carving I gave Teht'aa, she got away with only a bump on her head."

"I'm sorry to hear about her sister. They've both had a tough life, through no fault of their own." He sighed. "I'm so sick of the damage caused by these fucking residential schools. How many more generations are going to suffer because of the blind arrogance of the fucking whites?"

He spat these last words out with such force, I thought he was going to turn his anger on me. Instead, he unclasped our hands and turned away from me.

Though our love had overcome our differences, they would occasionally raise their ugly head. But never before had I felt such venom against my people. Mind you, it wasn't as if we didn't deserve it.

I held my hands open on the table, ready to receive his, and waited. Though his eyes were staring out the window, I sensed they were directed at nothing other than his own internal turmoil.

The sound of a chair scraping along the floor brought him back to me. "I'm so sorry, Meg." He reached for my hands. "I didn't mean to upset you."

"It's me that should be saying sorry." As if I could simply apologize for all the wrongs my people had done to his.

"Tell me, have you met Uncle Joe yet?"

"We've become the best of buddies. He's even taken me to his favourite noodle place."

"Know it well. You have definitely made it. He doesn't share noodles with just anybody, you know." His face relaxed as he broke into his familiar chuckle, which warmed my heart.

"I also met his son and family."

"Good guy, Malcolm, but I gather the two of them have had their differences lately. Something to do with a mining venture, which Malcolm is for and Uncle Joe against."

"They seemed on good terms last night."

"Maybe they've sorted it out. But when I talked to Uncle Joe a couple of months ago, he was hopping mad at his son. He refused to go into details other than to say Malcolm was set on destroying traditional lands, lands that are particularly sacred to his family. It was in some way tied into this purple flower embroidery, which Uncle Joe referred to as *dzièwà*."

"The same word Teht'aa and Lucy used. I gather it means blueberry. Did he say how it was connected?"

"He didn't know. Apparently, only Bluegoose women know the story behind the embroidery. But he did say that his sister Florence admitted it was a map."

"A map? To what?"

"Dzièwàdi."

"Blueberry Island. Gloria told me that the embroidery was made in memory of a young boy who died on an island covered in blueberries. I imagine it's the same island. But I've no idea how a design of flowers could be used as a map."

"He didn't know either."

"Who gave you the embroidery?" I asked.

"Teht'aa, last week, a few days before the attack. She wanted me to keep it safe. Said she'd be giving me other pieces, but … well, you know…."

"I know of at least three pieces. Do you know if there are others?"

"She never said. I'm not sure how pertinent this is, but Reggie Mantla asked me about the embroidery a couple of months ago."

"He's taken over your job, you know."

"Figures. He did all he could to win the election, including buying votes, but that's a story for another day."

I thought of the video Josh had tried to blackmail me with and decided to leave it for another day too.

"What did Reggie want to know?"

"If Teht'aa had such a piece. He took me completely by surprise. I thought no one but members of her family knew about it."

"What did you tell him?"

"Nothing, of course.

"Time's up," the guard announced, striding toward us, rattling his keys against his leg.

Eric's eyes glazed over. His face hardened. The spark that was my Eric vanished. He pushed himself away from the table.

The spark returned as we kissed with a passion I hadn't felt in a long time. But then it was gone.

I gave him one last hug and whispered in his ear. "Don't give up. I'll find a way."

Hope flashed through his eyes before he turned away and walked toward the door with the prison guard on his heels.

THIRTY-EIGHT

I waited until Derrick and I passed through the final door of the prison before tackling him about the missing phone.

"Do you know if the police have found Eric's cell?"

"They haven't said. Why do you ask?"

"We need to know who called Eric about Frank."

"The police don't need the phone. It's a simple matter of requesting the caller information from the service provider. But they need a warrant." He started walking toward the parking lot. "I've got to run."

"Do you know if they've asked for one?" I stuck close beside him.

"I imagine they have, since they'll want a statement from the caller to solidify their case against Eric. Like I've been telling you, it is an open-and-shut case. Pleading guilty to manslaughter is his only option. Sally thinks so too."

"How do you explain the missing phone?"

"He misplaced it."

"What if it was stolen?"

"I've already told you the police don't need the phone."

"Maybe the guy didn't know that, like me. So he stole the phone to keep the cops from identifying him. He could've grabbed it when Eric was lying unconscious beside the body."

"So?"

"Maybe the guy was smart enough not to use his own phone."

"That's for the police to establish."

"What kind of a defence lawyer are you?" I felt like I was ramming my head against a brick wall. "I thought you were supposed to find the holes in the case against your client and look for the real culprit, like Perry Mason."

"It's Sally's call, and she hasn't suggested hiring a private investigator." He lengthened his stride as if trying to put distance between us, but I kept up.

"Maybe you should. There is another reason why this guy wouldn't want the cops having the phone. Did you know that Eric never talked to him directly? Rather, the message was left on his voicemail. Another way to identify the caller and another good reason for stealing it."

He stopped so suddenly that I almost collided with him. "Where are you going with this?"

"I think Eric was set up. Someone lured him to Digadeh. And that someone is likely the guy who killed Frank and framed Eric for it."

"The evidence doesn't point in this direction."

"Of course it does, starting with the anonymous call. And don't forget Eric's convenient memory loss. Have you discovered its cause yet?"

"He's being taken to the hospital tomorrow for a more thorough examination."

"Are they going to check for drugs, like those date-rape drugs that make the victim forget?"

"Mrs. Odjik, please give us some credit. We've asked that an extensive blood analysis be done. But keep in mind, many of these so called date-rape drugs disappear from the bloodstream within hours. You should also know that he only agreed to do this at Sally's insistence. She threatened to withdraw from the case if he didn't."

"Good for her."

"You have to keep in mind that he is our client, and when a client doesn't want us to establish a defence, there isn't much we can do."

"What if I become your client? After all, it's my money that's paying your bills."

"That may be, but he is nonetheless our client." He paused. "If you really are serious in helping your husband's defence, there is one avenue you could pursue."

"Tell me."

"Hire a private investigator yourself. If he finds anything of value, you might be able to convince your husband that there is enough evidence to mount a defence." He opened the door to his car, which I realized was also a BMW, but a much larger SUV. Business must be good.

"They actually exist in Yellowknife?"

"Not the kind of investigator you need. Sally can refer you to the firm she uses for her Vancouver cases."

"Maybe he'll discover who Eric is trying to protect."

"Protect? What do you mean?"

"I think Eric knows who killed Frank, but for some reason he doesn't want them getting caught. I think it's behind his guilty plea."

He threw his briefcase onto the passenger seat. "Interesting that you bring this up. Sally said the same thing to me. Do you have any idea who it could be?"

"If I did, I wouldn't be standing here talking to you. I'd be giving the name to Sergeant Ryan. Does Sally plan to do anything about it?"

"Nothing without her client's consent. I do have one issue with your theory. If your husband was framed by the person who killed Frank, why would he want to protect them, if Frank is the man who assaulted his daughter?"

"Maybe Frank didn't do it."

"Doesn't matter. It wouldn't help his case. What is important is his mental state at the time of the murder. And as the police can prove, he believed Frank was the perpetrator."

"By the way, who found Eric?"

"I believe a neighbour of Frank's."

"Have you talked to them? Maybe they saw something that could help Eric."

"Like I keep telling you, our hands are tied." He paused while he watched a woman struggle to climb out of her car after wedging it into too narrow a parking space. "I shouldn't be telling you this, but I will. Neither Sally nor I believe he's guilty."

Thank God.

"We have tried to talk him out of this guilty plea, but he won't budge. If you hire an investigator, we'll provide you with the information you need, like the name of this witness. But you need to act quickly. We intend to start discussions with the Crown next week about having the charge reduced to manslaughter. After that it is a matter of scheduling a court appearance to register his plea."

"Okay. I'll call Sally now."

"I'll text you the name of the witness when I get back to my office." He climbed into the driver seat. "Sorry to cut this short, but I'm already late. I wish you luck."

Feeling considerably more upbeat, I was leaving a voice message for Sally for the name of the investigator by the time Derrick's car left the parking lot.

THIRTY-NINE

After trying unsuccessfully to find a room at Eric's hotel, I tried three others without success. Apparently a conference had snapped up all the rooms at the better hotels. When the clerk at the last one suggested the Gold Range Motel would likely have availability, I decided it was time to take Uncle Joe up on his offer.

With an invitation for dinner thrown in, I arrived to find Malcolm outside on the spacious deck barbequing moose steaks in the brightness of a northern evening. Uncle Joe was in the kitchen heating up a vegetable concoction — his words, not mine — that Shelagh had made before she went off to her meeting. The three kids still living at home had likewise dispersed, one to a friend's house and the other two to an indoor soccer game. My conversation skills wouldn't be in demand after all.

Under Uncle Joe's watchful eye, I fried up the bannock and placed it on the table, along with the vegetable concoction and three super-large baked potatoes.

"Never like baked potatoes until your husband show me special secret." The old man smacked his lips. "Sour cream. Lots of it." He placed a bowl brimming with the thick white cream next to the potatoes.

Between mouthfuls of food, the two men yakked about whatever father and son yak about. I wasn't listening. Instead I focused on trying to identify people for whom Eric would sacrifice three years of his life and his reputation. The first person who came to mind was his daughter. But she was in the hospital close to death when Frank was killed a few hundred kilometres away.

Raised voices brought Uncle Joe into my ruminations. I could see Eric making the same sacrifice for the kind-hearted gentleman sitting across from me, who at the moment was riled enough to jab his finger into his son's chest as he endeavoured to make a point. He had brought a lost young man under his wing and steered him along a course that the no-longer-young man was about to ruin. Would Eric do all he could to protect his mentor, who'd been more of a father than his adopted one had ever been? Yes, he would.

But Uncle Joe had been in Yellowknife, staying in this very house, at the time of the killing. Even if he had been in Digadeh and had for some reason killed his nephew, I doubt Uncle Joe would let Eric destroy his own life in order to protect him, an old man at the end of his.

I searched for other possibilities and came up empty except for Jid, and, I liked to think, me, and for obvious reasons we were out of the running.

Maybe I was wrong in thinking Eric wanted to keep the real killer from being caught. But what other reason would he have for pleading guilty to a crime he didn't commit?

I perked up at the word *diamonds* and turned my attention to the argument unfolding across the table from me.

"I no let you do it." The old man jabbed his son again.

"It's time to move out of the ice age, old man, and into this century."

This prompted another angry jab, this time harder. "You no 'old man' me. I do more in my life than you ever will."

"You need to get with the program. This mine will bring more money than our people have ever seen."

"We don't need your money," Uncle Joe spat out. "Our people live many thousand years off the land and will do it for another thousand years."

"Funny, you don't seem to mind staying in this house with the fifty-two-inch TV and your very own La-Z-Boy chair or eating the sour cream and chocolate ice cream Shelagh bought yesterday at a store. Besides, you know that the caribou herds are no longer large enough to sustain our people."

"Yah, because mines kill them."

"There is no hard evidence suggesting that mining is harming the herds. They are going through the downward trend of their cycle. Look, Dad, it's going to happen whether you want it or not."

"You ruin your heritage."

"I'm not ruining anything. I told you my boss said the company will respect the traditional lands. It'll be part of the agreement."

"Yah, right, by digging them up."

"We don't know that. We're only at the exploration stage."

"Yah, but—" Uncle Joe stopped and turned his head in my direction, as if realizing for the first time that I was listening. "You want ice cream?" He pushed a container of chocolate ice cream across the table.

"Thanks, I'll pass." I'd been gorging on forbidden foods since arriving. My jeans waistband was already feeling the pinch. Time to stop. "It sounds like you're talking about a new diamond mine?"

Both men stared blankly back at me. Neither uttered a word.

"Eric mentioned a mining dispute when I saw him today. Is this what you're talking about?"

"How did he know about it?" Malcolm demanded, glaring at his father.

Uncle Joe replied, "I told him."

"But we agreed to keep it to ourselves."

"He family," was the old man's succinct reply. "Meg family too."

"So how much does he know?" Malcolm shot back.

"Nothing much, only that your father is against it and you are obviously for it," I replied. "He also said the purple-flowered embroidery has something to do with it."

"Damn it, Dad, why can't you keep your mouth shut. How many others have you told?"

Uncle Joe raised himself to his full sitting height, a good six inches shorter than his son. "You must respect your *abà*. Not ask so many questions."

"But Dad, or *Abà*, if that's what you want to be called, we agreed not to tell anyone about any of this."

"Malcolm, your father didn't tell me or Eric about the embroideries. In fact, he kept his mouth shut despite my bugging him about them."

"How did you find out about them, then?"

"Teht'aa passed hers on to her father for safekeeping, and my piece was found near where Teht'aa was attacked."

"You actually had two of them. You better give them to me."

"I don't have them any longer. They were stolen."

"Fuck. Do you know who?"

"I suspect Hans Walther."

"Fuck."

"You should also know that Reggie Mantla is aware of them. He asked Eric about them a couple of months ago."

"Double fuck."

The sudden ringing of a phone from another room stopped the drilling. Malcolm raced off to answer it. He returned holding the portable phone out to his father.

"It's Teht'aa. She wants to talk to you."

Malcolm and I both kept our eyes glued to his father while he nodded and muttered the occasional one-syllable word. Finally he said, "Okay," and terminated the call.

Placing the phone on the table, he sighed. "Gloria gone."

FORTY

Left with too many unanswered questions after Uncle Joe recounted his conversation with Teht'aa, I phoned her back.

"Good, it's you," she whispered, afraid of waking her roommates. "I didn't know how to reach you."

"I have your dad's spare cell. Now tell me what happened with Gloria."

"She left after a visit from Father Harris. Said she'd only be gone a couple of hours, but it's over five hours now and I'm worried."

"Do you know what they talked about?"

"They were whispering, so I couldn't hear much. But I caught her sister's name and mention of the purple embroidery and I think my grandmother's name. I tell you, the way he hovered so close to her made my skin crawl. The way Gloria took off afterward left me feeling very uneasy."

"Why didn't the police guard stop her?"

"He didn't stick around. I guess he had more serious criminals to catch than a bail jumper."

"Did she say anything before she left?"

"Only that she'd be back and for me to make up excuses for the nurse. But I've run out of them, and now I have the nurse mad at me too."

"Do you have any idea where she could have gone?"

"I tried my apartment, but no luck, and she wasn't at the Northern Lites Tavern, her usual hangout. I'm really worried, particularly after what happened to her sister."

"Did you call Father Harris?"

"I left a message at his boarding house, but at this time of night he's usually doing his rounds."

"We need to start with him, so could you give me his address and his usual route, if you know it?"

After writing this down, including a short list of friends and their addresses, I asked, "Why does she hate the priest so much?"

"We've never talked about it, but I suspect it has something to do with her mother and the school where he taught. I gotta go. The nurse wants me off the phone."

Uncle Joe, Malcolm, and I agreed to split up our efforts. While Uncle Joe would search for Gloria in the Bimmer, I would go with Malcolm in his truck to look for the priest. On our drive past Teht'aa's apartment, the three of us stopped to confirm Gloria wasn't inside. Though the apartment was empty, it was evident that she had been by. Her purse, last seen on the coffee table, was gone, along with her puffy pink jacket. She'd also changed her clothes. The ones she had been wearing were strewn over her bed.

The neighbour living in the ground-floor apartment remembered noticing her arrival in a mud-splattered black truck. The truck's noisy muffler had roused her from the TV. A short while later she heard it leave. Unfortunately, she hadn't paid attention to the driver, but she was able to identify the truck as a Dodge RAM, because a friend had one just like it, which was the problem. According to Malcolm, black Dodge RAMs weren't exactly scarce in Yellowknife.

Since the driver was likely a friend, I gave Uncle Joe Teht'aa's list to follow up with while Malcolm and I continued our search for Father Harris.

As expected, he wasn't at his boarding house, a ramshackle two-storey affair in need of a paint job. After leaving a note under the door of the room we were told belonged to him by a wizened elderly gent grappling with a few beers too many, we set out along his route, starting with the alley behind the Gold Range Motel less than a block away.

The only people in sight were the two women I'd seen with Lucy. At first they were reticent to talk with us, but Malcolm managed to persuade them with the offer of a bottle of their favourite booze. It proved to be a wasted bribe, for neither had seen the priest that night, nor did they expect to, because it was Wednesday, and he never came on Wednesday.

As we turned to leave, one of the women tugged my sleeve. "You Lucy's friend."

"I know her sister and her cousin. He's a relative too. I'm sorry about Lucy."

She regarded Uncle Joe's son with renewed interest as she tugged on a hunk of black hair leaking out from her scarf. "It happens." She pointed to a spot on the asphalt that looked to have fewer butts. "She was lying there." She pointed to her friend. "Me and Izzy found her."

"I'm so sorry."

She shrugged.

"Did you see who did it?"

"Many bad men. They don't treat us too good." She reached into the pocket of her flimsy nylon coat and pulled out an all-too-familiar piece of hide. "Give this to Gloria, 'kay? It was Lucy's."

"Where did you find it?"

She glanced everywhere but at me. "I … ah … I took it … I like purple flowers. Pretty, eh?" She handed me the supple caribou hide with the tufted purple flowers. I noticed a blue bird in the corner.

I tucked it securely into my own purse.

"I hope Gloria not mad at me."

"Why should she be?"

"I tell her I don't know nothing."

"Did you see her tonight?"

She nodded. "She ask me about it. I give her Lucy's bag, but don't tell her I have the pretty flowers."

"When did you see her?"

"Don't know. A while ago."

"Was she with anyone?"

She shook her head.

"Did she come in a black truck?"

"She walk."

"Which direction did she leave?"

She pointed in the opposite direction from what I expected, away from the town centre, away from the direction of Teht'aa's apartment. But in the direction of Father Harris's rooming house.

"Thanks. If you see her again or you see Father Harris, tell them to call me." I scribbled the cell number on a scrap of paper and passed it to her with little expectation.

"What about my booze?" she called out as Malcolm and I walked back to his truck parked across the alley.

"Get in and I'll drive you to the liquor store," he answered. "What do you want?"

She named a brand of sherry that made my teeth itch at the thought of the sugar content.

Both women climbed into the back seat of the truck with a lift up from Malcolm to help them reach the step. There they sat as silently as two mice with only a mumbled thanks when Malcolm gave them the bottle hidden within the folds of a paper bag.

When we dropped them off at their alley hangout, the woman remembered. "Digadeh. Gloria say she go to Digadeh."

FORTY-ONE

Malcolm and I spent the next hour retracing Father Harris's route, but each time we stopped to inquire with the lost souls collected at the butt-strewn hangout, we received the same response. It wasn't the priest's night. No one knew where he went on Wednesdays, although someone jokingly suggested the bingo hall, which we checked without success. We paid one last visit to his rooming house to learn that he had returned, briefly, and left with a bulky pack slung over his shoulder. The last view his wobbly hall mate had of the priest was of him climbing into a black RAM.

"Are you certain it was a Dodge RAM truck?" Malcolm asked, trusting him as little as I did.

"Yup, a 2500. Used to sell 'em before drink got the better of me. If it helps, there was red lettering on the cab door, but I couldn't read it without my glasses. Also needs a new muffler."

We returned to Malcolm's house to find his father in the darkness of the den, slumped in his La-Z-Boy, snoring. We assumed that he had been equally unsuccessful in finding Gloria. Leaving him to his slumber, we retreated to the kitchen.

"It has to be the same truck," I said.

"Agreed. Too much of a coincidence," Malcolm replied.

"Any idea who the owner could be?"

"A black RAM with red lettering rings a bell, but for the moment I can't place it." He shoved his chair back. "This driving has given me a thirst." He sauntered over to the fridge. "I've got Molson Canadian and Coors Light. Which would you prefer?"

A beer would sure go down nicely. "Thanks. I don't drink."

"Right." He pulled out a Canadian. "How long has it been?"

"Coming on two years."

"Good for you. Dad was quite the drinker in his day but hasn't had a drop in a good thirty years. When we were kids, he made our lives hell when he was drunk. Used to be we'd look forward to when he was off on a job."

"I'm sorry to hear this. Not the kind of memories you want of your childhood. At least your kids will have good memories of a sober grandfather."

"When they were younger, Dad would take them into the bush, tell them Dene stories, and teach them how Dene lived off the land. It's been good for them. They have a great respect for their heritage, unlike a lot of Indian kids today. It seems to have rubbed off on Angus the most. He's our youngest. I swear he spends more time out on the land than he does in town. He's with his great-aunt at the moment, helping her out at the summer camp."

"You mean Florence?"

"That's right. I'm afraid being at the mine two weeks out of the month hasn't always given me the steady presence needed to be a good father. So Dad's been able to be here when I couldn't."

"What do you do at the mine?"

"I just got a promotion to Superintendent, Environment, which comes with a change in work hours. I'll be working four days on, three off. Shelagh will have to get used to seeing me more often." He laughed. "Look, you need something to drink. How about some tea or coffee?"

"I'm a tea drinker." I started to rise from the chair. "I'll make it."

"Stay put. In this house guests are to be waited on."

Remembering my call to Sally, I retrieved the phone from my purse and discovered a text with the name and phone number of the investigator. Figuring he wouldn't appreciate being woken up in the middle of the night, I set it aside to call him in the morning.

I also removed Lucy's piece of embroidery and spread it out on the kitchen table. "I have little doubt that this piece will fit with the two stolen ones."

"Nice piece of work," Malcolm said, placing a glazed blue pottery mug next to the hide. "Though I've heard about them, I've never seen one."

I rubbed my thumb over the tiny blue bird embroidered in the same corner as the other two birds. "One of the stolen pieces had a red bird and the other a yellow one. Do you know how many pieces there are?"

He shrugged and upended the beer bottle into his mouth.

"Or why the original was ripped into pieces?"

He continued guzzling his beer.

"I suspect there are four. The ripped flower in this piece should match up with the ripped flower in the one with the red bird. Which means the yellow bird piece needs a mate."

He continued ignoring me.

"I know you know something, because you got very upset when I mentioned that Hans stole the other two pieces. Why?"

This time I got a response. "Look, I'd rather not say. Let's just say in the wrong hands they could cause a lot of trouble."

"I think they've already caused trouble, with the attacks on two of your cousins and the death of the other. Why?"

"Second cousins, actually. It has to do with what they represent. And no, don't ask."

"Fine, but shouldn't you be concerned about the person who has the fourth piece? They could be in danger too."

"Jeez, my back is killing me," Uncle Joe growled, limping into the kitchen. "You shoulda woke me up. I can't sleep in that thing no more."

"Have some tea. It'll make you feel better." I walked over to the cupboard and pulled out a mug with a grinning moose wearing a Mountie hat. I poured in the remaining tea from the pot and carried it back to the table.

The old man slumped down in the chair beside me.

"I take it you didn't find Gloria," Malcolm said.

"No one seen her."

"We discovered that she's with Father Harris," I added. "Any idea why she'd go with him, when she hates him so much?"

"Bastard. He better keep his hands off her."

"What are you talking about? He's a priest," I exclaimed.

"Too bad he forget, when he—" he muttered but didn't finish the sentence. "Got any of Shelagh's cookies? Meg want one."

Malcolm brought a porcelain jar in the shape of Bambi to the table and slid it toward his father, who unsnapped the top and helped himself to a very large chocolate chip cookie before passing the jar to me.

"What's this about Father Harris?" Malcolm asked.

"Nothing." The old man slurped his tea.

"This have to do with Saint Anne's?"

Ignoring his son, Uncle Joe helped himself to another cookie.

"Was he accused of abusing students?" I asked.

Malcolm glanced at his father, who concentrated on his cookie.

"I don't know if he was ever charged," Malcolm said. "But there were rumours. Dad, what do we do about Gloria?"

"We find her."

"We have a better description of the truck, a black RAM 2500 with red lettering on the cab," I said. "Any idea who it could belong to?"

"Hans," the old man answered without hesitation.

FORTY-TWO

"He wouldn't hurt her, would he, Dad?" Malcolm queried.

In answer, Uncle Joe shuffled to the front door with more speed than I thought possible. "We take truck," he shouted, flinging the door open.

Malcolm hesitated.

"What are you waiting for?" I reached for my jacket. "He almost killed her yesterday."

I raced out of the kitchen after the old man. By the time I was running down the stairs to the driveway, I could hear Malcolm's footsteps thudding behind me.

The three of us scrambled into the truck.

"Do you know where Hans lives?" I asked as he backed onto the road.

"Small town. Everyone knows where everyone lives." He veered around a corner. "Unfortunately, it's on the other side of town."

He pressed his foot down on the gas pedal, thundered over the bridge, and onto Teht'aa's road. We whisked past the apartment so quickly, I barely had time to confirm that there was no black truck parked out front. Then it hit me. The colour of the truck I'd seen Hans fleeing in wasn't black. It was a shiny metallic blue. Had I made a mistake? But maybe he owned two trucks.

At one in the morning, the main road was free of traffic until we met up with an ambulance blocking the road by the post office. With legs twitching, fingers drumming, we waited for the paramedics to load the patient and take off with lights flashing. Malcolm stayed close behind until we reached a stop light. It was turning red. This time Malcolm didn't hesitate. He followed the ambulance through the light.

The ambulance veered to the right onto the familiar hospital turnoff. We whizzed past. A couple of streets later, Malcolm swerved onto a street lined with houses of varying shapes and sizes. He stopped in front of a nondescript bungalow, its windows dark. A barking husky strained on a chain at the house next door. The driveway was empty.

Malcolm and I jumped out, rang the doorbell, and checked the windows to see if anyone was inside. The neighbour, alerted by her dog, told us she'd seen his black truck leave several hours ago. It had headed off in the direction Hans took to go to his office at the airport.

Off we flew, narrowly missing a car backing onto the road. Malcolm's expertise at the wheel and heavy foot on the pedal made me wonder if he had learned from his father. But maybe it was the other way around, since cars likely weren't a part of Uncle Joe's life until he was well into adulthood.

For the first time, I noticed a full moon was lighting up the land with its silvery shimmer. It glinted off a lake bordering the highway. Another few minutes and the lights of the airport added to the brightness. We swerved onto the airport road and sped past the terminal along the road Uncle Joe and I had driven on our failed quest to see Eric.

A few buildings beyond the RCMP hangar, Malcolm braked to a halt beside the black truck with a silver logo of a ram's head on the tailgate. It was parked in front of a plain, flat-roofed building. The red lettering on the side panel spelled out "Walther Aerial Exploration International," the name on Hans's business card and the name on the sign beside the building's single door.

Malcolm banged on the door and tried to jiggle it open. With no windows facing us, it was difficult to know if anyone was inside. A chain-link fence prevented us from inspecting the sides and rear of the building.

I tried the doors and peered through the windows of the truck. It was locked and empty except for a pink scarf lying on the front seat.

"Gloria was in the truck," I yelled. "Where do you think they've gone?"

"They fly away." Uncle Joe peered through the fence at the empty asphalt behind the building. "See, no plane."

In the distance, a passenger jet's lights lit up the runway as the wheels touched down. It skidded along the tarmac and disappeared behind a building.

"Can we find out where they've gone?" I asked.

"Air traffic control will know," Malcolm said, walking back to his truck. "Hopefully he filed a flight plan."

"They go to Digadeh," Uncle Joe said, coming up behind us.

"How do you know?" I asked.

He pointed to a pickup truck parked on the other side of the black truck. When I initially noticed it, I gave it little thought. Now I realized its colour was the familiar metallic blue. "Who does it belong to?"

"Reggie Mantla," both men answered.

"But it can't be the same truck," I shot back in disbelief. "Reggie wouldn't risk his position as Tlicho Grand Chief or his position within the GCFN for the sake of a piece of embroidery."

"The man's done stupider things," Uncle Joe replied. "He don't always stick to rules."

"But you guys elected him, so he must be trustworthy."

"It isn't always about honesty," Malcolm answered. "It's about getting the job done. Reggie's very good at that. He's done more for our people since his election than any other chief, apart from the early ones."

"But if he was the man who broke into Teht'aa's apartment, he's the man who hit Gloria. And now they're on the same plane." I was still trying to get my head around the idea that it wasn't Hans. "We need to alert the RCMP in Digadeh."

Malcolm raised his eyebrows at his father, who shook his head in answer.

"We'd rather not," Malcolm replied. "This is better settled amongst ourselves. I'll have Jimmy, our chief, look out for Gloria when the plane lands."

"How long is the flight?"

"About an hour and a half."

"The plane will have already landed. She left the hospital more than seven hours ago."

"It's a small community of less than three hundred people. There are only so many places she can go. Jimmy will find her," Malcolm said.

"Say they didn't go to Digadeh? Where else would they go?"

"South to Hay River or Fort Smith, but not likely. I suppose one of the other fly-in communities. But Reggie and Gloria's ties are to Digadeh. Plus, Hans has interests there too."

"Oh? What's his connection?"

"His company is doing some mining exploration for my company, Nord Diamond, and is running it out of Digadeh. He also has a daughter living there."

"A daughter? I didn't know he was married."

"He's not. His daughter's about six. He visits her whenever he's in Digadeh, isn't that right, Dad?"

Uncle Joe grunted in agreement but chose to add nothing more.

Since Malcolm wasn't making any effort to use his phone, I pulled out mine. "What's Jimmy's number?"

"I'll call." He unclipped his from his belt, pressed a speed dial number, and immediately started talking. "Jimmy, give me a call. It's about Gloria. I need you to find her."

Putting his phone aside, he said, "Since it went straight to voicemail, I suspect the system is down. The service at Digadeh isn't the most reliable. I'll call someone else in case it's a problem with Jimmy's phone."

He hit another speed dial number, then shook his head.

"We'd better try the cops," I said, beginning to lose patience.

He glanced at his father again. "We really don't need to bring them in."

"I don't understand you guys. An hour ago you were certain Gloria was in danger. Now you aren't."

Uncle Joe gazed at the empty asphalt where Hans's plane should be parked before saying, "You right. We do it."

Malcolm pressed another speed dial number, but again without connection.

I didn't know if Gloria was truly in danger. But I didn't want to chance it. Nor did I care if I upset Malcolm or his father. I dialled the number Sergeant Ryan had given me and connected with her on the first ring, albeit somewhat sleepily. After explaining the situation, she agreed to contact the Digadeh detachment through their own satellite connection and alert them about Gloria.

After disconnecting, I said, "Sergeant Ryan will give us an update. She's also going to follow up on Hans's flight plan to ensure that Digadeh was the destination."

Though few words were spoken on the drive back to the house, I sensed their anger, particularly from the back seat where Uncle Joe slumped. But I didn't care. Gloria's life was more important than their distrust of the police.

Malcolm was parking the truck beside his wife's Focus when my phone rang.

"The Walther Exploration plane is at Digadeh," Sergeant Ryan reported. "It landed four and a half hours ago and four people disembarked, three men and one woman who was identified as Gloria Bluegoose. So far we haven't been able to locate Gloria or the men. My colleagues have done an initial check of Reggie's house,

Gloria's friends, and the house where the child lives. But no one has seen her or the men."

"They can't vanish into thin air. They have to be there somewhere. The officers need to check every single house and building."

"They are doing so as we speak. I'll get back to you when I know more. By the way …"

After she'd finished, I hung up feeling confused.

FORTY-THREE

I tramped up the stairs to the deck where the two men waited. Uncle Joe was resting in a Muskoka chair, his eyes closed. In the moonlight, his face appeared drawn and tired, mirroring my own exhaustion.

Leaning against the railing, his son gazed out at the lights of Yellowknife flickering on the shifting waters of the bay. On the opposite shore, the moon cast a silvery sheen on the buildings peeking out of the forest darkness.

"Gorgeous, eh?" Malcolm said as I drew up beside him. "I could've picked a site around the corner with flatter ground, but Shelagh and I decided it was all about the view. So tell us, what did the fair sergeant have to say?"

I conveyed all I had learned and ended with the sergeant's last bit of news. "Ryan doesn't think Gloria is in any danger. Apparently she was seen laughing with the men as they walked away from the plane. So did we get it wrong?"

"Dad, what do you think? You were the one who said she was in trouble."

The old man continued to breathe heavily while he summoned up the energy to answer. "The priest. I no trust him. Hans, I don't know. Reggie okay."

"I don't know what to think," I said. "Maybe she was in trouble, but it looks like not anymore. But why did she go off with them? Either of you hazard a guess?"

"Let's talk in the morning." Malcolm pushed himself away from the view. "There's nothing more we can do tonight, and it looks like the police have everything in hand, thanks to Meg." The icy tone of his voice expressed the full extent of his disapproval.

"What do you have against the cops? When you couldn't reach anyone at Digadeh, it was the only thing to do."

Uncle Joe sighed. "Gloria is problem. She no go to court when supposed to. RCMP catch her, throw her in jail. She cost me thousand bucks."

"Dad, you didn't. Not again. You don't have that kind of money to throw around."

"Family comes first." Uncle Joe clamped his lips shut and crossed his arms to stop further rebuke.

"They removed the guard at the hospital, so they can't think it all that important," I countered, trying to suppress a yawn. "I'm dead tired. Time for bed. Where would you like me to sleep?"

Malcolm showed me to a narrow room tucked under a gable on the second floor with a single bed covered by a thick, fluffy duvet. I was so exhausted, I barely spared the view of the moonlit bay more than a second before sinking into the soft mattress.

I slept the sleep of the exhausted. Nothing woke me up, not even the daylight seeping into the room, until the drumming cacophony of Eric's phone shattered my sleep.

It took me several seconds of bleary-eyed scrambling to locate and answer the phone.

I managed a garbled, "Hello."

"Sorry, I thought you'd be awake. Sergeant Ryan here."

I was amazed to discover that it was after ten. "Has Gloria been located?"

"No, nor any of the other passengers. But we believe we know where they went. The detachment learned this morning that she and the men were seen getting into Reggie's boat shortly after their arrival."

"But it was nighttime. Surely people don't take off on a boat trip when it's dark, especially in the wilderness."

"At the hour they purportedly left, there would've been sufficient daylight. Remember, you're in the north. At this time of year, it never gets pitch black. Besides, Reggie would be navigating. I imagine he could navigate those waters blindfolded."

"There can't be any nearby communities, so where would they be going?"

"Apparently the boat set out in the direction of one of the ancestors' trails, where the Mantla family has a camp. We assume that was the destination."

"Has anyone followed up to ensure Gloria is safe?"

"I'm afraid it's not possible. With only two officers at the detachment, we can't leave the community under-manned for a non-emergency situation."

"But this *is* an emergency."

"The officers don't believe so. Nothing points to Gloria being taken against her will."

"But they have an arrest warrant out for her."

"True, but she can only leave the area by plane from Digadeh. They'll take her into custody then. I've got to go. My apologies for waking you up."

I nestled back under the duvet, reluctant to leave its warmth. I had to assume that we'd read more into the situation than was warranted. Gloria was no longer in danger from any of these men. But did I really believe this? My gut told me no. Something fishy was going on, but what, I had no idea.

Despite a good eight hours' sleep, I was still tired and would've loved to linger longer, but knew Uncle Joe and Malcolm needed to be updated.

"You late, missy," were the words that greeted me when I entered the kitchen. "Malcolm no wait. He go."

Uncle Joe sat hunched at the kitchen table sipping his coffee. A trail of crumbs led from an empty plate beside a jar of jam to where he sat.

"You could've woken me up." I pulled a mug out of the cupboard, this one wrapped in a stylized Haida red-and-black eagle, and poured myself what was left of the coffee, barely enough to cover the bottom of the mug.

"Where do you keep the coffee?"

"Sit down." Uncle Joe ordered as he pushed himself out of the chair. "Your coffee okay, but I make better."

While the old man made the coffee, I told him about Sergeant Ryan's call. I finished by asking, "Do you know why Gloria would be going with these three men to Reggie's camp?"

"They don't go to his camp. They go to our family camp."

"Why?"

"Too early. Mantla camp not set up. Reggie don't harvest much anymore. Use it like summer cottage. But Florence and Angus already move to Bluegoose camp. Good fishing. Anita with them too."

"I believe Angus is your grandson, but who's Anita?"

"Gloria's daughter. She live with Florence."

"Do you think Gloria went with these men because she wants to see her daughter?"

"Yup. You hungry? I make bannock."

He poured batter from a bowl into a sizzling hot frying pan. Within minutes I was spreading strawberry jam over a piece of fluffy white perfection, which, I hated to say, was the best bannock I'd ever eaten. *Sorry, Eric.*

"You seem pretty calm about this now." I savoured another bite. "Why don't you think Gloria's in danger from the priest anymore?"

"She with the other two. They make sure he do nothing. Beside, he old man. Not easy to get it up." He chuckled to himself and tore off a chunk from my piece of bannock and smothered it with jam.

"So what do we do now? Nothing?"

"Go see Teht'aa. Tell her Gloria okay. She go see her daughter."

"You believe the police. You really don't think Gloria is in trouble anymore." Given his distrust of them, I was finding it difficult to accept.

He grunted a yes.

"Fine. But can you tell me what reason these three men have for travelling all that distance to your family camp? Or why they are even together, since they don't seem to have much in common, particularly Father Harris?"

He shooed me away with his hands. "Go."

I knew he wanted to get rid of me. But since I couldn't come up with a plausible reason for his sudden about-face, I left.

Two hours later, I returned.

FORTY-FOUR

I frantically rang the doorbell and hammered on the door, but it remained firmly shut. I walked along the deck to the kitchen windows and found it as dark and empty as the rest of Malcolm's house.

I wasn't surprised.

After Teht'aa had finally divulged the full story, I knew Uncle Joe would be on his way to Digadeh. I'd raced back to Malcolm's hoping he had more sense than to make this desperate trip. At least he wasn't alone. With the truck gone from the driveway, I knew he was with his son.

The second I told Teht'aa about Gloria, I saw from the fear in her eyes that she didn't believe her cousin was safe. It took her another hour to reveal the reason.

Before the attack, she'd been working on a story about the relationship between mining companies and First Nations communities. She wanted to highlight the challenge small communities like Digadeh faced in balancing the interests of older members who wanted to preserve traditional lands and the old ways with those of younger members who wanted to make the community more economically viable.

"What I found was far more troubling," she said, eyeing the two women in the beds across from her. One was sleeping, the other watching TV. Neither seemed interested in our conversation. Fortunately, the bed beside her, the one with her nosy fan, was empty.

"I stumbled across emails between two mining officials suggesting that a senior member of the Digadeh community would help pave the way for community approval if appropriately rewarded. He wasn't named, but I have my suspicions."

"His initials don't happen to be R.M.?"

She laughed. "Let's just say there's a fancy new house in one of the most expensive neighbourhoods in Yellowknife. With all my documentation gone, I can't go any further with this. But it's not only the story I'm worried about. If I tried to take it to the Digadeh council without concrete proof, no one would believe me."

"I take it this was on your computer."

"That and other material just as damning. Hans is also involved. I found two of the emails on his computer. They were forwarded to him by someone with the email address purpledream@gmail.com."

"There's that word 'purple' again. Did Hans identify the person?"

"I was, ah … looking for something else when I came across the messages. He was showering at the time. When he saw me on his computer, he freaked. I pretended I was checking my own email, but he didn't believe me. We ended up in a shouting match. I haven't seen him since."

"I thought he wasn't your boyfriend."

"He's not. We … ah … just … you know…." She smiled sheepishly. "He's not bad in bed."

"Did you come across Malcolm's name in your investigation?"

"No, why do you ask?"

"He and his father were arguing rather heatedly over mining. Malcolm is very pro-mine. It sounded as if he had a specific project in mind. Maybe it's the same one."

"He's never mentioned anything to me, but he does work for Nord Diamond, so it could be related to one of their claims. In this case the officials were with an international mining company that has no working mine in the Territories. Although a lot of gold, silver, and diamonds, even tungsten have been dug up over the years, people could make millions with the amount still buried under all that rock."

She reached for her water glass on her bedside table with the ease of a patient who was well on the road to recovery. I hoped by the time Eric finally saw her, she would be walking.

"We need to talk about your father. I think he's protecting someone. That's why he insists on pleading guilty. He probably thinks he can handle jail better than they can."

"The stupid idiot. Isn't it just like him. Do you know who it is?"

"If I did, Eric would already be free. I was hoping you might know."

"Well, we're his only family, and it's not us. He can be such a bleeding-heart. It could be anyone. Like someone he feels is worth redeeming. Or someone he doesn't want to see ruin their life any further by going to jail. You know how he is."

Didn't I. It was what I loved about him. But never had his compassion gone so far as to jeopardize all he held dear. "Does anyone come to mind?"

"No, but I'll give it plenty of thought."

"Could you also do what you can to convince him to change his mind?"

"I'll try."

"I thought I might do some of my own snooping," I continued. "His lawyer gave me names of people who might have seen something. I want to fly to Digadeh to talk to them. Maybe they'll point me in the direction of the real killer."

"Be careful. He's killed once. He won't hesitate to do it again."

"Don't worry. You know me, I'm not the bravest. I'm also hiring an investigator. But don't tell your dad. He'd kill me."

It took a second for the irony to sink in before we both broke into giggles. We sputtered and gasped like a couple of silly girls until it finally spent itself.

"Oh, that felt good," I said, wiping the tears from my cheeks. "I needed it.

Teht'aa, trying to suppress one last giggle, nodded in agreement.

"On to more serious things. I want to talk about the purple embroidery. I know you don't want to, but it seems to be connected to everything that's happening at the moment. I've heard bits and pieces about it from various people. Your uncle even called it a map."

"Fuck," was her only response.

I persisted. "At this very moment, Gloria is travelling to your grandmother's camp with the two men you've just identified as being involved in some underhanded mining dealings. Both men wanted your family's purple embroidery enough to steal it. I have no idea what is going on, but I don't think it's good. So please tell me what's so damn important about this embroidery."

She glanced over at her roommates. "Okay. But let's go elsewhere."

At that moment, Teht'aa's neighbour arrived in a wheelchair pushed by an orderly. I claimed the wheelchair and with the aid of the orderly settled Teht'aa into it. Wanting to make some calls, she brought her cellphone, and off we went in search of privacy, as if it were possible in a hospital.

FORTY-FIVE

Teht'aa and I found an empty corner in the cafeteria away from the tables of gossiping nurses and doctors. Figuring hospital coffee would be worse than my own, I bought two teas and a couple of donuts and sat down beside Teht'aa.

She bit into the donut. "Chocolate. Love it." She took another bite. "You know that my great-great-grandmother made the embroidery as a reminder of her son's death."

I nodded, sinking my teeth into my own donut.

"*Mamàcho* Teht'aa—" She saw my raised eyebrows. "Yeah, I'm named after her. Anyway, *Mamàcho* Teht'aa wanted it to serve another purpose, too, and she did it through a story. We Tlicho are great storytellers."

"Explains your terrific broadcasting skills. It's in your DNA."

She laughed. "Storytelling keeps our traditions and history alive. We even use stories to identify good hunting and fishing locations and the routes taken to reach them."

"Like an oral map."

"Exactly. When my grandmother gave me my piece of the embroidery, she recounted *Mamàcho* Teht'aa's story. It's in Tlicho and too long to recount now."

"I didn't know you spoke Tlicho."

"Not much anymore, but amazingly, I remember every word of the story. Most importantly, not only does the story recount the history of the embroidery, but it's also an oral map."

"The map Uncle Joe was talking about."

"Exactly. It describes a trail through various lakes and rivers with identifiable markers, like rock outcrops, types of vegetation, beaches, and so on."

"Is the destination an island, like Gloria mentioned?"

"Yes, with purple flowers."

"But both Lucy and Uncle Joe called it Blueberry Island."

"Did they use the word Dzièwàdi?"

"Sounds right."

"In our language *dzièwà* means both blueberry and purple. *Mamàcho* said it was called Purple Island because of the purple flowers growing on it."

"Gloria said they sparkled."

"*Mamàcho* used the Tlicho word that means 'sparks from a fire.' A curious way to describe a flower, don't you think? I'm starting to wonder if the flowers aren't something else. Rocks can sparkle. Maybe they are purple rocks."

Remembering the quartz with the glimmering fragments of gold I once found on an island back home, I said, "You could be right."

"It would explain Hans's interest. Apart from sex, all he's interested in is geology and making his millions on a major discovery, like gold."

"Amethysts are the only purple rocks I know of, but I don't think their value would be great enough to generate millions, unlike gold or diamonds. Maybe these sparkly purple flowers are diamonds. But have you ever heard of purple diamonds?"

"Nope. The diamonds that are currently mined in the Territories are known for their pure white clarity." She paused to sip her tea. "Did Gloria tell you how she learned about the embroidery?"

"Lucy told her."

"She wasn't supposed to. *Mamàcho* made us vow never to tell anyone. Threatened us with the Dene equivalent of the boogeyman."

"Why would your grandmother entrust Lucy with such a secret and not Gloria? The Lucy I met couldn't even remember what day it was, let alone a lengthy story."

"Gloria was too young. When Lucy was younger, she had a very good memory. She could remember conversations word for word. It didn't matter if the words were in Tlicho or English. Sadly, the booze pretty much destroyed her memory."

"Besides you, Lucy, and Frank, who else has a piece? I think there are four of them."

"Frank wasn't supposed to have it. The embroidery and its story belong to the Bluegoose women. He should've given it back to *Mamàcho* after he found it in Aunt Connie's belongings. Aunt Connie's piece is identified by the red bird. I have my mother's piece, the one with the yellow bird, and Lucy her mother's, which has the blue bird."

"I thought the red one was yours. That was the piece you gave your father."

"No, it was Frank's. I took it from him when he came to me wanting to know more. Gloria had told him some of the story, but he knew there was more to it, particularly the part about Dzièwàdi. He also wanted my piece. I started to worry he was going to do something with them, so I told him he would be betraying our family if he did. I also invoked the anger of *Mamàcho*, a key figure in his life, as she has been for all of us. I thought I was getting to him until he took off in a snit. But by then I'd already snuck his out of his pocket." She chuckled.

"What did he do when he found out?"

"Left me some angry messages. I was afraid he'd go after Lucy. That's why I was in the alley the night of the attack. I was going to ask her to give me hers for safekeeping."

"Good, your memory's coming back."

"Only parts. I still don't remember who attacked me."

"It sounds like it was Frank after all?"

"I don't know. But wait, I haven't told you about my purse. Someone turned it in. When Sergeant Ryan was here yesterday, she returned it to me. Amazingly, my phone was still inside, along with my wallet. Only the cash was missing. When I checked for messages, I found one from Frank. Here, listen to it."

She withdrew her iPhone from her sweater pocket and clicked on the message.

"Hi, Teht'aa. It's Frank." His voice was deeper than I expected. "I'm sorry I got mad at you. You've got a point about family, so I wanted to let you know that I'm not going through with it."

"When did he leave it?"

"The day before he was killed."

"You don't know what the 'it' is?"

"Like I told El, he only talked about the embroidery."

"El?"

"Sergeant Ryan. We jog together."

"Do you think he guessed that the sparkling purple flowers could be more than simple flowers?"

"It depends on how much Gloria told him."

"Do you think she knows everything?"

"If she does, I worry that Reggie and Hans will use her to take them to the island. If it does turn out to be a big diamond deposit, she could be in real trouble. A big find is something most prospectors want to keep quiet until the claim is fully staked and registered."

"Don't forget about Florence. They could use her too."

"Oh God, I've got to call her." She fumbled for her phone.

"You can't reach her. She's at the summer camp. Uncle Joe's convinced that's where Reggie and the others are also headed."

"Oh, hell. You've got to warn them."

She glanced at the time on her phone. "You have to leave now to catch the flight."

I started to wheel her out of the café. "Stop," she cried out. "There's no time. I'll get myself back to the room."

"Okay, but call your friend El first. You should have better success convincing her to send someone to Florence's camp than I did."

After confirming that neither Malcolm nor his father were home, I drove straight to the airport. I had fifteen minutes before the Digadeh flight left.

FORTY-SIX

"The boarding gate is closed," the agent said when I arrived gasping at the check-in counter. Through a nearby window, I could see a small turboprop plane taxiing toward the runway. With a sinking feeling, I watched it lift off into the deep blue and turn north toward Digadeh.

Citing privacy regulations, the agent refused to acknowledge that Uncle Joe and his son were on the passenger list. But a middle-aged woman checking in for her own flight overheard my shrill demand. She confirmed that he had boarded the plane with his son. Thank goodness for small towns, where everyone knows everyone.

I'd already left three messages on Uncle Joe's voicemail. It was pointless to leave another, particularly when he was in the air. Yesterday the phone service was down in Digadeh. Would I trust two people's lives on it working today? No. I had no choice but to fly to Digadeh.

Finding another flight proved a bigger hurdle. The next scheduled flight wasn't until tomorrow, same time, same gate. But tomorrow was too late. Besides, tomorrow was the day Eric would be released, and I needed and wanted to be with him.

The woman offered the name of a couple of charter services. When I inquired on my cell, the fee was astronomical, considerably more than I wanted to pay. But I decided it would be worth it if it saved two lives. While the one airline had a plane available this evening, the other wouldn't have one free until tomorrow morning. I nixed the next-day option and kept the evening one open in case I couldn't find another way to Digadeh.

An elderly man wearing an embroidered moosehide vest and an Oilers baseball cap suggested I could travel the way they did in the old days, by canoe. But that was a three-week trip, if the winds on the lakes behaved.

Driving was out. There were no roads. Flying was the only option, but that looked as if it wasn't going to happen in time to be of any help to Gloria or Florence.

Maybe I should stay put, which would likely please Uncle Joe. He could've mentioned the trip over breakfast but he hadn't. He had also tried to put me off by pretending he was no longer concerned about the safety of his grandniece. Yet as far as I knew, he had only one reason for rushing off to Digadeh, and that was to save Gloria. Keeping the trip a secret made little sense, unless he wanted it to remain within the family.

I didn't know why I felt compelled to help Gloria. She was no relation to me. While I liked her feisty spirit, I barely knew her. Yet with her sister murdered, her mother dead, and her father a man no one mentioned, she seemed such a lonely soul, with only her cousin and her great-uncle looking out for her. I discounted Malcolm. Judging by the disparaging remarks made at dinner, he and his family had little respect for a woman who hadn't followed the straight and narrow path they'd taken.

My purse suddenly vibrated with the insistent drumming of Eric's phone.

"Fuck, you're still in Yellowknife," was Teht'aa's greeting.

"I missed the flight, but Uncle Joe and Malcolm caught it."

"Double fuck. You have to find a way to get to Digadeh and warn Uncle Joe. I've just learned that Malcolm is in on it."

"In on what?"

"He's working with Reggie and Hans."

Now it was my turn to curse.

"He told Reggie about the embroidery. I just finished talking to Shelagh. She asked me what I knew about the purple flowers, because Malcolm had brought them up with her. Said they were going to make them rich."

"It still doesn't mean that he has joined forces with Reggie and Hans."

"Shelagh said the flowers had to do with some deal Malcolm was involved in with Reggie. She wanted to know why they were so important. You have to get to Digadeh as fast as you can."

"I found a plane I could charter, but it's not available until tonight."

"Too late. See if there are other flights going there today. I'll call a couple of airlines I know that deliver supplies and get back to you."

"Before you hang up, did you have any success with Sergeant Ryan?"

"Couldn't reach her. She's off on a call somewhere. Damn, I wish I could leave this goddamn hospital."

She hung up without a goodbye.

I walked over to the security clearance line to the woman who'd been so helpful. "You wouldn't happen to know if there are other flights going to Digadeh today? Like those that deliver supplies or mail."

"Most times the mail and supplies go in the same plane as the passengers," she replied. "I suppose one of the mining companies could be sending a plane up there. But I don't know how you find out about them. Sorry." She glanced around at the other passengers waiting in line. "Anyone else know?

Most shook their heads, but a young man clothed in Gore-Tex with a backpack propped against his knee spoke up. "You might be able to hitch a ride with Plummers."

I followed up with the arctic lodge company and bingo, I lucked out. They had a flight leaving for their fishing camp on Great Bear Lake and would be making a stop in Digadeh to pick up an employee. The only catch was I had ten minutes to get to their hangar, or the plane would leave without me. I had to pay them double the scheduled flight amount.

With the cellphone clutched to my ear, I gave her my credit card information while I raced out of the terminal to the parking lot. I braked to a halt in front of the hangar. One of the pilots was waiting at the door as I scrambled up the rickety metal stairs and into the small plane. With little more than a perfunctory nod, he closed and locked it before returning to the cockpit. I squeezed past the five male passengers dressed in rugged outdoor wear to the only empty seat. Before I had completely buckled myself in, the plane was rumbling down the runway.

I was on my way, not knowing what awaited me.

FORTY-SEVEN

We flew over a jigsaw puzzle of equal parts water and bare rock broken up by intermittent stretches of dark-green forest and sand. Unlike the canoe routes to the south, which followed identifiable water courses, the maze of rivers and lakes below offered no discernable route. Yet the Dene had travelled these bewildering waters for thousands of years without benefit of GPS or printed maps. But as I had discovered, they had their oral maps. I realized a guide was imperative if I were to venture out on my own to Florence's camp.

A rising plume of smoke marked a forest fire, as did another farther to the east. Apart from the odd solitary cabin on a lake, the land bore no scars of man's presence until Digadeh loomed into view. A clutch of buildings occupied a peninsula jutting into a broad river. I could see the single brown line of a runway.

The airport was devoid of aircraft when the wheels of my plane touched down on the gravel and taxied toward a single-storey building proclaiming itself the Digadeh airport. Any wishful thoughts of Uncle Joe's flight being delayed were nixed the minute I asked the airport agent.

The return Yellowknife flight had taken off seven minutes ago.

The woman was more reticent when it came to telling me the direction Uncle Joe had taken. Eying me with suspicion, she at first denied knowing him. After I countered that in a community of less than three hundred it was unlikely she didn't know one of its elders, she admitted she might have seen him but was too busy checking in the outgoing passengers to notice where he had gone. To avoid giving me his address, she picked up her ringing phone, turned her back to me, and answered the phone instead.

I walked out of the airport hoping to find someone more forthcoming, or better yet, catch sight of the two men. But I was greeted by a long stretch of empty road lined on either side by stunted evergreens that looked more like bottle brush cleaners than trees. I was going to have to trek to the distant houses of Digadeh to find them.

Though the day was warm, the biting black flies and mosquitos forced me to zip my Gore-Tex jacket up tightly and pull the hood down over my brow. By the time I reached the first bungalows, I was sweating and cursing the bugs.

I stood in the middle of a gravel road that t-boned another several hockey rinks away in the direction of the water. Vinyl- and wood-clad bungalows, some in better repair than others, were scattered along either side of the street. In addition to muddy ATVs and skidoos, most had canvas tipis erected in their yards. I later learned these were used for smoking fish.

A gaggle of school-aged girls were playing in front of one house, while a man on an ATV sped away from me.

But I didn't see the limping figure of Uncle Joe or his striding son.

I approached a couple of elderly women coming toward me. Each carried plastic bags bulging with goods, likely bought at the windowless grey building at the bottom of the street with a faded sign announcing it to be the Digadeh General Store. They were wearing what I would also learn was the usual outfit worn by women of a certain age: a pleated skirt made from a bright satiny material, white ankle socks with dark shoes, a colourful nylon jacket, and a head scarf with cherry red, shocking pink, or royal blue as the colour of choice. An old friend, also a scarf wearer, had once told me the scarf kept her dreams from flying away.

As was later pointed out, the outfit closely resembled the uniform these women would've worn at residential school when they were being taught to be well-behaved Catholic girls. The main difference was in the brightness of the colours, as if in defiance of the dull browns and greys the nuns would've decreed.

The moment I saw the blank stares in answer to my question about Uncle Joe, I knew I had a language problem. We exchanged embarrassed smiles and continued on our respective journeys, though when I glanced back, the two ladies remained standing where I'd left them, eyeing me suspiciously. I gave them another hearty wave and continued walking.

The gaggle of schoolgirls didn't suffer from the same language difficulties or reticence as the airport agent. They gleefully told me where Uncle Joe lived and skipped along beside of me to the t-bone junction and pointed out his house, a white bungalow with a new red-shingled roof midway down the water side of the abutting street.

His yard also sported a tipi and next to it another larger house-shaped canvas tent with a sprawling rack of caribou antlers guarding its entrance. The only mode of transportation in his weed strewn yard was a skidoo, an Arctic Cat with the sheen of newness barely rubbed off, the kind of machine Jid drooled over. I sensed Malcolm's role in its acquisition.

I tramped up the wooden stairs to the front door and knocked, at first lightly and then harder. This door, too, remained firmly closed.

"Joe's in Yellowknife," a man called out from the house across the street.

"He's back. Came in on today's flight. Do you know where he could be?"

"Try the community centre." He pointed to a larger newish building farther along the water side of the street, newish only because its brown paint hadn't faded. "He might be at Florence's place too. She lives near the church." I could see a steeple rising above the houses behind him. "Though come to think of it, she's gone to their camp." He grew silent and stared at me for a minute or two before asking, "Whaddya want with Joe?"

I thought if I mentioned my relationship to the elder, he would be more amenable to sharing what he knew with me.

Instead, by the time I finished introducing myself as the wife of Eric Odjik, a longtime friend of Uncle Joe and father of Teht'aa Bluegoose, I knew I had made a big mistake.

"That the guy who killed Frank?" His eyes narrowed.

"He's innocent," I retaliated.

"Not from what I saw. He had the bloody knife in his hand."

It took a few seconds for his words to sink in. "You found him." I walked closer to reduce the need for shouting. I didn't want the whole neighbourhood listening in. "I've been wanting to talk to you."

"What for? I told the RCMP all I know."

"I'd like to know if you saw anyone else close by."

"RCMP never asked me that." He paused as if debating whether to tell me. "What you gonna do with it if I tell you?"

"Use it to prove my husband innocent."

"Your man's a good guy. Teht'aa's done good by him. She was having a hard time before they linked up. Yah, I'll tell you what I saw."

He clambered down the stairs and stopped within whispering distance. "Frank had it coming, but Eric don't need to be the man to take the fall, so maybe what I seen will help. Yah, I seen somebody. No one else was behind Frank's house, except Frank and your man. But I seen someone running away. Caught a glimpse of their back when they run around the corner of the house next door."

"Did you recognize them?"

"I seen them later in an ATV going to the airport."

"How do you know it was the same person?"

"They were small."

"Like a woman?"

He pulled a crumpled package of cigarettes from his jacket pocket and lit one. After a couple of puffs, he continued. "They was wearing a pink jacket."

Pink jacket. I knew one person who wore pink. "Could this person have been Gloria Bluegoose?"

"Like I said, I didn't see much." He spewed out a stream of smoke and stared at me as if daring me to ask the next question.

"Does anyone else in Digadeh wear a pink jacket?"

He ground the toe of his running shoe into the dirt. "Larry's kid. Her auntie give it to her. But she's away at a school."

I think I had my answer. "Gloria has gone to Florence's hunting camp. I need someone to take me there." I was hoping he would offer, for I was suspecting that Uncle Joe and Malcolm had already left.

"Joe can take you."

"Do you know where I can find him?"

"Sure. Turn around."

I whirled around and almost fell into the old man.

FORTY-EIGHT

Without a word, not even a grunt of greeting, the old man shuffled across the street to his house with me trying to walk slowly enough to keep from bumping into him.

"Want me to send the RCMP to the camp?" his neighbour called out.

"Nope," was the clipped reply.

"But Uncle Joe," I said, mounting the front steps after his lumbering form. "Gloria might've killed Frank. That man saw her leaving the crime scene."

"Yup."

"Yup what? That you knew she killed her cousin or that she was seen leaving?"

"He beat Gloria up. Send her to the hospital many times." He opened the door and stepped inside.

"Did they live together?" I followed him into a surprisingly neat kitchen. Surprising, because I'd never known a man to put anything away, not even Eric.

He grunted an answer I couldn't decipher.

"Is Frank the father of Gloria's child?"

Another grunt, which I took to be a yes.

"What about Teht'aa? Did he beat her too?"

"He hurt her real bad, long time ago."

"What about the assault last week?"

"Gloria know."

"Are you saying that Gloria went after Frank because of what he did to her cousin, the only person, besides you, who cared enough to help her?"

Another grunt.

"Why haven't you told this to the police? It would prove Eric's innocence."

"It take time. He understand."

"Is Gloria the person he's protecting?" I could see my husband wanting to help someone he viewed as a victim. He would want to prevent her from ruining her life completely, especially if he thought the killing was justified.

"Ready to go?" he asked, avoiding my question.

I gave up. "Go where? To the camp?"

"Yup."

"Where's Malcolm?"

"He already gone."

"Why didn't you go with him?"

"I wait for you."

"I thought you didn't want me."

"You stubborn. I know you come." His eyes twinkled.

He opened various cupboards, telling me to take the food I wanted. Since it was more than a day to Florence's camp, we would be camping overnight.

"You like sleeping under stars? I got no tent."

"No problem, but I don't have a sleeping bag."

"I have plenty gear."

"Wait a minute, I can't go. I have to be back in Yellowknife tomorrow for Eric."

"More better you come with me."

"Why? What do you mean?"

Once again I was treated to his avoidance tactic as he clamped his mouth shut and focused on a bulky vinyl canoe pack leaning against the fridge. He dragged it into the middle of the kitchen with more strength than I thought he had in him. He crammed my selection of two soup cans and one of baked beans between faded Hudson's Bay Company blankets and a battered metal pot.

He added a bag of flour. "For bannock. We eat fish too. You good fisherman?"

"Nope." I didn't have the patience.

"I teach you."

Before I went any further, I had to ask the question. "Are you aware that Malcolm is part of this mining scheme with Reggie and Hans?"

"Yup," he answered without hesitation.

It so startled me that I took a good minute to hone in on the implication. "Are you involved too?"

"No more talk. We go." He cinched the pack up tightly and with a mighty heave, thrust his arms through the straps and hefted it onto his back.

"You bring beer." He nodded in the direction of a red Coleman cooler standing next to the back door.

"Beer?"

"Good for talking. Beer don't work, I use gun." He picked up the rifle propped against the wall and headed outside. "Close door behind you."

I lifted the heavy chest with both hands, balancing it on the outside railing while I dutifully closed the door and clambered down the stairs after him. I stumbled on an unseen rock, almost dropping the weight on my feet before regaining my balance. I let it drop on the sand beside an aluminum motorboat lying within dragging distance of the water. While the boat looked as if it had encountered numerous rocks over its lifetime, the raised 50 hp Mercury outboard motor still wore the manufacturer's stickers. Another gift from Malcolm, as I suspected the fancy canoe pack was.

Feeling confused and nervous, I decided to try again. "Why don't I run over to the detachment and get the police to come with us?"

"No RCMP," he growled.

"We could be heading into a dangerous situation."

"It family matter. You don't like, you stay."

He pushed against the boat's bow in an effort to shove it into the water. It didn't budge. I joined him, and together we managed to move it a half foot until it ground to a halt.

"Move, aside, Joe," a familiar voice ordered.

Uncle Joe's neighbour and another man easily dragged the boat into the water. The neighbour walked it out until it floated while the other man hefted the heavy pack onto his shoulder and dumped it into the boat. He smiled broadly as he placed the cooler beside the pack. "Party time, eh?" He tossed the rifle and a paddle with a clatter into the aluminum hull.

"Whaddya doing with the beer, Joe?" the neighbour asked. "Ya know it ain't legal. You even approved the alcohol ban when you was on council."

Ignoring him, the old man waded out to his boat with little regard for the water lapping against his high-sided moccasins. The neighbour helped him climb over the side and into the boat.

"You coming?" Uncle Joe asked.

When I hesitated, he said, "Don't matter you tell the RCMP. They don't know where camp is."

I sought support from the neighbour, but he merely motioned for me to get in the boat.

In the end Uncle Joe made the decision for me. The frailty he was to trying so hard to pretend didn't exist convinced me that I couldn't let him go alone.

I removed my trail shoes and socks, rolled up my jeans, and stepped into the water. Gasping, I almost jumped back out. It was cold, bloody cold. I didn't think I'd ever stepped into such icy water. I waded as quickly as I could without getting my jeans soaked, tossed my purse into the boat, and climbed in with a boost from the neighbour.

His whispered words, "I tell Kirk," made me feel marginally less uneasy, as long as "Kirk" was the name of one of the cops.

He pushed us out into deeper water. Uncle Joe had the motor revving with one click of the starter. We putted out into the deeper water. With a brief wave of thanks to the men on shore, the old man turned up the throttle, and off we shot into the great unknown.

FORTY-NINE

I have paddled many miles by canoe, but farther south where the trees lining a shore can blot out the sun, the rivers are more narrow than broad, the water more turbulent than flat, and the lakes mirror the surrounding forests as much as they do the sky. So I wasn't prepared for the vastness of this northern land.

When Teht'aa first mentioned her community of Wolf River or Digadeh, I'd assumed it lay beside a river. But the broad expanse of water, the wind-whipped waves crashing over the bow of Uncle Joe's boat, seemed more like a lake to me. Though both shores were fringed with trees, I doubted even the tallest would blot out the sun. Down south I barely paid attention to the sky other than to note that the sun was shining or rain was on its way. I couldn't avoid it here. It filled the frame from north to south, east to west. This land of the Tlicho could give Montana hefty competition for the moniker "Big Sky Country."

At that moment the sky was a brilliant deep blue, but a stretch of intermittent white suggested clouds were moving in. Given the force of the wind that had buffeted us on shore, it wouldn't take long. A wind, I might add, with few natural barriers. The surrounding land was for the most part low, with only the occasional rise of a hill to interrupt its passage. It was also the kind of wind that would keep canoeists wind-bound on the shore. Though I preferred the quiet propulsion of a paddle over the ear-shattering roar of an outboard, I was glad we had fifty horses to power us.

From the grin on Uncle Joe's face, he was liking it too and taking full advantage of motor's unfettered acceleration. He piloted the boat like he did the BMW, swerving in and out of a string of rock islands as if they were course obstacles. While I half expected the bottom of the boat to be torn out by a submerged rock, I knew it wasn't likely. The old man would have every hidden obstacle on this river memorized.

I hung on to the gunnels to keep from being knocked out of the boat by the pounding waves. After a particularly strong one almost drowned me, I turned around and watched the buildings of Digadeh retreat. Although my Gore-Tex jacket kept me dry, it didn't stop the icy water and wind from sending shivers down my spine. The wet patches on my jeans didn't help either. But there was little I could do. My extra clothing was locked inside Malcolm's house. At least I had gloves. I put them on.

Despite his wet moccasins and the soaked jeans clinging to his legs, not to mention the thinness of his nylon jacket, Uncle Joe appeared not the least bothered by the cold. But he must've noticed my shivering, for he shouted "Blanket" above the engine's roar, pointed to the pack, and gave it a kick in my direction.

I pulled out a blanket and wrapped it tightly around me. Worried it could be my bed for the night, I took special care to keep it away from the water sloshing around in the bottom of the boat. Though Uncle Joe had reduced the speed to prevent further deluges, the engine noise was still too loud to talk. I admired the passing scenery and worried over what awaited us at Florence's camp.

I was confused. While I could understand and accept Gloria's killing of Frank, I couldn't see her deliberately framing Eric for the murder. At no time in our conversations had I sensed a dislike for my husband, a dislike so strong that she would willingly ruin his life. Nor could I see her planning the murder in such a cold, calculating manner.

The young woman I had come to know struck me more as the kind of person who gave little thought to her actions. She operated on emotions. If she did kill Frank, it was either a spur-of-the-moment response to something he did to her, such as another beating, or it was revenge for his assault on Teht'aa. The only way she had known to stop the never-ending abuse was to kill him.

But the steps taken to frame Eric, like the anonymous phone call and drugging him unconscious, spoke of a premeditated murder. Since it was unlikely that anyone other than the actual killer would have sufficient motive to frame someone else for a murder, Gloria wasn't Frank's killer after all.

Still, I couldn't ignore Uncle Joe's neighbour, who had seen her running away from the body with Eric lying unconscious beside it. There was also her strange apology. Maybe she was trying to tell me that she was sorry for what she'd done to Eric.

I could see Eric wanting to protect someone like Gloria. He would think that three years in jail would have considerably less impact on his life than it would on hers. Going to prison would likely send her into a downward spiral from which she might never recover. And there was her child. A child who would become just another statistic in the cycle of indigenous children growing up motherless.

Although Eric would never admit it, he would view this as a way of appeasing the guilt he felt from having been given opportunities by his wealthy adoptive family during his early years, opportunities that were beyond the reach of most indigenous people of his generation, opportunities that hadn't been available to Gloria.

I was confused by Lucy's death too. Two deaths in the same family suggested the same killer. But I couldn't believe Gloria would kill her own sister. She'd been genuinely upset by her death. Moreover, the proximity of Teht'aa's sexual assault to Lucy's murder suggested the same culprit, which could not be Gloria. It had to be a male.

My only other suspect was Hans. But he supposedly had an alibi for the attack on Teht'aa, and his murdering Frank wouldn't explain Gloria's presence.

I was, however, certain of one thing. The purple-flowered embroidery and the sparkling purple flowers on Dzièwàdi were behind everything. Though I didn't know how the pieces fit together, I knew I would find the answer at Florence's camp, where all the suspects were congregating. Once I had the answer, I would have the means for proving Eric's innocence.

FIFTY

Although the sun was nowhere near close to setting in this land of the midnight sun, my rumbling stomach and aching bones told me it was time to call it a day. Uncle Joe's slumped posture hinted at the same degree of exhaustion, but with his eyes riveted on the route ahead, it didn't look as if he were prepared to stop anytime soon.

"When are we stopping?" I shouted over the noise of the motor.

The old man rested his squinting eyes on me but acted as if he hadn't heard.

"Food. I'm hungry." I pretended to eat.

He pointed to the cold chest.

Forget the beer. "Food," I yelled louder.

He pointed to the pack with the canned goods.

I shook my head. I wasn't going to eat cold baked beans in a freezing, wind-whipped boat.

"I'm tired. You're tired. Time to stop." I pretended to sleep.

Nodding vigorously, he pointed beyond me. I swivelled around to face forward, cinching my hood tighter to prevent it from blowing off. I tried to glean what he was pointing at, but the way ahead looked no different than the retreating view I'd been watching for the last five hours: rock, trees, and water with the occasional patch of bobbing ice pans or chunks piled onto the shore. Yes, ice. Little wonder the water was so frigid. The river had broadened into a large lake. We no longer travelled down the middle but kept the shore within shouting distance.

He shouted, "Campsite," and waved his hand at some undefined feature in front of us.

At least he agreed it was time to camp, so I stopped fretting and hoped this invisible campsite wasn't another hour away. I did wonder, though, what was so special about this distant site, when the flat expanse of rock on the near shore or the grassy knoll on the island we'd just passed looked perfect for camping.

A short while later I noticed a shift in the boat's direction. The bow had a tree-covered island within its sights. As we drew closer I made out a narrow band of sand. Another few minutes and I was pulling the bow onto the coarse sand. I dropped the gear onto a worn spot in the tangle of bushes that seemed intended for such a purpose. After helping him out of the boat, the two of us hauled it farther onto the land as best we could. I glanced around for a tree or rock to secure the bow rope, but with a dismissive wave, he grumbled that the boat wasn't going anywhere.

Muttering, "Too tired. You bring," he waved in the direction of the gear before picking up his rifle. Not waiting for a response, he turned and shuffled up a low incline toward a break in the trees that I sure hoped was our campsite.

Intent on doing only one trip, I hefted the pack onto my back and picked up the cooler. Deciding the combined weight was manageable, I lumbered up the trodden path Uncle Joe had taken through sedges and low shrubbery and sighed with relief when I saw the familiar clearing of a campsite tucked into a stand of stunted birch, aspen, and bottle brush spruce. The old man was resting on a large boulder, one of several scattered around the site. I gratefully dropped the gear onto the ground and joined him.

We were sitting at the clearing's edge next to a fire pit formed by a circle of blackened rocks with scavenged branches neatly stacked beside it. Though the trees were barely higher than a bungalow, they were dense enough to keep us from being buffeted by the wind that helped lessen the fury of the bugs.

From our perch we had an unobstructed view of the way we had come. I scanned it carefully, something I had been doing for much of the trip. I was hoping to catch sight of a boat that would tell me the cops were on their way. But the lake continued to be as empty as it had been the entire trip. Nonetheless, I wasn't yet ready to give up. I still held out hope that Uncle Joe's neighbour had alerted Kirk.

"Best camp spot on lake," Uncle Joe declared. "Bears no visit in the night." He chuckled. "Is traditional Bluegoose camp. My ancestors use it since time of Yamoria."

"Yamoria?"

"Medicine man. Prophet. Lawmaker. He live many, many years before you people come. Our stories say he come from another place, lived with us, and went away. He had much medicine power. He made our world safe.

Give us laws. We use them today, like share what you have, help each other, be respectful."

A saviour, like other religious figures, I thought.

Though it was close to eight thirty, the sun had a ways to go before it sank below the low hills of the western shore.

"How far are we from Florence's camp?"

"Tomorrow afternoon."

Not what I wanted to hear. It could jeopardize catching the Saturday flight back to Yellowknife.

"You think this long time. In old days, it take a week by canoe."

"How long do you think we'll be staying?"

"Until it done. Why hurry? You in Tlicho land. You follow Tlicho time."

"But I need to get back to Yellowknife. I don't want to leave Eric alone for more than a day after his release."

He grunted. "He big boy. He okay without you. He go see Teht'aa."

But I wasn't okay without him. "I thought you wanted to get to the camp as fast as you could to protect your sister from Reggie and Hans."

He continued surveying the empty expanse in front of us. A slight upturn of his lips was the only indication that he might have heard my question. Maybe he wasn't worried because he'd discovered Reggie and the others weren't going to his sister's camp.

"Sergeant Ryan said Reggie's camp is somewhere along this route. Is it far from here?"

"It back there." He waved his hand toward the end of the lake. "I check. Camp empty."

"Do you still think he's going to Florence's camp?"

"Yup."

"When will they reach it?"

"Late tonight. He don't stop."

Despite my body telling me it needed sleep, I suggested, "Maybe we should only stop long enough for dinner. I don't think you want your sister spending more time than necessary alone with them."

"Florence tough."

Like you, I thought.

He continued, "Malcolm make sure nothing happen. He don't stop. Get there when sun come up. He got faster boat than Reggie." He let out a loud guffaw, then stood up with more vigour than when we'd arrived. "Time to catch dinner."

FIFTY-ONE

The fish was delicious, a lake trout large enough to feed the two of us with leftovers for breakfast. Considering it was fried in lard in a blackened aluminum frying pan over an open fire without seasonings other than smoke and ash, it would rival any of the tantalizing fish dishes Eric prepared.

The key to this campsite was the excellent fishing. Uncle Joe had fond memories of this island, which was named Inooda after the lake trout that lived in the surrounding waters. He recalled catching a very big one that was almost as big as he was when he was a young boy. The best spot was on the rocky side of the island, where a granite cliff plunged to the kind of depths lake trout liked.

Using fishing rods stored under a pile of spruce boughs, the old man caught four good-sized trout. Amazingly, with plenty of tips and encouragement from him, I caught one of equal size. If only fishing were always this easy and quick, I might be convinced to take it up.

He had me store four of them in the cooler, which I discovered didn't contain beer, but frozen haunches of moose. He was taking them along with quantities of tea, flour, and other goods to his sister's camp to add to her food supply in case her unexpected visitors consumed most of it.

I silently patted myself on the back after he complimented me on the bannock I cooked under his critical eye. The pairing of beans and bannock, along with the trout, made for perfect camping fare. We finished it off with hot tea and chocolate-chip cookies from the box I'd snuck into the pack. While he made the tea, I washed the few dirty dishes at the water's edge using sand to scrub them clean.

With mug and cookie in hand, I returned to the boulder. I wrapped the red blanket snugly around my body and sat down to watch the transformation of the land into night, or what served as night at this time of year; a soft purplish-grey twilight. The last orange remnants of sun rippled across the lake, igniting the hills on the eastern shore. I could feel a chill I hadn't felt before. I snuggled further into the blanket and hoped it would keep me warm enough overnight. I cast an eye at the cold ground and hoped I was tired enough to ignore its hardness. I doubted the old man had a Therm-a-Rest hidden inside his pack.

"Denendeh. Dene land. Beautiful, eh?" Uncle Joe slumped down beside me. Like me he had a cookie in one hand and a mug of hot tea in the other. But he hadn't bothered with the blanket.

A stillness descended with the dying of the wind. I swore that if a mouse stepped on a twig, I would've heard it, so quiet had it become, apart from the whine of mosquitos, which were starting to discover us. We were alone, just Uncle Joe and me, in this vast, silent, empty land. Until a wolf's howl in the distance reminded me we weren't. I wondered if wolves could swim.

"*Diga*." Uncle Joe jerked his head in the direction of the howl.

"So *deh* must mean river."

He nodded, then without preamble began to tell me about his sister.

"Florence special. She older. Six or seven years. Don't know for sure."

"That would put her in her early eighties. I'm surprised she'd be out on the land at that age."

"She with Angus, Malcolm's boy. But she tough old lady." He slurped his tea before continuing. "In old days, families live on the land. Priests visit families and mark down new babies in book and bring them to God's family. Priests don't come often. They guess dates when babies born. My brother is two or three years older than me. My mother had more babies, but they died. Hard living on the land."

"I imagine it would be, especially during the long, dark days of winter." I tried to picture myself huddling in the dark in a tent with nothing but caribou hide to protect me from the fierce Arctic wind, but couldn't.

"But it was good times too. We Tlicho were strong. Knew how to live on the land. We followed the caribou. Herds cover the land. Today caribou gone. We not strong. Too used to modern stuff. Look at me with my big motor." He flicked his hand in the direction of his boat. "We forget how to live on the land. Our kids spend too much time on fancy phones and watching TV. They don't want to go out on the land. Florence don't like new life. She don't like how it change our people. She spend more time on the land than in Digadeh."

A rustle in the underbrush had us both turning around. I half expected to see the wolf and instead saw the long bushy tail of a fox sneaking up on the cooler I'd forgotten to close. Behind her scampered four little ones, their bright eyes gleaming in the light from the dying fire. They scurried after their retreating mother when I rushed over to close the container. But I doubted they'd gone far, so I set it on the ground by our feet.

Uncle Joe chuckled. "That's *Dek'oo*. Means red in Tlicho. She live on the island. When she look for a boyfriend, she swim to mainland." Another chuckle. "She want fish. She like it. Give her a piece and she be happy."

I cut a generous portion and laid it down on a flat rock at the edge of clearing where she and her children had disappeared.

Within seconds of returning to the boulder, I heard a rustle, a scrape, and then silence. When I looked over, the fish was gone.

But foxes weren't the only ones who liked fish. "Won't it attract bears?"

"You scared of bears?"

"I don't fancy waking up to a grizzly smacking his lips over me."

"I have bear alarm. When it make big noise, I wake up and shoot him, okay?" He grinned and waved his rifle in the air, which I realized was never far from his reach, even when he was cooking.

I laughed nervously. But I was thinking our island location was likely protection enough, until he asked me to take the cooler down to the boat, a goodly distance from where we would be sleeping. I kept my ears peeled for strange sounds all the way down to the beach and all the way back. I only relaxed when I was sitting safely beside him.

"Florence look after me and my brother," he said, continuing the story. "At Saint Anne's she make sure priests don't beat us too hard. My brother tell me she have a bad time there. But she never talk about it. After school, she come back to Digadeh and never leave. She never go to Yellowknife, not even when she have babies. She marry, but her husband die in a hunting accident after girls go to school."

"Besides Charmaine, Claire, and Connie, are there other children?"

He stared thoughtfully at the shimmering lake in front of us, where the moon was lighting a path through its purple darkness. "Pretty, eh?" He paused again. "It hard for Florence with her girls dead and two grandkids dead too. But she got Gloria's girl, Anita. Pretty little thing. I call her *Gòmoa*, Butterfly. She dance like one." He flutters his hands like butterfly wings.

"When her girls little, she didn't want them go to Saint Anne's. She afraid. She want them live Tlicho way. Her and her husband hide them from Indian agent. They travel many, many days on ancestor trail to *hozìi*, where nobody go. Barren Lands, you call it. No trees grow there. Bear attack Connie and hurt her real bad. Florence had to make tough decision. Let her daughter die or go to a doctor? They go to Deline on Sahtu, Great Bear Lake. Connie get better, but RCMP take girls away and send them to Saint Anne's."

"The school where Father Harris taught."

"Yup."

"Since you are both the same age, he wouldn't have been at Saint Anne's when you were there, so why do you dislike him so much?"

"I hate all priests. They treat us Indians like we shit at Saint Anne's."

"Did they sexually abuse you and the other kids?"

He fidgeted with his empty mug. "No one talk about it. We only started talking about it at the Truth and Reconciliation Commission."

I sensed a reluctance to talk about himself, but I thought he might be more forthcoming with the next generation. "Do you think it could've happened to Florence's girls?"

"Maybe, maybe not. I never ask. But I see things. Make me think maybe. Claire never settle down. She back and forth between Digadeh and Yellowknife. She drink too much, got into fights. She with many men. They beat her up. Authorities try to take away her girls, but Florence look after them when it not going well for Claire."

"What about Teht'aa's mother, Charmaine?"

"She don't talk much when she live with me and Mary in Medicine Hat. She good girl. She don't drink. She never talk about Saint Anne's. But she never go to church."

"And Connie, Frank's mother?"

"She try to live on the land with her mother, but it too hard. She too used to living like white man. She lived in Digadeh. Her man was good to her. They didn't have any kids. Maybe why they took on Frank when his mum died."

"I'm so sorry," I mumbled, feeling the insignificance of the words, when it was my people who had caused the harm.

"It been hard on us, but better now. With self-government, we have more control over our people and our land. We run our own schools. We teach both Tlicho traditions and the white man ways. The kids born today will do better job of living in both worlds."

"Was Father Harris teaching at Saint Anne's when Florence's girls were there?"

"Yup."

"Do you think he was involved in the abuse?"

He spat on the ground.

"I take that as a yes. So tell me, why is he going to your sister's camp?"

He was saved from answering by a sudden splash and a loud thump that had us both leaping from the rock and peering through the half-light to the shore below. I made out a large black shape moving beside the boat. It was banging against an object lighter in colour, which I realized was the cooler.

Uncle Joe fired his rifle and hollered in Tlicho. I knew he was yelling at the bear to get the hell away. The animal lumbered over the chest and scrambled into the forest. The old man fired two more shots.

"I knew putting fish in the cooler was bad idea. But I thought *sah* was far away. Guess not. He be back. He want fish more than he scared of us. We got to go."

Though we were both drooping from exhaustion, I didn't argue. With my ears on high alert for his return, I threw the still wet dishes into the pack along with my

314

blanket. Ignoring the pack's weight, I hoofed it down to the boat, where Uncle Joe waited with his rifle.

I only resumed normal breathing when the island had finally blended in with the shadows of the land.

FIFTY-TWO

The first few hours after our close encounter melded into a blur of wakefulness and sleep. Though it was light enough to see our way over the water, the land slept. The drone of the outboard had me fighting to stay awake. Much to my shame, Uncle Joe, a good thirty years older, sat solidly upright with his hand firmly gripping the tiller, his gaze steady, without hint of the tiredness he'd shown earlier.

He insisted that I curl up in the bow with the blanket and the sleeping bag his son had given him, which I declined for fear of getting it wet. I didn't remember using my lumpy purse as a pillow, but when a jolt woke me up, I found my head wedged between the purse and the side of the boat and a painful bump on my forehead. I sat up into the glare of the sun's first rays streaking over the undulating hills of the eastern shore.

Uncle Joe had barely shifted his position beside the motor. Though his posture was more hunched and his eyes less bright, he continued to stare unwaveringly at the route ahead.

Apart from a narrowing of the shoreline, the lake behind us appeared to be a mirror image of the lake with the bear. "Are we on the same lake?"

He slowed the boat to a putter, making it possible to talk without shouting.

"That lake was Nodlàati. Lots of *nodlàa,* cloudberries. Very tasty." He smacked his lips. "This lake is Edahbàati. Mary used to pick pretty roses that grow here. *Edahbàa,* we call them."

The boat was slowly wending its way through scattered pans of ice. Ahead, where the lake narrowed into a river, they bunched up into a more substantial barrier. But as we approached, I could see that it wasn't impenetrable. The line of ice chunks took on a life of their own as they bobbed and moved apart in the river's current. Some were a good half-metre or more thick, though I imagined at breakup they would've been considerably thicker. I was tasked with shoving the pans aside with a paddle.

The boat moved easily, with only an occasional thrust of the paddle to push the stubborn ones out of the way. Several times we were stopped by chunks jammed so hard together that despite my best attempts, they refused to break apart. Uncle Joe tried to ram them apart by increasing the speed of the boat. When this didn't work, I joined him in the stern, and he launched the now lighter bow onto the ice. Then I'd return to the bow and jump up and down as best I could without falling over the side. The theory was that my added weight would be enough to force the ice apart. It worked, though I wasn't certain I appreciated the compliment.

We reached an impasse at the narrowest part of the river, where the ice pans were so firmly wedged together that no amount of ramming or jumping would break them apart. Beyond, smooth, ice-free water beckoned. Fortunately, the river was flowing freely over a section where two chunks were being forced downward. Uncle Joe eased the bow onto this dip while I pushed the paddle against the blockage to keep us moving forward. With the water's momentum on our side, we slid over the ice and into the clear water beyond. Our passage broke the jam. Within seconds, ice pans were tumbling around us, along with the rush of water. The old man revved up the engine and we left them behind in a bobbing wake.

But our ice adventure took a toll on the old man, so I insisted we stop for a break on a rock knoll jutting into the river. Though four in the morning was early for breakfast, we gobbled up the remaining cooked fish and leftover bannock. When I learned that the next part of our trip was simply to follow the river until it emptied into another large lake, I insisted on taking over.

After satisfying himself that I knew how to handle an outboard motorboat, he bedded down in the bow inside his sleeping bag with the folded up blanket as a mattress and my purse as his pillow. He warned me to wake him when we reached the treeless island that looked like a grazing caribou at the end of the next lake. He ordered me to stay in the middle of the river and watch out for submerged rocks. He also insisted that I go no faster than the easy pace we were currently travelling. He estimated we would reach his sister's camp in time for an early lunch.

While he gently snored in the bow of the boat, I wondered how he could be so calm about his sister. If his time estimate was correct, Reggie and the others should already be at her camp. With only her grandson for protection, Florence was entirely at their mercy. Uncle Joe was acting as if he didn't think she was in danger. But I had my doubts. She had information two of these men desperately wanted.

I hadn't trusted Hans since our first encounter. I believed him hot-headed enough to resort to force to get what he wanted, like attacking Teht'aa and killing Frank and Lucy for information about a valuable mineral deposit, like diamonds. I had little doubt that he would threaten Florence with harm to get her to reveal the location of Dzièwàdi.

I didn't trust Reggie either. Despite being Florence's chief, he was the kind of man who would do anything to get what he wanted, even if it meant harming one of his people. Moreover, if the blue truck did belong to him, then he, not Hans, had broken into the apartment and hadn't hesitated to hit Gloria in his frenzied attempt to steal the embroidery.

I wasn't certain how big a threat Gloria posed. Though she might've killed her cousin, would she harm her own grandmother, the woman who had been more of a mother to her than her own and the woman to whom she entrusted the care of her daughter? I doubted it. But she might do what she could to convince her grandmother to give in to the demands of the two men.

While a cleric wasn't supposed to be of a danger to anyone, this particular priest was suspected of abusing children, possibly hers. But did he pose a threat to Florence? On the contrary, I hoped he would try to prevent the other two men from harming her, like Malcolm was supposed to do.

But since Malcolm was in cahoots with Hans and Reggie, how far would he go to protect his aunt? Perhaps his only contribution would be to prevent the others from being too rough, while he added his own persuasive voice to get her to divulge her secrets.

Since taking over the boat, I had dutifully obeyed orders by sticking to the middle of the river. There had been a few narrow misses with unseen rocks and one scrape of the bow before I jerked the boat away. But I hadn't noticed any submerged rocks for the last hour, and the water ahead was flowing more easily. I decided to go against orders and increased the speed.

The faster we reached Florence's camp, the better.

FIFTY-THREE

The sun was little over halfway to its midday position when Uncle Joe pointed out a jutting, tree-fringed point where Florence's camp was located, about midway down the long narrow lake we were entering. Tatseati, he called the lake, after the falcons that nested on the cliffs at the far end, where I could see clouds of smoke rising from the hills behind.

I'd first noticed the heavy cloud a couple of hours ago hovering slightly above the horizon. It had steadily grown in size the farther north we motored. At first I thought it meant bad weather until Uncle Joe told me otherwise. A forest fire, he informed me in his simple way. But I was not to worry. It was a long, long way away. Well, it looked as if we'd finally reached it. It seemed to be consuming the forests on the other side of the hills at the end of Florence's lake, which I told myself was still a goodly distance away.

The past couple of hours had been a confusion of lakes, big and small, and a labyrinth of connecting rivers, some narrower than others, one so shallow we had to drag the boat over the rocks. This last river had been more ice-choked than water-filled. Both of us had ended up with freezing wet feet from our struggle to drag the boat through. My teeth were still chattering.

From this distance, I could make out several objects lighter in colour than the surroundings. A couple lay close to the water's edge, while two others stood higher up on the land. But we were too far away to identify them.

"Do you think we should sneak up on them?" I asked.

"What we do that for?"

"To surprise them."

"They already know we here." He jerked his head in the direction of the motor. Though we were travelling at little faster than a crawl, the engine sounded like a mosquito in the dead of night.

As we drew closer, two of the lighter patches became boats hauled onto a beach, one with an aluminum hull and the other white fibreglass. Higher up on the point's backbone, next to a copse of scrawny birch, flapped the other light patches, a couple of dirty white tents. A man stood at the entrance to one of them, but at this distance I couldn't tell who it was. Gloria I recognized only because of her pink jacket and small size. She stood beside several racks draped with what I took to be fish. A child played at her feet.

"White fish," Uncle Joe confirmed. "Florence been fishing. She dry them."

Malcolm strode down to the water's edge to meet us, with Reggie and Hans sauntering down the incline behind him. I tried to read threat in their body language and couldn't until I noticed the rifle Reggie had slung over his shoulder.

"Where Florence?" Uncle Joe shouted.

"On the other side," Malcolm answered.

"Fishing." He chuckled. "She never stop."

Malcolm dragged the boat far enough onto the loose stones of the beach for me to jump out of the bow without getting wet. Mind you, it didn't matter. My feet were still damp after their recent soaking. Actually they felt more numb than wet, which caused me to stumble when they touched the ground and fall into Malcolm, who managed to keep me upright before helping his father out of the boat.

While Malcolm and I emptied out the boat, Hans and Reggie watched, their faces expressionless. Neither greeted us. Nor did Gloria, who stared silently down at us from atop the ridge.

Uncle Joe nodded at Reggie's rifle. "Bear troubles," he said more as a sarcastic remark than an actual question.

Reggie responded by planting his feet farther apart. Hans smirked.

Only the child was happy to see us. She ran down the incline, her face aglow with delight, shouting, "*Babàcho, Babàcho*," though technically he wasn't her grandfather. He swooped her up into his arms and smothered her with love.

I was confused. I'd been expecting to find a camp under guard. This was too casual. Yet I couldn't help but sense a sinister underpinning.

I figured I might as well be polite. "Hi everyone, fancy meeting you here."

No response, not even a crack of a smile.

"A long way from Yellowknife, isn't it? But what a fabulous part of the world." I opened my arms to embrace the stark beauty around us.

I noticed both Uncle Joe and Malcolm hanging back, as if waiting to see the reaction.

"We're wet and cold. Is there a fire where we can warm up and get away from these godawful bugs?" I hadn't stopped slapping the incessant biters since we'd come ashore.

Gloria was the first to rouse herself. "Up here, Meg. I'll get the fire going again." She disappeared behind one of the tents.

Leaving the heavy cooler for Malcolm, I hefted Uncle Joe's pack onto my back and started up the incline. Hans and Reggie blocked my way. Not wanting to give into their bullying, I headed straight for them. They broke apart at the last moment but left barely enough room for me to pass between them.

"I'm surprised to see you," Reggie said. "Isn't your husband being released today? I thought as dutiful wife you'd be waiting with open arms — that is, if they free him."

"He'll be released. He's innocent. I'm here to prove it."

"You're wasting your time. Your husband's guilty."

I caught a flash of pink out of the corner of my eye and looked up to find Gloria watching us before ducking behind the tent.

"We'll see." I thrust past the two men and trudged up the incline. I could hear Uncle Joe puffing behind me. The ground levelled off onto flat, solid rock with scattered tufts of sedge and shrubbery. The tents had been erected on softer ground in a copse of scrawny birch and spruce.

Used to the luxurious and towering growth of trees in my part of the world, these spindly specimens were beginning to grow on me. With their myriad shapes formed by the harshness of the subarctic climate and the short growing season, they seemed to have more distinctive personalities. But their use was limited. They were too small to be used to build anything other than a rustic one-room cabin.

The peaked canvas tents were identical to the one in Uncle Joe's yard. About the size of a one-room cabin and high enough to stand upright, their support came from an elaborate frame of external poles made from thin, tapered tree trunks. So there was a use for these trees after all. Both the canvas with its numerous patches and the weathered texture of the poles spoke of many seasons of usage.

"We call them McPherson tents," Malcolm said. "They're made at Fort McPherson on the Mackenzie River. Because trees are used for the poles, you only have to transport the canvas shell. Prospectors and the RCMP also use them. I swear these are the same tents Auntie had when I was a kid. We Bluegoose don't take kindly to change." He laughed. "It doesn't look like Auntie has the stove going. Not cold enough for her." He pointed to a chimney angled out of the side wall of the nearest tent. No smoke seeped out the top. "But Gloria has a good fire going in the pit."

With the young girl skipping beside him, his father limped over to the blaze rising from the circle of blackened rocks set in front of the tents. He collapsed into one of two aluminum lawn chairs with pink and green plastic webbing, which he moved as close to the fire as he could without igniting himself. Pulling a small object out of his pocket, he closed his eyes and muttered a few words before throwing it into the fire.

"Dad's feeding the fire," Malcolm observed. "He's thanking the Creator for a safe journey."

"I'd like to thank the Creator too. Am I allowed to feed the fire?"

"Of course. Throw in something that has meaning to you."

I groped around in my pockets, fingered clumps of dirty Kleenex before settling on Shoni's dog biscuit. Perfect. It spoke of home and my precious visit with Eric. Whispering a prayer for him and his daughter, I tossed it into the flames and watched it ignite.

"Is your aunt all right?" I asked Malcolm.

"Never better." He nodded in the direction opposite where we'd beached the boats.

Through the trees I could see the shimmer of water and thought I could make out a bright blue scarf. A strong female voice called out in Tlicho.

"She's telling my son where to set the nets."

"I thought you and your father were rushing here because you were worried Reggie and Hans were going to harm her."

"Guess we were wrong."

"So why did you come?"

Instead of answering, he turned away and walked over to meet the two men who were cresting the rise.

Was this his way of confirming his involvement?

Figuring the other lawn chair was for Florence, I dropped onto the ground beside Uncle Joe. I removed my wet shoes, drained the water, and placed them on a rock next to the fire. I did the same with my socks before placing my feet within striking distance of the flames. My toes tingled with the heat.

"Uncle Joe, why are we here?"

"Patience, my *t'eekoa*," was his answer.

I was beginning to think coming here was one giant mistake. I should be in Yellowknife where I was really needed, with my husband and my stepdaughter.

FIFTY-FOUR

Gloria tossed more branches into the fire, sending sparks skyward. I flicked a glowing ember from my jeans and jerked my feet away when a wayward flame kissed them. I was feeling toasty. The bottom of my jeans was almost dry, and my socks no longer seeped water when I squeezed them. My trail shoes, however, would take considerably more heat before they would be dry enough to wear.

Though the smoke was making me cough and my eyes tear up, it was keeping the mosquitos away. But they hadn't gone far. I could hear their hungry buzzing behind me. I inched closer to the smoke.

Gloria sat cross-legged across the fire from me. She picked at a thread in her pink jacket. Without the heavy eye makeup and bright red lipstick, she looked younger, almost girlish, an impression reinforced by her long braids. Except for the purple streaks in her hair, all vestiges were gone of the hard-assed young woman who roamed the streets of Yellowknife looking for the next john.

She no longer wore the bandage, but the shaved patch of hair and redness marked where she'd been struck.

"How is your head?" I asked.

"Okay."

Normally bursting with words, today she had few.

"Why did you leave the hospital? You could be putting yourself in danger if your brain starts to swell."

She shrugged.

"Do you have a headache?"

"Nope." But the rigid way she held her head made me suspect that it was hurting.

"How about vomiting?"

She grimaced.

I took that for a no, which was a good sign.

Though I didn't like the damage she'd done to my husband, I didn't want her to die. "You should lie down. It will help the healing process."

"I had a good sleep after we got here. Feel better now."

The little girl ran up to her mother to show her a sparkling white stone. Gloria gently kissed her on the forehead and admired the stone.

"You have a lovely daughter."

"Thanks. I don't see her much. It's good to be here." She brushed wayward curls from her daughter's eyes. Her child's light-brown hair was a sharp contrast to her own inky blackness.

"Is this why you left the hospital? To see your daughter?"

She appeared startled, then she murmured, "Yah. That's right, eh, Little Bird?"

"Uncle Joe calls her his butterfly."

The old man snickered beside me.

"Yah, she's that. Never keeps still, eh, Little Bird?" The child, suddenly quiet from the unlooked-for attention, settled into her mother's lap and cast her shy grey eyes back at me. Gloria smoothed her hair and kissed the top of her head.

Watching them, I could understand Eric's reason for wanting to keep this young mother out of jail. It wouldn't be one life destroyed, but two. It left me in a difficult quandary: accept Eric's decision or get her to admit she killed Frank. But it might not be such a difficult choice. If Gloria killed the man because of his abuse, she could plead self-defence and spend no time in jail. Not so with Eric.

I was about to query her on her relationship with Frank when a man I'd completely forgotten about shambled toward the fire.

"Hello, Mrs. Odjik, I didn't know you were coming." Father Harris groaned as he lowered himself into the other lawn chair. "These old bones sure can't take it anymore. Used to be I could travel for days in a canoe without feeling an ache."

I watched the reaction of Uncle Joe and his grandniece to the priest's arrival. Uncle Joe clamped his lips shut and glared, much the way he had done at the hospital. Gloria pulled her child closer, while pushing herself with her feet farther away from the man, surprising considering they'd travelled in close quarters for more than a day.

He appeared unfazed by their contempt.

"I'm surprised, Father Harris, to find you here, sharing the fire with people who don't hold you in much regard."

"I was invited."

"By whom?"

"Florence, a lady whom I highly respect. Do you know that nearly fifty years ago I sat in front of this same fire and recorded the births of her children. I later came to know them at Saint Anne's. As you know, I look out for her grand-children." He paused to flick a piece of ash from his jacket sleeve. "I'm sorry about Lucy. One of God's special people."

"Why did Florence invite you?"

"You will have to ask the lady yourself."

His smugness only made me want to delve deeper.

"As you know, the Truth and Reconciliation Commission has finally revealed the terrible abuse, much of it sexual, that was inflicted on native children at the various residential schools. I know that not all the teachers were involved, but I am wondering about you?"

I sensed Uncle Joe's sudden alertness and saw Gloria sit up straighter.

"These good people know that since retiring I have been trying to atone for the terrible things done at Saint Anne's. I look out for my students and the others who have gone astray. It is God's calling."

"Did you teach Florence's three girls?"

"Not—" He stopped talking, then continued. "I taught her children, as I did other Tlicho children."

"Did you abuse them?"

He jerked his head back as if I'd punched him, which I was sorely tempted to do.

Gloria answered for him, "You hurt my *Mamà*. When I was little *Mamà* would have nightmares. She'd wake up screaming, 'Don't, please don't.' My friend's mother had the same bad dreams. She said it was because the priest had hurt her mother at school."

"I'm so sorry, Gloria, for everything that my church has done to your people. We meant well. We thought we were saving you for Christ."

"Shut up, you stupid old man," Uncle Joe growled. "Always same excuse. Tell her. Did you destroy her mother?"

The two men stared at each other across the flames, one with hate in his eyes, the other imploring.

Father Harris dropped his gaze. "Such pretty little girls. Their dancing skirts, flying braids. So pure and innocent…." His voice faded into nothing.

FIFTY-FIVE

I waited for the shouts and accusations. Instead the old man and his grandniece remained silent. Tears trickled down Gloria's cheeks as she hugged her daughter closer. Even rock-solid Uncle Joe was brushing tears from his eyes, almost as if he were reliving his own school memories.

Behind him stood Reggie, his rifle gripped tightly at his side.

I could feel the hatred pouring out of him. Of course. He would've gone to Saint Anne's too. He raised the gun and with his finger on the trigger pointed it straight at the priest. Father Harris raised his head. He made no attempt to duck or back out of the way. He merely stared back at his former pupil and waited.

But it was not to be.

After several tense minutes, Reggie lowered the rifle.

"Not worth it," he muttered. Turning his back on his abuser, he walked away from the fire.

Uncle Joe hobbled after him. Reggie stopped short of the trees. The old man placed a hand on his shoulder. The younger man stared silently into the woods before turning around and gripping the old man in a tight hug. I wasn't certain who was comforting whom. Likely they were both consoling each other.

"Dear God, forgive me …" mumbled Father Harris.

He pushed himself out of the chair and limped away. Gloria spat at his retreating back as he disappeared behind the tent.

"Are you okay?" I asked.

"Yah. I always knew he abused my mother. She used to say she was worthless shit, not good for nothing. I guess that's why she drank. It killed her, you know. Grandma brought me up, just like she's doing with Anita." She ruffled her daughter's hair. "Maybe I should move back to Digadeh. Little Bird, you want Mummy to come live with you and *Mamàcho*?"

Anita nodded vigorously. "We play with Bèbi." She held up her doll, a soft Raggedy Ann kind of doll made from moosehide and wearing traditional Dene clothing that looked as if it had been treasured by more than one owner. "*Mamàcho* showed me finger pull and snowsnake. We play, okay?"

"You bet." Gloria tickled her daughter and soon had her giggling.

Then she looked up at me. "I couldn't do it. It scares me. I don't know how to be a mother."

Such sad lonely words. "Most new mothers feel the same way. Besides, you'll have your grandmother to help you."

"Yah, I guess."

I could see she was already backing away from the idea.

"Uncle Joe told me about Frank. Is Anita his child?"

"Nope."

"I gather Frank used to beat you."

"Yah. Happens a lot around here."

"Did he hurt you recently?"

"Whaddya mean?"

"Someone saw you leaving the place where Frank was killed. Did he—"

"Who?" she cut in.

"I'd rather not say. I'm wondering if Frank hurt you that day."

"Why would he? We didn't live together no more."

She rubbed her arm where I'd seen her rubbing it before. It reminded me of the rubbing I would do whenever I thought of my ex-husband, on the exact spot where my arm broke when he threw me against the kitchen counter.

"Maybe for old time's sake," I said.

She firmed her lips.

"You know you can plead self-defence."

She scowled. "Hunh?"

Without another word, she grabbed her daughter's hand and strode off in the opposite direction to the one the priest had taken, leaving me discouraged. At least she hadn't denied leaving the crime scene, but she was far from admitting she'd killed her one-time lover. I hoped she would reconsider once she digested the import of a self-defence plea. Surely when she realized she would be acquitted, she wouldn't let Eric go to jail.

Everyone had scattered. Through the shimmering heat of the fire, I could see the priest standing on a rocky knoll at the edge of the point with the wind buffeting his clothes. He faced outward, away from the camp and his accusers. I wondered what he would do now, for I suspected this was the first time anyone had confronted him about his abuse.

Beyond the motionless figure, I could see the smoke billowing over the hills at the end of the lake. It looked no worse than when I had first seen it. Since no one in the camp seemed worried by it, I wasn't either.

In her rush to escape, Gloria had sped through the trees behind the tents before veering down the slope to where her grandmother was fishing. Out of the corner of my eye, I'd seen Reggie break free of Uncle Joe and disappear into the woods. Since Hans wasn't within sight, I assumed they were together. Malcolm had joined his father with a consoling pat, and together they'd wandered down the hill to the boats. I was alone.

My dried socks felt snuggly warm as I pulled them over my feet. I shifted my still-damp shoes to a sunnier spot, careful to keep them within heating distance of the fire. I stretched out on the ground in the warmth of the noonday sun and closed my eyes.

A voice jerked me awake.

"What are we going to do about the old woman?" came Hans's guttural tone.

"Don't talk about her that way," Reggie replied. "She's a respected elder."

It sounded like their voices were coming from the other side of the tents.

"How long is it going to take to get her to tell us? I don't have all day. I have a business to run."

"You're on Tlicho time now. It'll happen when it happens."

"You're sure she's going to tell us where the diamonds are?"

"Shut up! The trees have ears."

I froze.

"Remember, we don't know if they really are diamonds." He dropped his voice so low, I barely heard the last word.

"Are you changing your mind? We have a partnership for only one reason, to find these fucking diamonds."

"Shshhhh…. Remember, Frank wasn't certain. He just suspected they were from the things Gloria said."

"You realize if it really is a purple diamond deposit, we could make millions."

"Shshhhh…. I know, I know. Come on, let's get Florence. She's caught enough fish for today."

I continued lying in stunned silence, barely daring to breathe while I listened to their retreating footsteps.

So Teht'aa and I had been on the right track. Purple diamonds really did exist.

I waited a good five minutes after hearing the last rustle before standing up.

I had to warn Uncle Joe.

FIFTY-SIX

I found Uncle Joe resting against the bow of his boat. His son stood a short distance away at the edge of the water. Both were silently watching the billowing clouds of smoke. A gust of wind brought its warning smell.

"Do you think the fire will reach us?" I asked.

"Hard to say," Malcolm replied. "It's a good five or six kilometres away, but with this strong north wind, it could quickly move our way."

"Thank goodness our return trip is in the opposite direction."

I remembered the blistering heat of another forest fire and knew I didn't want to race through this one.

"Okay, guys, no more pretending you don't know. It's time you told me about the purple diamonds." I braced myself for the denials.

Malcolm wheeled around to face me. "How did you find out?"

"I overheard Hans and Reggie talking. Besides, Teht'aa and I had already guessed. I want to know how involved you are with Hans and Reggie."

Malcolm looked over at his father, who nodded. "Tell her. She family."

"Okay." Malcolm walked over to the boat and leaned against it beside his father. "The diamonds have to do with a story that has passed down through the Bluegoose women."

"I know. Teht'aa told me."

"That surprises me. But I guess she thought the time for secrecy was over. Anyway, a few months ago Dad caught wind of something going on when Frank starting asking him questions about the purple flowers. Like me, he wasn't supposed to know anything about them."

"Yeah," Uncle Joe chimed in. "I only find out about the purple flowers when I ask Florence. She say they are Bluegoose secret for women only. Men get greedy and kill people for them."

"Did she know they were diamonds?"

A strong gust blew the cap off his head, but he ignored it. "She only know they valuable. She tell me story about *Mamàcho* Teht'aa. She grandmother of Florence and me. She found the island with the purple flowers, Dzièwàdi."

"I know."

"When *Mamàcho* Teht'aa leave Dzièwàdi, she took some purple flowers. Her husband, my *babàcho*, took them to the Hudson's Bay Company trading post in Fort Rae. The trader got real excited. Wanted to know where they come from. But *Babàcho* ran away. The trader sent men after them. *Babàcho* and his brother got killed. But *Mamàcho* Teht'aa escape with our mother. Her little boy died at Dzièwàdi. She realized flowers were valuable. Something men want and kill for. But she thought they might someday be important to Bluegoose family, so she made embroidery to remember them and to use like a map to find them."

Malcolm took over. "After both Frank and Reggie started asking about them, Dad wanted me to see what they were up to. That's when I learned about the possibility of a purple diamond deposit. I inserted myself into their partnership and have been working with them since."

"I'm surprised by the secrecy. Wouldn't a deposit this valuable bring a lot of money to the Tlicho?"

"Dzièwàdi a sacred place," Uncle Joe answered. "Little boy buried there. We don't disturb where our people buried. It Tlicho tradition."

"Now Dad, let's not go there again." Malcolm couldn't hide the exasperation in his voice. Turning to me, he said, "We've been keeping it secret because Hans and Reggie are playing it that way. I want to see how far Reggie will take this. We suspect he's more interested in filling his own pockets than those of his people."

"But he's your grand chief."

"He told me he intends to resign. He even had the nerve to ask if I wanted to take over from him." He shook his head. "He now spends more time in Yellowknife than Digadeh, probably as a way of cutting his ties to the community."

"I saw his fancy new house."

"Exactly. There's another reason for keeping this quiet. We weren't certain if the island lay within the Tlicho boundaries agreed upon during the self-government negotiations. The Tlicho would have no rights to a share of the mining income beyond these borders, even though much of this land is also considered traditional. It's what Reggie is hoping for."

"What about Hans? How did he get involved?"

"After Frank told him about the diamonds, Reggie approached Hans to see if he could find the deposit with his aeronautical exploration equipment. Hans has ties to our community, so I imagine Reggie thought he could be trusted."

"I gather he has a child living at Digadeh."

Uncle Joe, who'd been focusing on the smoke, shifted his eyes back to me but remained silent.

"That's right," Malcolm answered. "But the territory is so large that despite many months of searching, Hans still hasn't located it. After Frank told them that the embroidery was a map, they figured by putting the pieces back together they would find the diamonds."

"Hence the thefts. Do you know if they have located the fourth piece?"

"They think Florence has it. I know they have the two stolen pieces because Hans showed them to me before you guys arrived. I brought Lucy's piece with me, the one you left on the kitchen table, but I've kept that from them."

"Sorry, I forgot all about it. Do you think they know about the story?"

"I'm not sure what they know. They keep saying Florence will tell them where the diamonds are."

"Will she?"

"No," Uncle Joe bellowed.

"But you suspect they'll force her."

"Those guys will do anything to get at those diamonds. I'm hoping Dad can talk some sense into them."

"Greedy buggers," Uncle Joe said, taking me by surprise. This was the first time I'd heard him swear. "I no let them hurt my sister."

"Teht'aa told me something interesting about Frank. The day before he died, he left a message on her cell saying that he had told the guys he was no longer in. I bet the guys were Hans and Reggie. Do you think it possible that one of them killed Frank in a fit of anger?" But if they had, where did Gloria fit in?

"I've wondered that myself," Malcolm replied. "I know they both flew to Digadeh last Saturday."

When he mentioned Saturday, I realized with a jolt that less than a week had passed since that disastrous phone call. It seemed more like a lifetime.

"A friend of mine is a mechanic at the airport," Malcolm continued. "He complained to me about an argument he got into with Hans last Saturday morning over a rush job on his plane. He later saw Reggie board the plane with Hans. An air traffic control buddy told him that it had flown to Digadeh."

Bingo. "Do you know what time of day? Maybe we could tie it into the timing of the murder." I'd thought all along Reggie was capable of framing Eric.

"Nope. But the police can check the flight plan."

I thought I heard a shout drifting on the wind. "Did you hear that? We'd better check on Florence."

FIFTY-SEVEN

I scrambled after Malcolm, leaving Uncle Joe to follow at his own pace. The shouting continued, but as we crested the backbone of the point, I couldn't tell whether it was an argument or a boisterous conversation. We slipped and slid our way down the shifting stones of a steep incline to another bay, more like a shallow indentation in the lake's undulating shoreline. The bow of an aluminum boat was pulled partway onto the beach. Three people were dragging a fishnet through the water. Its content writhed and thrashed with silvery objection.

One was a young man in his early twenties wearing his Oilers ball cap backward over long, glossy black hair. With jeans rolled up past his knees, he waded through the frigid water as if it were a southern lake at the end of summer. His facial features, namely the largish nose, were too much like Malcolm's for him not to be Angus. The second person could only be Florence. Her royal-blue scarf and wisps of grey hair flickered in the wind as she half stood, half sat in the boat. Beside her stood Gloria, helping her to pull the heavy, writhing net alongside the hull toward the shore.

"Gloria, tell your grandmother to stop fishing," Hans shouted from atop a granite outcrop overlooking the boat. "I'm not going to wait any longer."

Reggie stood farther away as if trying to distance himself from his partner. His rifle hung loosely at his side, while Hans had a firm grip on his, a more modern-looking model complete with a scope and sling.

"I told you, she won't answer any of your stupid questions until she's finished with the fish," Gloria screeched back. "We got to fillet the fish while they're fresh."

"Fuck that." He jumped down onto the beach and strode toward the two women, his gun clasped in both hands.

"Hey, back off, man." Angus dropped his end of the net and thrashed through the water toward the German. "Don't you lay a hand on *Mamàcho*."

"Stop where you are," Malcolm yelled at the same time as Reggie shouted. "Hans, this won't get us anywhere."

But a determined Hans kept going.

Meanwhile, the fish, seeing their chance to escape, started slipping through the dropped end of the net.

The old woman, oblivious to the advancing man and his rifle, cried out in Tlicho and tried to climb out of the boat after the fleeing fish. But Gloria caught hold of her and wouldn't let go, despite her struggles to break free.

"The fish be here tomorrow," a puffing Uncle Joe called out as he came up behind me.

By now the net was empty, apart for a few stragglers. But no one noticed.

A determined Angus stood in front of the boat, feet apart, arms crossed, facing a snarling Hans, who towered over him by a good half foot. "Leave Auntie alone," he hissed.

"Get her out of the boat." Hans pointed his rifle at the boy.

Angus stood his ground. Behind him in the boat, Gloria had her arms around Florence as if to protect her, but the old woman had other ideas. She broke away and clambered unsteadily to the bow of the boat, where she stood as erect as her hunched back would allow and cried out in Tlicho.

Uncle Joe shouted back an answer, which seemed to satisfy her, for she smiled and nodded and sat down on the bow seat.

Reggie had raised his gun and was pointing it in the direction of the boat, but it was impossible to tell the intended target.

Behind me I heard Uncle Joe lift up his rifle. He aimed it at Hans's back. I was afraid he was going to shoot until he lowered it and muttered, "Not this way."

He shouted, "Everyone relax. You come here to talk. We talk Tlicho way. Not with guns. Put them down."

Hans continued to stand his ground.

As if daring him to shoot, Angus inched forward so that his chest touched the barrel.

Neither Malcolm nor Reggie lowered their guns.

"Drop it, Hans," Malcolm called out. "Or I will shoot."

"Hans, please," Gloria pleaded. "Not this way."

He raised his eyes to the young woman, who looked back at him with a tentative smile.

"Okay." He lowered his rifle. "Sorry, I meant no disrespect. I'm just worried the forest fire will reach us before we finish."

I sniffed the air. The intensity of the smoke had increased, while the clarity of the air had taken on a brownish tinge.

Uncle Joe began retracing his steps slowly back up the hill.

Reggie, lowering his gun, strode over to his partner. "It's better this way."

The two of them walked briskly after the old man.

The old woman teetered at the side of the boat as she tried to climb out with Gloria's assistance. I ran down to help, but Angus reached them first. He deftly lifted his great-aunt out of the boat and settled her gently on the solid ground. She shoved a flying strand of hair under her scarf and patted down her pleated skirt before turning her red-rimmed eyes up to me. Easily a head shorter, her grin revealed more gaps than teeth, but the web of wrinkles couldn't hide the chiselled features that defined Teht'aa's beauty.

"You Meg," she said, followed by more words in Tlicho.

"She doesn't speak much English," Gloria said. "She's saying that she is very happy to finally meet you, after hearing so many good things about you from Teht'aa."

I felt myself blush. "Please tell her that I am happy to meet her too."

"She thinks of you as another granddaughter," Gloria said as the old woman wrapped her arms around me.

I hugged her back and felt her frailty. I could do with another grandmother. Both of my real ones were long dead. One, remembered only as a smiling face, passed away when I was small, the other when I was in my twenties. Distant and stern, she hadn't been the twinkle-eyed, warm, embracing sort of grandmother I suspected Florence was.

Breaking free, the old woman shambled over to Malcolm and hugged him too. "Good nephew." She patted him on the back and started her slow way up the hill with Malcolm supporting her elbow.

Anita, who'd been sitting wide eyed on the beach, watching the skirmish unfold, ran over to her mother. "I'm scared, *Amà*."

"Don't be. Everything's going to be okay." Gloria clasped her hand, and together they followed Florence and Malcolm.

While Angus hauled the boat further onto the shore, I slogged up the hill to join the others. Partway up I caught sight of Father Harris. He hadn't moved from his perch on the end of the point, except now he was facing the camp.

I thought I saw flames flickering in the thick black smoke rising behind him. Though the fire looked to be on the verge of breaching the hill, I wasn't overly worried. It would have to leap over several kilometres of lake to reach us.

I expected to find everyone standing around glaring at each other, waiting for the talking to begin. Instead, Reggie and Malcolm were standing beside one of the tents, arguing. Hans was sitting cross-legged on the dirt, his rifle forgotten beside him, staring at the fire blazing with renewed energy. The anger I'd seen on the beach was gone.

Uncle Joe was balancing a kettle as blackened and battered as his own on a warped grate set over the fire. Florence was sitting on a flat rock filleting the lake trout her brother had caught the previous night. On seeing

Gloria, she called out and the young woman disappeared into the nearest tent.

Meanwhile, her daughter stepped shyly toward the prospector. "*Aba.*" She stopped a couple of feet from him. "You okay?"

When he opened his arms, she ran into them.

FIFTY-EIGHT

I never suspected that Hans's child could be Gloria's daughter. But seeing them side-by-side, I saw the resemblance. Anita shared more of her father's features than her mother's. From the way he was smoothing her curls and laughing with her, I could tell he loved her and she, with her bright eyes shining up at him, loved him in return.

I suspected Gloria, who kept casting adoring looks in their direction, loved him too, which surprised me given her derogatory comments about the man. But we had been talking about his relationship with Teht'aa. Perhaps jealousy had interfered. Hans hadn't minced his words about his love for her cousin or lessened his despairing comments about her. Was jealousy influencing her relationship with Teht'aa, and even Eric? Was it strong enough to make her retaliate?

I assumed she would do what she could to protect her grandmother. Now I didn't know what she would do if the man she loved forced her to choose.

Florence fried the fish and the bannock over a Coleman stove set up on a wobbly table made from plywood and

spindly tree trunks. Though I'd eaten mostly fish and bannock since arriving in the Territories, I wasn't yet tired of
it. Starving, I served myself a goodly amount along with a
mug of tea and sat down on the ground in front of the fire.

Across from me, Uncle Joe attempted to lower himself
into his chair with a plate piled with food in one hand and
a mug overflowing with tea in the other and ended up
sloshing the hot liquid onto his pants. He brushed it off
with a shrug and a few flicks of his hand and commenced
eating. When Reggie attempted to use the other chair, Joe
stopped him with a gruff, "It Florence chair." She sat down
only after everyone had served themselves and silently
crossed herself before dipping her fork into the fish.

We'd all found a spot around the fire, except for Father
Harris. He remained at the end of the point, though he'd
shifted his position. He now sat with his feet dangling
over the edge with his back once again to us. Was he trying to ignore his guilt by turning away from his accusers?
Or was he finally facing up to the damage he had done
to the Bluegoose children and all the other lonely and
homesick students?

Though the man might be a pariah, he still had to eat.
I started to rise to load up a plate for him but Angus beat
me to it. But when the young man placed the full plate
and mug on the rock beside him, the priest ignored it.

We concentrated on eating. Anita, oblivious to the
tensions seething around her, chattered away while she
played with her doll, showing it off to her mother and
father sitting on either side of her. While Hans ignored
Gloria, she couldn't stop herself from glancing at him
when he wasn't looking.

Florence chatted with her brother between mouthfuls of food, as if they were having a pleasant family conversation. But since it was in Tlicho, I didn't know whether they were discussing their tactics for handling the two men or simply commenting on the weather.

Reggie, sitting next to me, jiggled his knees with impatience. Finally, unable to wait any longer, he set his partially eaten plate on the ground and began speaking in Tlicho. The only words I caught were "*Ohndah* Florence" before he switched to English.

"I'm worried the forest fire will cause us problems, so let's not waste any more time. Since Florence speaks only rudimentary English, we'll conduct it in Tlicho. Mine is pretty basic, so Gloria can be our translator."

"I guess," she muttered. "Except I don't understand everything."

"Joe will help out." He jerked his head in the direction of the old man, who acknowledged with a reluctant grunt, while continuing to shovel the remaining food into his mouth.

"*Ohndah* Florence, Hans and I want to—"

The old woman cut him off with a string of Tlicho.

"She wants Father Harris here," Gloria said.

"What the fuck does she want him for?" Reggie shot back.

"I don't know," Gloria replied, "but she's not going to do anything without him."

Sensing Reggie was about to argue, I jumped up. "I'll get him."

The old priest seemed to be waiting for this call, for I met him on his way back to the camp.

"Is she ready?" he asked, slipping a tattered bible into his jacket pocket.

When I first met him, I'd sensed a certain energy, a zest for life. It was gone. In its place was a man shattered by his wrongs who stumbled as if he were sleepwalking. Worried he would fall, I took him by the elbow and guided him over the uneven rock.

The silence was deafening as we approached the fire blazing with more strength than when I'd left it. Every pair of eyes was trained on us, some filled with hate, others with bemused curiosity. When no one shifted their position to let the priest join the circle, I led him to the only empty spot, mine, and helped him lower himself to the hard ground. At the last moment, Angus ran inside the tent and returned with a folded canvas chair, which Father Harris declined by turning his head away, despite the obvious pain as he struggled to cross his legs.

"I'll take that," Reggie called out to Angus. "Bad back." Wincing, he raised himself carefully off the ground and sat with more ease in the sagging director's chair. "Okay, let's begin. *Ohndah* Florence, we want to—"

Uncle Joe cut in, "We thank *Nòhtsi*." He chanted softly in Tlicho and was joined by his son and Florence.

Angus, who'd been heating a hand-held drum at the edge of the fire, began tapping on its translucent hide surface with a flat drumstick.

Anger flashed across Reggie's face as he opened his mouth to object, but he clamped it shut, realizing it would put himself deeper into Florence's bad books. He stood up with his plate in hand and joined in the singing.

One by one, they approached the fire and let the remaining food on their plates fall into the blaze. When it came to my turn, I wasn't certain what to do. I'd been so hungry that I'd gobbled down every succulent morsel and wiped my plate clean with the last of the bannock. Florence, seeing my dilemma, placed a piece of leftover fish on my empty plate. Thanking her, I said a silent prayer for Eric and Teht'aa as I tipped the food into the flames and watched the fire consume it. I returned to my spot and let the drumming sweep over me.

It took me a few minutes to realize the singing had stopped. The tension of impatience had been replaced by an armistice of calm. Reggie no longer jiggled his leg like a man focused solely on satisfying his own greed. Instead he wore the respectability of who he was, Grand Chief of the Tlicho. Hans appeared more interested in playing with his daughter than in interrogating Florence. Both rifles lay forgotten on the ground.

The ceremony had no effect on the priest. He remained hunched over, staring at the bible he'd placed on the ground in front of him. It seemed to be lying on a folded piece of moosehide. With a start, I caught a glimpse of purple peeking out from the edge of the fold.

FIFTY-NINE

"Good. You bring," Florence said in her quiet way, nodding toward the hide.

With trembling fingers, the priest unfolded the hide and spread it out carefully on the ground. Two flowers and a partial one emerged purple in the sun. Their beaded centres sparkled. He ran his fingers gently over the tufts, as if caressing something precious. I noticed a tiny green bird embroidered in the same corner as the others.

Florence spoke a few words to Gloria, who turned to Hans and said, "*Mamàcho* wants the embroidery you brought."

"The two stolen pieces," I added.

"He only took one piece. Reggie stole the other." She raised questioning brown eyes to her daughter's father. "That's right, isn't it?"

When he didn't respond, she continued, "But that's what you told me."

"No fucking way did I steal it!" Reggie broke in.

"It had to be you," I said. "I saw you getting into your blue truck."

"Wasn't me. I sold my truck to Hans a week ago."

"Hans, was it really you?" Gloria pulled their child closer and wrapped her arm around her as if to protect her from the father. "Did you hit me?"

The prospector remained studiously silent.

"But why? I was going to give it to you."

"Why in the hell didn't you tell me?" he shot back.

"I did. I left you a message."

But as if he hadn't heard he continued, "You knew I needed it. Did you really expect me to go shouting up and down the halls of the Gold Range Motel looking for you with your latest fuck?" He spat this last out with the full venom of his distaste.

Gloria shrivelled within herself, looking everywhere but at us.

Her grandmother didn't need to understand English to know the despair her granddaughter was feeling. She motioned her to come over and hugged her tightly. Gloria sat down on the ground beside her and wept silently into her lap while she faced the truth that the father of her child, the man she loved, had almost killed her.

"You broke into Teht'aa's apartment the first time, didn't you?" I accused the prospector. "Why? The embroidery wasn't there."

"I didn't know that. The stupid bitch wouldn't give it to me. When I learned she was in the hospital, I raced over to her apartment to get it."

"And took her computer instead. Why?"

"I wanted to see how much she knew."

"And stop her from exposing you," I retorted.

He shrugged.

"That's why you attacked her. When she refused to give you the embroidery, you tried to kill her."

He held his hands up. "I never touched Teht'aa. I couldn't. I love her too much."

For some strange reason I believed him.

The more Hans revealed, the further Reggie leaned away from him. Finally he said, "Look, I knew nothing about any of this."

"Don't you dare plead innocence," Malcolm lashed out. "You wanted the diamonds as much as Hans and were willing to do whatever it took to get them. Isn't that the reason you're here? To frighten an old lady into telling you where they are?"

When Gloria finished translating the conversation, Florence straightened up as best she could with her hunched back, pulled the scarf tighter around her head, and smoothed her skirt. "No more talk."

She rested her steely gaze first on Reggie and then on Hans and said via Gloria, "You should be ashamed of yourselves. Reginald, you do great dishonour to the Tlicho. As do you, Hans."

The two men squirmed but remained silent until Reggie, bowing his head, said, "I'm sorry, *Ohndah* Florence. I meant no disrespect."

Florence grunted in disbelief and continued. "You have come to learn about the purple sparkly flowers my grandmother found. I will tell you. It is time to tell their story and time for them to serve the Tlicho."

With a smug smile, Hans nodded at Reggie, who ignored him.

"First we look at the beautiful embroidery *Mamàcho* Teht'aa made. Hans, give me your pieces. And Malcolm, the one you brought."

We watched as Gloria fitted the three pieces together on the ground.

"Claire, Charmaine, and Connie," Florence whispered, smiling wistfully at the emerging bouquet. "My daughters."

She gazed a while longer at it before saying, "Father Harris, yours please."

As he struggled to get up, Gloria snatched it from his hand and set it down beside the other three.

From the puzzled expressions on everyone's faces, I knew we were thinking the same question. How in the world did the embroidery end up with Father Harris?

The old woman kissed it and clutched it to her shrivelled breast. Tears trickled down her withered cheeks. "Carol … my daughter," she whispered.

SIXTY

We all sat in stunned silence, apart from Uncle Joe, who sorrowfully nodded while gently patting his sister's hand. But before she would tell us the story, she insisted that we fortify ourselves with more tea.

Though the campfire smoke was blowing away from me, my eyes were tearing up from smoke. I twisted around to discover that the forest fire had finally breasted the ridge of the far shore and was a line of flame racing down to the lake. But since it had to jump over several kilometres of water, I told myself that there was nothing to get excited about. I did, however, notice that the edges of the fire seemed to be spreading outward.

Once we had our mugs of steaming tea and Dad's cookies, thanks to Angus, Florence began her story. As impatient as I was to get to the crucial parts, I knew after her first words that she had her way of telling the story, and she wasn't going to be rushed. So I dunked my cookie into the tea and told myself to sit back and relax. I could see Hans forcing himself to be patient too. But the others, used to Tlicho ways, were already in a state of relaxed anticipation, except for the priest. He remained focused

solely on his bible. It was impossible to tell if he was paying attention to Florence's story or was too caught up in
his own miseries.

She spoke of Tlicho life as it was in her grandparents' day, moving from camp to camp along the ancestors'
trails in search of food. A favoured fishing spot here, a
good one for grayling there, a plentiful cloudberry spot on
the ptarmigan island, another one where the waters rush.
As she spoke of these places, I realized she knew them
firsthand, for these were the locations where she harvested
her own food.

Every fall her grandparents travelled the ancestors'
trails in search of the caribou herds. But one year, the
herds were late. With winter arriving, the family travelled
to a place that lay deep within the Barrens, a place they
knew only from the old stories. She described the journey
right down to the lake with the island and its magical,
sparkling purple flowers, Dzièwàdi.

Hans perked up at their mention. I could see he was
dying to ask the location of the island. But he didn't know
that she'd already told him. As she took us through the
various parts of her grandparents' journey, I came to realize she was giving us the oral map Teht'aa and Lucy had
memorized. She was telling us where to find the diamonds.

Reggie, on the other hand, had recognized the story
for what it was. He no longer relaxed backward into the
chair but was leaning forward, elbows resting on his knees,
listening intently. But unless he had total recall, it would
be nearly impossible to remember the ins and outs of the
journey, which I imagine was hundreds of kilometres
long, possibly even a thousand. Dzièwàdi could only be

reached under the guidance of Florence or someone else who knew the story, like Teht'aa.

Florence continued her story between sips of tea replenished by her granddaughter. Much of what she related I'd already learned. The drowning of the son, the death of her grandfather at the hands of the HBC trader's men, along with the theft of the purple brilliants and the fleeing of her grandmother with her daughter and her brother-in-law's family to a distant part of the territory, where few Europeans dared venture. They never returned to Dzièwàdi, but Florence's grandmother, believing the sparkly purple flowers could one day be important for her people, recorded the memory in an embroidery and the location in the story.

She used the hide and hair from a caribou her husband had shot prior to his death and blueberries to produce the purple dye, not only to represent the purple stones, but also to remember that the island was also covered in blueberry bushes. She decided on seven flowers with seven petals, because that was the number of days they travelled beyond their fall camp before discovering the island.

When she finished translating this part of the story, Gloria matched the fourth piece with the other three.

The old woman sucked in her breath. "It is many years since I see the embroidery like *Mamàcho* Teht'aa made it." She ran her gnarled fingers over the seven flowers, which seemed to float above the suppleness of the hide, and smiled. "Beautiful, eh? My grandmother was very good with a needle. But she didn't destroy the beauty. I did."

The petals that had been ripped apart had lost too many tufts to return to their former glory. Nonetheless, the embroidery retained a magical exquisiteness.

"My mother found the pretty purple sparkles," Florence continued. "When the white men stole them from my grandfather, they paid no attention to the young girl who'd kept a couple for herself. She put them in the head of her dolly to make it look pretty." Turning to Anita, she said, "Child, the doll please."

The young girl hesitated before giving her precious doll one last kiss and handing it to her great-grandmother. "Please, don't hurt her," she said in Tlicho.

The old woman took up the doll. "Like Anita, I loved playing with Blueberry when I was a child, as my own daughters did, even Gloria. Blueberry was the name my mother gave her to remind her of the pretty island. She once had hair more purple than blue, made from the tail of a caribou, but it fell out many years ago. She really isn't very gorgeous, but I loved her, like Anita does." She caressed the soft curls of her great-granddaughter.

"Sorry, child, I have to do this." She took a hunting knife and began digging out one of the doll's black eyes. Soon, minute tufts of black were flying away on the wind, along with tiny feathers that had been the stuffing.

After removing a fair amount of stuffing, deflating poor Blueberry's head, she inserted her finger into the hole. "They're in here somewhere. My mother told me she'd inserted them behind the eyes so the bad men wouldn't get them. Ah … here is one." She dropped it onto her palm and closed her hand around it while she searched for the other, which soon joined the first one.

"My dolly," Anita cried out. Sobs wracked her slight frame, as she clung to her mother.

Florence bent over, kissed her weeping great-granddaughter, and spoke to her softly in Tlicho, which seemed to soothe her.

She then straightened up and opened her palm.

No one spoke. Two tiny pieces of translucent stone sparkled in the sun. One was about the size of a thumbnail, the other a fingernail. I'd been expecting to see a rich purple, like amethyst. Instead I saw a much paler, almost ethereal hue. But there was no denying it was purple, like the lilacs I'd left behind at Three Deer Point.

"Let me see." In his excitement to check out the stone, Hans knocked over his half-full mug while he rummaged through his pack. He extracted an instrument of the sort I'd seen gemologists use to ascertain the quality of a gem, a loupe, I thought it was called.

Not trusting him, Florence passed him the smaller stone.

Amidst "ohs" and "ahs" he examined it using the loupe. He rolled the stone around in his hand in order to catch the refraction of light. "*Wunderbar! Unglaublich!*" He salivated with lust.

Finally, he turned back to us. "I have never seen such a good-quality diamond. The clarity is near perfect, with no fractures, and the colour is the truest I have ever seen for a purple diamond. Very rare. You can get a lot of money for this one stone. It could be cut down to about a carat with little wastage. I'd like to see the other."

Florence held out her hand for the smaller stone before relinquishing the larger one.

This one received the same pronouncement. When Hans started to slip it into his pocket, Gloria jumped up and snatched it from his hand. She returned it to her grandmother. "Greedy bastard," she muttered, resuming her place by her child.

Unfazed, he demanded, "Where is the deposit?"

Florence was about to respond when Reggie cut in. "She has already given it to us." He held up his iPhone. "I've recorded it."

I should've known.

"Let's get out of here." Reggie stood up. "Thank you for your kind hospitality, *Ohndah* Florence."

He and Hans were walking down the hill to their boat when Uncle Joe called out, "You guys have big problem."

"You trying to stop us, old man?" Reggie called back.

"Fire do that," came the succinct reply.

SIXTY-ONE

Unfortunately for the two men, the trail to the diamonds led north, directly through the forest fire. But the fire wasn't the only thing stopping them. Ignoring Florence's entreaty to stay, Reggie and Hans kept walking, more like running, down to their boat.

"They're going to get Hans's plane," Malcolm said. "They want to stake the claim before anyone else does."

"But can they?" I asked. "If the land doesn't belong to them."

"The deposit isn't in Tlicho territory and therefore not governed by our self-government agreement. It's considered Crown land, and the first person to register a claim owns it."

"So are you going to let them get away with it?"

"They won't find the deposit. They'll try to follow Florence's trail from the air. But I know from experience it is impossible. Many traditional markers can only be recognized at ground level. Besides, we have another trick up our sleeve."

He and his father exchanged smug grins.

A few minutes later we discovered their secret when the two men stomped back into camp.

"What in the hell did you do to my fucking boat?" Reggie shouted. "The damn thing won't start. Yours won't start either."

Chuckling, Uncle Joe opened his palm to reveal a dirty spark plug. Malcolm showed two more. Angus dangled a fourth. The three men burst into raucous laughter, which served to make Reggie angrier. He lunged at Uncle Joe, who slipped the spark plug into his pocket before the other man could snatch it away.

"Stop," Florence said. "We not finished. Drink more tea."

"I'd rather have a Scotch," Reggie muttered under his breath as he flopped onto the director's chair, almost tipping it over.

Hans, on the other hand, wasn't deterred. "You can't stop us. We will find the diamonds before you."

"Already have," Malcolm grinned. "Show them the papers, Auntie." He repeated it in Tlicho.

She spoke to Angus, who ran into the closest tent and returned with a handbag made of shiny blue plastic, complete with a rhinestone clasp, the kind of bag that belonged in a suburban mall and not in the wilds hundreds of kilometres from nowhere. She pulled out a thick envelope.

"For Tlicho." Smiling, she passed it to Malcolm.

"Auntie, Angus and I found the deposit three weeks ago and staked the claim in the name of Mamàcho Teht'aa Inc. A fitting name, don't you think?" He pulled out a document and unfolded it. "Though the deposit lies outside the boundaries of the agreed Tlicho territory, it still is on land traditionally used by Tlicho."

"You double-crossing bastards," Reggie hissed. "You're gonna keep the money all to yourselves. Hardly the way of our people."

"You mean the way you were going to share?" Malcolm sneered.

Reggie snarled.

"I am president of the company, and Florence is chairman, or should I say, chairwoman. The rest of the board comes from Digadeh, including my father. The company's mandate is to share the proceeds with our community. We are currently in discussions with Nord Diamond."

He pulled out a leather pouch from his jacket pocket and tapped out a stone onto his palm. About the same size as the smaller of the doll's two, it sparkled the same lilac hue in the sun.

"Here." He tossed it toward the Grand Chief. "This is as close as you're going to get to the diamonds. Keep it as a memory of your betrayal of our people."

It marked a sparkling mauve arc until it landed at Reggie's feet. He ignored it. Hans didn't.

Malcolm continued, "After Auntie Florence learned of your interest in the diamonds, she realized the time had come to fulfill her grandmother's legacy. She sure knows you, Reggie. She knew she couldn't trust you, so she decided it was up to her to make sure our people received their due.

"We set up the company before heading out onto the land to follow *Mamàcho* Teht'aa's trail. It took us several weeks of a lot of trial and error through some pretty rough conditions. There was a fair bit of snow and ice, which covered some of the trail markers. But we finally found

Dzièwàdi. What a magical moment. They really do look like sparkling purple flowers. It's hard to say how large the deposit is, but Nord Diamond is going to send out an exploration team once we agree to the terms. It's not going to be cheap to develop with most of the deposit likely under the lake. But if the entire deposit is made up of purple diamonds, it's going to bring in one hell of a lot of money for our people."

Throughout his discourse, I thought I heard crying and looked over to see Gloria weeping softly into her grandmother's lap. While the young woman muttered in Tlicho, the old woman gently patted her head, but the expression on her face was not the one I would expect from a woman who'd just wrested a diamond mine out from under the grasp of a greedy man. Rather, it was one of resigned sorrow.

"What's going on?" I asked Malcolm. "Why is Gloria so upset?"

"I'm afraid she suffered from the same disease as Reggie and Hans. She's telling Florence how sorry she is, that she didn't mean to cause harm."

"What harm?" Though as I asked the question, I knew the answer.

"I'm not sure, but I think we're about to find out."

Gloria straightened up as if summoning her courage. "You bastard," she shouted at Hans. "I did it all for you."

He shrugged in response while continuing to fondle the diamond.

"It's all your fuckin' fault. You made me betray my people."

"You did it to yourself. I merely gave you the reason."

Was she admitting to killing Frank?

In a rage she lunged at her former lover, who casually stepped aside, causing her to fall to the ground. Sputtering, she picked herself up and pummelled him with her fists. He grabbed her wrists and held them tightly as she struggled to break free.

Finally she stopped, gasping.

"You finished?" he said.

She glared at him before wrenching free.

She rose to her feet. "Okay everyone, listen up."

"Remember, it's your word against ours," Hans said.

"We'll see. These are my people, not yours."

Nonetheless, a shadow of worry crept over her face as she backed away and positioned herself so she could see the entire circle. "You want to know who killed Frank?"

I noticed that Malcolm brought his rifle closer to his side.

"It wasn't Eric."

At last.

She swept her eyes slowly over everyone, one by one, until they landed on one man. "It was him." Her finger pointed at Reggie.

But her chief was prepared. He'd already raised his rifle.

"Look, she's got it all wrong. Eric did it."

"*You* did. I saw you put the bloody knife in his hand," Gloria shot back, despite the rifle being pointed straight at her.

"You gonna believe a hooker over me, your chief?" He inched backward while keeping his eyes trained on us.

With his rifle aimed, Malcolm started walking toward him. "Put the gun down, Reggie. It's over."

Reggie looked around wildly as if trying to find an escape route.

Uncle Joe joined in. "You're too soft, Reggie. You wouldn't last one week out here on your own."

In the meantime, Angus, also armed, silently crept up behind the man. Frank's killer stopped when he felt the barrel of the rifle in his back.

He dropped his gun and held up his arms. "Okay, okay. You win. Yes, I killed the fucker. He was going to ruin everything. He called me from Digadeh to tell me he had a crisis of conscience." He spat out the words. "Fancy words, eh, for a dropout? Probably learned them from that fucking Teht'aa. Said he didn't want to screw our people, so he was going to tell Florence everything.

"I couldn't let it happen. I needed those goddamn diamonds. Hans flew me in so I could convince him not to. But he wouldn't listen, and as the saying goes, one thing led to another and he was lying on the ground bleeding. It was Hans who came up with the idea of framing Eric. He knew how much I hated the guy."

If looks could kill, mine would. I didn't think I had ever hated someone so much.

"We hid the body in Frank's tipi. Trick was getting Eric to come to Digadeh. Hans had heard about the attack on Teht'aa, so he called Eric and told him Frank had done it."

"Did Frank really do it?" I blurted out.

"How should I know? But it worked. Eric nabbed a ride with Plummers and was in Digadeh before I had a chance to figure out how I was going to do it. It was Gloria who came up with the idea of using Special K, that right, babe?"

She crossed her arms over her breast and scowled at him.

"She got it off one of her johns, one of those date-rape drugs that makes you forget."

"Yah, he tried to slip it into my drink," she finally admitted. "Wanted free sex. Jeez, did I make him pay. Made him give me all his drugs and money or I report him to the cops. Look Meg, I'm really sorry. I know I shouldna given your man that stuff, but I was in a crazy space…."

"You know he was about to go to jail for you because he thought you had killed Frank."

"Fuck, I didn't know. Oh, I feel awful. I'll make it up to you. Promise."

"At least you're doing the right thing now."

"Yah, I shoulda never done it."

Though I wanted to throttle her, I merely mumbled, "Yup."

Once he finally admitted to the murder, Reggie couldn't wait to spew it all out. "I couldn't believe how fast it worked. He was stumbling about within minutes of finishing the Pepsi Gloria gave him. She steered him to Frank's tipi, where Hans and I waited with the body. After he passed out, I took his knife and stuck it into the wounds on Frank's body and put it in his hand. Then we got the hell out of there. Hans dropped me off in Yellowknife then headed back into the bush. Gloria left later on the daily flight."

"You know someone saw you, Gloria," I said.

"Yah, you said, but there was no one around when I went back. I made sure."

"You went back?" Reggie exclaimed in disbelief. "Why, for god's sake?"

"I lost my earring. I had to go back to find it. And I did. Right next to Eric." She shook her head to ensure we noticed the two dangling beaded earrings.

"How could you betray your cousin like this?" I said. "Teht'aa has done so much for you."

For the first time she looked truly chastened. "Sorry," she said in a small voice. "Eric was a good guy. I liked him, but Hans told me I had to do it … for him … and our daughter. Besides, Teht'aa didn't love him, I did."

She whirled around to Hans and yelled, "You bastard! You're never getting near Anita again."

She ran over to her daughter, picked her up, and retreated sobbing to the tent.

SIXTY-TWO

Gloria might not have done the actual killing, but she had helped frame my husband and had been willing to let him go to jail for a murder he didn't commit. Any sympathy I might've had for her was gone.

Hans attempted to run after her, but Malcolm stopped him with his rifle and forced him to sit on the ground beside Reggie. He wanted to tie up both men, but his aunt wouldn't allow it, reminding us, as her brother had, that there was no place for them to flee.

I expected people to jump up and start loading the two men and Gloria into a boat. The sooner we handed Frank's killer and his accomplices over to the RCMP, the sooner Eric would be set free. Even so, it would still take a full day to reach Digadeh. If only we'd brought a satellite phone.

But no one made an effort to leave.

"Why aren't we going?" I asked Uncle Joe.

"Too soon," he replied. "Better for Eric we stay. He want to know who hurt his daughter too."

He clamped his mouth shut and refused to explain further.

I was awfully tired of the old man's obstinance. Wanting relief from the craziness, I jumped up and stomped into the woods behind the tents. There appeared to be a path, so I followed it, thinking it would lead me to the fishing beach. It didn't. After I didn't know how many minutes, I slowed as my anger slowed and I realized the path was no more.

I heard rustling.

Remembering the bear from the previous night, I froze. I debated calling out but feared it would betray my city foibles, particularly if it ended up being a small, defenceless animal like a squirrel or rabbit or whatever could survive a subarctic winter. Besides, if it was a bear, I didn't want to upset it.

I scanned the bushes around me and tried to peer around the slender tree trunks. Nothing. I waited. Nothing but empty shrubbery, burgeoning with new green leaves. And then a branch twitched. At first I made out two grey, upright ears. Then I spied two unblinking yellow eyes staring back at me.

Not a bear — too small and the wrong colour. But too large for a fox, so it had to be a wolf. I could almost sense him licking his chops at the sight of me. But I didn't sense a threat; more like curiosity. Still, I was reluctant to move, so I stared back. An eye-blink later, the eyes disappeared, along with the ears. I waited several more minutes until I was satisfied he'd gone.

I returned as nonchalantly as I could to the fire and casually mentioned the wolf.

"That's Nodi." Angus laughed. "He's a big puppy, about a year old. Likes to play with Anita's ball. He's been hanging around since we arrived. No need to worry about him."

I felt a tad foolish. But I couldn't forget that he was a wild animal that wouldn't hesitate to kill. On the other hand, there was a man sitting across from me who hadn't hesitated to kill. I decided if I had the choice of being alone in these wilds with one of them, I would take the wolf.

Angus was passing another pot of tea around, while Malcolm continued to guard Hans and Reggie. Florence returned from the tent where Gloria had fled and was settling herself back into her chair.

The air had become smokier. Stray bits of ash floated on the wind. I could see flames leaping at the edge of the distant shore and fanning out to the shoreline on either side.

"Guys, the fire's coming our way. We should go." If getting these men into custody wasn't going to get them to leave, maybe the fire would.

"Plenty time," Uncle Joe replied. "We not finished."

He spoke to his sister for several long minutes, then leaned back into his chair and took a long slurp of tea before beginning. "Florence want me to tell you about Carol, her daughter."

If all eyes weren't focused on the old man before, they were now.

"No one know about Carol. I think I only person. She was pretty, like her mother."

Embarrassed, Florence hid her smile behind her hand.

"Carol was born in the bush. She was first baby for Florence and George. She good girl, help look after her baby sisters. Florence didn't want her to go to school, so they stay in the bush. But the RCMP find them and take Carol away when she eight years old. The other girls too small, still babies. When she leave, Florence give Carol purple embroidery."

Florence interrupted.

After another short exchange, Uncle Joe continued. "Like Florence say, this purple embroidery very important to us Bluegoose. I remember seeing it when little, but never knew it was about diamonds. The secret was for women, not men, because men greedy."

He gave both Hans and Reggie a long hard stare before continuing, "*Mamàcho* Teht'aa give it to our mother. She was oldest girl. Our mother give it to Florence, the only girl. Like I said, Florence had four girls, so she take an axe and cut the embroidery into four pieces. When RCMP take Carol, she give her purple flowers with green bird to take with her. But Carol never come back from school, and Florence never see Carol's purple flowers again.

"Florence try to find out what happen to her daughter, but no one tell her. She don't know if she alive or dead. Her other girls don't know. They only know that one day Carol was at school, the next day she gone. Many, many years later, Father Harris come to Digadeh and tell her that Carol is dead, but he don't tell her how. He also don't tell her where Carol is buried. Florence pretty sure he knows. So she waits. She believes in God. She believes God is looking after Carol in Heaven. She was a good Catholic girl. She believe one day before she die, God will tell her about her daughter."

He swivelled around in his chair to face the priest, who, with his eyes still downcast, continued to remain disconnected from the people around him. He thumbed his bible.

"That day is here," Uncle Joe spat out.

Florence leaned forward and jabbed a finger at Father Harris. "Why my Carol die?"

We waited.

I heard a rustle from the tent behind me and looked around to see Gloria clutching her daughter, tiptoeing toward us. I pushed myself along the dirt to give them enough room.

Father Harris raised his eyes heavenward and crossed himself. He muttered something, likely a prayer, before directing his gaze fully on Florence. "I'm so sorry. I should've told you many years ago. But I worried it would upset you." He paused and looked heavenward again before continuing, "She died in childbirth. Please, I'm so sorry."

I could see Florence was confused by his English. I waited for Gloria or Uncle Joe to explain in Tlicho, but both seem too dazed, so I said, "*Ohndah* Florence, I'm so sorry, your daughter died having a baby."

"Baby?" she said.

"Yes, a baby. She died—"

Uncle Joe took over in Tlicho.

"Baby, where baby?" Florence asked, her eyes brimming in tears.

The priest hesitated and crossed himself before saying, "I'm sorry, he died too."

He's lying was my immediate thought, but before I could challenge him, Florence whispered, "Boy? Girl?"

"Boy. He lived for only a few hours. He was too small to live."

"Name?"

"I baptized him Edward…." His voice trailed off to such a low murmur that I wasn't certain anyone other than myself caught the rest. "After my brother, who died when he was a boy." He raised his eyes once more to heaven.

"I don't believe the baby died," I interjected. "I think you did something with him, like put him up for adoption."

Hope filled Florence's eyes until he replied, "I buried him beside his mother."

"Where?" Florence shot back.

"At the Grey Nuns mission, where I sent your daughter when I knew she was with child."

I could see her searching for the English words. Once again neither Gloria nor Uncle Joe came to her aid, so I asked the most obvious question. "Who was the father? One of the other students?"

He moved his mouth up and down, but no sound came out.

"Or you?" I hissed.

"She was so beautiful," he whispered, followed by another heavenward plea. "Father, forgive me, for I have sinned." Crossing himself, he murmured his confession.

Only then did I notice the scratches on his face where there had been a bandage. It was as if someone had scraped their fingernails down his cheek.

SIXTY-THREE

"Priests." Uncle Joe spat onto the dirt. "You make me sick. You say God protect us. But he sure as hell don't protect us from the likes of you."

Tears seeped from under Florence's closed lids as she crossed herself in prayer.

"I'm so sorry, *Mamàcho*." Gloria embraced her grandmother. The two of them wept entwined in each other's arms, each alone in their own grief.

"Get out of here," Uncle Joe rasped. "You destroy my sister's family. You don't deserve to live."

The priest struggled to rise from the ground, but the old woman intervened.

"Stay. Teht'aa? What you do?"

Teht'aa? What did the priest have to do with Eric's daughter? Unless … but how would Florence know?

With a deep, painful groan, the priest dropped back down. He sighed, brushed the sweat from his brow, though the day was more cool than warm, and touched his scratched cheek.

No longer bothering to pretend otherwise, he spewed out another sordid confession. "Teht'aa wanted Carol's embroidery. Florence, you must've told her I had it. She said it belonged to her family, that I had no right to it. But I couldn't let her have it. It was my only memory of Carol … and my son. I never dreamed I would have a child…." Another deep sigh.

"Florence, I know it was against God and the Church, but your daughter was the only woman I ever loved. She may have been only sixteen, but she was my angel with the innocent purity of the Virgin Mary. After she died I never touched another girl. It was God's retribution."

"Did you rape my daughter?" I hissed.

"Teht'aa, a lovely name. Beautiful like her mother and just as headstrong. Charmaine bit me the first time I loved her. I smacked her and she screamed and brought the nuns running. So I smacked her daughter. She threatened to tell the police if I didn't give her Carol's purple flowers." He glanced at the woman whose daughters he had ruined. "You've known all along about Carol, haven't you, Florence?"

With considerable reluctance and distaste, Gloria returned to her job as translator.

When she finished, Florence replied, "When you told me Carol was dead, you didn't look me in the eye like an innocent man. Answer Meg's question. Did you rape my granddaughter too?"

"So beautiful, lying on the ground after I smacked her. It had been many years since I sinned with your daughter. Too old, she didn't have the virgin purity I liked, but I thought, one last time before I die. She fought like a she-cat, just like her mother." He touched his cheek again. "It only made me want her more. I remember little. A car horn brought me to my senses."

"You left her to die," I said. "Like a piece of roadkill."

"People use that back alley all the time. I assumed someone would come by soon enough."

"When she lost all memory of the rape, I bet you thought God was still on your side. I sure hope your reason for wanting to visit her in the hospital wasn't to kill her. But you killed Lucy, didn't you? She saw you attack her cousin."

"I'd already sinned enough. I thought one more wouldn't matter. I didn't know she had seen me until she said something in her confused way that told me she had. I doubt the police would've believed her, but I wasn't going to chance it."

"Why did you come here? You were safe. No one was looking at you for the crimes."

"Because *Ohndah* Florence asked me to. I have always had a deep respect for her."

"Just not for her girls." I so wanted to slug the smirk off his face.

"She also asked me to bring Gloria."

"I'm surprised she trusted you with her."

"God told me it was time to make my confession."

He raised himself carefully from the ground and limped over to Florence.

He lowered himself painfully to his knees. "In the name of the Father, the Son, and the Holy Spirit. My last confession was …"

Thus began his lengthy confession to the woman he so horribly wronged.

SIXTY-FOUR

It turned out Malcolm had had the smarts to bring a satellite phone. Unbeknownst to the rest of us, apart from his father, he had called in the RCMP. I heard the drone of their plane long before it buzzed over us and landed on the lake.

The priest had finished his confession to Florence and was bowing his head, seeking forgiveness. Amazingly, she gave it. After crossing herself, she placed her hand on his wispy grey hair as if she were blessing him.

I found it incredible that she wasn't filled with hate. I couldn't say that about myself. I knew I didn't have it in me to forgive the man for his vicious rape of Teht'aa. The same way I would never be able to forgive the monster who raped me.

There. I said it. Finally. In our talks at the hospital, Teht'aa wouldn't leave me alone until I admitted it. She kept insisting that the healing wouldn't begin until I said the words out loud. I was raped.

After the police loaded the four prisoners into their plane, there was no room for me, despite my desperate entreaties, particularly when I learned they were flying straight to Yellowknife. But they left with a promise to arrange a flight for me from Digadeh. Uncle Joe, Malcolm, and I left within minutes of the plane's departure, leaving Florence to the solitude of her camp.

Her brother had tried to convince her to come, but she wanted no part of the fuss and bother of Digadeh. She was perfectly content to remain in her solitary, if somewhat smoky, world with Malcolm's son, her great-granddaughter, and their friendly wolf, who watched as we puttered away from the camp. At least she agreed to leave if the fire came too close.

The police were good on their promise. Within an hour of our arrival at Digadeh, the RCMP plane was whisking me off to Yellowknife. After leaving a message on Sally's phone to expedite Eric's release, I reserved a rental car, intending to head straight to the prison. It proved unnecessary.

My husband was waiting for me on the tarmac. Looking thin in the clothes I'd finally delivered to the prison and forlorn after his ordeal, he stood uncertainly beside the police car that had brought him. My heart wrenched. When his face creased into his much-loved dimpled smile, I ran without hesitation into his arms and we hugged and kissed several lifetimes away.

Close to a month later and the hugging and kissing hadn't stopped. We waited until Teht'aa was strong enough to make the trip. Once our plans were firmed up, we arranged for Jid to fly out to join us but had to leave poor Shoni behind in the care of Janet. We chartered a plane to fly us into Florence's camp, along with three canoes. Eric felt it only fitting that we make this momentous trip into the past the traditional way, the way *Mamàcho* Teht'aa would've travelled more than a century ago. We brought both Gloria and Uncle Joe with us.

Though Gloria didn't have the best track record when it came to obeying authority, Sally, whom I'd hired to defend her, convinced the judge that the young mother was truly repentant, ready to turn her life around and abide by the conditions of her release. The woman Eric and I picked up at the courthouse was a considerably subdued version of the hip-swaggering, gum-smacking hooker who'd lurched drunkenly into my life. Gone was the heavy makeup, the too-tight skirts, the chip-on-her-shoulder stance. In their place was a chastened young woman who was more than sorry for the trouble she had caused. During our month-long paddle to Dzièwàdi I came to like the caring yet steely person Eric and Teht'aa had perceived under the hardened veneer.

Florence wanted to make one last visit to her grand-mother's island before it was changed beyond recognition. Drilling would soon begin to determine the extent of the kimberlite and the mine-worthiness of its diamond content. If the only diamonds were the surface ones delivered millions of years ago by a glacier from a distant kimberlite source, the land would remain undisturbed. But if the deposit proved financially viable, the long process of mine development would begin, transforming this magical island and its crystal-clear lake into a no-man's land. Florence regretted the destruction but knew her people needed the money.

It was a journey of discovery. Not only were we paddling through a harsh, barren land of tundra and tree-fringed eskers that most of us had never seen before, but Eric, Jid, and I were discovering that we were very much a part of the Bluegoose family. Without hesitation, they welcomed us into their lives.

It was also a time for Eric and me to rediscover our love for each other. Too traumatized by the rape, I'd been afraid to let him come close. Not only did I fear other men touching me, but I wouldn't let my own husband either, apart from a cursory kiss or hug, which I had to brace myself to do. To compound our difficulties, I'd been unable to tell him about the rape, so his response to my withdrawal had been anger and a slow drifting away.

The long hours spent watching an unconscious Teht'aa had given me time to reflect. The distance from where the assault had happened helped too. When she finally awoke and treated her rape in such a matter-of-fact manner, I knew I had to confront my own. Teht'aa was the first person I told. It was like uncorking a fizzy bottle close to bursting. All my pent-up fears and confused emotions came tumbling out. We talked and talked as the tension slowly drained out of me.

When I saw the only man I'd ever loved standing on the tarmac wanting my love, but not knowing whether he was going to get it, the last dam broke. We spent long hours alone at Teht'aa's apartment sharing our fears and concerns and finally our love. This trip had become our second honeymoon. Eric had bought us a two-man tent, along with a double sleeping bag, so we wouldn't have to sleep with the others in the McPherson tents. Every morning when I woke up in Eric's arms, I pinched myself twice: one pinch to ensure I wasn't dreaming, and a second, more painful pinch for being such a stupid fool, not telling him about the rape sooner.

Not wanting to overtax Teht'aa, we took frequent breaks, once to watch wolf cubs cavorting outside their den, another time to explore an ancient stone fence that had been used to funnel caribou to waiting hunters. Eagle-eyed Jid managed to spy one of their tiny stone spearheads amongst the thousands of stones littering the ground.

We stopped to do our own caribou hunting. Eric was the first to see a few of the rangy animals with the tree-like antlers along a ridge. It was Uncle Joe's first caribou sighting in almost twenty years. He became so excited he almost fell out of the canoe. The men bounded over the ridge with their rifles while we women set up camp.

Afterward, we snuck up onto the ridge and looked down upon a sight only a privileged few ever see: a sea of undulating antlers spreading from horizon to horizon across the tundra. Florence couldn't stop smiling as we listened to the rhythmic clicking of their hooves on the ground and watched the newborns wobble on spindly legs as they strove to keep up with their mothers. Previously convinced that the great herds of her childhood had disappeared forever, she thanked God for being given this one last chance to marvel at one of nature's wonders.

Each man shot a caribou, including a beaming Jid, using Uncle Joe's rifle under his expert guidance. It required all of us taking turns to drag them back to the camp, where I learned that skinning and butchering the carcasses was woman's work. Though squeamish about such things, I felt I had to hold up the Odjik end, so I found myself skinning my first animal ever under Florence's skilled direction. We spent the next two days at the camp preparing the meat, readying the skins for drying later, and eating caribou stew. Of course, we had our share of fish too. Jid and Uncle Joe bonded over the fishing rod and tried to out-fish each other.

At the outset of our journey, Florence insisted that Teht'aa be our guide. Dredging up *Mamàcho* Teht'aa's story from the depths of her memory, she only made a couple of mistakes that sent us in the wrong direction before her grandmother turned us back on the right course. She would excitedly point out the markers as we approached them: the point with a rock that looked like a waiting ptarmigan, the yellow splash of ripe cloudberries carpeting a tiny island, a sandy beach with a long spit running far out into the lake, and so on.

Each time she recognized a marker, she would exclaim, "I don't believe it. This oral map really works."

Florence would patiently reply, "Ancestors very wise."

It was a vast, empty land we paddled through. With only low hills to obstruct the view, the horizon seemed limitless, apart from a few days of rain, when clouds cloaked us in misty drizzle. After paddling through the still smouldering lands of the forest fire, we travelled northward. The smattering of short, scrubby trees grew sparse until disappearing altogether. We had travelled beyond the treeline.

We were utterly alone. The only sign of human presence we came across was a line of gasoline barrels a plane had stored on a beach for its return trip. But we were reminded that civilization was only a satellite call away by the daily overhead flights. Mere specks in the sky, they were flying over the pole on their way to the bustling cities of the modern world.

A day's paddle from our destination, we saw our first claim stake. Knowing it wasn't one of the stakes Malcolm had hammered into the ground, Eric climbed up the slope to check it out but couldn't identify its ownership from the tag other than to note that he didn't think it had seen a winter. We assumed it belonged to Nord Diamond. If it didn't, it could cause problems if the kimberlite source for the purple diamonds spread beyond the boundaries of Mamàcho Teht'aa Inc.'s claim.

We saw a couple more along the river that Florence said fed into the lake before she pointed out the first stake Malcolm had placed to designate the boundary of the claim. Another bend in the river and a vigorous paddle through a rock garden before our three canoes spilled out into what we came to call Mamàcho Teht'aa Lake.

Expecting something momentous, I felt let down to see it appeared much like all the other lakes: the same crystal-clear waters with a shoreline that barely rose above the height of the water. I searched for the island and saw several shimmering in the distance. We paddled toward them.

"There's the pretty island," Anita suddenly called out.

I'd forgotten she had been here before.

Once again I felt let down. It looked the same as all the other lichen-covered mounds of rock I'd seen rising from the water. And then I saw a sparkle in the bright sun.

We beached the canoes on a narrow, stony beach, barely large enough to hold the three of them. Together we climbed the steep rocky slope to the top. Angus helped his great-aunt, Eric helped his daughter, and I, Uncle Joe. Jid and Anita cavorted behind us with Gloria.

Huffing and puffing, with a few scrapes on my palms from slipping, we reached the top together.

Not one word, one sigh, one exclamation was spoken.

In awe, we stood transfixed by the sparkling purple flowers.

ACKNOWLEDGEMENTS

Once again, Meg and I were off travelling together, this time to Yellowknife in the Northwest Territories. It was my second trip to that fair North-of-60 town, and I enjoyed it as much as my first trip with my husband, Jim, before we set out on our canoe trip on the Thelon River through The Barrens. I also travelled to Behchoko to join the Tlicho in their celebration of the tenth anniversary of self-government.

I love the North. It is no cliché to say everyone is so friendly. They are. Many went out of their way to give me a better insight into living in the North, including Cara Bryant. Two incredibly helpful and informative RCMP officers opened the window for me on policing in NWT. I'd like to thank Corporal Kirk Patrick Hughes and Corporal Elenore Sturko. Sue Glowach and John Nahanni with the Department of Justice helped me better understand various aspects of the justice system in NWT. Lydia Bardak, with the John Howard Society, also provided valuable information. I mustn't forget the many Tlicho who took the time to chat with me during their grand celebration.

I'd also like to thank Hayden Trenholm, who proved invaluable in increasing my understanding of life in the north, Terry McEwan, who helped simplify the Canadian legal system for me, and Dr. Carly Pulkkinen, who helped sort out medical procedure for me.

A book never comes to fruition without the help of many. I'd like to thank Allister Thompson and Carrie Gleason, my editors, and all the other people at Dundurn who turned my manuscript into a living, breathing book.

I relied on several books to increase my knowledge of the Dene. They include: *Yamoria, The Lawmaker* and *Trail of the Spirit: The Mysteries of Medicine Power Revealed*, both by George Blondin; *Walking the Land, Feeding the Fire* by Allice Legat; *Living Stories: Godi Weghàà Ets'eèda* by Therese Zoe, Philip Zoe, and Mindy Willet; and *Way Down North: Dene Life–Dene Land* by René Fumoleau.

I always save the most important person for last: my husband, Jim, without whom this writing journey could not be possible. Many, many thanks for your patient and enduring support.